W9-CNS-721

"Mr. Carmichael, are you all right?" Kat leaped to her feet.

He opened his mouth, then shut it again. He seemed to struggle to keep it closed, but words poured forth as if they had a life of their own.

"Ms. Piretti, I apologize . . . but I have a message for you."

Kat sank into her chair. "From what sort of being, Mr. Carmichael? Casper the Friendly Ghost?"

He shook his head violently. "I don't know who it's from," he said in a low voice. "Believe me, if I had the choice, I'd never talk to you again."

She rolled her eyes and reached for her coffee.

"Sure. You just can't help it. The stars are configured just so, and you've got a Ouija board stashed under the table."

"You're right about Peter's death."

The coffee cup dropped from her grasp, cracking both itself and the saucer on which it landed. Kat began to tremble so violently that Stephen instinctively reached out to hold her.

"Let go of me," she managed to say in a hoarse voice. "Let go of me."

"I'm sorry. Whatever I said, I . . ."

But Kat had wrenched herself free, and fled.

ANGEL CAFÉ

JILL MORROW

PARAVIEW POCKET BOOKS
New York   London   Toronto   Sydney   Singapore

The sale of this book without its cover is unauthorized. If you purchased this book without a cover, you should be aware that it was reported to the publisher as "unsold and destroyed." Neither the author nor the publisher has received payment for the sale of this "stripped book."

This book is a work of fiction. Names, characters, places and incidents are products of the author's imagination or are used fictitiously. Any resemblance to actual events or locales or persons, living or dead, is entirely coincidental.

An *Original* Publication of PARAVIEW POCKET BOOKS

PARAVIEW
191 Seventh Avenue, New York, NY 10011

POCKET BOOKS, a division of Simon & Schuster, Inc.
1230 Avenue of the Americas, New York, NY 10020

Copyright © 2003 by Jill Morrow

All rights reserved, including the right to reproduce this book or portions thereof in any form whatsoever. For information address Pocket Books, 1230 Avenue of the Americas, New York, NY 10020

ISBN: 0-7434-7573-9

First Paraview Pocket Books mass market printing July 2003

10 9 8 7 6 5 4 3 2 1

POCKET and colophon are registered trademarks of Simon & Schuster, Inc.

Front cover photo illustration by David Stevenson

Manufactured in the United States of America

For information regarding special discounts for bulk purchases, please contact Simon & Schuster Special Sales at 1-800-456-6798 or business@simonandschuster.com

To Tom, who has always believed.

Prologue

~~~

THEY WERE CERTIFIABLY NUTS, ALL OF THEM, BUT THE LEAD was intriguing, and Peter Dulaney had endured worse than a few hours of psychic mumbo jumbo to get a story. He stood in his apartment living room and ran a final check: notebooks, pens, tape recorder ready to roll. He'd even remembered to wind the tape to the proper starting point. Tonight's interview would smoothly follow the last interview he'd conducted in this dopey investigation.

For this he'd passed up an evening with Katie?

He shook his head. What a good little doobie he was!

This story probably wasn't worth the sacrifice. He already felt more like a reporter for the *National Enquirer* than for the respectable Baltimore *Sun*. Here he was, traipsing around after psychic readers, disembodied spirits, and cult members. Even his Journalism 101 professor would have recoiled in disgust.

There'd been, however, something undeniably pathetic about the quaver in his source's voice, about his utter conviction that a very real danger existed. "Please be careful," Mr. Toohey constantly implored, and while Peter doubted that the cult could do anything worse than bore him silly, Mr. Toohey's fear was too real to dismiss without adequate investigation.

Peter checked his watch. Maybe the cult members would cast a spell on him, turn him into a newt or something.

Seven forty-five. Time to hit the road. He bent toward his notebooks, then snapped ramrod-straight as a now-familiar chill crept up his spine. Damn, it was happening again! Worse, the attacks were definitely increasing in frequency. They'd started sporadically, right after he'd begun investigating this story. Now he could count on at least two a day.

The chill raced through his body. His teeth began to chatter. Resigned, Peter sank to the sofa to wait it out.

Now he'd be late.

No doubt about it, tonight's attack was worse than usual. The chills raced up and down as if searching for corners they might have missed. His stomach felt like a goddamned roller coaster.

"Okay!" he said as violent spasms racked his body. "I'll see a doctor. I promise!"

A bang on the front door made him jump. The chills stopped. Maybe they were like hiccups, requiring only a good scare to startle them out of the system. Peter leaped from the couch and hurried toward the door, then stopped halfway to reconsider. He wasn't expecting visitors and had no time to waste with Girl Scouts, Jehovah's Witnesses, or salespeople. Why answer? Surely whoever stood in the hallway would take the hint and leave.

Another thud. Peter furrowed his brow. Sounded like the next approach would involve a battering ram. He shifted his weight somewhat uneasily and took a tentative step forward.

The chills were back, but they were different from anything he'd experienced before. His apartment felt frigid. He passed a shaky hand in front of the window air conditioner. No, the air blew as ineffectively as always.

He suddenly recognized that the cold emanated from a definite source. Swallowing hard, he turned to stare at the front door.

The knock pounded again, more insistently. Peter drew in a wavering breath. "Okay," he said.

He walked cautiously toward the door, stopping only to press the red button on his tape recorder.

1

~~~~

KATERINA PIRETTI WAS A SMALL WOMAN, AND THE DENSE weight of the Wagner file was commensurate with Mr. Wagner's great importance to the firm. Kat lugged it from her credenza to her desk, barely noting that the late April sky outside her office window had progressed from a pink-streaked dawn into a full-blown day. Muffled footsteps trod the carpeted hallways of Harper, Madigan and Horn. The attorneys trickled in, the earliness of their arrivals depending partly on their workloads and partly on how far down the firm's letterhead they were. Kat had beaten everyone in that morning, as she did nearly every morning. She'd been associated with the firm for only eight months, which meant she received enough plodding research projects to keep her billable hours well above the firm average.

Eight months of real-life law. She knew Harper, Madigan and Horn's law library so well that she could file away regional digests faster than the librarian could. She required daily amounts of coffee large enough to fill a small garden pond. Every other week she received a healthy paycheck. One of these days she hoped to find time to spend it.

The Wagner file. Her mentor, a junior partner named Harold Banks, had dropped it on her credenza at six the night before.

"Hit it first thing in the morning," he'd said. "It's simple research, but potentially time-consuming."

Well, it was morning. And the file was still there, waiting. Kat wrinkled her nose as an unprofessional snort lifted her dark bangs from her forehead. The Wagner file was larger than most Thanksgiving turkeys she'd seen. Her secretary, whom she shared with Hal, would need a handcart to lug it back to his office.

With a resolute flick of the wrist, she opened the manila file.

Hal's giant red scrawl met her gaze: SECRETARY'S DAY.

Kat blinked. Then, of its own accord, her left hand reached for the phone. Hal answered after one ring.

"What's this note in the Wagner file?" she demanded.

"A reminder. Today's Secretary's Day."

"It is? How was I supposed to know that?"

"Haven't you been in any card stores lately? This is, I believe, a Hallmark-created holiday."

"Hal, I haven't been off the seventh floor of this building lately."

She was lucky to have him as her mentor, and she knew it. Hal looked out for her. Although nine years away from his own first year as an associate, he remembered clearly the pitfalls and confusion that came with the turf.

"Okay, okay," she said with a sigh. "So I'm supposed to be extra nice to our secretary today."

"You ever want to get to an appointment on time again, you'll be extra nice to her *every* day."

"What should I do, Hal? I didn't get her a present. Why didn't you warn me about this yesterday?"

"You don't need a present. Take her out to lunch."

"Lunch? What is that? I've forgotten."

"Very funny."

"Lunch with my secretary isn't billable, is it?"

"Sorry, Kat."

"What about you? She's your secretary, too."

Hal chuckled. "I've got a deposition today. Besides, I thought ahead. My flowers should arrive by noon."

Kat slumped in her chair. Lunch. With Devon. Devon was a dynamite secretary, but Kat saw no point in trying to cultivate a friendship with her. They weren't buddies, for Pete's sake. It was hard enough maintaining a boss-secretary relationship when your secretary was only three years younger than you were. And, although Devon was twenty-four and perfectly pleasant, Kat doubted that they had anything in common.

She sighed. "Hal, couldn't I just write Devon a nice note and then get back to work on my career? That's really why I show up here every day."

He ignored the comment. She could picture him, horned-rimmed glasses sliding down his nose, right hand tapping his ever-present pen against the top of his desk calendar as he quickly checked his watch.

"You could use the break too, Kat. Look, here's what you do. Leave a nice note on Devon's desk inviting her out to lunch today. Okay?"

"Out to lunch where?"

"Oh, Kat, Kat, Kat. Must I do all the thinking for you? Where's my star associate?"

"Out to lunch," Kat replied without a trace of humor.

"Devon's easy. She talks all the time. You'd have to be deaf not to know she's dying to try Angel Café."

Deaf or buried up to your ears in legalese. But at least Kat had heard of Angel Café. It was a trendy new restaurant in South Baltimore.

"Now," Hal said, "take my little note out of the Wagner file. Rip it to shreds. Underneath is a note regarding a couple of issues I need researched. Can you turn out a cohesive memorandum by tomorrow night?"

"*And* do lunch with Devon?"

"The research is straightforward. I'm counting on you, kiddo. Wagner's Big Man on Campus these days." Hal hung up the phone.

Lunch with her secretary. A memo on the Wagner file. An empty coffee cup. It already felt like Monday, even though it wasn't.

"I just love Federal Hill, don't you?" Devon sat in the passenger seat of Kat's car, her tall, strawberry-blond prettiness set off to perfection by the deep green suit she wore.

Kat had been born in Baltimore. The blue-collar Federal Hill she remembered from her childhood bore little resemblance to the pristine, yuppified version that now attracted touring suburbanites like Devon. This version of Federal Hill was very pretty, but the one Kat knew had been a lot more interesting.

Fortunately, Devon seldom required responses to her comments.

"I made a reservation," she said. "I was lucky to get it, too. This place is super popular."

"I hope you told them one-thirty, because it's going to take at least half an hour to find a parking place."

"I see a place over there if you think you can squeeze into it."

"I can squeeze into anything." Kat clicked on her turn signal and expertly glided into the space.

It was easier to exude confidence while both she and

Devon remained seated. Devon, a leggy five foot nine, always made Kat feel like a cute little puppet. Additionally, Devon possessed an air of sophistication that harmonized with her creamy porcelain skin and well-coiffed helmet of hair. Kat was only five foot one. She needed a stool to reach the top bookshelves of the law library. Her wide brown eyes and delicate bones made her appear younger than she was, no asset where attorney-client relationships were concerned. She suspected that if she didn't possess such a big mouth, judges would simply pat her on the head whenever she appeared in court.

She watched glumly as her secretary unfolded herself from the car. Devon should have been the attorney. No way anyone would ever ignore her.

And, as usual, nobody did. Devon's elegant, smooth curves strolled languidly toward the entrance of Angel Café, oblivious to the stares of male admirers.

Angel Café, tucked between an antique shop and a film-processing store, occupied a three-story row home. Its facade was white brick, accented by mauve trim. Tied-back lace curtains framed the large front picture window. A gauzy scrim blocked a clear view of the room immediately within, but a carved, painted sign positioned above the window said it all:

ANGEL CAFÉ

NOURISHMENT FOR BOTH BODY AND SPIRIT

"How wonderful," Devon said. "So perceptive, don't you think? Somebody should have opened up a place like this years ago."

Kat ran her fingers up the brass handrail. She had nothing against angels; it was kitsch she couldn't abide. A small brass cherub sat firmly on the top of the rail. Two attached cherub heads graced the doorknocker, reminding her of some weird celestial mutant birth. True perception, she thought, might have hired a better decorator.

Devon had been smart to call ahead for reservations. The tiny lobby of the restaurant was crammed with people. The sentimental whimsy of the surrounding Victorian memorabilia made the restaurant's patrons seem larger than life-size. Business-suited professionals wedged themselves between bowls of rose petal potpourri and carved cupids. There were, not surprisingly, angel images everywhere. Kat had never seen so many lithographs and paintings together in one room. Fat little putti rolled distorted round eyes up toward heaven. Plump, dimpled angels arced well-padded arms above innocent children.

"I love angels." Devon's smile lit the room. "God, Kat, don't you love this place?"

Kat averted her gaze from a melodramatic rendering of a drippy angel leading a rejoicing soul to Heaven.

"I prefer my angels to have edges," she said.

"Edges?"

"Victorian angels are too round. I like more fire and brimstone, a dash of medieval angst, perhaps."

Devon laughed and shook her head. "You would," she said.

They approached the hostess, who, swathed in a gauzy, ethereal dress, waited behind a burnished wood counter.

"Hi," Devon said, naturally accustomed to shielding her boss from unwanted entanglements with the outside world. "We have a one o'clock reservation. The name is Katerina Piretti."

"Pretty name," the hostess said, and Kat managed a small smile. She felt awkward, as if she blended right in with the other tiny knickknacks displayed about the room.

"Your table will be ready shortly," the hostess said. "Feel free to find yourself a stone and relax." She gestured toward a large, hand-woven basket on the end of the counter. Inside were hundreds of smooth, tiny stones. Each one sported a delicate "Angel Café" decal.

"What are we supposed to do with these?" Kat whispered to Devon as the hostess turned away.

Devon had already begun sifting through the stones, sampling individual ones with a thoughtful rub between thumb and forefinger.

"It's therapeutic. Let yourself feel each stone until you find the one that best matches your vibrations."

"What?" She knew she was on the edge, dangerously close to laughter.

"Once you find the stone whose rhythms suit your own, you can use it to calm yourself in times of stress. You, of all people, could use a meditation aid. Oh, look! This one practically glows pink. And it feels marvelous. It's just waiting for me!"

The words "Oh, give me a break!" pushed at the back of Kat's lips, dying to escape in a burst of derision. She bit them back.

"Ms. Piretti." The hostess tapped Devon on the arm. "Your table is ready. Please, follow me."

Kat sighed, not surprised that the hostess had chosen Devon as the one in charge. So much for psychic perception.

The cacophony of the crowded lobby faded away as they entered a serene dining room. Kat noted that Angel Café was composed of several small dining rooms, following the original floor plan of the structure's residential days. The hostess led them into one of the smaller rooms, a high-ceilinged area dominated by an intricately carved fireplace mantel.

"I bet this was a formal parlor," Devon said. "The lady of the house probably received all sorts of exciting men in here. Can't you just imagine the intrigue this room has seen?"

The room held five small tables, all filled with smiling diners. The angel motif of the lobby had been carried through here as well. Angel prints lined the walls. Papier-mâché angels descended delicately from the ceiling, attached by braided gold cords. Still more angels reclined on the mantelpiece in stone-carved splendor, sleeping, whistling, or blowing kisses. Crystals dangled in the windows, shooting the room with rainbows whenever the sun caught a facet. Tiny bowls of rose potpourri decorated each table.

"They've thought of absolutely everything." Devon shook her head. "This place is incredible."

Kat perused the menu. *Incredible* wasn't the word. *Expensive* was. She could raise her consciousness on her own at half the price.

The menu consisted mainly of salads, soups, sandwiches, and light fare. Kat noted that the café opened only for breakfast, lunch, and tea. That accounted for the lack of heavy entrées. Her eyes skimmed down a list of herbal teas.

"Welcome." Their waitress grinned. "I'm Molly, and I'll be your server today. What can I get you to drink?"

"I'll have the Orange Blossom tea," Devon said.

"Good choice!" Molly was entirely too chipper for Kat's taste. She looked as wholesome as fresh grain, apple-cheeked and blond, as if she'd just blown in from a meadow.

"Coffee, please," Kat said.

"Cappuccino, espresso, mocha . . ."

"Don't you have just plain coffee?"

Molly pondered her as if she were a poor, unenlightened being bused in from an underprivileged reality.

"Certainly," she conceded. "Decaf?"

"Caf. And lots of it."

Molly eyed her thoughtfully. "Sure. Did you pick out a stone while you were waiting?"

"No."

"Go choose one while I fetch the drinks. They're very soothing."

So was Valium. Everything about Angel Café rubbed Kat wrong, and she couldn't even say why. It shouldn't have been that way. Really, the room was sunny and comfortable, and some of the angel statues were very pretty. She liked the fact that none of the fine china pieces on the table matched. The patterns were beautiful and interesting, pulling the table together in a haphazardly charming way. The rose potpourri smelled pleasingly sweet. And yet, it all felt studied and contrived. Bogus.

A quick glance around the room proved she was the only one who felt that way.

"Look how relaxed everyone is." Devon leaned back in her chair. "You can bet that most of them left hectic offices to come here, too. This place is so serene."

"It's the stones. They each picked one hell of a vibrating stone."

"Maybe you're right." Though a crackerjack secretary, Devon wasn't very good with sarcasm.

Kat narrowed her eyes. "Don't you find this place the least bit commercial? You know, kind of riding the New Age wave?"

"Oh, no. This place is a welcome relief. It's like an oasis from the stress of everyday life. But I'm into self-discovery. I like exploring my potential on all levels."

"What does that mean?" Kat started to ask, but Molly had appeared tableside with a large cup of herbal tea and a ridiculously small cup of coffee.

"I'll need at least five more cups," Kat said.

Molly smiled reassuringly. "Don't worry. I'll take care of you. Will you ladies want readings today?"

"Readings?" Devon's face lit up.

"Why, yes. Nearly everybody who comes to Angel Café has a reading done. It's an additional fifteen dollars, but it's worth it. Stephen comes around to your table and speaks with your spirit guides. They've usually got a message for you."

Devon turned a pretty pink. "Let's do it, Kat."

"Fifteen dollars?" Kat's eyes widened. "For somebody to deliver a message from something I can't even verify exists?"

Molly, able to forgive a caffeine addiction, could not overcome Kat's latest breach of etiquette. She turned resolutely toward Devon.

"Are you interested?"

"Yes," Devon said firmly. "I'd love a reading. I've wanted to meet my spirit guides for ages."

"I'll sign you up, then. And I'll take your lunch order now, if you're ready."

Devon ordered the Sunshine Sprout salad, a rabbit-happy concoction that clocked in at $8.75. Out of pure peevishness, Kat ordered a slice of chocolate cake. She stared down the disapproval in Molly's eyes until the server was forced to retreat toward the kitchen.

"Kat," Devon said once Molly had gone, "I want to learn more about you. We work together, but we don't talk."

Great. Now her secretary wanted to be her confidante. Kat instinctively pressed herself against the back of her chair.

"I worry about you," Devon continued earnestly. "You work all the time. You're behind your desk when I get to the office every morning, and you're still there when I leave at night."

"Not so." Kat set her jaw. "Sometimes I'm in the law library, and occasionally I even make an appearance in court."

Her secretary plowed right on. "I can tell from my pile of dictation that you spend hours in the office on weekends, too."

"It goes with the territory, Devon. Big firms don't hire associates based on their ability to relax."

"But you work harder than all the other new associates put together. It's like you've got some sort of death wish. I was just telling my husband the other night, 'Kat's such a sweetheart, such a regular little doll-baby, I wonder why she pushes herself so hard?' You don't even leave yourself time for a social life."

Kat's heart slammed against her chest. She couldn't

afford to become Devon's pet project. Her mind cast frantically about for a diversion.

"Tell me about spirit guides," she said abruptly. "I've never heard of them."

Devon's gray eyes observed her reproachfully. "Okay, but don't think I don't know you're trying to change the subject. I don't get it. You're beautiful, you're smart, and you want to spend the rest of your life up to your ears in paperwork."

"If you don't tell me about spirit guides this minute, I'll mumble incomprehensibly through every dictation tape I give you for the rest of our lives."

Devon leaned back and lifted her teacup to pearly mauve lips. "Each of us has at least five spirit guides to help us through our daily lives. There's a high teacher, a doctor, a chemist, a saint, and an Indian guide."

"An Indian guide?" Once again, Kat stifled a desperate urge to laugh. "What's that for?"

"The Indian guide balances you with the forces of nature. That helps center you."

"Devon, there's not much nature in my background. My grandparents came over on a boat from Italy and settled in the city. As far as I know, no American Indians came with them."

Devon sighed and shook her head. "There you go again. You get defensive the minute anyone talks about anything other than work. Honestly, you won't open yourself to anything."

Kat glanced up, unnaturally grateful to see Molly bearing down on them with their lunches. The conversation was getting too personal for comfort.

"Here we go," Molly said in her perkier-than-thou voice. "A salad for you, a piece of cake for you. Stephen will be over in a few minutes to do your reading. Enjoy!"

Devon mournfully shook her head as Kat sunk her fork into the velvety chocolate icing of her cake. "You don't eat right, either. If you don't take care of your body, it won't take care of you."

That was probably true. It dawned on Kat that her father would love to have a conscientious, health-oriented daughter like Devon. Devon, neat and organized, efficient in a ladylike job . . . Devon, who'd fulfilled parental dreams by marrying young. Due to Devon's habit of chatting throughout the workday, Kat even knew that her secretary had been trying for at least a year to get pregnant.

A grandchild. Her father would swoon with delight.

She swallowed hard.

"Look, Devon, let's not talk about me anymore. It's a boring topic. I appreciate your concern, but it's not necessary. I'm fine, really."

"It's just that I like you, Kat. Most attorneys cop attitudes, but you're different. I think of you as a friend."

That was probably because she totally lacked authority.

"Greetings, ladies."

Kat and Devon turned as one to the man who stood beside their table.

"Stephen Carmichael." He extended a hand. "Welcome." He pulled an empty chair from a neighboring table and placed it deftly beneath him. "Which one of you requested a reading?"

"Me." Devon stared dreamily at Stephen Carmichael. Kat had to admit he was worth staring at. His hair was black and his eyes, the palest of greens, commanded attention in an evenly tanned face.

"No reading for you?" he asked her.

"No, thank you." She took another determined forkful of cake.

Devon leaned forward in excited expectation as Stephen turned her way. He reached across the table and, with a charming smile, grasped both her hands in his.

"What's your name?" The relaxed, intimate tone of his voice told Kat that most people were more than happy to put their faith in Stephen Carmichael.

"Devon. Devon Alexander."

"Pretty. Devon, I'm going to take a few quiet seconds to get a sense of you, and of your guides."

He closed his eyes. Kat watched as his strong, slender fingers rhythmically traced Devon's hand. An unexpected image of those fingers caressing her own hand flashed across her mind, sending an odd flutter through her chest. She brushed the image away. It made her angry, somehow. Besides, she had no intention of becoming involved with anyone, least of all someone who claimed to be in touch with invisible entities.

"You're married," Stephen said, eyes still closed.

"Yes, that's why she wears that ring on her finger," Kat blurted out. Her hand flew to her mouth. She thought she detected a look of annoyance flicker across Stephen's handsome, even features, but he continued as if she hadn't said a word. "You haven't been married all that long, though."

This time Kat managed to keep her thoughts to herself. Of course Devon hadn't been married long. She was only in her mid-twenties. How long could she possibly have been married?

Stephen opened his eyes and fixed Devon with his steady, green gaze. "There have been discussions about children within your household."

Devon's mouth dropped. "How did you know?"

Kat stifled a groan. He knew because Devon was a young, married woman. Of course she and her husband discussed children, whether pro, con, present or future.

Stephen once again stroked Devon's hand. "Two of your guides are here with messages for you. One is a tall woman dressed in flowing violet robes. She has long blond hair."

"Well, that counts her out as your Indian guide," Kat said. This time she was certain that Stephen was not pleased.

"Who is she?" Devon asked, intrigued.

Stephen closed his eyes. "She says her name is Sapphire. Her message concerns children. She wants you to know that all is happening as it should."

Devon let out a long, relieved breath. "Ask her why I can't get pregnant."

Kat studied the confident set of Stephen's mouth and abandoned all hope of tact. "Can't she hear you, Devon? Where is she, Mr. Carmichael? Levitating above the table? Sitting on the mantel?"

Stephen threw her a barely perceptible glare from beneath lowered lids. "She says to relax," he said, and for a moment Kat wondered if that message was more for her than for Devon. "Drink chamomile tea. Dream. Drink of yourself."

"Oh!" Devon cried, clearly impressed.

"What does that mean?" Kat demanded.

Devon rested her chin on her hand. "It means that I

should listen to my inner voice. I should like myself for who I am and stop measuring my worth by whether or not I get pregnant. It's truly profound, Kat."

Kat let out an exasperated sigh. "I'm sorry, Devon. I'm trying to be open-minded, here, but I just don't get it."

Devon blushed a lovely pink, unsure how to tactfully counter her boss.

Stephen Carmichael waded into the fray. "Your other guide is a very old soul, possessed of great depths. He stands behind you with the golden ring of knowledge balanced over your head."

An impish expression crossed Kat's face. "Why, Devon, his help must have gotten you through law school."

Devon looked confused, but Stephen Carmichael snatched up the clue and ran with it.

"Oh, are you an attorney?"

"She is," Kat said, unable to stop herself. "A damn good one, too. I should know. I'm her secretary."

"Kat!" Devon's jaw dropped.

"She works for Harper, Madigan and Horn," Kat continued. "Perhaps Mr. Golden Ring has a message regarding her law career stashed away in his little bag of tricks."

Devon nailed her with an angry glare, but Stephen had already closed his eyes in concentration, and she dared not break his communication with her guide.

"Yes," Stephen said, "he does. He did indeed help you through school. He helped provide that extra push you needed during long nights of study. And he is still available to you now that you are practicing law."

"Good thing," Kat said. "You're going to need him."

"You have a fine legal mind," Stephen said, "and you are undoubtedly effective in court."

"Undoubtedly," Kat echoed.

"Your secretary is very supportive." Stephen passed Kat a puzzled glance. "I'm sure, Devon, that you have a question or two to ask your guides. Please, feel free . . ."

"Kat!" a voice called from across the room. Kat jerked her head up sharply to see Joe Turner, opposing counsel on the Haggerty case, striding her way.

Why was the timing in her personal life always so impeccably off? And this was going to be even worse than usual because Joe, stopping smack at their table, leaned over to greet Stephen as well.

"Stephen, buddy. Great place. I love it."

"Thanks, Joe. I'm glad you stopped by. I'll be with you in a minute, I promise."

"Take your time. I can understand being bumped for Katerina Piretti."

"You?" Stephen asked Kat.

She nodded her acknowledgment.

"Watch your words, though," Joe said. "She looks small and innocent, but she's a killer. Kat, no chance your client will reconsider our last offer?"

Kat shook her head. "We're still laughing about it."

"Didn't think so. Oh, well, we'll duke it out in court next week, then. Stephen, you've done wonders. I bet you make loads of money with this place."

Kat's eyes widened. "You own Angel Café?" she demanded, staring at Stephen.

"You're an attorney?" he countered coldly.

"Gotta go." Joe lowered his voice. "I brought my secretary for Secretary's Day. I don't want to leave her hanging out alone in the lobby."

"What a coincidence," Kat said, throwing Stephen a challenging glance. "I brought my secretary, too."

"See you next week, Kat." Joe took off, unaware of the tempest he'd left behind.

"Well," Stephen said, icicles dripping from that one word, "I suppose I'd better be moving on."

Kat nodded her agreement. "Yes, I suppose you'd better."

"But I have questions for my spirit guides!" Devon protested.

Both Stephen and Kat stared at her, amazed by her singular lack of perception.

"I'm sorry to cut our session short, Ms. Alexander," Stephen finally said. He delivered a gracious smile. "I won't charge you for it."

"As well you shouldn't." Kat could seldom leave well enough alone.

Stephen, who'd already begun to stand, froze midway.

"Ms. Piretti, was it? I'm sorry if I've offended you. Please, feel free to dine elsewhere in the future."

"No problem, Mr. Carmichael. No problem at all."

He stood and, still glaring, turned toward the lobby. Suddenly he clutched his midsection and paled. He reached frantically for the edge of the table, his eyes fixed on Kat in disbelief.

"Mr. Carmichael, are you all right?" Kat leaped to her feet.

He opened his mouth, then shut it again. He seemed struggling to keep it closed, but words poured forth, almost as if they had a life of their own.

"Ms. Piretti, I apologize . . . but I have a message for you."

Kat sank into her chair. "From what sort of being, Mr. Carmichael? Casper the Friendly Ghost?"

He shook his head violently. "I don't know who it's from," he said in a low voice. "Believe me, if I had the choice, I'd never talk to you again."

She rolled her eyes and reached for her coffee. "Sure. You just can't help it. The stars are configured just so, and you've got a Ouija board stashed under the table."

"You're right about Peter's death," Stephen said tonelessly.

The coffee cup dropped from her grasp, cracking both itself and the saucer on which it landed. Kat began to tremble so violently that Stephen instinctively reached out to hold her.

"Let go of me," she managed to say in a hoarse voice. "Let go of me."

"I'm sorry. Whatever I said, I . . ."

But Kat had wrenched herself free and now stood, a deep flush of scarlet flooding her cheeks.

"Here." She reached into her wallet and pulled out a twenty-dollar bill. "Devon, I'll meet you at the car." She turned and fairly flew through the lobby door.

"What just happened?" Devon jumped to her feet.

"I don't know." Stephen stared into space, absently fingering the bill Kat had pressed into his hand.

Devon laid a comforting hand on his arm. "Don't worry. Kat just doesn't believe in angels yet."

But Stephen remained staring straight ahead as Devon gathered her belongings and left the table.

2

~~~

"WHAT I NEED TO KNOW," PETER SAID SERIOUSLY, "IS whether you cook like your father or like your aunt."

Kat, sitting beside him on the front stoop of her father's row house, grinned.

"Why?" she demanded. A tiny breeze stirred the stagnant air for a moment before giving up in the dense humidity of the early summer evening. Kat lifted her heavy hair from her neck and breathed deeply.

"Why?" Peter repeated, wrinkling his nose. "That should be obvious. Your father cooks like a dream. A vision. Food in heaven is going to taste like the ambrosia he serves. Your aunt . . . God, Katie, please don't tell me you cook like your aunt Francesca. If dinner tonight was the best she can do, she didn't willingly leave the convent. They kicked her out."

Kat's smile, wide and relaxed, dissolved into laughter. She reached out to push a strand of red hair from his eyes. "Aunt Frannie never cooked in the convent. Poor Peter. You're wilting out here. Let's go back to your apartment. At least you have air-conditioning."

"You're evading my question, Katie. Can you cook?"

She shook her head. "Sorry."

"Christ." He buried his head in his arms. "How could

someone who loves to eat fall in love with someone who can't cook?"

Four row houses down, the DiPaulo girls played hopscotch on the sidewalk. Kat serenely watched as little Gina threw her stone and, when her sister wasn't looking, surreptitiously pushed it off the line with a tiny tap of her toe.

"Peter, I just finished my second year of law school. It should have been clear to you long ago that I'm not planning to spend my life trapped in a kitchen."

"I know. I'll just have to take cooking classes."

She shrugged. "It's no big deal. I'll scrounge off my dad and you can eat carry-out for the rest of your life."

Peter, already pink from the heat, managed to turn even pinker. "Um . . . that's not going to work because . . . um . . . damn, I was going to be all debonair about this. I figured it was no big deal . . . but it *is* a big deal."

He rummaged through his pants pocket in a desperate search. He'd come to Kat's house directly from work, and now dragged up the day's accumulation of old receipts and gum wrappers before finally locating a crumpled plastic sandwich bag.

"Katerina Piretti," he said, digging into the bag, "please, please, you've got to marry me."

Kat stared as he drew out a tiny diamond ring.

"We can live together forever," Peter continued earnestly. "We'll starve, but we'll be blissfully happy. You get two seconds to decide. Then we break the news to your dad and Aunt Frannie. And then, unfortunately, I've got to get back into reporter mode. I'm hot on a story."

But Kat didn't need the two seconds. Quietly she

held out her left hand. Peter, usually so cocky and confident, shyly slid the ring onto the proper finger.

"Hey," he said, "I've got to admit I was a little bit worried, there."

Kat silenced him with a kiss.

"Angel Café was marvelous." Devon staunchly deposited herself into Kat's passenger seat. "Sometimes, Kat, I just can't figure you out."

Her indignant tones rose and fell in a faraway buzz for the ten minutes it took to reach the curb of their office building. Then her eyes grew round. "What are you doing? Why aren't we parking in the garage?"

"Happy Secretary's Day." Kat yanked the emergency brake. "As a special treat, I'll be out for the rest of the afternoon. Tell Hal not to worry; he'll get his memo on time."

"But . . ." Dazed, Devon slid from the car.

Kat reached across the seat and slammed the passenger door shut. The squeal of her car tires served as goodbye.

Damn him! Tears stung her eyes, making her blink rapidly in order to maintain solid vision. She swerved her car out of the path of a turning delivery van.

Damn him!

But she wasn't thinking about Stephen Carmichael, with his trendy little restaurant and sinuous good looks. Instead, her curses were for Peter, who'd made her love him, had promised to stay with her forever, and now lay peacefully buried in a pristine cemetery plot while she was forced to plow through the grim day-to-day reality of life without him.

She pulled a sharp left through a red light and

headed up the expressway, traveling seventy in the fifty mile-per-hour zone. A car horn honked behind her, but as long as flashing blue lights did not accompany it, she didn't care.

She'd been better off before she'd met him. Before Peter, she'd coolly attended to her life, acing her college classes and everything else she did without a trace of vulnerability. Her father and Aunt Frannie had provided solid security that eliminated any need to leave her safe cocoon.

Then Peter had come along, passing a corny wink at her from across their college sociology class. He'd appeared at her shoulder in the cafeteria, materialized in doorways at the very instant she passed by. Suddenly, everywhere she looked, Peter Dulaney was waiting for her, urging her to open herself to his vibrant sense of the world.

And where had it left her? Alone, with memories too painful to acknowledge, but impossible to ignore. Stuck with longings she couldn't begin to reconcile.

Her room at home remained the same. Her father and Aunt Frannie still cared as much as they'd always cared. And yet, none of this was enough anymore. Loving Peter had revealed possibilities she'd never before recognized. His words, his touch, his kiss . . . none of that could be duplicated by the souls he'd left behind to comfort her. There was a large, gaping hole in the fabric of her life, emptiness she couldn't imagine filling.

"Damn you." She angrily blinked back an errant tear, stemming the flow before it could begin.

In the days following Peter's funeral, her father had spoken gently of the necessary tears he'd cried twenty-one years earlier at her mother's death. Aunt Frannie had firmly advised that it was cathartic to cry. But Kat had known the truth even then: Peter was gone and he wasn't coming back. Crying would only get in the way.

The cemetery was small, and empty whenever she visited. She trudged by rote up the green hill to Peter's grave, reluctantly relinquishing her anger with each step. By the time she reached his gravesite, only a deep, dull emptiness remained where her rage had burned.

After nearly two years the simple gravestone looked as if it had always been part of the landscape. That made Kat want to scrub it clean, to make it clear that the vibrancy of Peter belonged to the living and would never blend in with this bucolic setting. She reached out a hand to brush away a streak of dirt, then withdrew it sharply before it could touch the stone. The gesture reminded her too much of the way she'd always brushed Peter's hair from his eyes. She'd done so only hours before his death, on the night he'd proposed.

Although she'd replayed his death in her mind a thousand times, it still made no sense. Suicide, they'd told her. The gun was found in one hand; a nearly empty bottle of Scotch sat nearby. His blood alcohol level had soared above the legal limit, yet he'd managed to shoot straight and clean. No note, but a clear, obvious conclusion that Peter Dulaney had killed himself.

Except that Peter hardly ever drank, was never depressed, and had no reason to kill himself.

"Oh, Peter." Kat closed her eyes, helplessly lost in memories. "You're never coming back to me. Why can't we let go? What exactly do you expect me to do?"

Suddenly a sharp image of Stephen Carmichael ripped through her mind. The vision was so intense that Kat reeled backward, as if physically struck. Her eyes flew open in shock.

Peter's gravestone, along with each individual blade of grass touching it, glowed in a band of strong, white gold light.

It was not in her nature to scream, so the shriek she needed now lodged itself firmly in her throat before it could reach the air. She hastily backed away from the grave. The light grew undeniably brighter.

Fumbling for her keys, Kat turned to race for the safety of the car. She jammed the key into the ignition and, gunning the motor, hazarded a last terrified glance toward the grave.

It looked the same as usual, peaceful and serene, a harmonious advertisement for the eternal life to come.

"Damn you, Peter Dulaney!" she gulped, leaning her head against the steering wheel. Her temples throbbed. "I'm never coming back here again, do you hear me? You can't do this to me! You can't hold on to me anymore!"

3

STEPHEN CARMICHAEL HAD A B.A. FROM CORNELL AND AN M.B.A from Wharton, and he knew a profitable trend when he saw one. He was thirty-five years old and had already planned to open his own restaurant when commercialized angels began showing up all over the place. Suddenly he couldn't go anywhere without encountering them. They cooed at him from bookshelves, smiled down benevolently from shop displays, and transformed themselves into serious talk-show fodder. Why, all one had to do at a cocktail party was reverently whisper the word *angel,* and half a dozen women appeared at your side! Stephen had discovered long ago that if he spoke gently, with deep eye contact and soft touches, most of those women would find him far more astute and sensitive than he actually was.

Personally, Stephen suspected that angels were a bunch of hooey. What was the point of ethereal, otherworldly beings popping in and out of human existence at will? What, was the spirit world incredibly dull? Were the visiting angels tired of halos and sick to death of harp music? The whole concept of spiritual assistance made him roll his eyes. If the spirit world couldn't pick up the tab or find a good parking space, then he had little use for it. He preferred his reality to be stone-hard practical.

He had to admit, though, that New Age spirituality provided some great pickup lines. And the women he met were even fun before their earnestness got in the way. He enjoyed the romance of their clothing, which flowed gracefully as they glided toward him. Their jewelry, inevitably silver-crafted mythological symbols, chimed pleasantly when they swayed to the open tones of his *Nature's Signature* CD. He acquired a lot of lady friends through that CD. The relationships never ran deep or lasted long, but that was okay. At least he was never alone.

For Stephen had found that he could speak "New Age" fluently, even though it was not his native tongue. It was almost like being the only sober person at a party. He learned a lot more about human nature than the humans involved would ever have wanted him to know.

Maybe angels didn't do windows or share secrets, but they obviously made money. It hadn't taken long to decide that his little restaurant would be filled first with angels, then with customers.

He'd succeeded beyond his most optimistic hopes. Angel Café, only a few months old, was a smashing success. It was still open only for breakfast, lunch, and tea, but business was so good that Stephen was contemplating a trial run for dinner as well.

Although angels were a great hook, Stephen had known all along that they were not the ultimate hook. Angel Café would need something else if it was going to distinguish itself from the other New Age-ish eateries sprouting up in yuppie pockets of the city.

"Maybe I could install Ouija boards beneath glass at each table in the restaurant," he'd mused early one morning.

"Don't do that!" Victoria, who'd already lasted a record-breaking four months as his companion, had stared in horror through the steamy cloud of her herbal breakfast tea. "God, Stephen, who knows *what* you'll attract!"

"I'll attract customers." They were sitting in his kitchen. He liked the way the morning sun played in Victoria's hair, turning its usually flat red into vibrant copper.

"You'll attract lost souls. I certainly wouldn't want to be around a bunch of lost souls, I can tell you that."

"Lost souls?" He'd wrinkled his nose in an attempt to hold back his laughter.

"Of course! Spirits speak through that board, Stephen, and not all of those spirits are happy and content."

"Of course they're not. AT&T is so much better."

"Stop it." Victoria looked hurt.

"Okay," Stephen relented. "So sometimes you hear from pissed-off souls. Then why do people use Ouija boards in the first place?"

"Because there's always an interest in knowing more than you can see. Don't you feel that way? Don't you want to learn about your future, or about your past lives?"

He pondered the question. "No. This life is enough for me. Each day takes all the concentration I've got. I'm a busy man."

"Even busy men need to make space for their souls."

He let that one slide by. Victoria, all the "enlightened" women he allowed into his life, came equipped with oblique statements that he just didn't feel like pondering too closely.

Her comment about Ouija boards and "lost souls," however, made him think. His thoughts had nothing to do with the souls themselves, since he relegated them to the same category as he did those nonexistent angels. What concerned him was the dangerous fact that the very clientele he wanted to reach might be repelled by the "bad vibes" of Ouija boards. He could not afford a major marketing gaffe.

Yet people harbored a vulnerable desire to know more about themselves, past and future. Stephen had a pet theory: Most folks were egotistical enough to buy into any story in which they could be the central player.

He wondered.

"Hey," he said casually. "Want a psychic reading?"

Victoria set her teacup down, surprised. "You can do those?"

Stephen shrugged. "Sure," he lied.

Victoria was as good a test case as any. Okay, so she was gullible, but Stephen felt that most people were. And she was no lightweight. She was a marine biologist, for heaven's sake. If she had a penchant for New Age stuff, well, it was that very penchant he counted on from the general public to make his new restaurant a great big hit.

"So, what do you do?" Victoria asked. "Read tarot cards? Use a crystal?"

What did he do? Stephen quickly reviewed several months' worth of cocktail chatter.

"I talk to your spirit guides," he said in a hushed voice. "In fact, I sense yours now."

"Too cool!" Victoria leaned forward.

"They've been with you since birth. One in particular has much to say today. His name is . . . Myrial."

"You're kidding. My God, Stephen, what does he look like?"

"He's difficult to visualize. He's on a higher spiritual plane and finds it awkward to translate himself into physical reality. He always guides you, though, and he cares for you very much."

Victoria's eyes widened with excitement. Good grief, she was buying every word!

Stephen continued his foray into the spirit world. He brushed a hand through his shaggy black hair and then nodded intently, as if listening to a faraway voice.

"There isn't time for everything today," he said, "but Myrial wishes to share one past life of significance. You, Victoria, have always been searching, growing toward the light. Once, centuries ago, you were a Tibetan monk. I see you there, standing on a mountain, before the monastery, practicing cool, clear tones of meditation in an effort to center yourself."

He would have laughed at his own fable had Victoria not been staring at him as if he'd just told her she'd won the lottery.

"Tell me more," she said. "This explains so much."

The hallway clock chimed him back into reality.

"Jesus, Vic, it's getting late. I've got to get moving, here."

"Tell me more!"

"Um, more. Myrial stands behind you, hands raised in benediction. He says you are the mistress of your destiny, beginning with this very moment. He reminds you to be as a stream, rippling and glistening over the rocks that may cross your path. The sediment of life will remain behind. What is good and necessary will travel with you. Okay, Vic, he's gone."

"God, Stephen." Her voice was throaty now, the way it always got when she wanted him. "I'm very impressed. Maybe I could come back tonight and you could tell me more. I had no idea you could do this."

Stephen was not surprised he could do this. Anybody could do this. What surprised him was that other people were so willing to buy it. As he reached out an arm to pull Victoria toward him, the idea blossomed: Angel Café would provide psychic readings and, in a brilliant stroke of economy, he would be the reader.

For the most part, it had worked beautifully. Stephen, handsome and smooth, found that all one had to do for mystical credibility was turn on the charm.

Unfortunately, the method wasn't foolproof. There'd been that slight mishap when he'd delivered a message "from beyond" from a spouse not yet dead. He'd covered it well, though, advising the woman that the message came from a spouse in a past life. (He'd provided a detailed account of that past life at no extra charge.) He'd also accidentally predicted a promotion for a woman just fired. Flowery talk about the fluidity of time had done the trick. The lady was soon happy again, knowing that a promotion awaited her sometime in the magic future.

Then there'd been that misadventure with Katerina Piretti. Fortunately, her dining companion had been gullible enough to ignore the entire fiasco. Still, the incident had been too close for comfort. Stephen cursed himself for forgetting that skeptics such as he would also flock to Angel Café, mainly to laugh at its spiritual pretensions.

The last thing he needed was for whispers of fake readings to slip out. That was why he now sat in his tiny restaurant office, diligently interviewing a bona fide psychic reader to take his place.

"You'd do readings between eleven o'clock and three o'clock, six days a week," he told the woman seated before him. "Table to table, about five to ten minutes with each customer. Could you handle that?"

It was the third time he'd uttered that stupid phrase: "Could you handle that?" Stephen was not one to repeat himself, but the woman, Tia Melody, did not inspire confidence. She looked nothing like the sort of reader he'd envisioned floating mysteriously through Angel Café. Her skin, thick and tan from too many days in the sun, made her look older than the forty-five years she'd listed on her job application. There appeared to be no requisite connections to Mother Earth or the universe. Even Tia Melody's hair was a color not found in nature, a shiny blond that broke the boundaries of platinum and verged on white. It was teased within an inch of its life, defying gravity to remain upswept in a beehive bubble. Tia Melody's eyes were violet. The clothing that clung to her tall, skinny frame made Stephen feel as if he were part of a sixties revival. She wore an orange poor-boy shirt, striped hip-hugging bell-bottoms, and platform sandals.

She'd come highly recommended by a friend of Stephen's who visited her regularly for private readings. He wanted to remember to ask that friend why.

"Mind if I smoke, hon?" Tia Melody asked in a voice made hoarse by decades of smoking.

"Well, actually, yes, I do."

"Don't worry." She broke out her pack of Camels. "You're not fated to die of lung cancer." She reached for her cigarette lighter, deftly lit the Camel, and leaned back in her chair. "You've been real informative, hon, and a charmer into the bargain. Now I've got some questions of my own."

Why don't you just read my mind, hon? Stephen thought peevishly, aware that she'd ask her questions whether or not he acquiesced. "Go right ahead, Ms. Melody," he said.

"Tia. Nobody calls me 'Ms. Melody.' It's my true name, too, in case you were wondering. Someone must've known I was going to grow up to be a psychic reader."

Or a stripper. Stephen glanced at his watch. It was 11:15. Soon the lunch crowd would stream in, and he'd need to make himself available.

"I'll be fast." Tia smiled. Her teeth, at least, were good: strong, even, and incredibly white for a smoker. "I work here eleven to three, right? I still want my private readings at home. I mean, that's not a problem, right?"

"I wouldn't care what you did on your own time, if you got the job. This isn't a done deal, remember. I still need to think on it."

The brilliant smile remained on her face. "Oh, it'll be a done deal, Mr. Carmichael. Let me do some readings for your customers today. Free. Kind of like an audition."

Stephen could not submerge the doubtful expression that flashed across his face.

"You don't like my clothes?" Tia asked, still grinning.

She was starting to remind him of the Cheshire cat in *Alice in Wonderland*. Worse, she was beginning to make him very, very nervous, and Stephen Carmichael was not accustomed to feeling nervous.

"Let's just say," he said politely, "that you're not dressed in a way my customers might find convincing."

"Oh, I get it. I don't go with the furniture." She took a long, deep drag of her cigarette. "You mean I'm not wearing ninety pounds of beads and filmy robes."

"Something like that."

"I could wear those things, hon, but it would look stupid as shit. Trust me, okay? It's words that count."

Stephen studied her. She was as far from the restaurant's New-Age ambience as one could get. His business sense, however, told him that this was not necessarily a drawback. Readers who looked like Tia Melody had to have talent. There was no other reason they'd get hired.

A tap on the door snapped him from his reverie.

"Hey, Stephen." Molly, his head waitress, leaned into the office. "A couple of folks want readings."

"Tell them I'll be right there, hon," Tia said forcefully before he could even open his mouth.

Molly glanced at Stephen, who nodded.

"Do me a big favor, though," he told Tia. "Don't smoke in my dining rooms."

"Oh, I wouldn't. Kills business." Tia ignored his grimace and dunked her cigarette butt into what was left of his coffee.

Stephen inadvertently rolled his eyes as he followed her out the door and over to Molly. This woman was a loon.

"Who wants the reading?" Tia demanded.

"Three people have already requested one." Molly peeked through a dining-room doorway and discreetly pointed out three individuals at three different tables.

Stephen recognized Devon Alexander right away. She was sitting with a group of friends, looking as beautiful as she had the first day he'd seen her. The open, trusting expression on her face made him feel a little guilty that he'd tried to pull one over on her.

Tia Melody's gaze rested thoughtfully on Devon. "Her."

"Pick another," Stephen said.

"Why?"

It was impossible to escape that penetrating violet stare. Stephen, feeling like a small boy forced to confess a petty crime, actually squirmed as he gazed down at his boots. "I destroyed her reading last time."

Tia Melody appraised him carefully. Her gaze took in his long legs, broad shoulders, and dark hair. Then she reached out a hand and, gently holding his chin, stared into his clear green eyes.

"Well, of course you did. God knows you're good-looking, but you don't have the gift. I'll handle it. You just watch and keep your mouth shut."

Devon's smile broadened as they approached the table.

"Hi, Mr. Carmichael," she said shyly. "I was so intrigued last week that I decided to come back. I didn't bring Kat, though. I brought some friends of mine instead."

No Kat. Stephen breathed a bit easier. There was obviously not a skeptic to be found among the women clustered about the table. They smiled up at him expectantly, as if he held the key to their innermost secrets.

Two of them eyed him boldly, obviously more than willing to know him on a non-psychic level.

Devon was lovelier than any of them, but Stephen remembered all too clearly the feel of that wedding band on her finger. Once, years ago, he'd tried an affair with a married woman. He'd been lucky to escape with his nose and teeth intact and, after that, required no psychic prodding to stay away from women already taken.

"Ladies." He flashed his winning smile. "A pleasure to see you today. Let me introduce Tia Melody, who will do your reading."

"Oh, you won't be the reader?" Devon looked disappointed.

"Mr. Carmichael taught me everything he knows," Tia said, pulling up a chair. She briskly took Devon's hand in her own. "Give me a moment to get a sense of you, hon."

Stephen watched closely as Tia slowly, rhythmically, ran her fingers gently up the inside of Devon's forearm. The gesture, nearly unconscious on Tia's part, seemed to mesmerize Devon.

"What's your name, hon?"

"Devon. Devon Alexander."

"No more wondering if your husband loves you, Devon, okay?" Tia closed her eyes. "He's a good, faithful man. He loves you a lot. He's just got quiet ways of showing it."

Devon colored. "How did you know . . ."

"Been on your mind all morning, right?"

"Well, yes, I . . ."

"His name begins with a *C*, but I can't make it out. He's blond, though, about your height."

"Jesus." One of Devon's girlfriends giggled nervously. "What did you do, Devon, show her a picture?"

Tia Melody continued as if she hadn't heard a word. "You're wasting your energy worrying about him. You haven't been married long, and you're both still adjusting. Long marriage, though. It will go through many changes, but it's solid."

Damn, Stephen thought as he watched Devon cross one long, shapely leg over the other.

"And, hon," Tia said, "do not even consider buying that new car at this time. Your finances aren't stable. I don't know what your husband does . . . oh, yes, I see. Sirens?"

Devon's eyes widened. "He's a cop."

"Well, it's honest work, but you need those paychecks for a down payment on a house. So lay off the car."

Devon's jaw, seemingly unhinged, dropped. Stephen could only assume that the same conversation frequently occurred at home.

He had to admit that Tia Melody did this stuff well. She didn't rely on past lives and broad predictions the way he had.

A slight shiver ran up his spine as Tia correctly informed Devon that, as the middle child of three, she was in constant search of a stabilized identity.

It was a little spooky. He glanced at the enthralled faces around the table, all staring at Tia Melody as if she were a minor deity. He suddenly longed for the skepticism of Katerina Piretti, of anyone who could take the essence of this odd woman and return it firmly to the South Baltimore row house whence it had come.

"How do you know all this?" Devon asked moments

later. "Are you talking to my spirit guides? Is Sapphire here?"

Tia Melody paused. "Sapphire?"

Stephen cleared his throat. "That's one of Devon's guides," he said, praying that Tia wouldn't blow his cover. "I spoke to her."

Tia passed him a sour look. "No, hon, I don't talk to your guide. I talk to mine. He's in better touch with the psychic world than I am. I sense lawyers around you, but you're not in trouble. Oh, I get it. You work for a law firm."

"Right," Devon said.

Tia stopped suddenly, as if listening. A puckered line appeared between her eyes as her face contorted into a frown. "Steer clear of your boss. She's not a friend; she's just a boss."

"Oh, no, Kat's different."

"Steer clear! The more distance between you two, the better. Get me? Unless, of course, you bring her to me."

Stephen registered the shocked expression on Devon's face. He'd have to tell Tia to tone down the vehemence in the future . . . if she got the job.

But it seemed inevitable that she would. Each comment she made elicited a little yelp of recognition from Devon and ignited an excited buzz from her entourage. Tia Melody, for all her eccentricity, was damn good at what she did.

"Okay, hon," Tia said after a brief rundown of Devon's lucky days and numbers. "Give me something of yours to hold."

Without hesitation, Devon worked her wedding ring off her finger and deposited it into Tia's open hand.

"Now, hon, I want you to think about a question, a question you really need answered."

Devon closed her eyes and concentrated.

Tia carefully stroked the wedding ring, her manicured finger tracing each groove and line upon it. "That's not hard," she said softly. "We can fix the problem."

Devon opened her eyes, surprised. "What do you mean?"

"I mean, hon, that there are psychic reasons why you can't get pregnant."

Devon turned white and hastily averted her gaze to the silverware before her. "Why, then? We've been trying so hard."

"You're not at peace with the universe, but I can't fix that here. If you want to visit me at my place, I'll channel Valentine. You can talk to him about it."

"Valentine?"

"My guide."

Stephen opened his mouth to protest, but Tia silenced him with a sharp glare.

"This girl's in pain. She needs help. You want me to ignore her need?" She reached into her pocket and pulled out a business card. "Call me," she told Devon. "We'll discuss rates and set up an appointment. Yes, you can have that baby. But first you need to get yourself in harmony with the rest of existence. Okay?"

"Okay." Dazed, Devon took the card.

"Ladies, excuse us." Stephen latched his hand under Tia Melody's elbow and raised her upward from her chair. She allowed him to escort her out of the dining room and back to his office.

"How'd I do?" she asked smugly once the door had closed firmly behind them.

"Is every reading you do at Angel Café going to turn into an advertisement for your own personal business?"

" 'Sapphire.' Don't give up your day job, hon. No, every reading is not going to turn into business for me. Some will, though. Sometimes I'll find it necessary to go deeper than a little lunch deal can provide. I've already got a thriving business, Mr. Carmichael. I'll be doing readings here as a favor to you, not the other way around." Her chin quivered indignantly, causing Stephen to wonder whether she could cast spells, too.

Once again, Molly opened his door. "Stephen, all the other women at that table just signed up for readings."

"I'll be there in a minute," he said.

Molly colored. "They don't want you. They want Ms. Melody."

"Oh." Slightly miffed, Stephen straightened.

"Well, hon, do I get the job?" Tia once again flashed her perfect teeth.

"On a trial basis. Fifteen bucks a reading, you get half."

She stared him down. "Fifteen bucks a reading, I get ten."

"Tell them she'll be right there." He narrowed his eyes, refusing to break eye contact as Molly quietly closed the door behind her. "Just remember, Ms. Melody, that I am still the boss."

"Undoubtedly."

"And that I am thoroughly unimpressed by the psychic world."

"Oh, I wouldn't take the psychic world lightly, Mr. Carmichael. Most who do live to regret it."

"I'll take my chances. You can leave your things in my office if you'd like. I believe you have customers waiting."

Her hand, clawlike, rested briefly atop his. He felt a shiver race like an electric current through his body.

"By the way, hon," Tia said, "that redhead you've been seeing? Dump her. She's got some other dude. Valentine won't give me the name, but it begins with a *G*. Don't worry, hon; she's no prize. There's somebody else out there just dying to snag a hunk like you."

Stephen stood open-mouthed as Tia strode from the room. Victoria? Seeing somebody else? It would certainly explain her recent reluctance to stay overnight and her current unavailability on weekends.

"Snap out of it!" he ordered himself sharply.

Okay, so occasionally Tia hit the target dead-on.

It was still a load of garbage.

4

KAT WEARILY PROOFREAD THE TYPED MEMORANDUM OF LAW
that Devon had tossed onto her desk. Hal had wanted
this memo hours ago. Kat had completed the research
quickly, placing a clear, concise Dictaphone tape on her
secretary's desk before leaving for home last night. She'd
been unpleasantly surprised to discover at three-thirty
this afternoon that Devon had not even touched it.

"Well, I was busy!" Devon had snapped.

"With what? The tape was top priority."

But Devon, unwilling to explain, had snatched her
earphones and whirled toward her computer screen.

Now, eyes skimming the draft, Kat could see that
she still didn't have a finished product for Hal. Devon's
usually flawless work had gone awry, producing a
memo filled with typos and creative spelling. Kat raised
a limp hand to her forehead. These past three weeks
had boiled down to one colossal headache.

Ever since that ill-fated lunch at Angel Café, Kat had
felt herself crumbling. The tough, blasé facade she'd
struggled to construct after Peter's death had somehow
met up with a wrecking ball. It wasn't even a question
of patching up weak spots and forging ahead. She felt
invaded, as if the wall around her had shattered. Her
emotions, usually guarded, suddenly seemed vulnera-

ble and unprotected, exposed to anyone who chose to look.

Devon was noisily fishing through her purse when Kat leaned against her cubicle doorway.

"I need some corrections on this."

Her secretary looked up, eyes hard and jaw set. "I'm leaving for the day."

"It's four forty-five. You can pound out these changes in fifteen minutes."

"Sorry. I've got an appointment. I guess I forgot to tell you."

Kat unconsciously drew herself up to her full height. "This is important. Hal wanted a finished draft hours ago."

Devon's hand flew to her hip. "That's not my problem. I can't help it if you decide at the last minute to change what you wrote. I've got a life, you know."

Kat's temper, always too hot, required extra effort to control. "I didn't change anything I wrote. All the mistakes are yours. Misspellings. Repeated sentences. They're careless errors, just like most of the errors you've made this past week. You used to take a lot more pride in your work. Is there a problem I should know about?"

Devon narrowed her eyes. "No problem other than you. Valentine was right!" Nose in the air, she brushed past Kat, leaving only a cloud of "Lauren" behind her.

"Valentine?" Kat repeated, puzzled. She sank into the chair before Devon's computer, amazed that she'd reached the point of offending people without even trying.

She recognized, of course, that she'd behaved badly at Angel Café. Nobody in the firm knew about Peter, so she would have understood anger from her secretary following that unexplained debacle. Devon's sudden coolness, however, had no connection with Secretary's Day. She'd actually been extra kind and solicitous during the week following their lunch date, as if she'd felt that kindness might soothe whatever troubled her boss. The following week, too, had been uneventful, except for a secretarial "field trip" to Angel Café. Kat had heard laughter as a few secretaries gathered in Devon's cubicle to leave for lunch.

"We're going to your favorite restaurant," Devon had announced playfully. "I'll be back in an hour."

Good, Kat remembered thinking. Maybe Stephen Carmichael would pull up a few famous past lives. Maybe Cleopatra was typing her mail and she just didn't know it.

Now she recalled that Devon had returned to work in a subdued, silent mood and that the mood had only intensified since then.

Maybe Devon had finally seen through Mr. Carmichael and was suffering the embarrassment of her own gullibility. Kat could certainly understand the letdown of disillusionment. The mood, however, was lasting entirely too long. Worse, Devon's work had become careless and sloppy.

"She's starting to make me look bad," Kat grumbled, scanning the computer screen to catch all of Devon's mistakes. "It's not a personal matter anymore when it affects my career."

She wondered if Devon's marriage was in trouble. Chris Alexander's picture, however, still occupied a prime position on his wife's desk, right next to the rosy stone Devon had chosen at Angel Café. Kat suspected that Devon was the sort who, if angry at her husband, would turn his photo facedown. The thought made her grin.

The grin practically hurt, so unaccustomed was her face to making it. And, just as the grin appeared, so did a familiar flood of taunting thoughts: *At least she's not alone. At least she's loved!*

She pulled in a tight, painful breath, angry that the words had once again broken through. The past three weeks had been crammed full of these horrible reminders that Peter was gone and she was alone. No matter how hard she tried to battle the hateful voices, they refused to retreat.

She slammed her finger onto the Print button. The whir of the printer was oddly comforting. It reminded her that work was eternal. Work had been, in fact, even more of a refuge than usual these past few weeks. The other new associates shook their heads in disbelief as they left her in the law library at seven o'clock each night. Even Hal had joked that the firm allowed time off for good behavior.

But time off didn't matter to Kat, as it meant only the opportunity for her imagination to take over. Her mind seethed with weird images of Peter, of the graveyard, even of Angel Café. It was as if those thoughts, unprocessed, with nowhere to go, searched furiously for an exit she could not provide. Even sleep, her best friend in the weeks following Peter's death, had become her enemy. Her nights were filled with turbulent, surreal dreams, the kind that made her wonder whether she was asleep or awake.

She was exhausted. Aunt Frannie had actually been the one to turn off the jangling alarm clock at four o'clock that morning. Aunt Frannie, whose room was clear across the hallway!

"Go back to sleep," she'd told her niece firmly.

"Gotta go to work," Kat had mumbled into her pillow.

"Gotta go to sleep." Francesca had rested on the side of the bed, her long, gentle fingers smoothing Kat's tousled hair. "Katerina, my darling, you can't dive into the grave after him."

Those words had been enough to send Kat flying out of bed. She'd raced down the hall to the shower, desperate for the cool neutrality of Harper, Madigan and Horn.

At least work was dependable. It was always there, solid and endless.

Kat stifled a yawn with the back of her hand and pondered which project to begin next.

The dream visited her again that night, closing in like a wide, smothering pair of wings. She was back in the same cave, wearing her business suit and clutching a briefcase as she felt along the glistening walls for a way out.

And, once again, she could hear Peter in the distance, calling her name over the rush of unseen water.

"Katie!"

He didn't sound frightened, only impatient, as if wondering when she'd finally reach him. As always, Kat started toward the sound of his voice, frustrated by her inability to walk freely in high heels and hampered by the extraordinary weight of her briefcase.

A cloud of bats flew out of the darkness, screeching like B movie veterans. Kat threw up a practiced hand to protect her face.

"Katie!"

Toward the end of the dark corridor, she could see a faint glow. An opening! If she could just make it to that point, Peter would be accessible, waiting for her.

At this stage of the dream, Kat always glanced down to see a long, thick snake begin its slimy ascent up her leg. Once it reached her knee, disembodied hands would grasp her throat, squeezing until she gasped for breath against the heavy currents of sleep. Then she would jolt awake, sweat pouring down her body as she sat shivering alone in her bed.

Tonight she looked wearily down to the floor of the cave. Sure enough, there was the snake, forked tongue flicking in and out of its diamond-shaped head. It appeared eager to begin the odious ritual they'd some-how developed together.

"Katie!" Peter called again, more urgently than ever before. "What's keeping you? You're smarter than this!"

The snake began to slither along its expected path across the floor.

She *was* smarter than this. As if in a trance, Kat lifted her heavy briefcase. It dropped like an anvil onto the hideous head. The snake's body jerked violently before lying still.

The light at the end of the corridor burned brighter. Now a radiant circle of white, tinged with blue, spilled onto the cave floor. Kat had never before reached this part of the dream. Hesitantly she took a step forward.

The light intensified. She found herself walking, then trotting, then finally running toward the blazing-bright opening.

"Katie!" Peter's voice grew stronger, and she knew she'd almost reached him.

The light beckoned, flirting with color as if it had a personality all its own. The soft blue tinge gave way to violet, then pink, and finally gold. Kat dashed toward it, through the doorway, and to the other side.

Once through the door, the light became so brilliant that she shielded her eyes, unable to bear the radiance. When she could finally squint, she noticed first the racing, swirling stream that flowed only a short distance from her feet. It was clear turquoise, and as her eyes adjusted to the brightness, she could see straight down to the tiny shells that lined its bed. Foam on top of the water warned of the stream's speed. Still, it was only three feet across, easily jumped.

And Peter stood on the other side.

"Katie." The tender note in his voice unleashed the pain she'd held at bay for so long. Frozen, she drank him in.

He wore the clothes she'd last seen him wear, his tie loosened, shirt opened at the neck, shirtsleeves rolled to the elbows. She could see the reddish-gold hair on his arms, the pale freckles across the bridge of his nose. She smelled the cologne he'd always worn, even though he stood far enough away that she shouldn't have noticed.

Her fingers ached to run through his hair. Her body screamed to feel his arms wrapped around her.

"Peter." Dazed, she took a step toward the stream.

"No, Katie. You can't come to me."

"You've got to let me! I'm so close! You can't send me back, not now!"

Peter opened his arms as if to embrace her, and a rush of warmth enveloped her.

"My Katie, I'm so sorry. I know it's hard. But you've

got to be strong, baby; you've just got to. You can't stay here. It's not time. You still have so much to do."

She nearly shrieked her frustration. "You're dead, and I'm alone! There's nothing left!"

"There's the truth. For all that I meant to you, for all that you know is right, you've got to see this through. You've got to get to the truth."

The soothing glow emanating from his outstretched arms calmed her. She furrowed her brow, puzzled.

"Truth? About your death?"

"About everything. I can't be the one to lead you, but I'm with you, Katie."

He was backing away, receding into the swirl of a light even more powerful than the brilliance that surrounded her. He didn't need to tell her that she couldn't follow. She knew in her core that she could never bear such light while hampered by physical form.

"Peter!" She reached out for him.

"Stephen can help you, Katie. And my love is always with you."

"But—"

"Don't back down. Don't hide from the truth."

He was gone. Kat opened her mouth to howl her grief, but no sound came. Instead, she felt strong, gentle arms lift her from the ground. With the touch of those arms, the sorrow of her wail slowly siphoned itself away.

"Let it go," a melodic voice told her, although she did not hear it through her ears. Gentle fingertips rested on her eyelids like a mother's touch on the forehead of a feverish, troubled child.

Peace such as Kat had never known wrapped itself

about her. "I should be scared," she murmured, but she couldn't be. The soft touch on her eyelids prevented her from opening her eyes, but she heard the rustling, constant whir of wings, and she felt a pleasant rush of wind brush across her hot cheeks.

The deep, debilitating grief that had lived so long within her soul was gone. Instead, a quiet sadness made its inevitable home within her heart, leaving room for hope to settle there as well.

Suddenly she was floating down, down to her bed. Her head hit the pillow with a tiny bounce. Her eyes opened, and she saw that she was alone, once again clothed in her nightgown.

Her bed had never felt softer. Her heart, bruised but not anguished, beat in a steady, serene rhythm. Kat stretched out across her mattress, carefully allowing her body to rest.

"But," a nasty little voice interrupted as she drifted off to sleep, "you can't be happy. He's still stone-cold dead."

"And you," another taunt chimed, "will die old, ugly, and unloved."

The insistent whir of wings once again echoed through the room. Now-familiar hands covered Kat's ears. With a screech of defeat, the voices stopped.

For the first time since Peter's death, Kat slept deeply and well. She didn't even stir when Francesca resolutely shut the offending alarm at four A.M.

Francesca examined the serenity of her niece's sleeping face.

"Thank you," she said quietly, "for answering my prayers as wonderfully as you always do."

5

"STEPHEN." MOLLY STUCK HER HEAD INTO HER BOSS'S OFFICE. "I have a question about our reservation policy."

Stephen glanced up from his accounts ledger. He'd been expecting this question for days. "Go ahead."

"Somebody called to ask if he could make a reservation for a psychic reading. He only gets an hour for lunch, so he wants a guarantee that Tia will get to him. He's going to call back for an answer, so I thought I'd better—"

"No reservations for readings. He'll have to take his chances like everyone else. If Tia doesn't get to him in time, he'll just have to come back."

"Okay." Ever a team player, Molly nodded her acknowledgment of his rule. "I'll tell him." She turned to leave, then hesitated. Her fingers absently tapped the heavy wood of the doorframe. "What do you think of her?" she asked.

"Of whom?"

"Tia."

Stephen raised an eyebrow. "Well, she's certainly doing her job, isn't she?"

"She's incredibly good at it." Molly's nervous fingers moved to the gaily colored fringe of her hand-woven Mexican belt.

"Incredibly good at what, Molly? Making up the sorts of stories that people want to hear?"

Molly squared her shoulders. "I'm going to her house tomorrow night for a personal reading."

"Oh, for heaven's sake." Stephen tossed his pen down onto the desktop. "I gave you credit for more intelligence than that."

Molly fidgeted, blue eyes wide at his reaction to her comments. "You don't understand. I have . . . um . . . a problem. Tia said that Valentine could help."

"Valentine?"

"Her guide. He's the one she gets her messages from. She channels him at her house."

"Oh, right." Stephen did remember Tia mentioning something like that. He could just imagine the theatrics she'd provide for that little spectacle. God knew she was odd enough without the inspiration of an adoring audience. He wondered if she used light shows and table raps when she lowered her voice in imitation of "Valentine."

"Molly, this psychic stuff is bullshit. You know it is."

"I don't think so." A bright scarlet blush settled across Molly's cheeks. "Tia says the most amazing things, Stephen. Things she couldn't possibly know."

Stephen's face hardened as his thoughts flickered briefly over Victoria. He was still smarting over her walk-out two weeks ago. Okay, so Tia's prediction of a rival had been accurate. That could be chalked up to coincidence, however, and was certainly not enough to convince him that strangers could improve his life through magic communication with the unseen. People became successful through their own sweat and abilities, not with the help of mysteriously spouted psychic voodoo.

"Molly, you're a smart woman. I can't believe you're falling for this."

Molly transferred her weight from one foot to the other. Dismayed, Stephen noted that she would not meet his gaze. This disturbed him. He had hired Molly because of her easygoing, friendly personality. He'd appreciated her ability to feel completely at ease during her interview, and he had enjoyed the confidence of her steady eye contact with him.

"What did Tia tell you?" he asked, amazed by her transformation.

Molly stared at the floor. "I never told you this, but my mother has been ill for years. She's got multiple sclerosis. It's grown worse these past few months, to the point where she needs constant assistance."

"I'm sorry."

"Me, too. But, Stephen, don't you see? Tia knew that Mom was sick! She came up to me one day and told me that Valentine said I had a sick relative."

"Fair guess. Don't we all? Did you jump in at that point and tell her it was your mother?"

He'd never before seen Molly's temper rise, but it did so now. Her eyes flashed as she took an angry step toward him.

"It wasn't a guess! She told me she sensed a female relative . . . close to death. She told me that Valentine might be able to prevent that death."

Stephen felt his fingertips tingle. "For how much money, Molly?" he asked quietly. "How much will it take for Valentine to play God?"

"What would it matter? There is no medical cure for MS, and it's worth any amount of money to see my mother well. Don't waste your breath telling me how stupid I am to believe what Tia says. My family has spoken to more doctors than I can count. None of them has ever offered this kind of hope. Valentine told me you wouldn't understand. I guess I just hoped he might be wrong!" She turned and marched stiffly from the room, slamming the door behind her.

"Whoa." Stephen let out a low whistle and sank to the top of his desk. What had just happened? He and Molly had always gotten along beautifully. He'd been, in fact, half-toying with the idea of asking her out. Now it appeared he'd be fortunate if she ever spoke to him again.

He drew in a deep breath, wincing as the stale smell of cigarettes met his sinuses. True to her word, Tia did not smoke in the dining room. She did, however, smoke in his office. A lot. He would be the first to admit that he had vices of his own, but tobacco was not one of them. The fact that Tia smoked freely and without permission in his office made him want to spit nails.

She was driving him crazy.

He stood and, in search of clean air, wandered out into the lobby.

Although the lunch rush should have been over, Angel Café was overflowing. People were willing to wait over an hour for a table and, as much as they praised the freshly squeezed juices and whole-grain breads, Stephen knew that they did it because they wanted a psychic reading from Tia Melody. Profits were up . . . way up, far beyond even his most optimistic expectations. Hiring Tia was the smartest business move he'd ever made.

It didn't make him happy. An odd sense of foreboding had recently settled over him. Stephen, whose crackerjack instincts had never before strayed beyond the realm of business, did not have the language necessary to express these alien emotions. He knew only that his little gold mine of a restaurant no longer felt as light and airy as it had before and that the only change to account for that was the addition of Tia to his staff.

He pasted a charming smile onto his face and waded vigilantly through the crowded dining rooms.

"I brought a list of questions to ask," he heard a diner tell her companion. "This psychic reader was dead-on about the Addams account last week. I want all the information she can give me."

Stephen inadvertently shuddered as he passed by.

Tia sat before a deuce in the main dining room. Her patrons, a couple in their mid-forties, stared at her, mesmerized. Today she wore a bright purple leotard and flowered bell-bottoms, but Stephen suspected it was those weird violet eyes that captivated people. They commanded full attention before the "messages" even began.

"I'm glad what I told you a couple of weeks ago worked out," Tia said.

"Oh, your advice was right on the money," the man replied solemnly. "That's why we're back. We've been asked to help finance a new business. Should we?"

Tia flashed her perfect grin. "Well, hon, no time to lose when it's money involved, right? Let's see what Valentine has to say."

Stephen turned away, a tight little knot working in the pit of his stomach. The conversation illuminated the very root of his uneasiness. In the beginning, Angel Café had been a harmless outlet for those who fancied themselves more spiritually attuned than the rest of the population. Their earnest gullibility, easily fed with past-life experiences and lucky numbers, had provided not only profit, but a good laugh as well. Now, however, Tia had a large following of people who came seeking concrete guidance regarding each and every step of their lives. They would not, could not, make a move unless Valentine authorized it. Their lives, in a sense, had been expertly lifted from their own control and placed in the hands of somebody else. Worse, they seemed more than willing to let that happen.

Suddenly Stephen no longer found his little joke particularly amusing.

"You look ill," a velvet voice said from behind him. "What did you do, overdose on sprouts?"

She was small, with dark, wavy hair tumbling down to her waist. The jeans and long-sleeved T-shirt she wore showed off the curves that her business suit had covered, but Stephen realized at once that he was staring into the wide brown eyes of Katerina Piretti.

"You're out of uniform," he said.

"I took the day off."

"To eat here? I don't believe it."

"You don't have to. I wasn't planning to eat here. In fact, I thought lunch would be over. Your restaurant is very popular. Congratulations."

"Thank you." He waited.

Kat did not keep him in the dark for long. "I need to talk to you privately," she said.

"Why? Still mad about my reading? Want to hit me up for fraud?"

"I'm off duty. Besides, Mr. Carmichael, your reading wasn't quite as fraudulent as you may think."

The silence that followed was broken by Tia's shrill voice.

"Valentine says your friend's business has the life expectancy of a fruit fly. Don't get involved, hon. But if you want to get into some good deals, what say you visit me at home for a private reading some time? Then Valentine can really let loose with his advice."

"Christ," Kat said. "Who's the dingbat?"

Stephen's tone remained neutral. "That's my new psychic reader. Her name is Tia Melody. Apparently she's very accurate. Most of these people are back for more of her wisdom."

"Oh, give me a break."

"Don't you want a reading? I could arrange it . . . to make up for last time."

"No." Kat nearly spat the word. "Do I look that gullible to you? I'm not interested."

Stephen studied her thoughtfully. Perhaps she had behaved badly when last here, but he was curiously relieved to find that she could not be swayed by the promise of Tia's psychic certainties. Every other face he saw in Angel Café these days reflected a mixture of adoration and awe where Tia was concerned. Lately, he felt worse off than that knowing little brat in "The Emperor's New Clothes," the one who had pointed out that the emperor was stark naked. At least in the story the emperor actually *was* naked. Here at Angel Cafe, Tia's words usually proved true enough to convince her increasingly large following that she possessed a psychic pipeline to their personal well-being. Stephen could point to no solid basis for his disbelief. And yet, neither could he escape the nagging, creepy feeling that something was very wrong.

Now Kat stood before him, the disgusted expression on her face an indication that she, too, did not comprehend how anyone could get swept into all of this nonsense.

He reached out a hand to touch her shoulder. "Come on. I'll buy you a cup of coffee."

"Not here," she said quickly.

"There's a coffee shop a few doors down."

Kat inadvertently shuddered as they stopped before Molly in the lobby. She did not remember the angel memorabilia looking quite as bloated and predatory as it did today.

"Molly," Stephen said, "I'll be back shortly."

"Whatever you say," Molly replied frostily. "You're the boss."

"Is all your help so pleasant and accommodating?" Kat asked as they hit the street.

"Molly's not always like that. We got along great until this morning. We had a disagreement about Tia."

Kat stopped short.

"Are you okay?" Stephen asked.

"Just wondering. Did the name 'Valentine' pop up during your discussion?"

"I believe Molly mentioned him. I'm not sure what that has to do with anything, though. I don't even think that Valentine exists, if you want to know the truth."

An image of Devon flashed through Kat's head. *Valentine was right*, Devon had proclaimed through a snarl. "I'd like to believe you, Mr. Carmichael, but I'm starting to wonder."

"Stephen. And you, I believe, are Kat." Puzzled, he guided her toward the coffee shop.

Kat waited until steaming mugs of coffee had been served before looking up to meet his questioning stare. "My impression is that you went to the 'make-it-all-up' school of psychic reading," she said.

The heat of a deep blush crossed Stephen's face. "I thought we'd already established that. No hard feelings, okay? I apologize. It was a business move, pure and simple. As you can see, I don't do it anymore."

"Because getting caught would be a lousy business move."

"Damn straight. I don't believe in this psychic garbage. I run my restaurant according to the bottom line."

"I want to know, then, how you knew about Peter."

As quickly as the color had come to Stephen's face, it now drained away. He'd spent the past weeks trying to forget the feeling of urgency that had forced him to deliver that last message. Such moments were better left unexplored.

"Oh," he said, licking dry lips. "That."

"Yes. That." Kat's liquid gaze, nearly as compelling as the force which had produced the message, held him.

"Honest," he said, "I don't know where that came from. Let's just forget about it, okay? It was no big deal."

But her eyes refused to let him off the hook.

"It was an extremely big deal," she contradicted. "Because Peter's death was very real, and your words made perfect sense to me."

Stephen finally tore his gaze away. "Don't tell me that."

Her hand rested atop his. The fingers, small and delicate, gave his clenched fist an urgent squeeze. "So you see, I've got to know why you said what you said."

There was no way out. He leaned back in his chair, resigned. "There's not much I can tell you. Nothing like that ever happened to me before. There was just an overwhelming push to tell you that you were right about Peter's death. I can't explain it any further than that."

"Did you hear a voice?"

"Other than my own? No. But the words weren't mine."

"Whose were they?"

"I don't know."

"You've got to think!"

"Ms. Piretti, I'm not some witness on the stand. You're not going to wear me down. I don't know where the words came from. Furthermore, I hope that never happens to me again."

"It will," Kat said quietly.

The assurance in her voice made Stephen shudder. He rushed to change the subject. "So, who was he?" he asked, trying hard to keep his voice casual.

"Who?" The troubled pucker in Kat's brow deepened.

"Peter."

An expression of raw pain flashed across her face. She mastered it quickly.

"He was a reporter," she said. "For the Sunpapers."

"And?"

"And he was found dead in his apartment nearly two years ago."

"What happened?"

Kat stared down at the table and swallowed hard,

but when she looked up, her eyes were clear and her jaw set. "I don't know. There was a gun in his hand and a bullet through his head. The place reeked of alcohol. His death was ruled a suicide."

"But you don't think it was."

"More than that. I know it wasn't."

Stephen nodded slowly. Whoever Peter had been, he'd been more important to Kat than she cared to share. Boyfriend? Brother? Colleague? Hard to say. She sat across the table with the cool detachment of the professional she was. Only that previous break in her facial expression, the smallest slip, had given away the depth of her need to know the truth about this one man's death.

And Stephen, with a fledgling restaurant and employee troubles, knew without a doubt that he had absolutely no intention of getting sucked into what promised to become a dandy little obsession.

"Hey," he said uneasily, raising a hand to catch the waitress's attention, "I'm concentrating right now and I'm not getting any information. No messages. Must have been a fluke. Sorry." The waitress appeared with a pot of coffee. "Just the check, please," Stephen told her gratefully.

"You don't want to get involved."

He reached for his wallet. "Let's just say that I find it a little too weird for my tastes, okay? Look, I don't even believe in this stuff."

"Me, either. But that doesn't seem to prevent it from happening."

"Sorry, Kat."

"Try. One more time. Just try to hear something!"

She looked so desperate that he actually paused for

a moment, head cocked in anticipation of celestial whispers he hoped would never come.

"Nope," he reported, relieved. "The only thing I hear is a reminder that I left a lot of people in my restaurant."

"Okay. Here." Kat fished through a pocket and pulled up a business card. "I can't push you. But, please, Stephen. Promise you'll call if you hear anything. Will you do that?"

"Absolutely," he assured smoothly, taking the card. He'd promise her anything, then run like hell.

"And, Stephen . . ." Once again, the insistent little hand was on his. "Please be careful. I don't know who's playing games here, but I'm not as convinced as you are that they aren't tangible."

He'd never in his life been so glad to see a waitress deliver the check.

"My treat." Kat abruptly tossed a five-dollar bill onto the table.

Stephen watched as she left the coffee shop.

"Do you ever get the feeling," he asked the waitress, "that you're the only sane person left on the planet?"

"Sure," the waitress said. "All the time. Which means I lump you in with all the other weirdoes of the world. Thank your girlfriend for the tip, okay?"

He gazed at the business card in his hand, noting that Kat had carefully written her home phone number on the back of it, just in case.

6

~~~

A CURLING WISP OF JASMINE INCENSE JOLTED CHRIS ALEXANder from his motorcycle magazine. He wrinkled his nose, then twisted in his bed to check the clock on the nightstand. It was nearly midnight. The swirl of incense came from across the bedroom, from the tiny alcove Devon now called her "temple for meditation." His wife sat there, eyes closed, body rigid against her straight-backed chair, bare feet planted flat on the floor. Her palms turned upward. Chris noted the slight pull of a smile at the corners of her mouth and burrowed deeper into the cocoon of his bed. Smile? Incense? Ever since Devon had taken up with Tia Melody and this Valentine character, this was her idea of foreplay.

"Don't even think it," he called across the room.

"Shh!" Devon said. "I'm grounding."

Chris ran a hand through his short, blond hair. His wife was beautiful, especially in that gauzy white thing she'd started wearing at night. Any man would trade beds with him. Lately, though, sex had deteriorated into a calculated, mechanical ritual. It always began with Devon's little grounding session. "To attune me to the powers and vibrations of nature," she explained gravely. Chris, ever polite, would bite his tongue rather than blurt out that perhaps they might have more fun if she attuned herself to him.

But grounding was the easiest part, because once Devon finally floated into bed, Valentine's advice would float in with her. Most of that advice seemed calculated to provide Chris with the most miserable sexual experiences he'd had in his whole twenty-eight years of existence.

"Hold it right there, Chris," Devon had admonished last night as he'd reached eagerly for her nightgown. "Don't maul me. And leave the nightgown on. Valentine says not to confuse lust for love."

Chris had frozen mid-pant. "What?"

"Make love to me with dignity. Approach me as you would a holy icon."

"*What?*" Was this the same woman who'd dragged him into the backseat of the car during their dating days?

"It's the only way, Chris. Valentine says that our child will only be conceived in an atmosphere of mutual respect."

Their child would never be conceived at all if this kept up.

Devon reached for the china cup that sat on the windowsill. Chris knew it contained an herbal tea guaranteed to promote pregnancy. Devon meant business, and she meant it that night.

"I'm beat, Devon," he said firmly. "Not tonight."

She glared at him, gray eyes stormy. "Yes, tonight. It's the perfect time of month."

"I need to be in at seven-thirty tomorrow."

"Your job can wait, Chris. Valentine said that this week is *the* week. I want that baby."

He studied her. Her delicate collarbone was even more prominent than usual, and her face looked drawn. Dark circles rimmed her eyes.

"Devon," he said as she walked toward him, "let's talk."

"I don't want to talk." Her fingers ran down his body. "I want to—"

"No."

"But Valentine—"

"Damn Valentine!" Chris shouted, and Devon stumbled backward in amazement at the outburst. "Valentine has been a third party to our marriage for weeks! I want to talk to *you*, Devon, not to Valentine, and not to that weird witch who channels him! Do you understand me?"

Her voice grew distant. "I understand that you're not willing to grow."

Grow. Harmonize. Open up. He was sick to death of all the "enlightened" activities he wasn't willing to do. Ever since Devon had begun making biweekly pilgrimages to Tia Melody's house, all she could notice was how psychically stunted he was.

And all he could notice was how much money she spent on readings, balms, candles, and herbal teas. Tia Melody's house might as well have been an outlet for some exotic holistic supply company. Devon, eager to conceive, anxiously bought every item suggested.

He reached for her hands, cradling them softly in his own. He was a cop, damn it. He'd talked down would-be suicides, counseled kids in reform schools. Surely he could talk to his own wife. He wrapped her in a hug, noting the quick beat of her heart against his chest as he held her tight.

"Devon, tell me again about Valentine."

"I tell you all the time," she said, voice muffled.

"Try again. I'm listening."

She gazed up at him, her eyes shining in a way he hadn't seen directed toward him in weeks. "Oh, Chris, he's wonderful. He's so loving. He wants only what's best for us."

He prayed that a real flesh-and-blood rival would never inspire such enthusiasm in his wife. "Does he . . . uh . . . talk to you every time you visit Tia Melody?"

Devon nodded. "He's been saying that you should come, too. That if you do, the things we want in life will happen so much more quickly. Please, come with me tomorrow night."

He stared into her pleading face, caught by the vacant expression he saw there. Devon was hooked.

"Okay," he said slowly. "I'll go."

Tia Melody lived in a three-story row house south of Federal Hill. She lived alone, but the house was so crowded with knickknacks, candles, and incense burners that Chris felt large and ungainly in the cramped living room.

"Is this the mister?" Tia had asked cheerfully, ushering them in.

"Oh, yes." Devon's smile had been wide.

"Pleased to meet you, hon." She'd extended a bony hand. Chris had given it a rather limp shake, careful not to impale his palm on one of her fingernails. They were at least an inch long, layered with sparkles over deep purple polish.

Then, complete with fake leather miniskirt, orange cashmere sweater, and four-inch spike heels, Tia had tottered back to the kitchen to fetch a pot of herbal tea before "the others" arrived.

"Others?" Chris asked Devon.

"We've never been more than five in this circle."

"Devon, how much is tonight costing us?"

"Let me show you around." His wife sidestepped the question. "We have a few minutes. See those pictures?"

He followed her pointing finger to four oil-crayoned drawings positioned along the stairwell. Each picture was a head-only portrait, with two of the subjects male, one female, and one utterly androgynous. Their features were nearly identical. Only their hairstyles, coloring, and collars differed.

Devon continued before he could remark that the artwork was primitive at best. "Those are some of Tia's spirit guides."

"You don't say." He struggled to keep his face expressionless.

"They were drawn by a man who can actually see them. The woman is Shera. She's been with Tia through many past lives. The man in the turban is Tia's High Teacher, Isynth, and the blond man is Machiel. The other being is from another planet."

"Oh, Devon."

"Well, why not? You aren't close-minded enough to believe that Earth is the only inhabited planet in the universe, are you?"

He did not reply. Devon grabbed his hand and pulled him toward the cluttered mantelpiece. "Don't touch anything," she said. "Tia doesn't like anybody else's vibrations disturbing her energy flow. Do you see that crystal propped against the Buddha?"

Chris's eyes rested on an amethyst-tinged crystal. It reminded him of one of Tia Melody's fingernails.

"Valentine materialized it," Devon said. "It was a gift to Tia during one of their first channeling sessions. Isn't that incredible?"

Chris was saved from replying by the gentle chiming of the doorbell.

There proved to be four of them that night, and Chris gathered from preliminary small talk that Devon had met the others before. Van was a stockbroker in his early fifties. He'd come straight from his office, still dressed in his customized three-piece suit. Marcy had come from the gym, her stringy brown hair tied back in a sloppy ponytail, her jaws in constant motion around the wad of chewing gum in her mouth. Chris was surprised to learn that she was a doctoral candidate in English lit. Both Van and Marcy had, like Devon, met Tia Melody at Angel Café.

"Did we all have a good few days?" Tia asked, dragging her chair into the living room. "Chris, hon, pull your chair closer so's that you can be part of this circle. We won't bite." She reached for the rheostat to dim the lights. As if on cue, Devon, Van, and Marcy closed their eyes.

"That's it," Tia said. "Let's hear that nice, deep breathing. We're going to breathe deep down to our toes. We're going to feel energy running up from the soles of our feet through the tops of our heads. You are one with Mother Earth and the god within you. Get with the program, Chris. Close your eyes and breathe deep. You'll feel better."

Chris obediently closed his eyes. He smelled sulphur as Tia struck a match and heard the rustling of her clothing as she lit candles and incense. Within minutes the familiar scent of jasmine wafted past his nose. He opened his eyes a slit. Tia had returned to the circle, where she sat placidly, apparently awaiting some sign of spiritual readiness.

In the semidarkness the spirit pictures along the stairway observed them from a surreal stupor. Candlelight ricocheted off crystal facets, causing odd reflections of light to paint the room. Devon, Van, and Marcy had established a mutual rhythm. Chris noted their chests rising and falling in unison.

He was perhaps unenlightened, but the pit of his stomach felt distinctly queasy. Reflexively, dredged from the depths of childhood memory, the Lord's Prayer echoed through his thoughts. Grateful for anything familiar, he allowed the words to fill his mind.

"Okay," Tia said. "We've dropped those earthly pressures, right? I can sense your guides here. Got a quick message for you, Marcy: Park somewhere else tomorrow. I don't understand it, but maybe you will."

Marcy's face contorted. "But I love the view from the roof of the garage. Do you really think there's danger?"

"I think," Tia said, "that I would do what your guide says. Or maybe you want to risk it and let us all know what happens, if you're able. Okay?"

Marcy blanched. "I'll park downstairs."

"Now," Tia continued briskly. "Any questions or comments for your guides before we move on?"

Devon shot a hesitant glance at Chris. "I just want to thank all my guides for helping me get my husband here tonight. I'm very happy about it."

Chris furrowed his brow, certain that "guides" had

nothing to do with his appearance at Tia's this evening.

"Devon, hon, you know what we say," Tia reminded. "The universe lends its positive power to all who strive to be in harmony with it. Ask and you shall receive."

Devon nodded vigorously. "I'm asking, I'm asking!"

An appreciative chuckle traveled around the room.

"Chris," Tia said, "you're new here tonight. I guess Devon's explained quite a bit to you, but I want to make sure you're comfortable. Are you familiar with spirit guides?"

"Yes."

"Then you'll want to know more about yours." A warm smile broke across her face. "They're very glad you're here. They hope this will be the beginning of a deep spiritual journey." She paused to study him. Chris suddenly felt a kinship with mice used in experimentation.

"I see," Tia said slowly. "You were very close to someone who died unexpectedly last year."

A prickle crept up his spine. Devon gasped.

"A man." Tia's eyes expertly searched Chris's face. "A colleague."

His face grew hot as jumbled images crashed through his mind. Carl, his partner, his buddy since the Police Academy, his acquaintance since high school . . .

"It wasn't your fault," Tia said in a monotone.

He needed air, fast. His eyes darted about, searching out an exit.

"He wants you to know that," Tia added.

Bullshit, it wasn't his fault. If he hadn't been sick that night, if he'd been the one to answer that domestic violence call, Carl would never have taken the bullet that . . .

Tears started down his cheeks. He stared helplessly at Tia, silently urging her to stop.

"It's all right," Tia said soothingly. "We're friends, here. It's all right to let that emotion out."

But it wasn't all right. It wasn't all right to be vulnerable before strangers who had no knowledge of who he was and what he felt. It wasn't all right to be laid open before them, as if they had a right to assimilate and join in his every life experience.

He remained caught by Tia's glittering violet eyes. He'd seen that expression before on the faces of criminals. She was planning to shoot again, and quickly. Of course, that made perfect strategical sense. Once you've disarmed your victim, you'd better act fast before he can recover his weapon.

On automatic pilot Chris again let the Lord's Prayer race through his mind. *Our Father, Who art in Heaven . . .* A drop of sweat dripped down his forehead as he concentrated on the words. He averted his eyes from Tia and let the prayer unwind through his head. When it ended, he realized that he knew no other way to block the sound of Tia's voice. He allowed the same words to begin again, a broken tape player with no Off button.

Tia's mouth opened, then closed again. She leaned back in her chair, puzzled. "It's gone. I was getting it clear, but now it's gone. That's your fault, hon. If you're gonna close up on me, I can't be expected to read your messages."

Chris swallowed. Good.

Van cleared his throat. "I've got questions for Valentine," he said.

"Me, too," Marcy and Devon echoed eagerly. Chris

saw that Tia was simply the warm-up act. Valentine was the reason everyone had bought tickets.

Tia cast one last reproachful glance in his direction, then shrugged. "Sure," she said. "I know he's got plenty to say tonight. Maybe he'll even be able to open our closed friend here."

She shut her eyes, and Chris watched the others lean forward in their seats. Tia breathed deeply as mouths dropped in anticipation.

The room grew dimmer. The candle flames wavered. The cloying scent of jasmine made his eyes water.

Then a burst of cold air started at his feet and shot through his body.

He lost count of the "Our Fathers" that tumbled about his ears.

"Well," Devon said during the drive home. "What did you think?"

"I think I'll go back with you next time."

Chris noted his wife's confident smile and knew that he'd just confirmed what Valentine had assured her would come to pass.

7

━━━

"I'M GLAD YOU'RE HOME FOR DINNER," JOSEPH PIRETTI TOLD his daughter, "but what good will it do if you don't eat? Frannie, pass Katerina the spinach, will you? Get some vitamins into her."

Francesca placed a serving bowl of spinach before her niece.

"Take some." Joe gestured with his fork. "I want to see some pink in those cheeks again."

Kat tapped a small mound of spinach onto her plate. Francesca watched her neatly push it beneath her untouched steak.

"So they let you out early today, hmmm?" Joe's appetite rarely failed him, and tonight was no exception. He speared a second baked potato and reached for the butter.

"I left at five o'clock for a change," Kat said.

"Good. Because I'm going to the Pasquinis' tonight to play cards. Their bachelor son Ralph is visiting. You come with me. You'll have a good time."

"No, thanks." Kat set down her fork. "I've got work to do."

"But you're home!"

"I'm going to work here tonight, Dad."

Francesca observed the set of her brother's jaw and

sent him a swift kick under the table. He stared at her with wide, innocent eyes and purposely ignored the hint.

"Listen to me," he said, pointing his fork at his daughter. "I don't like what I see in your life these days."

"You don't have to." Kat bristled. "It's my life."

"I'm worried about you. You're going to work yourself into a lifetime of loneliness. When are you going to get out and meet a good man? When am I going to see you safely married, baby?"

Kat's cheeks burned red. "I'm not interested."

"Katerina." His tone softened as he reached for her hand. "What happened with your Peter was a tragedy, and nobody's denying that. But it's almost two years gone. You're a young woman with a long life ahead of you. It's time to move on."

Francesca watched, waiting for the glassy, closed expression that always veiled Kat's face whenever Peter Dulaney was mentioned. It didn't come. Kat's color remained high, her chin raised. Surprised, Francesca peered more closely at her niece.

"I'll move at my own pace, Dad," Kat said. "If that makes you nervous, I'll get my own apartment. I'm strong enough to do that now. Just say the word."

"No," Joe said. "The word is *no*."

"For now. Because soon, Dad, I'll need to go." Her chair scraped the hardwood floor as she pushed away from the table. "I'll be in my room."

Joe shrugged his shoulders as his daughter's muffled footsteps sounded overhead. "So tell me, is it so terrible that I care? So suffocating that I want to see her safe and happy?"

Francesca shook her head. "Of course not. The trouble is you want everything now."

"So?"

"So, Joe, in my experience, God doesn't work that way."

"I'm not talking God. I'm talking Katerina."

Francesca lifted her wineglass. "So am I."

He slumped back in his chair with a heavy sigh. "Sometimes, Frannie, you forget you're not in the convent anymore. Maybe God talk worked there. Out here in the real world, you've got to take action. Nobody knows from God's time. You want something, you make it happen. If I want my Katerina to find a good man, I introduce her to good men. I don't sit waiting for God to bring me a miracle."

"That's a pity," Francesca said. "Because sometimes, Joe, miracles can be more wonderful than anything you'd choose on your own."

"Oh, Frannie . . ." His voice trailed. His younger sister, calm and focused since earliest girlhood, had always exercised a soothing effect on him. He'd never known how or why. He seldom understood her words and only vaguely comprehended her philosophies. Still, there was something in the quiet confidence of her voice that never failed to convince him that she was right.

Francesca studied the ruby wine in her glass. "For a long time after Peter died, it was hard to even think about Katerina. She was so shattered, so raw and angry. I couldn't touch her, physically or spiritually. So I did what I always do: I prayed for her. Oh, how I prayed for that girl. There wasn't an hour went by that I didn't ask that she be healed, opened to Light.

"Joe, lately I feel that those prayers have been answered. When I think about Katerina now, I sense a strong white light about her, heavenly protection, if you will indulge me. Positive changes are beginning, despite Katerina's resistance."

She looked so resolute, so certain. Joe groaned.

"You know I'm right," she said, a small smile tugging the corners of her mouth.

"What I know is that you've never let me down. You came to live with us when I thought I couldn't survive another day. With your strength, I did. You helped me raise that little girl, Frannie. I owe you for that."

"You owe me nothing."

"I owe you my trust."

She considered. "That would be nice," she said, and the smile broke full across her face. "Good, truthful things are happening with Katerina. Please, give her your blessing and let her be."

A loud bang sounded from overhead, followed by several muffled thuds.

"Jesus Christ, what's she doing up there?" Joe demanded. "What kind of work did she bring home, anyway?"

"Sounds like she's rooting through her closet."

"For what? Buried treasure?"

The thumping stopped.

Maybe. Francesca rose to clear the table.

Kat's heart slammed against her chest as she stared at the metal box resting near her toes. It was the size of a shoebox. She had, in fact, just toppled several shoeboxes from her closet shelf in order to claim it.

"Damn." She sank to the floor. Her fingers absently

twisted the shag of the carpet as her eyes wandered along the pink walls she'd known since childhood. Every aspect of this room was achingly familiar. She was twenty-seven years old and sitting only yards away from the ballet trophy she'd earned in second grade, her framed high-school diploma, and a faded rose plucked and dried from a bouquet Peter had given her years ago.

Her life had become a living time capsule, left in a rut for all eternity by the man who'd once owned that metal box.

Mechanically her right arm reached out to tug open her nightstand drawer. Eyes still fixed on the box, Kat groped until her fingertips hit the cool metal smoothness of a key.

The box was green, with the initials "P.J.D." etched into the lid. Until Peter's death, it had stayed in his desk at the newspaper. He'd kept the key in his pocket during the day, placing it each evening in the change tray on his dresser, alongside his high school ring and the pocket watch he'd inherited from his grandfather.

"I keep notes in this box," he'd told Kat during one of her rare visits to his office cubicle.

"Under lock and key?"

"Not all my notes. Only my very favorite ones. Certain sources require more protection than others. And, frankly, some of my first drafts are dear to my heart, but so bad that I'd hate them to fall into unsympathetic hands."

She'd laughed. "You're ridiculous."

Peter had wrapped an arm around her waist and peered down into her eyes. "Dear, dear Katie. The box contains the only secrets I'll ever keep from you. But should anything ever happen to me, take it. Okay?"

"Okay," she'd said, sure that nothing would happen to him.

She still didn't know what force had pushed her to filch the key, the ring, and the watch from his apartment in the days following his death. She couldn't say why possession of the box had become such a need that Peter's editor, unable to fight her intensity, had handed it over to her without questioning its contents.

And she certainly didn't understand why, in nearly two years, she'd been unable to face opening the thing.

The key trembled in her hand as she aimed for the lock.

The lid popped open easily, as if there hadn't been a two-year lull between calls to do so. For some reason, Kat had expected clouds of dust to puff forth from the box. Instead she saw a dense pile of assorted papers gathered loosely in a rubber band. On top sat a card she recognized well; she'd sent it. The picture showed a dark-haired girl of perhaps eight, wearing a baseball cap, striped shirt, and jeans. Hands on hips, she thrust out her chin. "Okay, you win," a bubble above her head proclaimed. Kat didn't need to open the card. "What are you going to do about it?" the inside said, and she remembered adding in purple ink, "You made me love you, Peter Dulaney, and now you're stuck with me!"

With a sigh, she set the card gently on the floor beside her knee.

The next piece of paper was folded into eighths. Kat opened it. Her eyes met Peter's fluid scrawl, identified by "Journalism 101" in the upper right-hand corner. "My grandfather was the most amazing individual I ever met," she read silently. That sentence had been crossed through with red. "What makes an amazing individual?" Peter had tried on the next line. That sentence, too, had been scratched. "Amazing. Individual," he'd written next and, beneath that, " 'Grandpa,' I asked innocently one achingly bright spring day, 'how does an individual know if they're amazing?' "

Kat smiled. The student attempts at originality were awful. "I know why you kept these under lock and key," she said out loud.

Her shoulder grew warm, as if the slight pressure of fingers rested there. Startled, she snapped her head around, but no one stood beside her. Her hand began to tingle. Slowly she refolded the page.

A silent, subtle push made her reach back into the box. She rummaged past a list of names, stopping only long enough to ascertain that they'd been compiled in connection with a long-ago story on the state legislature. She ignored an essay about male bonding at a local Laundromat. The tingling in her hand increased. She searched the bottom of the box until her fingers scraped against a small spiral memo pad.

The tingling stopped.

She felt warm, as if a low-grade fever had set in. Hands trembling, she drew out the pad and slowly opened it.

A pink telephone message fluttered out. It was dated the April before Peter's death and said: "Call David Toohey. Needs to talk to reporter." Kat noted that the phone number was a local exchange.

Peter's scribbling filled the next sheet, but was nearly indecipherable. She managed to make out a South Baltimore address, along with the name "Tia Melody."

That name was familiar. Now, where had she heard

it? Kat furrowed her brow and returned to the pad.

Peter had tamed his notorious scrawl on the next page. Kat studied the chart he'd neatly drafted. There were three columns. The left caption read "Individual." The center title was "Corporation." The right column represented "Amount Spent."

"Holy shit," Kat whispered. Most of the individuals listed were associated with major local and national corporations. She recognized not only the names of several Harper, Madigan and Horn clients, but of some local attorneys as well. The common thread seemed to be that each person had spent big bucks.

For what?

A familiar name headed the list: David Toohey. He was listed as vice president of Kaleidoscope, a computer software corporation. Mr. Toohey, either individually or on behalf of Kaleidoscope, had managed to put out more than $50,000.

Kat turned the page. Peter had written a few sentences that struck her as being either titles or story angles: "Swept Into the Unseen." "The Celestial C.E.O." "The Valentine Connection."

Valentine Connection?

Tia Melody?

Of course. Tia Melody was the reader at Angel Café. But she was just a dippy lady making a living off the gullibility of others. If she were worth any story at all, it would only be a lighthearted feature in the "Today" section. And it would never be anything worth locking up in a metal box.

Only one other page in the notebook had been used. There Peter had written: "June 8. Meet with Tia Melody."

Kat felt a surge of nausea swell in the pit of her stomach.

Peter had died on June 8.

She plunged her hand back into the box, feverishly searching for the rest of the story. Peter would have had notes, maybe even a cassette. There would have been more leads to follow, interviews . . .

She knew already she'd find no additional clues in the box.

"Oh, Peter," she murmured with frustration. "How am I supposed to do this?"

And, as it had once before, a sharp image of Stephen Carmichael flashed through her head.

"No!" she protested, remembering her last meeting with the annoying Mr. Carmichael. "Find another way! If we can't do better than him, let me bury myself in law for all eternity, make a ton of money, and forget that you ever, ever existed, Peter Dulaney! Do you hear me?"

Her voice died away into the silence. She was quite alone.

I'm going crazy, she thought bleakly, staring into the empty air. She had to be. She was sitting in her room talking to nothing.

What could anyone possibly want from her? If this weren't some awful, sick joke, somebody had to let her know.

The house remained quiet. Kat registered the ticking of her alarm clock, the swish of car tires traveling the road, the padding of Aunt Frannie's feet as she mounted the stairs.

This, then, was her reality: solid, calm, predictably dull . . . excruciating.

A rap sounded on her door. Then Francesca, not waiting for a response, opened it. Kat reflexively shielded the metal box with her hand.

"Katerina, you have a visitor."

Visitor?

"He says that you know him. His name is Chris Alexander."

Startled, Kat scrambled to her feet. "That's my secretary's husband," she said, heading for the stairs. "I hope everything's all right."

Chris Alexander stood in the front foyer, keys jingling in his hand.

"Ms. Piretti." He shifted his weight from one foot to the other. "I'm sorry to intrude, but—"

"Is Devon okay?"

Chris paused briefly before answering. "Physically? She's fine. But if I could just have a few minutes of your time. I need . . . damn, this is hard. But I've thought it through and . . . does the name 'Valentine' mean anything to you?"

"Just give me a minute to get my house keys," Kat said.

8

~~~

Kat had met Chris Alexander at Harper, Madigan and Horn's Christmas party. She remembered him planted beside Devon, looking every bit as out of place as she herself felt. With his short blond hair, squared shoulders, and solid stance, she'd pictured him more at home on a motorcycle than in the banquet room of a downtown hotel, dressed in a good navy suit and forced to make small talk.

She didn't remember his face appearing as drawn as it did now.

She'd left her house intending to steer them both down the street for a cup of coffee. Chris, however, had begun talking the second the front door closed behind them. Since there seemed to be no break point in his story, they'd kept walking.

"So Devon's been acting weird ever since she began seeing this Tia Melody," he said. "I want to know if you've noticed a change at work."

"Yes." Kat studied the sidewalk as they rounded the same block once again.

"Go on."

"She used to be conscientious. Now everything she does needs to be done again."

"Any personality changes?"

She hesitated, aware that this man was practically a stranger. "I feel like I'm tattling to some kid's father."

"Well, tattle away. I have a lot more to tell you."

"Why me? It's not like Devon and I are good buddies. I only see her at work."

It was Chris's turn to hesitate. His pause lasted so long that Kat stopped walking and turned to appraise him.

"I'm telling you," he said, "because Devon thinks very highly of you. She considers you a friend."

An embarrassed blush crept across Kat's face. Most of her recent thoughts about Devon had been totally derogatory.

"Also," Chris continued, his voice returning to a businesslike plane, "if what I suspect is true, I may need a lawyer."

Kat walked briskly up Exeter Street, shoulders hunched against a nonexistent chill. "Okay. If you must know, Devon's been surly, rude, and uncooperative. Angry. Frankly, I haven't liked her very much lately."

"Neither have I."

They walked in silence until they reached St. Leo's Church. Forehead puckered in thought, Kat seated herself gingerly on the church steps. Chris sank down beside her.

"But this isn't all you want to tell me," she said.

"No. I've done some investigating. Devon handles our household accounting, but I pawed through last month's credit card bills, and our checkbook, too. It seems my wife has forked over nearly a thousand dollars to Ms. Melody and her little enterprise."

Kat gasped. "Are you kidding?"

"I wish I were."

"But, why? Why would anyone—"

"Devon wants a baby," Chris said flatly. "She wants that more than anything in the world. And, as you may know, she hasn't been able to get pregnant. Apparently, Ms. Melody and her friend Valentine have promised to fix that."

"But how could anyone fall for that crap? Good grief, it's not as if Tia's running a fertility clinic. She's just a loopy dingbat making a little . . . a *lot* . . . of money at Angel Café. Why would anyone believe she could solve their problems?"

"Oh, you'd be surprised." Kat detected a razor-sharp undertone in his voice that told her he was finished underestimating Ms. Melody's influence. "Tia runs private sessions at her home. The people who go are not the ones you'd expect. They're stockbrokers and doctors, teachers and lawyers . . ."

. . . vice presidents of software companies. Peter's list, the one with all those names, titles, and financial figures, emblazoned itself on Kat's mind.

"But the most amazing thing," Chris continued, "is that Tia's readings are dead accurate. She makes predictions, and people straighten up and listen like she's some kind of oracle. Because it turns out she's usually right."

"How do you know this?"

"Devon's told me enough. And," his voice wavered, "I have personal experience."

"Oh?"

"I went to the last circle meeting with Devon. She's so wrapped up in this that I figured I'd better see what the deal was."

Kat nodded slowly. "And?"

He steadily met her gaze. "Tia Melody is a skilled con artist. She's incredible. She starts the session with mumbo jumbo about light and universal focus. She throws in a few comments about your past, gives out advice. And I'm telling you, Kat, she's absolutely accurate. But then she tops herself. She brings on this Valentine character. I swear to God, the people I met at her house would jump off a bridge if Valentine suggested it."

While in high school Kat and two of her friends had taken the bus down Eastern Avenue to visit an old Gypsy fortune-teller. Kat still remembered the mysterious feel of the salon, how vulnerable and intimidated she'd felt standing in her parochial school uniform amongst the candles, religious pictures, and icons which decorated every available space in the tiny room. Even her thoughts had seemed transparent, out of her own control.

"Fortune-tellers create an environment that inspires self-doubt," she conceded. "But surely that's not enough to make people automatically believe everything Tia says. If they do, that's their problem. Isn't it?"

Chris rested his chin on his hand and stared at a point beyond the scuffed toe of his boot. "I'm not so sure. I'm starting to think this is a grand case of fraud."

"Fraud?" She jolted upright.

His face grew animated. "Look at it, Kat. All these people are forking over large amounts of money because they believe Tia Melody will deliver their dreams."

"But to support a fraud claim, you'd need to provide a damn good reason why they relied on her promises.

That's a problem. Why would anybody in their right mind actually believe a word Tia says?" She grimaced, aware that she'd just insulted this man's wife.

"Like it or not, Tia is very believable. She knows things about people. She knows what they're thinking."

"Psychology 101. Spend five observant minutes talking to an individual, and you'll come away knowing plenty about them."

"But she presents information that she couldn't possibly know."

"So she researches. She uses a computer. She perks up her ears in conversation and puts together the pieces. Chris, I can call any number of agencies to get information about defendants. With one phone call I can uncover credit reports, criminal records, driving records, insurance . . ."

"My point, exactly. She can and does get the information."

"But why?" Kat slapped a hand to her knee, exasperated.

"Oh, I don't know," Chris said. "It might have something to do with all the money she's making. Seems to me that the more desperate a person is, the more they're willing to spend. Tia probably pulls down a hundred thousand dollars a year."

Kat mentally reviewed Peter's list. Tia pulled down more than that.

"Valentine is her master stroke," Chris said seriously. "It's an amazing performance. Academy Award material."

The fortune-teller on Eastern Avenue had not attempted any sort of channeling. She'd stuck to her tarot deck, telling Kat about some unlucky karma she'd carried in from a past life, karma that the woman herself would be more than willing to confront if Kat could come up with the money. Even as she'd laughed at the obvious ploy, Kat had found herself wondering just what she'd done to deserve the black cloud of negative energy that had attached itself to her existence.

"What exactly happens?" she asked.

Chris rubbed the back of his neck and stared up at the cloudless sky. "It's hard to explain. You're watching Tia, waiting for this Valentine to speak up. Then all of a sudden, you feel like you're not watching Tia at all. The voice that comes out of her mouth is deeper, more elegant. Her body starts to move real smoothly. It makes perfect sense. If I were going to try to fool people this way, I'd pick a character as far away from my own personality as possible. I can see why people fall for it. She's got the act down pat."

"And you want her stopped."

"You bet. It isn't right, what she's doing. Tell me, Kat, do you think we have a case?"

Kat leaned back against the cool concrete of the step. Peter had obviously thought there was a case. His story, she realized suddenly, had perhaps meant to unmask Tia Melody, to expose her for the charlatan she was.

Perhaps that was why someone had killed him.

"I'm interested," she whispered. "I might even have some leads."

Chris's eyebrows rose. "Oh?"

Kat brushed his implied questions away with a wave of her hand. "My source stays anonymous. If you want my help, that's the way it has to be. It'll also be extracurricular. Harper, Madigan and Horn won't handle it. They're a white-glove firm."

"And not a word to Devon."

"Of course not."

They rose from the steps, awkward in a new partnership that had no logical foundation.

"Obviously," Chris said, "I can't call you at work."

Work. Kat bent her head. She could remember each and every case she'd handled since becoming associated with Harper, Madigan and Horn. But once outside the glass doors of her safe, sterile office building, life became a blur. If she pushed through her mind hard enough, she could almost glimpse what it had felt like to be alive. Once, she'd possessed the courage to press forward in search of answers.

"Call me at home tomorrow night," she said in a low voice. "I'll arrange for a leave of absence."

She knew immediately that their partnership would be fruitful. Chris, who'd surely caught the tremor in her voice, asked no questions.

Instead, he nodded curtly as they started up the street. "I'll keep visiting Tia with Devon," he said. "With both of us on the trail, this shouldn't take long at all."

Good, because they were already running two years behind.

9

―――

"LOOKS LIKE I CHOSE THE WRONG PROFESSION," CHRIS SAID AS he guided his motorcycle past the palatial homes of Guilford. "Maybe *I* should have gone into computer software, too."

"It's his mother's house," Kat reminded. Her arms tightened about his solid abdomen as he executed a too-sharp turn. An unexpected shiver raced through her. When was the last time she'd actually touched a man? The feel of Chris's hard body beneath his leather bomber jacket stirred longings she preferred remain dormant.

"Mr. Toohey apparently gets loads of free time, too," Chris said. "Didn't that ding-dong receptionist at Kaleidoscope say he conducted most of his business from home?"

"Don't insult her. She was trying to be helpful. If she was naive enough to give out his mother's phone number, then I'm eternally grateful for her dopiness."

"And I'm eternally grateful for how official you sound on the phone."

That was just about the only place. Kat's leave of absence from Harper, Madigan and Horn had become official that morning. To her own surprise, she'd based it on Peter's death, letting Hal believe that Peter had died the summer before she'd joined the firm. She hadn't gotten over it as well as originally thought, she'd said. It wasn't exactly a lie, but it certainly wasn't the truth. She suspected that she was functioning as well as she ever would. It had worked, though. Hal had gallantly offered to buy her as much time as she needed.

How frightening that someone who valued honesty could bend the truth with such conviction. Kat had next informed Mrs. Toohey that she was conducting a legal investigation into local psychic readers. She hadn't even felt guilty implying that she could produce a subpoena should David Toohey refuse to speak voluntarily.

"Turn right," she said, cheeks burning at the memory of her deceit. "You know, Mrs. Toohey sounded awfully eager to see us."

"Of course she did. You scared her." Chris slowed to check house numbers.

"No, it was more than that. She acted as if we'd be bringing gifts or something."

"Maybe she's got a bone to pick with Tia Melody, too." He pulled close to the curb, flicked the ignition key, and dismounted. "We should have T-shirts made. Little crystal balls inside red circles with slashes through them."

Kat snickered as she took his warm hand and slid from the bike.

The house was a large Georgian affair, the kind Kat knew she'd never afford in this lifetime.

"I wonder if there's a dress code," she said. Her leggings and sweater seemed suddenly tacky. She had the distinct impression that the women who lived in these palatial homes never walked out the door without a string of pearls clasped about their elegant necks.

"Just keep your cool. If you let them see you shake, they'll go for the jugular."

Kat had learned that lesson long ago. She straightened, marched up the front steps, and firmly lifted the brass doorknocker.

To her surprise, no butler appeared. Instead, the door flew open to reveal a thin, brown-haired woman with anxious gray eyes.

"I'm Janet Toohey," she said, extending a hand. "You must be Ms. Piretti."

"Yes." Kat seldom had the opportunity to meet with people at eye level. "This is Chris Alexander."

"Do come in."

The house, imposing on the outside, proved more welcoming inside. As they followed Janet Toohey through several rooms, Kat noted that the large, plush furniture looked comfortable and well used. There was ample evidence of foreign travel: African masks lined the hallway, delicate Oriental dolls posed on the living room mantel, and framed sketches of European cathedrals decorated nearly every room. Kat glanced at a signature in the lower right-hand corner of one: D. Toohey.

"Your son?" she asked, impressed.

"Yes." Janet Toohey continued down the hall, effectively squashing any possibility of small talk. Kat raised her chin against the thought that she had no business intruding here.

They passed through a large modern kitchen and out to a glass-enclosed sunporch. To Kat, born and bred in the heart of the city, the porch was beautiful, filled with green, leafy foliage and the subtle fragrance of blooming spring flowers. Plants occupied every available surface. Ferns and flowers hung in pots suspended from the ceiling. Tulips sat in vases atop pedestals; lilies and paperwhites occupied a table before the large glass windows. Kat was so immersed in the lushness of the flowers that she entirely overlooked the small man nestled in a recliner by the window.

"They're perfect, aren't they?" David Toohey said in a clear voice.

Kat and Chris turned his way, surprised. They saw not a powerful business magnate, but a small, frail man in his early forties. David, thin and obviously ill, smiled as he adjusted the afghan draped across his lap.

"My passion," he explained. "I used to have an incredible garden. Now I'm down to forced bulbs and plants that even a black thumb couldn't kill. I'm addicted, though. I must have my flowers."

Kat extended a hand. "Katerina Piretti."

"I know."

"Chris Alexander." Chris carefully shook his hand. "Thanks for seeing us today."

David nodded and pointed to an overstuffed sofa. "Please, have a seat. Of course I wanted to see you. I wouldn't have it any other way."

Chris sank onto the sofa. Mrs. Toohey positioned herself against the doorframe. Kat, aware that everyone awaited her lead, reached for a small round hassock and pulled it next to David's chair.

"Mr. Toohey," she said, seating herself before him, "tell us about Tia Melody."

He responded in a calm, even voice, as if she'd asked him what time it was or whether it was raining. "You must know something about her already. She's a psychic reader in South Baltimore."

"How did you meet her?"

"Through Kaleidoscope. She needed an accounting program for her business. Naturally, we got to talking, and when I found out she did psychic readings—"

"Tia Melody has a computer?" Chris interrupted from the couch.

David looked puzzled. "Nearly everyone in business has one these days."

Kat quickly picked up Chris's train of thought. "Did Ms. Melody ever approach you about programs other than the accounting one?"

"No."

Chris leaned forward. "Mr. Toohey, did you ever get the feeling that Ms. Melody was a computer hacker, that she could access data from . . ."

He stopped short as David Toohey began to laugh. The laughter obviously hurt. David clutched his abdomen as odd snorts escaped his mouth. He wiped tears from his eyes. "Sorry," he said, still grinning. "But have you ever met Tia?"

"Yes," Chris replied, startled.

"Mr. Alexander, she's no hacker. She couldn't even figure out the accounting system. She went right back to using a ledger."

"Oh." Chris looked disappointed. "Maybe somebody else in her operation uses a computer?"

"As far as I know, Tia works alone."

Kat threw Chris a glance. "Let's get back to your own experiences with Ms. Melody. Why did you decide to visit her?"

David's translucent skin took on a yellowish tinge. "I needed some answers. Tia said she could help."

"Valentine?" Kat asked gently.

"Yes." He lowered his eyes. "Exactly."

"And what did Valentine promise?" Chris asked.

"How do you know he promised anything?" David's voice grew thin. His mother stepped toward him, but he waved her back with a feeble flick of his hand.

"Because," Chris said, "Valentine always promises something."

David leaned back in his chair and closed his eyes. "He promised a cure."

"A cure?" Kat's eyebrows lowered.

He opened his eyes but did not meet her gaze. "I was HIV positive. Valentine said he could help."

"Oh, God. I'm so sorry."

"That's immoral!" Chris sputtered. "To raise hope in the impossible . . ."

With a surprising surge of strength, David Toohey lifted himself in his chair. "No," he said firmly. "It wasn't . . . isn't . . . impossible. Don't think I was some naive, desperate soul willing to believe anybody who threw a kernel of hope my way. I actually felt better when I followed Valentine. I grew stronger. Even my doctors were amazed. My T-cell count increased, and I had more energy than I'd had before my illness."

"How fortunate for you," Kat murmured.

"How much did it cost?" Chris asked.

"Between the readings, circle meetings, teas, balms, seminars . . . quite a bit, Mr. Alexander. But I had the money, and I'd have paid twice the amount to regain my health."

"Do you still visit Ms. Melody?" Kat asked.

His face closed. "No."

"Why not?"

David's strength ebbed. He slumped back against the chair. "I started to notice things I didn't like."

Eyebrows raised, Kat waited for clarification. David stared at her listlessly. Finally Janet Toohey spoke from her place by the wall.

"He realized that every moment of his life belonged to Valentine. He'd gotten to the point where he couldn't even choose orange juice over grapefruit juice in the morning without wondering which Valentine would recommend. And he noticed that he no longer had any friends outside of Tia Melody's circle. Valentine, you see, disapproved."

"But you felt better," Chris pressed, trying to understand.

David stared at the afghan. "I felt better physically, but I knew I was dying in spirit. I'd been had. It was a cult, a goddamned cult. All along I'd been encouraged to recruit new followers for Valentine, and I was good at that. I had a lot of social contacts, many employees. It was easy to get them to Tia's house, and once they were there, Valentine hooked them."

"I'm still not clear on why you left," Kat said.

"I saw what Valentine did to the people I brought in," David mumbled, finally able to meet her eyes. "Do you remember the story of King Midas, Ms. Piretti? You know, the king who wished everything he touched would turn into gold? Ultimately, all that gold came at the expense of his own happiness. Sure, Valentine could fulfill everyone's ultimate dream. But the costs were high. I watched a friend's marriage disintegrate because his wife wouldn't buy into Valentine. I saw enthusiastic employees turn into bland automatons, unable to deal with lives that seemed dull compared to the vibrancy of Valentine's unseen world. Valentine was evil, an insidious stain that bled into people's souls and refused to wash out. I wanted no part of that."

"Good for you," Chris said.

"There was more. . . ." David's voice trailed into the air. "I noticed that bad things happened to those who left the cult."

"Bad things?" Chris's eyebrows rose.

"Yes." David licked his lips before continuing. "Accidents. Suicides. Those who left the cult of Valentine usually ended up dead."

The thud in Kat's stomach felt like a kick. "Is that so?" she asked, voice hollow.

"Of course," David added, "it could have been purely coincidental. Most people who gravitated to Valentine had problems to begin with, so maybe they were predisposed to commit suicide anyway, or—"

"But you don't think so," Chris said.

"No. I didn't think so then and I don't think so now."

"Why didn't you go to the police?" Chris asked.

"I tried. They said that each death had been investigated and that they had no reason to suspect Tia or the cult. There were never any fingerprints, you see, never any clues pointing that way. In each case, either an accident or suicide made sense."

"But if all these people had been a part of Tia's circle . . ." Kat started.

". . . then all these people were certifiably unbalanced anyway," David finished. "That's what was implied, at any rate. So I called a reporter from the Sunpapers to help me dig up evidence. At the very least, I hoped he'd raise some doubts about the advisability of flocking to Valentine."

A wave of nausea swept through Kat. "A reporter?"

David nodded. "Smart young man. He investigated for a while, but I guess it never came to anything. I never saw anything in print, and I lost track of him."

Kat flinched. "He's dead."

David's fingernails scrabbled across the wooden arms of his chair as he struggled to pull himself forward. "What?"

"He's dead," she repeated, jerking her chin up. "He died on the night he was to meet Tia Melody. I believe he was murdered."

"Kat." Chris was beside her, urgent hand on her shoulder. "What are you saying? How do you know this?"

She stared into his wide blue eyes, and for a brief second he might have been Peter, so caring was his expression. Then she remembered that all she had left of Peter was the call to finish the investigation he'd begun.

"Peter Dulaney was my fiancé," she said in a hollow voice.

"Jesus." Chris wrapped a supportive arm around her, but Kat remained rigid by his side.

A dry, rasping sound escaped from David's mouth as he clawed at his throat. His mother rushed to his side.

"David!"

"It's what I told you, Mother! I will rot in hell for leading people to that monster! I will never be forgiven!"

"No!" Janet eased him back against the cushions.

"Mr. Toohey." Kat closed her cool hand over his. "It wasn't your fault."

"I take responsibility. I led innocent people into that darkness! No peace! I'll never find peace!"

"But you did it in good faith!" Kat cried. "You didn't know how deep Tia Melody's fraud ran!"

He turned glazed eyes to her. "Fraud?"

She nodded vigorously, relieved to have his attention. "She's obviously an accomplished actress, and well-versed in human nature. She can apparently access enough information to convince people that a spirit speaks through her."

David shook his head, amazed. "You don't understand, Ms. Piretti. Valentine is real."

Kat quickly exchanged a glance with Chris. As one, their heads swiveled to the bottles of medication arrayed on a nearby TV tray.

"No," David said. "My mind is clear. I'm not hallucinating. Valentine is real. Surely, your Peter Dulaney believed that, too. He gave up his life for that belief, just as I will do."

Kat searched for a delicate way to phrase her comment. "Valentine didn't cause your condition. You would have become . . . ill . . . no matter what."

"Not like this." David once again closed his eyes. "I was doing so well. I felt so good when I visited Valentine. When I left the circle, he promised me a horrible, painful death. He said he'd make it ten times worse than if I stayed with him. So you see, Ms. Piretti, I, too, will end up as dead as everyone else who tried to escape him."

Mrs. Toohey set her jaw. "It's time to say goodbye to your visitors." Her voice sounded so resolute that neither Kat nor Chris dared contradict her.

Kat reached for David's hand, but he did not open his eyes. "Thank you," she said.

"You can't stop him," David whispered. "He's too strong. Too powerful. Say a prayer for me, okay?"

"Okay." Kat succumbed to the pressure of Mrs. Toohey's hand on her arm and allowed herself to be ushered quickly from the room.

"He's wearing a morphine patch," Janet Toohey said as they walked briskly down the hall. "And he's on half a dozen medications. They might be affecting his perception of reality."

Kat hurried to keep up with her rapid footsteps. "Then you don't believe that Valentine is real, either?"

Mrs. Toohey stopped so suddenly that Chris almost plowed into her.

"All I know," she said in a brittle voice, "is that my son is dying. Right now he believes that his death was exacerbated by that damned Valentine, that something of a death sentence was laid upon him when he abandoned Tia Melody's circle."

"Impossible," Chris muttered.

Mrs. Toohey's eyes bore through him with laser intensity. "He also believes that he is condemned to hell because he brought others into Valentine's clutches. I invited you here today in the hopes that whatever you had to say would soothe him." She glared at Kat. "I had no idea, Ms. Piretti, that you would add another death to his conscience."

"Mrs. Toohey." Kat reached for the woman's hand. "I'm sorry. But we'll uncover Tia for what she is: A fraud, pure and simple. And once we've done that, David will see that he's blameless."

Mrs. Toohey studied Kat's eyes, shoulders slumped. "Do you honestly think you can do that?"

"Yes."

Chris cleared his throat. "You can help us, ma'am. Do you know anybody else we could talk to about this? Anybody else who got burned by Tia Melody?"

"I can get names."

Chris silently handed her a business card.

"Work quickly, please," Janet Toohey said sadly. "David doesn't have long. My last wish for him is a peaceful death."

"We understand." Kat reached for the door.

"We have a lot to do," Kat said as they approached Chris's motorcycle. "Hopefully, Mrs. Toohey will get back to us with more names, but in the meantime, I know of some people we can contact."

"Kat . . ." His voice caressed her.

"We need to see more of Tia's operation. You'll be there with Devon, but maybe I should start going, too. You know, at a different time."

"Kat."

"I could even visit her at Angel Café. She doesn't know me, after all."

"Kat." He caught her hand in his. "Why didn't you tell me about Peter?"

Kat squinted against the setting sun, turning away from the sympathy in his voice.

He stared down at their clasped hands. "How horrible for you."

"I don't want to talk about this," she said.

Startled, he looked at her closely. "Well," he said, swallowing, "aside from everything else, it's probably important that we do. We're in this together, now. It's important that I know what you know."

She extricated her hand. "Peter left a list of names. I think they're Tia's patrons. There. Now you know what I know."

He looked as if he wanted to say more. His head was cocked to one side, his mouth tight. She could imagine him saying, "Let me see your license and registration."

"Kat," he finally said, "I'm sorry. You'll let me at least say that, won't you?"

She turned calmly toward him. "How about you take me home?"

"Yeah. Sure."

They boarded the motorcycle, and Kat once again wrapped her arms around his middle. "You're working tonight, right?" she asked.

"Night shift for the next week. Devon's got a date with Tia this evening. She'll fill me in, though. She'll tell me more than I want to know."

"Except that now you want to know everything. Call me when you wake up, and we'll plan our next move. I've got a sudden urge to see Tia Melody behind bars."

Chris grinned. "You haven't met her yet. Bars would be most becoming."

Anything else Kat might have said was drowned out as he gunned the engine.

10

~~~

A TINY ANGEL-SHAPED SALTSHAKER SKITTERED ACROSS THE table and landed in shards at Stephen's feet.

"Oh, jeez," Devon Alexander said. "I'm so sorry."

"Don't worry about it." He caught the eye of one of his waiters, who hurried over, broom and dustpan in hand. "I can't get mad at one of my best customers, can I?"

Devon managed a wan smile. She sat alone at a deuce, a steaming cup of herbal tea before her, an untouched plate of multigrain toast pushed toward the edge of the table.

"Hey," Stephen said lightly, acknowledging the plate. "Something wrong with your order? Can I help?"

"What?" She gazed blankly at him, and the delicate purple shadows beneath her eyes took him by surprise. "Oh, no, Mr. Carmichael. Everything is just fine. I love your restaurant. Is Tia here yet?"

Stephen frowned and checked his watch. "Probably. It's nearly eleven."

"Please, I need to speak with her."

He knew that. Devon had visited Angel Café three times this past week. She always came alone, always ordered tea and toast, and never ate anything. Each visit ended with Tia stopping by the table for a five-minute chat. Stephen never heard their conversations, but it was hard to miss the strained expression that settled on Devon's face throughout them.

Ever observant where female beauty was involved, Stephen noticed that Devon had lost weight. Her once easy grace had been replaced by an air of jittery nervousness. No matter how hard he tried, it was impossible to banish the persistent feeling that Tia Melody was at the root of the change.

"I need to get back to work." Devon's fingers beat an uneven tattoo on the tabletop. "I know there's a sign-up sheet to see Tia, but it's really important that I speak with her before she gets involved in her readings today."

Stephen sucked in a deep breath and shot a glance at the sweeping waiter. "Thanks," he said. The waiter scurried away.

"I know it's not policy, Mr. Carmichael, but please, just this once. . . ."

Even with the weight loss and her harried sense of urgency, she was impossibly beautiful. Stephen wanted to reach out and cup that perfect face in his hands, to lean toward those full, beautiful lips and . . .

He remembered with a thud that her husband was a cop who probably carried a gun. It was enough to snap him out of the fantasy.

"I can't bend the rules," he said gently. "Next thing you know, everybody will need an emergency reading."

"But I really do!"

"Sorry, Ms. Alexander, but—"

"Good to see you, hon." Tia Melody swept over, a

vision in leather fringe and thigh-high boots. Devon brightened instantly. "You don't have to ask Mr. Carmichael about seeing me," Tia continued. "He's a softy, a regular softy. He's not going to say no, are you, Mr. Carmichael?"

Stephen opened his mouth to speak, then closed it again. Tia was already seating herself opposite Devon, reaching confidently for her hand.

"Scat," she told him. "I'll be on time. You just take down names for readings."

He'd been duly dismissed. In his own restaurant. By his own hired help.

"I want to speak with you later," he informed Tia evenly. "In my office."

"Of course you do, hon. I'll be there for a cigarette break in half an hour. Now, scoot."

Smoldering, Stephen turned to leave. Who did she think she was? God's gift to the restaurant world? He was immediately sorry he'd posed the question. As much as he hated to admit it, Tia Melody was a prime ingredient of Angel Café's booming success.

Devon's plaintive voice halted him in his tracks. "But Valentine promised!" he heard her say, and he could not stop himself from turning mid-stride. Over the back of Tia Melody's shoulder, he could see that Devon was close to tears.

Mechanically he paused at an empty table and began to rearrange the silver.

"It's gonna be okay," Tia said. "The universe takes its time, and you probably haven't gotten yourself ready."

"I've done everything Valentine told me to do, and I'm still not pregnant." Devon must have noticed how frantic she sounded. Her voice dropped to a low murmur. Stephen moved from the silverware to the flower arrangement. "Chris is trying to understand, just like Valentine said he should."

"Chris still needs help," Tia replied shortly. "Valentine told you that last time." Her voice, thank God, was a scratchy foghorn that could never be muted.

Devon defensively drew herself up. "At least he comes to the circle with me."

Well, forget me trying for even first base, Stephen thought. She was definitely in love with her husband.

Tia sighed. "Look, hon, only Valentine knows what the problem is."

"Then ask him."

"You can ask him yourself next week."

"I can't wait that long."

The flowers had been arranged to death, but Stephen realized that neither Devon nor Tia was paying the least attention to his hovering.

"Okay," Tia said after a short pause. "Okay, but only because you're one of my favorites." She reached into her purse to pull out a steno pad and pen. Stephen edged closer for a better view as she placed the tip of the pen to the paper.

At first nothing happened. Tia sat frozen, eyes closed. Devon leaned in, lips parted expectantly. Stephen forgot to find an alibi and stood openly staring.

Suddenly the pen scrawled across the paper, flinging Tia's arm out to the side. Both hand and pen returned immediately to the page, spewing out sentences at breakneck speed.

"He's got a lot to say, hon, but he's sure not going to say it all here."

As quickly as the writing had begun, it stopped. Tia's hand dropped to her lap.

"But he said something!" Devon cried. "What is it?"

"Here." Tia passed the pad across the table and slowly began to massage her wrist. "I hate doing the writing. Valentine forgets I'm not a robot, that my hand can only go so fast. I'd rather channel any day. Read it out loud, hon."

Devon cleared her throat. " 'More,' " she read. " 'More will support my way, your Christopher. Bring me a circle, and we will surround your husband with intent.' Tia, what does this mean?"

Tia smiled, and Stephen backed out of range of her peripheral vision. "Easy, hon. Your husband needs more encouragement. A community. Got any friends you can bring to our circle? Any people you work with?"

"Well . . ." Devon blinked. "I guess."

"Think about it. The more folks your husband knows who think like we do, the more he's gonna see how right we are. He's got to be in harmony with both you and the universe before you can have that little baby."

A flush of pink appeared on each of Devon's cheeks. Stephen watched in amazement as she squared her shoulders and actually smiled.

"Thank you, Tia. And thank you, Valentine. It makes sense."

"Sure it does." Tia absently reached across to pat her hand. "Now, think you can muddle through until our circle meets next week? Because I've got to . . ."

Stephen did not wait for her to complete the sentence. He turned on quiet feet and headed quickly toward his office.

What was happening? How had Tia Melody and her goofy Valentine managed to gain entrance into so many of his customers' private lives? He batted away the surge of guilt that had begun to appear with alarming frequency. Surely, he was not responsible for the actions of insecure morons too dense to see that they were being taken.

He slammed his office door behind him and leaned wearily against it.

Tia Melody was great for business, and his only responsibility was business.

Damn it. He should have stuck with his original idea of Ouija boards beneath glass tabletops. Perhaps Victoria had been right; perhaps that would have attracted a crew of disoriented, lost souls. He didn't see where that was much different from what he had now.

A curious scent piqued his nostrils, drawing him from the depths of his thoughts. It was vaguely familiar, but out of place. Stephen took a step forward.

Rosemary! That's what it was. He'd have recognized it at once in the kitchen, but it certainly didn't belong here in his office. His office, which had once tantalized with the aroma of freshly brewed coffee, lately reeked only of stale cigarette smoke.

Nothing on the menu today required rosemary. Besides, the kitchen was on the other side of the building. Stephen opened the door and stuck his head out into the hallway. It smelled as it always did . . . of rose petals.

"Did you need something?" Molly asked coolly from behind the cash register.

"Um . . . no." He retreated into his office.

The aroma had intensified. It swirled teasingly about

the room, inviting him to enjoy its presence. Without thinking, Stephen closed his eyes and drank it in. He'd always liked rosemary. It sharpened his senses, reminded him of cold, brisk days and clear autumn skies.

The herb of remembrance, he heard. He smiled in acknowledgment of the information.

His eyes flew open. He'd heard those words in his own voice, but they weren't his!

"No," he breathed. But there, once again, was that compelling urge, the one that had enveloped him on the day Katerina Piretti had first entered Angel Café. His hands flew to his ears. He thought he sensed gentle, chiming laughter at the sight of physical hands trying to block nonphysical sound.

He staggered to the chair behind his desk and collapsed into it. Kat had warned him that it would happen again. It couldn't. He wouldn't let it. He pulled his knees up to his chest, wrapped his arms around them, and buried his head. "Go away," he whispered.

The room grew warm, inquiring. Stephen lifted his eyes and thought the office looked brighter.

Tell Katerina she is on the wrong track. Tell her to talk to Francesca.

Francesca? Who the hell was Francesca?

Rosemary was, indeed, the herb of remembrance. Stephen dredged desperately through his memory for an explanation, stopping with relief at a reassuring image from childhood. His breathing steadied as he recalled his mother marching into his room, her mouth drawn in a straight line as she observed him arranging stuffed animals for protection against the monsters he knew would attack in the night.

"Stephen," she'd announced, pushing aside the animals, "there are no monsters in this world. Do you understand me? They do not exist."

"But—"

"Stephen," she'd repeated, seating herself beside him, "have you ever actually seen a monster?"

Of course he hadn't.

"No monsters. No ghosts. No fairies, no elves, no angels . . . Stephen, if you can't see it or touch it, it doesn't exist. Ever."

He'd accepted it then; he'd believe it now. If the rest of the gullible world wanted to jump onto the metaphysical bandwagon, they were more than welcome to do so. Stephen Carmichael would remain a man of cool, logical reason.

As for those unwelcome words in his mind . . . He glanced tentatively around the room. He saw no shadows, heard no weird noises. The room felt secure and warm, even welcoming. Still, he could not deny that a calm, patient question awaited an answer.

He drew in a deep breath. Stress played odd tricks on the mind, and he was a stressed, tired man. There was no other way to explain why Katerina Piretti still resided somewhere within his subconscious.

There'd be no Francesca. He'd deliver his message to Kat, who would stare in disbelief and tell him that it made absolutely no sense. Then he'd be free at last, and Kat would know once and for all that he was no oracle, no viaduct for ethereal messages from the amorphous "beyond."

He straightened in his chair and narrowed his eyes. "Find another dupe, Ms. Piretti," he said quietly. "I'm through with it."

The words once again intruded, confidently insistent: *Tell Katerina she is on the wrong track. Tell her to talk to Francesca.*

A corner of his mouth turned up. He would do that. He would definitely do that.

Calmly, nonchalantly, Stephen reached for the telephone.

11

~~~~

Francesca wrapped her hands firmly around a twelve-pound free weight and, with a grunt, hoisted it toward her chest. The pull through her biceps invigorated her. With a satisfied smile, she reached to the living-room floor for the other weight, then locked into a slow, steady rhythm. Right elbow bent, left elbow bent, right elbow . . . Contentment radiated throughout her, warming every inch of her body.

She had turned fifty last month, but was in better condition than ever before. Tall and lean, she possessed a smooth, feline grace that only hinted at her strength. Her eyes were gray, set off by high, defined cheekbones. Her hair—dark, shoulder-length, and shaggy—had only recently begun to register streaks of white.

Lifting weights was balm for both body and soul. Francesca closed her eyes and focused her thoughts on an image carried since her convent days. It was one of her favorites. A vibrant light pulsated in and out of itself in a flood of color. Even in imagination, it was almost too brilliant to view straight on, but Francesca, fascinated, could never pull herself away. The colors! The purest white, the most shimmering gold, the clearest tinge of rose. How wonderful to thrust oneself into the very center of such constant, beautiful energy!

She thought she heard Katerina's voice at the edge of the light. Perhaps. Kat had been on her mind lately, and on her heart. These days, the thought of her niece induced a reflexive mantra. Now was no exception. "Keep her safe," she murmured without missing a beat in her exercise. "Open her heart and guide her."

"Aunt Frannie." This time the voice was closer, and it penetrated Francesca's concentration. Startled, she opened her eyes. Kat stood before her, frowning.

It took a minute to readjust to the surroundings of the row house living room. Blinking, Francesca slowly lowered her weights. Kat, she saw, was not alone. To her right stood Chris Alexander. To her left was a tall, dark-haired man with clear green eyes. Despite the informality of his jeans, T-shirt, and tweed jacket, Francesca noted an elegant grace to the line of his body. He was handsome despite the troubled scowl on his face.

"Katerina. I didn't know we had company."

This was plainly not a social call. Kat didn't even bother to introduce her new acquaintance.

"Aunt Frannie," she said, "we need to talk to you."

The smile faded from Francesca's face as she reached for the towel draped across the back of the sofa. Her niece, doll-like between the tall men, nervously bit her lower lip. Were Kat a young high school student, Francesca might have feared that the bombshell was a pregnancy and wondered which of these two very different men was to blame. These days, however, she longed for any indication that her niece might be enjoying male companionship. She swung the towel across her shoulders. Kat was different this evening, but one look told her it had nothing to do with romantic entanglements. Chris Alexander's wedding band glinted in the light as he reached up to run a hand through his short hair. The other man stood with his fists jammed into his pockets, eyes focused on a lithograph mounted near the fireplace. No, Kat's heightened color had nothing to do with either man.

"Well," Francesca said. "Suppose we adjourn to the kitchen? I'm dying of thirst."

The three followed her down the short hallway. It reminded her of the days she'd taught elementary school. She motioned them all toward the kitchen table, opened the refrigerator door, and reached for the Gatorade. Kat seated herself in her usual chair. Chris sat beside her, his dark police uniform a jarring note against the cheery whites and reds of the kitchen. Their colleague chose to stand. He leaned against the tiled counter, eyebrows lowered, arms crossed against his chest.

"And you are?" Francesca inquired.

"Stephen Carmichael." He nodded curtly, but extended a hand to shake.

"Pleased to meet you. I'm Francesca Piretti." She caught a wince at the sound of her name. With a bemused smile, she reached for his hand. "You can call me Frannie."

"Aunt Frannie," Kat began in a rushed, embarrassed voice, "I've been working on a case about psychic readers, and I—"

"Case? I thought you'd taken a leave of absence."

"I did, but . . ."

Stephen pushed himself away from the counter. "Cut the game, Kat," he ordered, turning to Francesca. "I find it best to be direct. Let me tell you first that I own Angel Café."

"I've heard a lot about your restaurant," Francesca replied, eyebrow arched. "I understand you feature romanticized angels and fortune-telling. Congratulations. You've certainly tapped into a lucrative vein."

The chiding tone in her voice made Stephen blush. "Angel Café features psychic readings," he corrected. "My reader simply has a knack for delivering the sorts of messages people want to hear."

"No doubt." She raised the bottle of Gatorade to her lips.

Stephen had taken several steps forward and now stood behind Kat. He locked his elbows and leaned against her chair. "There's only one problem," he said tightly. "*I'm* the one who's starting to get messages."

"Messages?" Francesca set down the Gatorade, puzzled.

"Yes. Thoughts run through my head. They're in my own voice, but they're definitely not my words."

"Aunt Frannie," Kat said, "Stephen's last message was about you."

Francesca tilted her head. "I suppose you'd best tell me what it was."

Stephen opened his mouth to speak, but Kat's answer poured out first. "The message was that I'm going the wrong way, and that I should talk to you."

"Nobody would ever guess you were a lawyer, Kat," Stephen said. "You're weak on facts. How's she supposed to reach a logical conclusion with only a fraction of the story?"

Kat whirled in her chair to face him, an angry frown on her face.

Chris cleared his throat, short-circuiting the blow-up. "Frannie, you know that my wife, Devon, is Kat's secretary. A little over a month ago, Devon became involved in a psychic circle run by Stephen's reader, Tia Melody. Those who visit Tia at home get messages straight from Valentine, an entity Tia claims to channel. My wife . . . everybody who visits Tia . . . swears by Valentine. They all spend tons of money just to hear his advice, and then they follow whatever he says to the letter."

"Dangerous," Francesca said.

"You bet. Never mind the money; I'm losing my wife. She's so obsessed, so drained, that she can barely think for herself."

"It sounds like she relies on Valentine for that."

Chris sighed. "I'm afraid so."

"What is Devon's Achilles' heel?" Francesca asked gently.

"What?"

"Her vulnerability, Chris. What does she want so very badly?"

"A baby." He stared at the floor.

She reached across the table to touch his hand. "Everyone has a point of vulnerability. No matter how well we build our defenses, there's always someone who knows how to penetrate them. It's hard to resist an onslaught like that."

Chris nodded sadly. "I know. That's why I came to Kat. I figured I'd need a lawyer to handle a first-class case of fraud like this."

"Fraud?" Francesca looked blank.

"Sure. Tia invents Valentine as a mouthpiece and then makes promises that people rely on. It's easy. They keep paying Tia, and 'Valentine' keeps assuring them that they'll get whatever they want, provided they do as he says and keep handing over the cash."

"Aunt Frannie, you wouldn't believe how much money people have paid." Kat spoke so quickly that her words tumbled over themselves. "Tia's set for life."

"She's convincing, too," Chris added. "I've gone to her circle. Even the feeling in the room changes when she becomes Valentine. It makes the hair on my arms quiver."

Francesca thought for a moment before meeting Stephen's smoldering eyes.

"Why did you choose to come here today?" she asked.

Stephen colored. "I wanted to end this nonsense once and for all. I figured there'd be no Francesca, that a useless message would prove how stupid this all is."

"But you didn't feel forced to deliver the message?"

He sighed and stared down at the top of Kat's shiny, dark head. "Not forced. Urged, maybe. But the choice was mine. I could have refused."

"Why didn't you?"

He shrugged helplessly. "Delivering the message seemed like the right thing to do."

"I see." A tiny smile tugged at one corner of Francesca's mouth. "Stephen, you may not be the curmudgeon you'd like to think you are. I suspect there's hope for you yet."

She didn't give him a chance to respond, although the indignant look on his face indicated that he wanted to. "Katerina, anything to add?"

Kat squared her shoulders and lifted her chin. "We need to stop Tia Melody."

The room grew silent as Francesca studied her Gatorade.

Stephen cleared his throat. "So it's stupid, right? The message makes no sense to you, either, and we should all just forget about it, right?"

"Wrong. Actually, the message does make sense to me."

"I don't want to hear this," Stephen said as Chris and Kat leaned forward in their chairs.

"I think there's a fundamental flaw in your reasoning," Francesca said.

Kat gulped. "Flaw?"

"You're assuming that Valentine is Tia's creation. He's not. He's real."

"Jesus." Stephen groaned. "The whole family is crazy."

Francesca continued as if she hadn't heard him, the cadences of her voice falling over them in a soothing stream. "You can fight the concept all you want, but you can't fight Valentine unless you accept him for what he is. He's real. If he works through Tia, it is he who controls her, not the other way around. And money wouldn't be his motivation."

Chris had turned scarlet. "But . . . but that makes no sense."

"Money is *everybody's* motivation!" Stephen declared.

"A bit jaded, hmmm?" Francesca nodded at him. "Money may have been Tia's bait, but Valentine, whoever he is, has no use for money. It buys only physical things and Valentine isn't physical."

"I need a drink," Stephen snapped. "And I don't mean Gatorade."

"But . . ." Chris struggled for words, "if he's not physical, then . . ."

Francesca stood and reached into a cabinet above the sink. "I'm not sure what he is," she admitted, pulling out a bottle of bourbon. "But if he seeks total control and personal glory then he's certainly not an agent of the Light."

"What?" Stephen made a face.

She deposited ice cubes into a glass, poured the bourbon over them, and thrust the drink into Stephen's hand. "I think I've made myself clear," she said. "Whether or not you choose to believe me is your affair."

"Are you saying that Valentine is an evil spirit?" Kat asked gingerly.

"For lack of a better description, yes. At this point that's exactly what I'm saying. Of course, I don't know enough yet to be sure."

"No offense," Chris said, "but how would you know. . . ."

She cast him a quelling glance. It had once worked exceptionally well on her fourth graders. It worked now, even when aimed at a fully grown police officer.

"Let's just say that your angels have guided you to a source who has always believed in their existence," she said.

"Angels?" Kat's voice cracked.

"I am sane, Katerina, so wipe the grimace off your face. It's time to dust off our spiritual armor."

"And what is that?" Chris asked. His face alone remained open. Kat and Stephen stared at Francesca with outright incredulity.

" 'Put God's armor on so as to be able to resist the devil's tactics,' " Francesca quoted. " 'For it is not against human enemies that we have to struggle, but against the Sovereignties and the Powers who originate the darkness in this world, the spiritual army of evil in the heavens.' "

"Ephesians." Kat spoke slowly, dragging the word up from the depths of her memory.

"Good," Francesca said. "You remember. This is your background as well as mine, after all. Do you remember the armor itself?"

Embarrassed, Kat slid down in her chair. "Um . . . truth buckled around your waist, integrity for a breastplate, eagerness to spread the gospel on your feet, salvation as a helmet."

"Two more," her aunt prodded. "Two more intensely important ones. You forgot the shield of faith and the sword of the spirit. Don't leave home without them, Katerina."

Stephen flung back his head and downed enough bourbon to make his eyes water. "This is insane," he said, voice raspy. "And what's it got to do with me, anyway? Here I am getting messages I never asked for and certainly don't want. I don't believe in evil spirits, and I couldn't care less about Tia Melody. What the hell is going on?"

Francesca topped off his drink, then returned the bottle to its shelf in the cabinet. "You can't deny that you've been tapped. Your message was accurate. After all, you didn't know a Francesca, but here I am."

"I never heard of Peter, either," Stephen muttered. "Yet he seems to have lived and died despite my ignorance."

Francesca's head swiveled toward Kat, who avoided her probing gaze by studying the pattern on the wooden tabletop. "Oh?"

Stephen caught the bright red flush on Kat's cheeks

and recklessly plowed on. "Kat apparently doesn't share pertinent information. Oh, yes, the first message I received was for her. I was told that she was right about Peter's death, whatever that means."

"Katerina," Francesca said in a low voice, "is that what drew you into this web?"

"You know it wasn't what it seemed, Aunt Frannie." A shiver raced visibly through Kat's body, escalating until even her teeth chattered with the power of her shaking.

Chris Alexander wrapped a strong arm around her shoulders. "Breathe with me, Kat."

Kat leaned against him, rhythmically drawing in air to match the rise and fall of his broad chest.

Stephen studied them until the shaking stopped. Then he returned to his drink.

Francesca paced for a moment before turning to her niece. "Katerina, you know this is dangerous, don't you? There's danger any time you brush against darkness, and this feels as dark as anything I've experienced in years. Don't scoff at the idea of spiritual armor; you're going to need it."

"No," Stephen said. "What we really need is a heavy organ chord, followed by a loud scream and thumps in the hallway."

"I suggest you keep quiet," Francesca told him. "I've spent a lifetime trying to walk the path of spirit, and you, Mr. Skeptic, obviously have not. Katerina, look at me."

They all looked at her, stunned by the note of authority in her voice.

"I don't have a choice," Kat said unhappily. "I've got to make this right, Aunt Frannie."

Her aunt's stare bore through her, questioning. Kat held the gaze without a flinch.

"Yes," Francesca murmured, reaching out a hand to raise her niece's chin, "I can see that you do. You're the image of your mother, but I recognize your core as my own. If you plan to answer this call, then I've obviously been led to help you. And I will."

"Thank you," Chris said. "Because you'll be helping me, too."

Stephen set his glass down on the table with a loud bang. "Well, hope you all find the Holy Grail or whatever it is you're looking for. This is where I bail out."

"You can't," Kat said. "You're the only one who gets marching orders around here."

"Oh, I don't know. Your aunt probably has better radar than I do. I'll just tell the spirit world that my number has been disconnected. They can call her instead."

"You're an idiot." Kat circled the table to stand before him. "A pompous idiot. And if you don't stay and help, I'll find a way to tie you into any fraud claim I file, Stephen Carmichael. See if I don't!"

Chris placed a cool hand on her shoulder. "Easy. You can't make people do what they don't want to do. We can handle it without him."

Francesca smiled. "Stephen, don't you see that you can't leave us? Somehow, somewhere, God has a task for you in this."

"God?" He stared skeptically.

Francesca nodded. "I only work for the Light. I have no intention of messing with anything else."

"What makes you different from Tia Melody?"

Stephen demanded. "She speaks of Valentine as if *he* were a god!"

"Stick around," Francesca said. "See if you can figure out the difference for yourself."

He stared at her, his body rigid and his fists clenched. Her sharp gray gaze seemed to pierce his very soul, until he felt emotionally naked before her.

"If you leave us, Stephen, you will always wonder how you might have made a difference."

He pulled away from her stare and turned toward Chris. "Surely you understand," Stephen said, palms turned upward in appeal.

Chris steadily met his gaze. "I understand that you have a right to do what you want. As for me, I'm in it until the end."

There was no need to ask Kat. She stood smoldering before him, a tiny ember struggling against the dark.

"Damn." He reached up a tired hand and began to massage his neck. "Damn."

"I want to visit Tia's circle," Kat said. "I want to meet Valentine."

Chris shook his head. "I can't take you. Devon and Tia would know that something was up."

"I'll pick a different night and go alone. I can handle it."

"You can't go alone," Chris insisted. "It's too much. Take Frannie."

Francesca shook her head. "I think you'll need my help in a different capacity."

All eyes turned to Stephen.

"Damn," he said again.

12

ANGEL CAFÉ HAD CLOSED HOURS AGO, SO IT WAS DIFFICULT for Stephen to rationalize why he was still there. He could only be waiting for Katerina Piretti. Outside, the light of the summer sky had barely begun to fade. Inside, only the rhythmic ticking of the antique grandfather clock in the corner broke the stillness of the empty lobby. Stephen cocked his head to observe the steady sway of the pendulum. That clock had once sat on the landing of his family's staircase, its ticks, chimes, and gears reminding him that life continued in an accountable, coherent manner. Now the same noises mocked him. Normal life continued, yes. But somehow, he'd been pushed off its track.

Fifteen minutes before Kat was due to arrive. He could leave. She was smart; it would take only a few minutes of knocking before she'd figure out that he'd stood her up, that he had no intention of participating in this asinine chase. And what on earth could she do about it?

"Not a damn thing," he muttered beneath his breath.

He shook his head, still unclear about how he'd gotten swept into this. Certainly, he had not willingly chosen to waste a free Wednesday evening chasing spirits with Kat Piretti. He was not interested in spending *any* free time with her. She was pretty, but she was definitely not his type. He always fell for leggy, fair women . . . like Devon Alexander. Besides, even if Kat were seven inches taller and golden blond, Stephen would avoid her at all costs. There was a closed hardness to her that he found abrasive, far too difficult to break through. Winning her over would take too much work.

He wondered how she got that way.

The thought crept uninvited through his mind, but at least the words were his own and not some celestially planted conjecture.

Who cared how she got that way? She was hard and obnoxious, and that was all that mattered.

He leaned against the wall and folded his arms across his chest. Obviously, Peter had something to do with the crusty wall that surrounded her. Clearly, his death propelled her compulsively through this search. After all, she couldn't possibly care enough about Devon Alexander to waste time rescuing her from her own bad judgment.

He batted away his thoughts and glared again at the clock.

Ten minutes. He could still leave, locking the door behind him, refusing to look back as he slipped through an alley to his car. Sure, Kat would probably telephone him all week, but he wouldn't have to take her calls. Molly's demeanor was icy now, but she'd field the calls for him if she thought it was part of her job.

He glanced out the window. A city police car cruised to a stop at the curb in front of the restaurant. Stephen reflexively straightened, wondering what he'd done wrong. His nerves were not entirely appeased when Chris Alexander emerged from the driver's side.

Damn. There went any chance of escape.

With a resigned sigh, he unlocked the front door of Angel Café and wearily ushered Chris inside.

"Nice place." Chris removed his hat as he studied the angel prints on the wall.

"Thanks." Stephen did not care to be accommodating.

"I'm on my way home. I wanted to wish you luck tonight. I also wanted to tell you that I don't hold you responsible for what's happening with Devon."

"Well, gee, that's big of you."

Either Chris chose to ignore the sarcasm, or it failed to register. Blue eyes calm, he extended a conciliatory hand. "Thanks for your help. I know this isn't something you want to do."

Stephen managed a dry, barking laugh. "You can say that again."

"Be careful tonight," Chris said. "I know you think you can handle anything, but Valentine is downright spooky. Don't get sucked in."

"No problem there. Believe me."

"No, Stephen, you believe me. I felt the same way you do before I visited Tia. Wear that armor tonight."

"You've been hanging out with Francesca too long."

"I wish I could hang out with her tonight. Devon will be home, though. Frannie said she could handle it alone, but—"

"Handle it alone?" Stephen stared at him. "What's to handle? She won't be traipsing like an idiot to Tia Melody's house. What's she going to do, hoist a cappuccino in my honor?"

"I don't know what she's going to do, but I trust her." Chris glanced out the window. "There's Kat."

Stephen checked the clock. "Somehow I knew she'd be the punctual type."

Chris hesitated. "Take care of her," he said finally.

"Take care of her? I'd hate to run into her in a dark alley. She's a little pit bull."

"You think so?"

"Sure." Stephen cracked a tight smile. "She's ready to take on the whole world."

Chris shook his head, bemused. "I don't know why you think that. She's bleeding, Stephen, and she doesn't know how to stop the flow."

"What?" That made no sense. Stephen turned as Kat approached the door. She wore tight jeans and a loosely fitting black cotton sweater. The wind lifted her long hair, causing it to ripple behind her in a gentle wave. Her eyes met his as she reached for the door-knob. For one moment he lost himself in the vulnerability of her gaze. Stoically, he forced his stare to the determined set of her full mouth. "This one can take care of herself," he muttered, reaching for his key. "Anyone can see that."

Chris remained silent as Kat tugged open the door and strode inside.

"I'm surprised," she told Stephen haughtily. "I really didn't think you'd be here. I expected you to stand me up."

"Thanks a heap," he replied, offended.

Her expression softened as she noticed Chris. "What a surprise! Are you coming with us after all?"

"I can't. I just dropped by to see you off. Good luck, Kat. And please . . . be careful."

She flipped a lock of hair back over her shoulder. "Nothing's going to happen that I can't handle."

"Come on, Wonder Woman," Stephen said. "We'll be late."

"I'll drive," Kat said as they hit the sidewalk.

"No, I'll drive," Stephen corrected. "I told Tia you were my date. It'll look better if I drive."

"Your *date?*" Her voice cracked.

"Tia knows how I feel about psychic readings. I had to tell her that you were interested, and then I had to invent a damned good reason why I'd care enough to accompany you. You want to play detective, you have to roll with the punches."

Chris stopped before the door of his cruiser. "One thing. This sounds stupid, but it worked for me. If things get really bad in there tonight, pray."

Stephen rolled his eyes. "Sure, sure. And then I'll throw a pinch of salt over my shoulder. Or is it garlic? Am I supposed to be wearing garlic?"

Chris shook his head as his colleagues rounded a corner and disappeared from view.

"We could have walked this distance," Kat said as Stephen pulled his car into a space near Tia's house.

"You could have." He shoved the stick into gear with more force than necessary.

Kat eyed his custom-made leather cowboy boots. "More for looks than function, I see."

"I'm a hardworking man. I'm entitled to my luxuries."

She stared nonchalantly out her window. "You're the one who talked to Tia. Tell me about tonight."

"It's an all-Valentine extravaganza. He's the only

player on the bill this evening, and I had to work mighty hard to get you in."

"Why? Was he sold out?"

"Tia hates to disturb settled circles. We're in for two reasons. One, she thinks she's doing me a favor and that I'll owe her. Two, she had to let another new person in tonight anyway."

"Great. Another rookie."

"Not quite. This is his third visit. He's got a scheduling conflict, so he's switching to the Wednesday circle. As a special bonus, this guy happens to be someone Devon Alexander brought in."

Kat wrinkled her nose. "What's his name?"

"Hal Banks."

She felt the blood drain from her face. "He's my mentor at the firm. He thinks I'm taking a leave of absence to get myself together. How am I supposed to explain my appearance at a looney-tunes meeting like this?"

"Maybe this is how you're getting yourself together. Remember, Hal Banks doesn't think it's looney-tunes, or he wouldn't be there."

"Unless he's investigating, too. That's it. We're *all* investigating. Nobody's there for any other reason."

"Nobody else is stupid enough to investigate. Listen up, or we'll be late. You're my date. We're crazy about each other. That's why I discarded my dignity and begged Tia to let us come this evening. I suggest you keep any biographical details to yourself, even if it means squashing deep conversation with Hal. Got that?"

"I'm crazy about you?" Kat grimaced.

Stephen opened his car door. "I know it's a stretch,

but try to keep your revulsion to a minimum. Besides, I got us in free tonight. I'm worth knowing."

She watched as he slammed his door and rounded the car to open hers. Then she stepped out, a vacuous smile on her face. "How's this? The 'nothing in my head but lint' approach?"

"Very good," he said, striding up the sidewalk.

"Wait." Kat caught up and hooked her arm through his. "Let me prove what a good actress I am."

They continued arm in arm to Tia's front door.

Tia's hair glowed white against the darkness of the foyer as she flung open the door in answer to Stephen's knock. A deep purple caftan shot through with streaks of lavender hung from her skinny frame. The colors heightened the violet of her eyes, which were magnified tonight behind a pair of cat's eye rhinestone glasses.

"So glad to see you, hon." She extended a bony hand and drew Stephen into the room. "Is this the little girl you're so gaga over?"

Kat cautiously eyed her surroundings. Ivory-white candles decorated nearly every surface, their elongated flames shooting fingerlike through the darkness. In the far corner several people gathered in deep conversation. She could see Hal among them.

Stephen's arm snaked smoothly around her waist. "Tia, I'd like you to meet . . . Katie."

Her heart jumped. Of course he'd chosen a pseudonym for her, a name that might be less noticeable should Devon mention her in passing one day. But how had he managed to pick the one nickname that only Peter had ever used?

"Katie." Tia swooped toward her, reaching for her hand. Kat managed a weak smile, recoiling slightly when she realized that the hand would not be immediately released. "My, my, my," Tia gushed. "What a precious little thing you are. Far too good for Stephen Carmichael, hon, you can trust me on that one."

I do, Kat thought automatically, casting a sideways glance at Stephen. His arm tightened around her, and she noticed a defiant flush cross his cheeks. He threw Tia a withering glance.

He was going to see this through. He wasn't going to let her down. Startled, Kat let herself relax against him.

Tia's eyes raked over her. "Cupid's working, guys," she said. Her stroking fingers irritated Kat, who withdrew her hand with a polite smile.

Tia treated Stephen to a megawatt grin. "She's the one, hon. You can stop looking."

Stephen's jaw dropped. "Tia, Katie doesn't need the pressure of—"

"Truth is never a pressure," Tia said firmly. "Is it, Katie?"

Once again, Kat felt those weird violet eyes trained upon her. Tia reminded her of a vulture searching for prey. "No," she said. "Truth is never a pressure."

"Tia!" a voice called from across the room. "We have a question."

"We'll talk later." Tia absently patted Kat's arm. "We'll be good friends, hon, especially since you're fated to become the mistress of Angel Café. Take a seat. We'll begin in a moment."

They watched her depart, caftan swirling behind her in a gauzy cloud.

"Well," Kat whispered, "I can't say I think much of

her powers of prognostication. What's with you? You look like you swallowed a lemon."

Stephen shrugged uncomfortably. "I'm getting a message," he said.

Kat noticed that tiny beads of perspiration had formed on his upper lip. "You are?"

"You know I don't make this stuff up. We're supposed to put on our armor."

"Our what?"

"Like your aunt said. We're to visualize ourselves in the armor. Clothe ourselves in it. Don't ask me why, because that's all I know."

Armor. Kat swallowed hard as she searched her mind for an image. It was there. She stood small and strong on a grassy hilltop, looking somewhat like Joan of Arc about to lead the French army into battle. Her breastplate gleamed. A shiny sword rested comfortably in her right hand.

"Kat!" Hal Banks bore down upon her, and she managed a crooked smile of greeting. "I can't believe you're here!" He was more animated than she'd ever seen him. His expression changed to concern. "How are you?"

"Improving, Hal." She shifted awkwardly.

"Well, this is the place to do it. When Devon told me about Valentine, I thought it was just a load of garbage, but . . . you won't believe him, Kat. If anyone can heal you, Valentine can. Whatever led you here tonight, you won't regret the decision."

He looked so earnest, so intense. Kat narrowed her eyes, searching for signs of the laid-back, casual partner she'd known at the firm. Hal smiled at Stephen, obviously awaiting an introduction.

"Oh." She regained her composure. "Hal Banks, this is Stephen Carmichael."

Hal extended a hand, awed. "You own Angel Café, don't you."

"Guilty as charged," Stephen said.

Hal turned serious. "Valentine told me that my career will skyrocket if I surround myself with Believers. That makes sense. How about getting together for lunch to discuss doing business with our firm?"

A muscle in Stephen's jaw twitched. Kat placed a steadying hand on his arm. "He'd like that," she said, recognizing that her escort was momentarily incapable of speech.

"I plan to spread the word about Valentine," Hal continued. "His advice has made a remarkable difference in my life. But surely you're already aware of that, Mr. Carmichael."

Kat tightened her warning squeeze on Stephen's arm. Now was not the time to protest.

An image flitted across her mind. The scabbard of her sword was encrusted with tiny purple jewels. Amethysts.

"Let's begin," Tia called in her grating voice. "Some of us have to get up in the morning, you know."

"Me included." Hal smiled and turned to take the chair at Tia's right.

Eight people clustered in a loose circle about Tia. All turned expectantly toward Kat and Stephen as they waded through furniture to join the group. To Hal's right sat an attractive middle-aged woman in a business suit. Stephen and Kat sank into the vacant loveseat next to her.

"Okay, everyone," Tia said. "I know we all want to

hear what Valentine has to say, so I'll keep it brief. This here is Hal Banks, who has met Valentine before. He'll be a regular member of our Wednesday night circle. Over there's my boss at Angel Café, Mr. Stephen Carmichael."

A brief smattering of applause followed. Kat realized that most of these people had met Tia through the restaurant. She felt Stephen shift uncomfortably beside her.

"Anyway," Tia continued, "Stephen thinks this is all hogwash, but his little girlfriend knows better. That's Katie, and between you and me, don't be surprised if we hear wedding bells sometime real soon."

Appreciative chuckles. Kat studiously avoided meeting Hal's eyes.

Tia straightened. "Shall we begin?"

With a low murmur of excitement and a great deal of rustling, the members of the circle leaned forward in anticipation. An unwelcome chill swept through Kat's body. How ridiculous to feel nervous! They sat in an overheated, somewhat shabby living room, traffic flowing outside, an occasional siren breaking the stillness. There was nothing eerie here. If only Tia didn't have so many candles lit . . . and if only the others in the circle didn't stare with such rapt, goofy expressions on their faces . . . She moved closer to Stephen, who sat rigid beside her. He had suddenly become the most solid bite of reality in the room.

"Valentine." Tia's voice, usually a buzz saw, muted itself to sandpaper. She sat with her eyes closed, palms turned upward. "Valentine, we welcome you. We call you. We are ready to accept you."

The veterans of the circle leaned in closer, faces aglow.

"Please, Valentine," an elderly gentleman said, voice husky. "Come share with us tonight."

"Please!" the business-suited woman beside Stephen echoed. "We're ready to receive your wisdom."

Kat shivered as the room grew colder. Stephen reached for her hand. His eyes remained focused on Tia, but his skin had grown ashen.

Tia's head lolled forward. Her fingers, turned upward in supplication, flexed in smooth, graceful motions. Her arms lowered in an elegant sweep. Then one hand raised, index finger pointed in a fluid gesture of acknowledgment.

"Welcome," came a voice, so sonorous, so clearly male, that Kat could hardly believe it had come from Tia's mouth.

Tia's head began slowly to rise. Her face wore a haughty, sinuous smile. Her sharp features seemed gentler, blended together into a more harmonious balance. Her hand reached up to remove her glasses, and Kat gasped as the eyes, large and blackened by fully dilated pupils, raked the room.

"Welcome," Valentine said again, delicately placing the glasses on the TV tray beside his chair, "to all of you."

An appreciative "Good evening, Valentine," raced through the room.

Valentine leaned jovially against the back of his chair, smile widening. "I have much to share with you tonight," he said, satisfaction evident in his melodious voice. A gracious sweep of his arm encompassed the entire circle. "And I know that many of you have questions. It will be, as always, my pleasure to answer them. Knowledge is the key, my friends, to opening minds. But first, we must not forget our manners. Let me greet each guest who has come to me."

Kat's eyes widened as she tried to comprehend. This was Tia's body before them, yet it was not Tia. The voice, so lilting, so pleasing to the ear, was like nothing she'd heard Tia's vocal cords produce before. Even Valentine's patrician gestures were foreign. The personality before them possessed no rough edges.

He was like a prince . . . a Renaissance prince straight out of Machiavelli. She imagined him beautiful to behold, powerful and influential.

Valentine turned to Hal. "Welcome, Mr. Banks," he said with a grand nod of his head. His voice grew deeper as it gained strength. "May I expect to see you each Wednesday from now on?"

"Yes," Hal said eagerly. "Valentine . . . the advice you gave me about . . . certain matters . . . worked."

"Of course."

Hal leaned forward breathlessly. "I need to know if . . ."

Valentine raised a hand. "Ah, Mr. Banks, not yet. We will come to your requests. Let me first greet you and speak to your being. Your existence will flow with ease if you continue with us, and you should indeed continue with us. I sense a rough road ahead, but together, as friends and comrades, we can maneuver it."

"Rough?" Hal's eager expression faded.

"Your life flows like a stream, my friend. You will always find rocks in the streambed. You can flow around them or become lodged against them. The choice is yours."

The business-suited woman beside Hal pulled out a small steno pad and began scribbling.

Valentine let out a hearty laugh. "My dear Madeline. How you underestimate yourself. You are intelligent enough, my dear, to remember my words without props. But write if you must. My words are meant to be shared. They broaden our community. The more who bask in our message of peace and harmony, the better. For we are all brothers and sisters on this journey, are we not?" He laughed another rich laugh, and most of the circle joined in.

"Madeline," he continued kindly, "I see that the herbs I prescribed have made a difference. Your aura is so much clearer this evening. Are you centering yourself? Are you meditating?"

"Daily."

"You seem more grounded in the universal consciousness."

"Valentine," Madeline said, "do you think it would be all right if I stopped attending synagogue?"

Valentine raised an eyebrow. A teasing smile played about his mouth. "You would only ask if you doubted."

"I guess I'm nervous. I mean, I've gone since I was a child and. . . ."

"Afraid you'll rot in hell?"

"Well . . ."

"Of course, that is your concern." Valentine's voice grew paternal. "What a trick your religious leaders have played upon you! They've twisted your perception of your own nature. The power of goodness resides inside *you*, my dear, not within a building. Be true to your higher self, and the universe will operate through you. All your needs will be met in this fashion, and mankind will live together in love. Serve the god within you."

The glittering black eyes rested next on Stephen, who straightened in his chair.

"Ah!" Valentine's face lit with recognition. "You have come. Welcome. We've expected you."

"Expected me?" Stephen met the coal-black gaze.

"But of course. I have longed for the day you would enter my fold, dreamed of the time you would allow me to guide you. For your life follows a path I long to change."

"Oh?"

"Your potential is great. I've eagerly awaited your arrival."

Stephen blinked rapidly, eyes wide. Kat gave his hand a surreptitious squeeze, then turned to him, startled, as his fingers became limp and cold in her grasp. He stared into Valentine's deep, dark eyes, seemingly hypnotized.

"We will speak more, my son, and at length," Valentine promised. "You were wise to come tonight."

A spark of fear leaped in the pit of Kat's stomach. She quickly dug her fingernails into Stephen's palm, so hard that he gave a little jump beside her. He threw her a reproachful glare, but she was too relieved to glare back. She knew only that she'd broken Valentine's pervasive spell and that they were safe for the moment.

And now that insistent, liquid stare had turned her way.

There was no mistaking that this was not Tia. The depth of those black eyes was unfathomable, and they led to something far greater than the South Baltimore woman whose body sat before them.

Valentine remained still, studying her. Kat met his gaze dead-on, raising her chin in challenge.

Valentine's mouth opened, then shut again, as if he'd come to a difficult chapter in a book. He furrowed his brow. Then the great, terrible eyes widened as his hands, knuckles white, grasped the ends of the chair arms.

"You," he said in a low, ominous voice, "are not one of us."

Kat heard a collective gasp about her, but held her gaze. She drew in a deep breath and tried to imagine her armor. She once again caught an image of herself fully armed, ready for attack. Her breastplate grew clearer. She could distinguish intricate curlicues engraved across it. A helmet protected her head, while a skirt of chain mail hung to her calves.

Slowly she watched the arm which held her sword begin to rise.

"The havoc you will wreak." Valentine half rose in his chair. "You are *not* one of us!"

Kat barely noticed Stephen's arm tighten around her. Somewhere in the distance a clock chimed eight, the clear bell tones fading on the air.

A cloud of black had appeared in her vision. She saw it crest the rise of the grassy hill. Parts of it looked tangible, filled with tarry lumps and clods of straw and mud. As it rushed toward her, Kat heard human groans from within its midst.

She continued to raise her sword.

"Leave us be!" Valentine thundered. "Leave us be!"

The hideous cloud moved closer. Kat could smell the dark, pungent odor of sulfur. She started to gag. At first she assumed that her gasps existed only as fantasies within the strange vision. Then she realized that vision and reality had somehow merged. She was choking in

Tia's parlor, straining for air amongst the startled faces of the circle.

"Katie!" Stephen's hoarse voice cut through her consciousness. He grasped her shoulders and gave her a shake. She opened her mouth to tell him that she would handle it, but unseen smoke clogged her throat, blocking attempts to communicate.

She'd probably die here.

Her eyes widened as she reached for her throat. That couldn't happen! It wasn't possible!

Suddenly a column of white light shot through the vision. The cloud faded momentarily, as if hesitating. Then it began to whir toward her again.

Kat took advantage of the lull to pull clear air into her lungs, a fish thrown back into the pond just in time.

"The sword!" Stephen squeezed her arm. "Use the sword!"

Without thinking, Kat aimed her sword, then plunged it violently into the center of the cloud.

Valentine stared at her, mouth agape. Then Tia fell face forward from her chair, landing with a thud on the floor.

"Holy shit!" Stephen jumped to his feet.

"What did you do to Valentine?" Madeline shrieked at Kat. "What did you do?"

Stephen rushed to Tia's side, turning her onto her back. "Somebody get some water," he ordered. "Tia!" He gently patted her cheeks.

Tia's eyes fluttered open. For a second she stared vacantly about the room. But Kat, kneeling beside Stephen, noted that her eyes had returned to their usual violet shade. Tia was back. Valentine was gone.

"Hon," Tia said flatly to Stephen, "I don't suppose you just kissed me or anything, did you?"

"No."

"Shoot." She flashed a good-natured smile, then took in the white faces surrounding her. "I see that something happened."

"You don't know?" Stephen asked, incredulous.

" 'Course not, hon. I never know what's going on when Valentine's around. But I can find out." She rose quickly to her feet. "Anybody gonna volunteer the info, or do I need to go directly to the source?"

The room remained uncomfortably silent.

"All right, then." Tia stiffly returned to her chair. She shot them all one last annoyed glance before closing her eyes in concentration. A small frown creased her face.

"Stephen," she said, eyes still closed, "take your little girlfriend and get out of here. Valentine doesn't like her."

"Why?" Stephen asked.

Tia opened her eyes to appraise Kat, who endured the probe with a blank expression on her face.

"I don't know," she finally said, slumping back in her chair. "Something's blocking. I'm not getting anything but a bunch of noise where Katie's concerned. Party's over for the evening, folks."

"But, Tia." Hal's jaw dropped in dismay. "I have questions for Valentine."

Tia Melody had always come with sharp edges, but Stephen had never before seen her angry. A spot of red burned on each cheek as she whirled about.

"Too bad! Valentine's not a trained dog, you know! He's not going to show just because you want to talk to him! Something's tweaked him off tonight, and I don't know what it is just yet. We'll meet again next week. In the meantime, I suggest you all think real kindly of Mr. Valentine and send him some appreciative vibes."

"You're right." Madeline bowed her head. "We've been very ungrateful. Tell us, Tia, what we can do to help."

The members of the circle moved closer to Tia, obviously hoping to lure Valentine back.

Stephen and Kat edged toward the foyer. Then Stephen quietly opened the front door, grabbed Kat's hand, and pulled her out into the dark night.

13

~~~

STEPHEN PACED FURIOUSLY ACROSS KAT'S LIVING ROOM FLOOR, each step followed from the couch by Francesca's weary eyes.

"It was unreal," he muttered. "Honest to God, if I hadn't been there, if I hadn't seen . . ."

"Don't wear out the carpet." Kat leaned against the living room wall, a determined gleam in her dark eyes betraying her casual body language.

Stephen spun to face her, finger pointed at her nose, mouth opened to retort.

Francesca held up a warning hand. "Time out. Katerina's father is reading upstairs in his room. I think you'd rather he stayed there."

Stephen clamped his mouth shut and turned his back on Kat.

Francesca pulled her bathrobe more tightly about her body and tucked her slippered feet beneath her. "You've got a right to be upset, but anger won't solve anything. We need to discuss our next move."

"Easy," Stephen said tightly. "I fire Tia. Come tomorrow, she's out of Angel Café. Gone."

"Big mistake," Francesca said.

"Easy for you to say. You were here all snug and safe while Kat and I hobnobbed with the weird and misguided."

"She's right, though," Kat said from her place by the door. "Think about it. Tia never channels Valentine at Angel Café. For the hours she's there, not only do we know where she is, but Valentine remains dormant."

There was no way to refute her logic, so Stephen didn't even try.

"Fine," he conceded icily. "Just fine. But I'm out of this. I don't believe in this crap enough to get hurt exploring it."

Like a top spun loose from its string, Kat broke from her spot to challenge him face to face. "Don't be stupid! You can't drop out now!"

"The hell I can't! Look, Kat, I'm a nice guy. After what I saw tonight, it's clear I've already done more than my share."

Francesca's eyebrows raised. "And what exactly do you think you saw tonight?"

His arms dropped helplessly to his sides. "I'm not sure. But whatever it was, it was so wrong . . . so incredibly . . ."

"Evil," Francesca said.

Stephen grimaced.

"Can't bring yourself to even think it, can you," she continued. "That word is of biblical, mythical proportion, and you, Stephen Carmichael, are not gullible enough to believe in such superstitions."

He had the grace to flinch. "The word is unimportant. The bottom line is that Angel Café is not directly involved here, so this is none of my affair."

"You're so right to be careful." Francesca cracked a dry smile. "Once acquired, a conscience is a devilishly hard thing to lose."

"Fine," Kat said. "Leave. We'll handle it without you. I knew all along you couldn't hack it."

Stephen bristled. "It's hardly a matter of 'hacking it.' It's a question of intelligence. If you had any sense of reason, you'd drop this insane search, too. You almost died tonight!"

"I did not!"

"Don't give me that, Kat. I was there. I watched you gasp for air, turn blue . . ."

"May I ask exactly when this was?" A thin, steel wire ran through Francesca's voice, causing both Stephen and Kat to turn her way. Stephen noticed for the first time how tired she looked. Dark circles showed against the pale, delicate skin beneath her eyes. Tiny, fine lines etched the corners of her mouth.

Kat slipped onto the couch beside her aunt. "It was around eight o'clock. I remember hearing a church bell chime the hour."

Francesca nodded. "Now I understand."

"Care to clue us in?" Stephen asked sourly.

"I began focusing on you both at about seven-thirty. It wasn't hard. I had no problem bathing you in white light. My strength wavered a bit around seven forty-five, but I assumed you'd come in contact with some conflicting force at that point."

"That's about the time Tia began the meeting," Kat said.

"That's what I thought. I just prayed all the harder."

"Prayed?" Stephen looked blank.

Francesca furrowed her brow, remembering. "At about eight o'clock I grew so tired I thought I'd drop. That was odd; prayer and meditation usually invigorate me. This time, though, the drain was horrendous. I felt as if someone had flung a coat over my head. All I wanted to do was turn off the light and sleep."

"Why didn't you?" Stephen needled. "You could have."

"And leave you two out there without protection? Certainly not. I knew that if I felt so exhausted, you had to be in big trouble. I did my best to focus. I asked the angels of light to aid me. Then I saw a column of white light. Strange. Usually I envision the light as soft, incandescent. This time it was sharp, nearly laserlike."

"You're kidding." Stephen's voice was faint.

"What happened next?" Kat asked, breathless.

Francesca shrugged. "I did what I always do. I asked God to guide the light." She reached for her niece's hand. "Katerina, this will be far more difficult than I ever imagined. Whatever the force, it's powerful. I won't be able to protect you on my own. From now on, two or more will need to light you whenever you're in contact with Valentine."

Stephen stared at her in disbelief. How could this woman believe she'd been the least bit instrumental that evening? As far as he could see, she'd spent a spacey evening meditating at home, wrapped in the illusion that her thoughts could make a difference. He was tempted to inquire whether she could levitate.

"Prayer duty," he muttered. "Another good reason to count me out."

"I had no intention of doing otherwise," Francesca said. "I think Chris is a better candidate."

Stephen stiffened and sent a quick glance in Kat's direction. "Yes, everybody seems to prefer Mr. Alexander."

Kat did not even blink. "Some of us," she said, "prefer his wife."

Stephen flinched. She'd won that round hands down.

Francesca rose from the sofa, barely stifling a yawn. "I'm wiped out. If you'll excuse me, I'm going up to bed. I think more clearly in the morning. Good luck, Mr. Carmichael."

Stephen watched as she disappeared from view.

"Well," he said, turning back to face Kat.

"Well," she replied frostily. "I suppose you'll be leaving now."

There was no reason to stay. He'd certainly done more than his duty. The sooner he left this house, the calmer his life would become. Still, he could not deny that a strange truth had been planted inside him. Valentine was real, more real than anything he'd ever experienced. Life would continue as usual for everyone else in the world. They would shop, complain, work. But the tapestry of that humdrum day-to-day routine would never again be as vivid as what he'd seen at Tia Melody's that evening, and Stephen understood with startling clarity that very few people would recognize that fact.

Katerina Piretti would not only recognize it, she'd understand it.

"No use parting enemies," he said, straining for nonchalance. "I could use a cup of coffee before I go."

Kat paused for a moment before nodding her agreement. He wondered what hoop she'd pushed him through, what kind of test he'd just passed. With a touch of trepidation, he followed her back to the kitchen.

She reached for the coffee grinder, and the whir of beans crushed to grains filled the kitchen. She didn't speak, but Stephen suspected that she had much to say.

"You're quiet," he said, simply to break the silence.

"I got the impression you preferred it that way." She rummaged in a cabinet for a filter.

He arranged his features into a mask of neutrality. "Actually, I'd like to know what you're thinking."

"Oh, would you?"

Maybe not, he thought, but Kat flicked the switch on the coffee machine and, hands on hips, appeared more than willing to share her thoughts.

"Okay," she said. "I want to know why you told me to use the sword."

"Sword?"

"At Tia's. While I was choking. I saw a beam of light, and I guess that was Aunt Frannie, but then you told me to use my sword."

"Well, the cloud was coming straight for you again."

She cocked her head. "Oh?"

Stephen nodded. "It wavered when the column of light appeared, but then it picked up speed again. Your sword was already raised, so . . . Oh, Jesus." He sank into a chair and buried his face in his hands.

"There was no actual cloud in Tia's parlor. Whatever I saw, wherever I saw it . . . you saw it, too!"

"No!" Stephen groaned.

"Yes!" She stepped beside him and pulled his hands away from his face. He turned his gaze upward, and their eyes locked. "Don't you see, Stephen? You *can't* get out of this! The images will haunt you, I'm sure of it!"

He jerked his hands from her grasp.

She stepped away. "Besides, you're wrong when you say that Angel Café isn't involved."

"How so?"

She began to pace. He pictured her in court, ready to deliver a rousing closing argument. "Many of Tia's patrons met Valentine through Angel Café. Don't you feel the least bit responsible?"

"No!"

"Then let's try curiosity," she continued, an insistent hammer banging away at a nail. "My God, are you so bored, so jaded, that you don't want to know the end of the story?" She lit beside him, eyes glittering. "Don't you have questions you'd love to see answered?"

He stubbornly set his jaw. "Questions? About gullible, malleable fools? I wouldn't waste my time."

"No, Stephen." She lowered her voice. "Think harder. Who is Valentine, and what does he want? And if Tia is so damned wealthy from all this, why does she live in a South Baltimore dive? Where's the money going? Don't you wonder? There's more going on here than psychic readings, don't you think?"

He felt sucked from a cocoon, yanked out into the daylight despite deliberate yowls that he preferred the darkness of manageable walls. The room seemed to waver and fade away. He could see Kat's dark, questioning eyes, hear the drip, drip, drip of the coffee machine. Everything else vanished from reality.

"Those are interesting questions." He searched desperately for a way to regain control. "I bet your reporter asked them, too."

She blanched. "Peter?"

He nodded. The room rapidly refocused itself, but he did not turn his eyes from her troubled face.

"Yes," she said in a low voice. "I think he asked them, too. In fact, I suspect he got some answers. I just don't know where he hid them."

He wanted to ask about Peter, to find out who he was, whether she'd loved him. But in a flash, Kat closed up, a small tower well protected by an unscaleable wall.

"I need you." Her tone was indecipherable. "Please help me."

He looked away. With a sigh she reached for the coffeepot. Hot coffee sloshed into each mug. Stephen studied the rising steam as she returned the pot to the coffee machine.

"Katie . . ."

She swung around, eyebrows drawn together across the bridge of her nose.

"Sorry, Kat. It slipped out. Your sword . . . its scabbard . . . are those stones amethysts?"

She did not respond. She did not need to.

He shifted uncomfortably in his chair. "It's possible that this situation could have some financial impact on Angel Café."

She remained silent. He cleared his throat before continuing. "And since Angel Café is my business, I guess I have no choice but to . . ."

He was startled when she threw her arms around him, pulling him into a tight hug. He reflexively hugged back, then stared into her face as she pulled away in embarrassment.

"Sorry," she said, once again coolly detached. "But I think you've made a good decision."

They finished their coffee in silence.

14

SHE LIKED TO TELL PEOPLE THAT HER GIVEN NAME WAS TIA Melody, but the truth was that she'd been born Opaline Brenda Harper, sixth child of a poor sharecropper in southern Maryland. "Opaline" was a family name, and her mother had felt obliged to use it, especially since raising five sons before this little one had convinced Annie Harper that once she had her girl, there'd be no more babies. So she'd named her blond baby "Opaline," but she'd called her "Brenda" right from the start. Brenda was a glamorous name that reeked of shiny blue eye shadow and elegant cigarette holders. This little girl, Annie was sure, would live up to the image, because you could tell even at her birth that there was something special about her.

"Look at that!" the midwife had exclaimed. "The child's born with a veil! Means she's going to have an eye for the future, Annie."

Annie, twenty-eight years old and exhausted after hours of labor, had struggled to her elbows in time to see her newborn daughter jab at the caul with an angry little fist, tearing it from her face as if it were a mass of cobwebs.

And then, baby Brenda had opened her eyes.

"Gawd!" Annie sucked in her breath.

The midwife leaned over to take a quick look. "They'll change," she'd said indifferently.

But Annie had known even then that her daughter's eyes would remain violet. She'd never seen anything quite like Brenda's eyes, purple as the pansies that grew outside the town's white clapboard Baptist church. Brenda's eyes, her mother felt, were only one more indication that she was special.

That was the last moment Annie dwelled on Brenda's future. Life, as usual, had a tendency to get in the way, to sidetrack any hopes higher than housing the family and putting food on the table. Three more babies followed Brenda. They were healthy, robust boys, and even if Annie had once harbored great plans for her only daughter, she couldn't afford to act on them. She relied on Brenda too much for help with the washing, cooking, and cleaning.

Shortly before Brenda's ninth birthday, her father announced that he was tired of living hand-to-mouth. His cousin had written that there were jobs at Bethlehem Steel. Moving to Baltimore made perfect sense.

"Move? Us?" Except for an occasional shopping trip to Lexington Park, Annie had never been more than ten miles away from the small farm where she'd grown up. "We're not city folks! They'll eat us alive in Baltimore!"

But they went. And they prospered. Not only did Cal get a job in Bethlehem Steel's blast furnace, his two oldest boys got hired on as well. The paychecks brought in more money than either Annie or Cal had ever dreamed possible, and it was steady money, too.

The family crammed itself into a Dundalk row home, and, for the first time ever, Brenda found herself enrolled in school.

She was a plain, agreeable child, with soft white-blond hair and those unusual violet eyes. She was, however, nine years old and in the first grade. Even hunched shoulders could not disguise the fact that she measured several inches taller than her classmates.

"What's white and purple and dumb all over?" the fifth graders teased.

"Brenda Harper!" The response echoed through the playground at recess, ricocheted off the cafeteria walls during lunch, and followed Brenda on her long, lonely walk home each day.

"Fight back!" her brothers urged, but she knew that fighting back wouldn't make her one jot more popular. She didn't want to get even. She wanted to be liked.

One cold December morning, as she struggled to sound out the letters in her reading book, a girl swaggered toward her from across the playground. Brenda knew her. She was Ellen Davis, ten years old and the most popular girl in the fourth grade. Ellen studied her through slitted eyes, the tip of her perfect little nose red from the wind. Her bangs peeked out from beneath a fashionable hat, and her hands rested toastily inside a rabbit-fur muff. She tapped a patent-leather Mary Jane as if waiting for a late bus.

"What I want to know, Miss Brenda Harper, is if everybody in your family is as stupid as you?"

Ever placid, Brenda did not respond. The insults, though expected, never ceased to surprise her.

Ellen continued in her haughty voice. "Why are your eyes that weird color? What's wrong with you, girl? You're stupid, and you have strange eyes, so there's got to be a problem!"

A small semicircle of kids had gathered around Ellen. Brenda stared at them blankly.

"Don't be rude!" an oversize fifth grade boy called from the crowd. "Answer the question!"

Brenda stared at the ground, not sure that a question had been asked.

"We can make her," a girl taunted. "We can make those purple eyes cry!"

The crowd moved closer, and Brenda jerked her head up. Why did all these kids hate her so much when they didn't even know her?

Somebody picked up a rock.

Suddenly Brenda noticed a glow about Ellen. Funny, she'd never seen that before. She closed her eyes and then opened them again. The glow not only remained, it seemed to intensify. As she watched, it became a lovely lady clad in a long, flowing robe.

"What's wrong, pea-brain?" somebody jeered. "See a spook?"

The lady was not transparent, but shimmered so that Brenda could not clearly make out the outline of her figure. Words rushed through the girl's head. "Repeat what I say," she heard, and she dutifully obeyed.

"Ellen," she said carefully, "don't forget that your mama wants you to come straight home today. No dillydallying. Today's visiting day at the jail, and your daddy's expecting you."

Ellen gasped, cheeks scarlet. "How did . . ." She threw an embarrassed stare back at the crowd behind her.

"Your daddy's in jail?" Nancy Myer's mouth formed an O.

Ellen's mouth flapped helplessly as Brenda turned toward the fifth grader who'd harassed her earlier. "Howard, you got to give back those dollars you stole from your daddy's wallet yesterday. I know you're saving up for cowboy boots, but your family needs that money for rent. You guys ain't rich, you know."

Howard stared, speechless.

Brenda could not explain what was happening, but suddenly words rushed through her mind and out her mouth. The shimmering lady stood smiling throughout the recitation, but Brenda was so busy delivering messages that she had no chance to ask who she was.

"Grady, you ain't sickly like your granny says. You just don't get outside enough. You got to go out and run around with the rest of the kids. Amanda, stop stealing those chocolate bars. Stealing ain't right. Lucy, your sister's getting fat because she's going to have a baby. She's afraid to tell your parents, but you might as well let her know that she's got to."

Finally the torrent of words stopped. Brenda looked for the lady, but she was gone. All that remained was a crowd of school kids, white-faced and trembling. One by one, they drifted away, uncertain about what had just happened and how to save face. Only Ellen remained.

"How'd you do that?" she asked.

"I don't know."

Ellen moved closer. "What else can you tell? Can you tell the future? Can you tell what boy likes me?"

Brenda thought for a moment. "Right now I can't tell anything. But it'll happen again."

Whenever she recounted this tale in later years, she was most proud of the fact that the coming of her "gift" had seemed more inevitable than frightening. She hadn't been at all scared through the visitation, and she'd known without a doubt that the lady would return.

Nobody bothered her after that, partly because of her insights on the playground and partly because Ellen became her protector. Jailbird daddy or not, Ellen was the richest girl in the school, and her word was law. Brenda would never be popular, but she was sure as hell respected.

The lady returned periodically, but not as often as her messages. Soon Brenda could tell when a message was coming. The voice in her head was always her own, but she could sense a different personality authoring the words. The lady, who'd let the name "Columbine" drift across her mind, felt gentle. Her cadences fairly sang, something Brenda could not do. Most of the messages were for other people, but every once in a while, Brenda got one for herself: "You'll be okay without school, so don't fret if your grades are bad." "Share this gift of yours with the world." "Don't ever close this channel of communication."

When she was fifteen, the timbre of the messages changed, and she knew that she was no longer in touch with Columbine. The new voice was stronger, more definite. It spoke in clear, concise, capital letters. And it came with new instructions for her to follow: *Give me a voice in your world. Get a Ouija board.*

A Ouija board? Of course, Brenda knew about Ouija boards. She'd just never used one before. Still, a message was a message. With a little shrug, she took off in search of a board. She found one at Goodwill for a

quarter. Twenty-five cents was a small enough invest-
ment, so she bought it without a second thought and
carried it home.

She wondered who should use it with her. Immediately an image of her youngest brother flooded her
mind.

Are you crazy? she thought. He's ten years old! He's a
pain in the neck! That's the dumbest thing I ever heard.

But the message grew so strong that it gave her a
headache. Brenda had never become ill from a message, and it caught her off guard. Unbalanced by the
pain, she groped for the back door and called her
brother.

Donald had been playing softball with his friends,
but to her amazement, he ran in eagerly at the sound
of her voice. More surprising, he not only agreed to use
the Ouija board with her, he seemed happy to do so.

They crept down into the basement where they
wouldn't be found and, breathless with anticipation,
set eager hands atop the white, triangular planchette.

Instantly, propelled by a force all its own, the
planchette traveled gracefully over the curved alphabet
printed on the board. It examined the *yes* situated in
one corner, then the *no* in the other. One of the board's
previous owners had taken an indelible marking pen
and drawn an exclamation point and a question mark
at the bottom of the board. The planchette visited there
as well, and Brenda shivered at the feeling that somebody was laughing.

"What do we do now?" Her brother squirmed with
excitement, his freckles greenish in the odd half-light
of the basement.

"We wait," she said.

They did not need to wait long. With elegant precision, the planchette began to spell:

Welcome, though we have known each other long. I am Valentine.

A strange chill ran up her spine. "I'm Brenda, and this here's Donald. . . ."

The planchette nearly yanked itself from beneath their fingers.

You are not Brenda. Your soul answers to Tia. Tia Melody. You sense the rhythm of it, the harmony. You know I am correct. And you, my son, are Victor.

"Victor?" Her brother screwed up his face with distaste, but Brenda nodded slowly. He was right. She was Tia. The name flowed. It didn't bind her to earth, as did the boring "Brenda." She'd never heard the name before, but she understood that it was hers.

"Yes," she said slowly. "I am Tia."

And much more. Ah, Tia Melody, we are just beginning our work together.

"Can I go outside now?" her brother asked in a small voice. "This is creepy."

No, Victor. This is the beginning of freedom.

Tia hated the three-hour drive to Ocean City. She could tolerate it until she crossed the Chesapeake Bay Bridge. Then the land became so flat that just staying awake was a challenge.

At least she only had to do this one Thursday a month. And Angel Café closed early enough that she could make the round trip and still get home at a decent hour.

June was early in the summer season, but Ocean City was already crowded. Tia yielded to a crowd of pedestrians who, laden with bags and beach chairs, scampered across the street from the ocean. Strange. As often as she came here, she never set foot on the beach. She didn't like the ocean very much. Something about it scared her. Maybe it was because you had to travel clear across to Portugal to reach solid land on the other side of that vast expanse of water. Maybe it was the ships that rested on the ocean floor. Knowing they were there always gave Tia the creeps. She could imagine passengers pulling in water instead of air, terrorized by the realization that they were being sucked rapidly beneath that misleadingly calm surface of sea.

"Yuck," she said out loud, searching for a parking place. She'd recognized long ago that her thoughts were much more vivid than those of most people. Other folks seemed able to shrug off unpleasant images, but the pictures stayed branded on her mind for hours.

There was usually parking on the bay side of the city. There were plenty of rental units here, but people with money preferred to stay as close to the ocean as possible. That left the cheaper bay side for students working summer jobs or for those who didn't plan to spend much time in their lodgings anyway. Tia nosed her old Mustang into a space in front of her destination.

She hated visiting Donald. She hated the trip, hated his apartment, hated the sight of his smug face. At least he lived in Ocean City. The thought of him breathing down her neck in Baltimore was enough to make her stomach queasy.

With a sigh she reached for her purse, opened the car door, and began a resolute march toward the building.

Donald occupied the ground floor of a two-apartment rental unit. He lived there year-round and since the other unit rented only seasonally, usually enjoyed a degree of seclusion. Today, Tia noticed bathing suits draped across the upper apartment balcony railing. Great. Donald hated sharing his territory with other people. He would probably be even more annoying than usual.

She rapped loudly on his door, hoping he'd be out. But, of course, Donald never went out.

She heard the creak of his wheelchair as it rolled across the linoleum floor. She listened to the clicks of three locks and a chain. Then the door swung back, and Donald smiled out at her.

"Why, Tia," he said. "How lovely to see you."

He looked as calm and cherubic as always. His blond hair was a little longer than usual, but neatly brushed, with a perfect part on the right side. His smooth white skin reflected the fact that he never ventured into the sun. He looked younger than his age, which Tia knew was forty. He wore the usual clean T-shirt and neatly pressed Levi's. From the waist up he was a powerful man, with bulging biceps and a hard, muscular chest. His legs, however, were thin and useless. He'd been in a wheelchair for more than twenty years now.

"How was your trip?" he asked jovially.

"It ate shit, and you know it." Tia gave the wheelchair a little shove with her foot and strode into the room. "Where's Dana?"

Dana was Donald's paid nursing companion, the one who helped him with everything from bathing to cooking. Tia had long suspected that Dana was a big help in other arenas as well, but she didn't care enough to make a stink.

"I gave her the afternoon off," Donald said. "I thought that since you were making the drive anyway, we might enjoy a little visit."

"I don't want to visit. I have nothing to say to you."

"Not you." His voice was smooth. "Valentine."

She clamped her mouth shut and reached for her purse. "Here," she said, drawing out an envelope. "Your portion of this month."

"How much?"

"More than you deserve."

"Oh, I doubt that, sweet Tia. You owe me."

She tossed the envelope onto his lap. "Ten thousand."

She smirked with satisfaction as his eyebrows rose. Donald prided himself on presenting a cool, unflappable face to the world. She'd obviously impressed him.

"More than last month," he commented.

"I'm doing very well. And it ought to be enough to keep you quiet for a while."

He swung the wheelchair around with a mighty push on the right wheel. "Dear Tia. Nice Tia. Wouldn't you like some chips or something?"

"No."

"A beer?"

"Nothing. I'm out of here."

She always forgot how proficient he was with that damn chair. He rolled to her side faster than most people could run. She felt his hand around her wrist, the strength of his grip contradicting his damaged physical condition.

"I'm trying to be friendly," he said. "You obviously don't want to play. But I think Valentine does."

"Not today."

"Yes, today. And, yes, anytime I want. Because it's your fault I'm in this chair, Tia Melody, and don't you ever forget that."

She needed a cigarette. With forced cool, she raised her left hand and carefully pried his fingers from her wrist. Then she reached into her purse for her Camels, aware that his eyes followed her every move.

"Don't smoke in my house," he said.

"Sorry, hon." She inhaled slowly, glad for the prop. "You want Valentine, you gotta give some." It was a small victory, but at least it helped her feel as if she still retained some control over the situation. She knew how illusory that was, for Donald was not the only one eager to speak. She could feel Valentine pressing, longing for a physical voice. She couldn't fight them both.

She took another deep drag. Donald wheeled himself to a window and, with a great deal of unnecessary noise, shoved it open.

"Now," he said as she finally stubbed out the cigarette butt in his sink. "Let me talk to Valentine."

Early on, channeling Valentine had required intense concentration. Tia had once sat for nearly an hour before his essence pervaded her. These days it seemed that she had only to close her eyes before Valentine came crashing through, pushing her consciousness to some out-of-the-way corner of her mind. She couldn't say exactly where she was while Valentine used her voice, her face, her hands. She only knew that lately she felt trapped there, disturbed by a disorienting lack of control.

She settled herself ceremonially on Donald's couch. "I'll see if Valentine wants to talk to you."

But it was only a moment before Valentine engulfed

her like a wave, leaving her once again in that distorted prison she so disliked.

Donald viewed Valentine's arrival with some detachment. He'd seen it often enough to remain unimpressed, and he sometimes wondered which one crafted the drama, Tia or Valentine. He watched Tia's head drop to her chest, then rise again. He checked the eyes: deep and black. Good. Valentine was available for consultation.

"Greetings." Donald wheeled his chair closer. "Long time no see."

"Must I remind you that I am always with you?" Valentine asked, weariness dripping from each word.

"Yes, I know. I got the feeling you wanted to talk to me face to face today."

"You are correct. Astute. Perhaps you will yet reach your potential usefulness."

Donald hated when Valentine spoke in riddles like this. He always got the impression that Valentine put him in the same league as an organ grinder's monkey, only not quite so clever. "Hey," he said, "Tia brought a lot more money this month. Thanks."

"Money." Valentine waved a disdainful hand and swiveled to appraise his surroundings. "If you want it, it is yours."

"Of course I want it. I'm saving up. I've got big plans. Besides, I've got to pay Dana and . . ."

". . . all the other prostitutes who strike your fancy. But, yes, live as you choose. It is of little consequence. Greater amounts of money will flow your way, for souls are flocking to me, flocking to me as never before."

Souls. Sometimes Valentine sounded downright moronic.

"But I need more souls," he was saying. "Nothing must stand in my way. The Prince marches in full glory, and none must cast a shadow of doubt in the minds of those who bask in his grandeur."

Jesus Christ, the guy sounded like a fortune cookie gone berserk. Donald pinched the bridge of his nose between his thumb and forefinger and tried not to roll his eyes.

"I have brought you wealth," Valentine said. "Now I come to you with another mission."

Donald straightened. Valentine's missions were always the same. "Sure. What's up?"

"Hear me well." Valentine spoke slowly. He had a habit of slowly canvassing the room when he spoke, as if not quite accustomed to the feel and texture of physical reality. It reminded Donald of bad acting in B movies. "A danger is upon us, a danger long foretold. We must act now."

Valentine's victims were always "dangers," threats to existence. The last mission had involved some poor defector who'd come to equate Valentine's circle with cultism and who'd vigorously warned everyone on his campus to steer clear. College students were easy. The guy's death had been listed as an alcohol-induced accident.

Valentine fixed Donald with a fathomless stare. "A young woman stands in our path. She cannot remain."

"No problem. I'll try to get up to Baltimore in a few weeks."

"It cannot wait."

"Some things have to wait. I can't just climb into my

car and drive myself into the city. I've got to arrange it with Dana, work it out so that—"

"Work it out quickly, then. There is little time to lose. Too much has been lost already."

"Okay, okay." No way was he going to ask what had been lost already. He'd get a fifteen-minute diatribe about souls and spirits and victory on the battlefield. Been there, done that. Valentine, Donald thought, was only as good as the money he generated. Any threat to the cash flow was worth removing, but only in his own time. "I'll do the best I can."

"I will be waiting."

"What's this woman's name?"

Valentine stiffened, then again swept the room with his dark stare. "She is called Katerina Piretti. Make haste."

"I'll get there," Donald said, but he knew that Valentine had already begun his departure. Donald often wondered where he went. Did he hover around Tia like an invisible cloud? Did he live in a bottle or a lamp, like some ancient genie?

Tia sat before him, more sluggish than he remembered from past channeling sessions.

"Yipes," she said. "I feel like Valentine hit me over the head with a two-by-four. So what did he say, hon? Anything I need to know about?"

Donald turned a beaming grin her way.

"He said you're doing a bang-up job. Keep up the good work."

15

CHRIS ALEXANDER TUCKED THE TELEPHONE RECEIVER between his ear and shoulder, then popped the flip-top off his can of beer. He'd worked the eight A.M. to four P.M. shift all week and had just walked through his apartment door when the phone rang. Usually he let it ring, but he'd been unable to speak with Kat since her visit to Tia's two nights ago. That made every phone call potentially important.

"Chris." It wasn't Kat, but Francesca. Fear rose in his throat, but her voice sounded too calm for catastrophe. Her serenity, in fact, left him unprepared for the bombshell of Kat's close call during Tia's circle. He listened in open-mouthed amazement until Francesca ended the story.

"That's enough," he said. "Kat is out of this. Stephen and I will handle it."

"I wouldn't try telling that to Katerina. And Stephen is not committed. I'll need your help."

A key clicked in the front door lock. Chris glanced quickly toward the kitchen clock.

"You've got it." He lowered his voice. "Talk fast. Devon's home early."

"Pay attention to whatever she says. It could be important."

"Anything else?" he asked as the apartment door swung open.

"Do you work day shift tomorrow?"

"Yes." He waved at Devon, who seemed surprised to see him. She carried a large shopping bag in one hand and her purse in the other.

Francesca paused. "Call me from a pay phone on your way to work."

"Done."

He hung up quickly, his mind constructing various excuses. Devon would surely ask to whom he'd been speaking. He rejected the called-for-pizza explanation in favor of the message-from-work story.

Surprisingly, Devon didn't ask any questions. She'd kicked off her shoes and now stood unpacking the contents of her shopping bag onto the dining room table. Chris furrowed his brow, confused. His wife possessed a little jealous streak that usually prodded her to push for information. Puzzled and a bit put out, he approached the table.

"You're home early," he said, dutifully pecking her cheek.

Devon turned a lovely shade of pink, then averted her eyes like a guilty child. "You caught me. Honestly, honey, I forgot you'd be home this afternoon."

Chris shrugged. "You don't need my permission to play hooky from work."

She turned back to her bag. "Well, I've kind of abused the privilege lately. You won't believe what I heard at the office right before I left!" She whirled to face him, eyes alight. "You remember my boss, Hal Banks. Right?"

Chris nodded cautiously. Lately, he felt that every

move he made in his home required caution. One never knew where the mines were buried.

"Well, I talked him into visiting Valentine."

He hoped he could keep his face immobile. Francesca was right: Devon could be a fountain of information.

"He's very impressed with Valentine," Devon said. "So impressed, in fact, that he's recruited some of the other lawyers to see Tia. Anyway, Hal goes to the Wednesday circle now, and guess who happened to be there this week?"

"Who?" He steeled himself.

Devon put her hands on her hips and raised her chin in triumph. "Katerina Piretti, that's who!"

"My, my," he said faintly. "What a surprise."

"You bet. She's supposed to be in mourning or something, I don't know. But the next part's even better. Guess who she's dating?"

Dating? With a great deal of effort, Chris set his face into neutral lines. "Who?"

"Stephen Carmichael! Can you believe it?"

"Who's Stephen Carmichael?" he asked, remembering that he shouldn't know.

Devon sighed. "I forgot. You're a failure when it comes to who's who in this city. He's only the proprietor of Angel Café! He's hot news, Chris!" She peered into her shopping bag, then reached to the bottom for the final items. "I was there when they first met. I thought they were going to kill each other."

"Didn't get along, huh?"

"Cats and dogs."

Francesca had told him to listen, but Chris could see that asking might yield even more valuable information. "So how'd Kat like Valentine?" he asked casually.

"Kat?" Devon wrinkled her nose at him. "Since when do you call her that?"

"*You* call her that."

"Hal said the session was weird. He said Valentine got angry at Kat for some reason and threw her out."

"Threw her out?"

"Well, she left. Stephen went with her. Talk about devotion."

"Well, what do you know." His voice sounded weak even to his own ears. "I wonder what went wrong?"

"Me, too. Hal said Valentine came back after a while, but nobody could get him to talk about what had happened. It was business as usual as far as he was concerned."

"What do you make of it?"

Devon leaned against the table. "My guess? Kat's got a bad attitude. Stephen probably thought that bringing her to Tia's would help, but Valentine obviously couldn't teach through such friction. She'll have to do some serious thinking if she wants to return to the circle. She probably owes Valentine an apology."

"You can't believe that."

"Why not? Tia told me today that—"

"You saw Tia today?"

Devon flushed. "Oh, Chris, don't be mad at me. I just had to stop by Angel Café. And while I was there, Tia felt certain that Valentine had more to say, so I met her when she got off work and went to her house."

"How much did it cost this time?"

Devon blushed once again. She was starting to remind him of a velvety rose that colored delicately at the slightest touch.

"I wasn't there very long," she said contritely. "I only had one question for Valentine, so Tia cut me a break and didn't charge the usual price."

He felt his temper rise, but couldn't decide which made him angrier: that she'd once again spent money on this insidious obsession or that she'd grown so reliant upon Tia and Valentine that the responsibilities of her life were easily shoved into the background.

She was suddenly beside him, one graceful hand playing through his hair, the other tracing an invisible design across his chest. "Don't be mad," she said, lips close to his.

He didn't want to be mad. He wanted to once again feel as one with this woman, to look into her eyes and remember all they'd been to each other for the past five years. He gazed at her, longing to see a reflection of their shared life. Instead, he saw someone impersonating his wife. He searched Devon's even features. She was still there, he supposed, somewhere behind the too-sharp cheekbones, pasty complexion, and opaque eyes. Perhaps a spark of her original flame still struggled to remain aglow in her heart. But where Devon had always been spontaneous and fun loving, the woman before him coolly calculated every move. Devon leaned closer, a cat ready to leap upon the bird, and Chris turned his head away.

"What's all this?" he asked, pointing to the table.

She didn't notice the rebuff. "Oh," she said. "It was going to be a surprise."

A surprise. Lately, all "surprises" served as red flags. Chris warily surveyed the tabletop.

Twenty fourteen-inch scented candles. A small sack of rose petals. A new box of that infernal jasmine incense. More "fertility tea." A small vial of oil and a tube of massage cream.

"What's this?" He uncapped the cream and took a whiff. It was intensely aromatic, oddly enticing. "Where'd you get these things?"

"I bought them from Tia." She threw him a sideways glance from beneath slightly lowered lids. "You, my dear Christopher, are in for a very pleasant evening."

He froze. "I suppose that this is the perfect time of month to conceive?"

"Ye-e-s!" She hooked her arm around his waist.

"Did Valentine recommend all this stuff?"

"Better than that. He told me exactly what to do tonight."

A wave of nausea made him step away from his wife's embrace. "You mean he gave you a play-by-play description of how to make love to me?"

A broad smile lit Devon's face. "You're going to love it."

He was not going to love it. He'd be damned if he approached his bed feeling like some sort of experiment, an instrument for Devon's needs and Valentine's amusement. He couldn't help but believe that Valentine derived pleasure from his ability to manipulate the lives of his disciples. Was he voyeuristic? Would he somehow become a third party in their bedroom that evening, directing Devon's motions, telling her where to touch, when to apply pressure just so? He stared in disbelief at Devon. How could she mechanically comply with cold, step-by-step instructions for building the perfect baby? Didn't she notice that none of the instructions made any mention of love?

"Devon!"

She covered his lips with her own, smothering his strangled cry. Her body pasted itself to his. They were nearly the same height, and he'd always like that. It made him feel as if they were truly one when they stood like this, breast to breast, hip to hip. Despite his misgivings, he felt himself growing hard against her. "Devon . . ."

Her kiss began with brazen self-assurance, as if she planned to overpower him with brute strength if necessary. She tugged at the bottom of his shirt until it came away from the waist of his pants. Her fingernails traveled up his back. One hand massaged his hard, muscular shoulder while the other worked its way to his chest. Chris let out an inadvertent groan and reached for his wife. Quite suddenly Devon's kiss grew softer, almost questioning. Her mouth melted into his as if yearning for a moment from long ago.

In that split second Chris realized how very much he missed, longed for, his soul mate.

He cupped a hand behind her head and guided her into his own version of their kiss, gentle but insistent. Her body relaxed against his as she wrapped her arms around his neck. They remained locked together for a moment, swaying as one in the quiet room. Then, with a little gasp, Devon pulled away. Chris read not only surprise in her widened eyes, but recollection. Somewhere, somehow, Devon's heart had not forgotten his.

"Wait," she said halfheartedly. "We need to set up the candles in our bedroom like Valentine said. And we need to—"

"No." He kissed her deeply, strengthened by the familiarity of her body in his arms. He felt her tremble and knew that she, too, remembered.

There were, Chris realized with clarity, realms that Valentine could neither penetrate nor distort. Love, pure and untainted, was one such realm. At that moment Devon belonged to him alone, not to Valentine, not to Tia.

He gathered his wife close and defiantly banished all others.

16

PETER HAD TAKEN KAT ICE-SKATING ONCE.

"This should be hysterical," she'd said, struggling to lace her skates. "I've never been on ice skates in my life."

He'd brought his own skates along and laced them with lightning-quick accuracy. "Just remember, everybody on the ice was once a beginner."

"Are you good at this?" she'd asked, ankles turning inward as she struggled to stand.

Peter shrugged. "I used to play ice hockey in high school. I don't get out on the ice much anymore, though."

She'd known immediately that he was more proficient than he cared to admit.

He'd guided her out the door and toward the rink. "Take my hand."

"I'll go alone."

"Katie, you really should—"

"No."

They stepped onto the ice. Kat grabbed the side rail as her skates slid from beneath her.

"Sure you want to go alone?" Peter asked again.

"I want to try. You can rescue me if I need help."

He looked a trifle hurt as she inched away from the rail.

It hadn't taken long to admit defeat. Traveling on ice made her feel physically impaired, as if her limbs could not be trusted to do as they were told. She took a spill only yards away from the gate and looked up to tell Peter that he'd been right all along.

He wasn't there.

She scoured the rink with narrowed eyes. There he was, skimming across the ice as if she didn't exist. He never even turned to check up on her.

Her solo lap around the rink included one more spill and two near misses. She moved more slowly than anyone else, but she would have crawled had that been the only way to stay vertical.

Peter had met her at the gate. "Congratulations," he'd said.

"Where were you?" she'd demanded.

"Skating. You told me you could handle it alone."

"You were supposed to bail me out if I needed help."

He'd raised both hands to halt her words. "I didn't want to impose on your independence."

"I could have gotten hurt out there!"

"Hey! I do as I'm told. It's one of my most appealing traits."

Not always, Kat had thought. Sometimes, people needed to be saved from themselves.

Since most of Angel Café's clientele hailed from busy downtown office buildings, Saturdays at the restaurant were usually quieter than weekdays. Kat hoped this meant that Stephen had stayed home. She cased the foyer. He was nowhere in sight, an excellent sign.

"Hi." The hostess appeared before her, stack of menus in hand. "One for lunch?"

Kat recognized her as Molly, the waitress who'd served her the first time she'd visited Angel Café. Molly, thank God, didn't look as chipper today as she had then. Actually, she looked tired and somewhat gaunt. Kat longed to advise an increase in fiber intake, but a nagging tug at her heart made her wonder if Molly, too, had fallen prey to Valentine. She wore an expression that Kat recognized from Tia's circle . . . one of blind expectation, as if she were waiting eagerly for a bus at a discontinued stop.

"Yes, one for lunch," she replied. "I'd like to see Tia, too."

"Great!" Molly's smile confirmed her involvement with Valentine. She beamed as if welcoming a novice into final vows. "My pleasure. Tia's a doll. You won't be disappointed. Follow me."

She led Kat to the exact table she'd occupied before. Kat shuddered as reverberations from that visit raced through her. Then she straightened her shoulders and slipped resolutely into the chair.

"Tia will be by shortly," Molly said. "Can I bring you something to drink while you're looking at the menu?"

"Coffee. Thank you."

She waited until Molly had disappeared from view before turning to stare at the menu in her hand. She wasn't hungry. Anything she ordered would stick in her throat. Her eyes ran past salad and sandwich choices, then left the menu to survey the room.

Angels everywhere. She had to hand it to Stephen. He certainly knew how to cash in on a trend. Her gaze focused on a porcelain angel figurine perched on the fireplace mantel. That one was a new addition to the menagerie. Kat walked over to get a closer look.

The angel was meant to be beautiful. He stood approximately seven inches high, wings spread as if he planned to take flight. Long blond curls trailed down to his shoulders, and turquoise eyes languorously surveyed the world. To Kat's surprise, he did not wear the usual long white robe that most artists assumed angels wore. Instead, he wore a short blue tunic, rose tights, and brown boots. He appeared to have horns at the sides of his head, but upon closer inspection, Kat saw that they were all that was left of a broken halo.

He should have been beautiful, but he was not. He seemed smug and indolent, about as far from her perception of angels as possible.

"Do you like him?" a voice asked behind her.

With a sinking heart, Kat turned to face Stephen. One of his eyebrows was raised in inquiry, but she knew that his real question did not involve the angel. He wanted to know why she was there.

"No, I don't like him." She opted to answer the spoken question rather than the silent one. "He's too impressed with himself."

Stephen reached over her shoulder and lifted the angel from its place. "I found him at a flea market a few weeks ago. The lady selling him thought he must have been part of an old Nativity scene."

"No way. This one wouldn't be interested in Baby Jesus unless the manger had a mirror in it."

Molly ushered a group of three into the room. "Excuse me," she said, "but I was hoping to seat these people just about where you're standing."

"Oh . . . sorry!" Kat returned to her table, grateful that her coffee had arrived in time to serve as a prop.

Stephen studied her for a moment, then pulled over a chair to sit beside her.

"Why are you here?" he asked.

She took a quick swig of coffee, eyes watering as it scalded her tongue. "Don't worry. It doesn't concern you."

"Of course it concerns me."

"Hi." A fresh-faced waiter appeared before them. "My name's Tad. Are you ready to order?"

"She'll have the chocolate cake," Stephen said evenly.

"Sure, Mr. Carmichael. Can I get you anything?"

"Coffee, please. Thanks, Tad."

"Okay, then. Coffee and a piece of chocolate cake. Oh, and Tia's on her way." Tad departed, a vision of kinetic enthusiasm.

"Your staff is entirely too perky," Kat complained. "What do you do, make them watch *The Sound of Music* over and over again until they get it right?"

"You've asked to see Tia?"

"I . . . well, yes. I have. But I didn't invite you to be a part of it."

"You're mistaken. You did indeed invite me . . . Wednesday night, in your kitchen."

She colored. "I'm sorry, Stephen, but I have questions that are better handled alone."

"I take it your aunt doesn't know you're here."

She shot him a glare, then turned back to her coffee.

"Kat." He grasped her wrist. "We're all in this together, do you understand me? You and me and Chris and Francesca. You can't just go darting out on your own. It isn't safe . . . for any of us."

"I was going to fill you all in. Besides, nobody else

has any better ideas. This might help us figure out our next move."

"Cake's here." Tad grinned above them. "And here's your coffee, Mr. Carmichael. Enjoy!"

"And just a spoonful of sugar helps the medicine go down," Kat muttered at his departing back. She picked up her fork. "Here, Stephen. Take a bite of cake, and go about your business."

"I don't want any," he said as Kat aimed the fork at his mouth.

"Practicing for the wedding, are we?" Tia's voice, loud as always, ignited appreciative chuckles from the patrons in the room. "Gawd, Mr. Carmichael, I never expected to see the day I'd find you eating out of a woman's hand."

Stephen sullenly opened his mouth. Kat popped the cake in and then turned to Tia. "He was just leaving," she said demurely. "You know he's always got a ton of work to do around here."

"Maybe that's what he tells *you*." Tia seated herself opposite Kat. Today, she wore a rubber body suit with zippers zigzagged across the front, a pair of flowered elephant bell-bottoms, and silver high-heeled sandals.

Kat lowered her eyes. "Ms. Melody, I'm dreadfully sorry about what happened at your house the other evening. I still don't know what went wrong."

"Call me Tia, hon. And don't worry about it. You've just got some sort of personality clash with Valentine."

"But what did I do? Perhaps if I knew, I could fix it."

"I don't know what you did. Maybe you tweaked him off in a past life or something. Valentine's male, and males are persnickety. All's I know is that you're fated to be Mrs. Carmichael, so I'll deal with you on that level, woman-to-woman. We can be friendly. Just don't ask me to channel Valentine for you."

"I have questions that don't involve Valentine." Kat glanced down at the tabletop. "I don't want to ask them in front of Stephen, though."

He draped a protective arm around her shoulders and peered earnestly into her face. "Katie, you shouldn't have any secrets from me."

She wanted to smack him. "But I do. All women do, don't they, Tia?"

That was the ticket. Tia winked at her. "You bet. A little mystery adds spice, hon. Mr. Carmichael, suppose you give us gals a chance to get better acquainted?"

"Yes, Stephen." Kat smiled at him brightly, ignoring the flash of annoyance that crossed his face as he lifted his arm from her shoulders.

"You know how it is, Tia," he said. "I hate spending time away from her." He threw one last searching look Kat's way, then disappeared from sight.

"He'll settle down, hon," Tia said. "Don't you worry about that."

"I don't." She appraised the woman before her, all pretense of shyness gone. "I have some questions for you."

"You and everybody else here. Go for it."

Kat hesitated, then decided that the ambush approach was best. It would leave Tia no time for a glib response. "Tell me about Peter Dulaney."

Tia leaned back, puzzled. "That name doesn't ring a bell, hon."

Kat blanched. How could that be? She'd anticipated a nervous Tia, sweat beading her brow as she realized she was cornered. She'd even envisioned Tia in panic, desperately searching the room for an exit. She'd expected everything but nonrecognition. People didn't usually forget someone they'd murdered.

"Who is he?" Tia asked.

"You really don't know?" Kat leaned in closer.

"Nope."

"Can't you feel it . . . divine it . . . whatever it is you do?"

Tia sat quietly for a moment, then shrugged. "I'm not getting anything, hon. Of course, much of my information comes from Valentine, and we both know how fond of you he is. He's not talking. So suppose you fill me in on who this guy is?"

"He was a reporter for the Sunpapers. Do you remember ever talking to a reporter?"

Tia examined the ceiling. "Reporter. I remember talking to a reporter a few years ago, but I can't say I recall his name."

"Did you ever meet him?"

"Sure. A real nice guy. Said he wanted to do a story on psychic channeling. I didn't see much of him, mind you. He came to two circle meetings, that's it."

"Could you describe him for me?"

"Can't pull his features to mind, but he had red hair and real, real blue eyes."

She'd spoken to Peter. There was no doubt about it. A lump in Kat's throat threatened to take over. She swallowed hard and recklessly plowed forward. "When did you last see him?"

Tia thought for another moment. "I was supposed to meet him for an interview. This is going back a few years, so don't expect me to have much detail. All I know is that he never showed, and I never heard from him again."

"Where were you supposed to meet?"

"My house, of course." Her eyes narrowed. "I don't answer questions like these without a damned good reason. What do you want?"

Kat squirmed. "He was just someone I knew."

"But not just any someone," Tia said. "Why am I getting the third degree?"

"I thought you'd know something, that's all. People come to you with questions all the time."

"You're not asking for a psychic reading, hon. You're grilling me. What's the deal, here?"

Flustered, Kat quickly searched for a viable explanation.

A steady hand landed on her shoulder.

"Katie," Stephen said wearily, "why don't you just let Tia do the reading her way? She won't mind. I'm sorry, Tia. Katie still doesn't understand how this works."

Tia squinted up at her boss, considering. "It may not be much of a reading," she finally said. "I don't feel Valentine at all, so I'm going to have to rely on my own sixth sense, not that it isn't pretty damn good." She extended a hand. "Give me something of yours to hold, then. Let me get a sense of you."

Kat gazed from Tia's open palm to Stephen's blank face. Then she reached into her purse and drew out a pocket watch. She wordlessly passed it to Tia.

Tia closed her fingers around the smooth, golden surface of the watch. "This isn't yours," she said.

Kat gave a small nod of acknowledgment.

A troubled frown crossed Tia's face. "It's his," she said. "Peter's."

"Are you getting that information from Valentine?" Stephen asked.

"No. I told you, he's not here."

She closed her eyes and fingered the watch chain. Kat stared, fascinated, as every ounce of color drained from Tia's face. She looked waxen, as if someone had applied a thick coat of Halloween makeup.

"Peter is alone in his apartment. Someone's knocking on his door. It isn't you, Katie . . . he just left you. He's nervous, but he should be happy. You just agreed to marry him."

Kat gasped. Stephen reflexively covered her mouth.

Sweat glistened on Tia's waxy forehead. "Who's this talking to me?" A smile broke across her face, making her appear years younger. "Columbine! It's been so long!"

Stephen let his hand drop from Kat's mouth. Together they waited as Tia pressed the watch tightly into her palm.

"The knocking is louder," she continued slowly. "Peter's walking to the door. He's stopped at an end table, but I can't see why. He's talking, now, quietly. He's at the door . . . he looks through the peephole and . . ." Tia breathed a sigh of relief. "It's okay. It's all right to open the door and let . . . oh!"

Her eyes flew open. "Valentine's back, and he says I'm scaring the shit out of you. Sorry, hon. I don't usually go off like that on readings, but this watch you gave me . . . its vibrations truly kick butt!"

"What happened to Peter?" Kat whispered.

"I don't know. I've lost it." Tia glanced at the antique clock on the mantel. "I hate to rush you, but I don't have time to shoot the breeze today. Duty calls, you know."

"Who's Columbine?" Stephen asked.

"Oh, her. She's one of my guides. I haven't heard

from her in a long time, though. Once Valentine entered the scene, he just kind of took over. Kind of like wisteria, you know? It sure is pretty, but if you don't watch out, it chokes everything in your garden."

"But I need to know more." Kat's voice shook. "I need to know what happened to Peter."

"Sorry." Tia rose from her chair. "I'd invite you to the circle, but Valentine . . ." She straightened slowly, head cocked curiously. "I take it back, hon. Valentine wants you to come this Wednesday evening."

Kat blinked. "What?"

"Don't ask. I've never known him to be this fickle. He says you should come back. He says you're more than welcome."

"Is he going to behave himself if we come?" Stephen demanded.

"I never know what to expect from Valentine and I have no idea what he says when I'm in trance. If you come, you come at your own risk." Tia set Peter's watch down in the middle of the table. "Incredible. This old thing still keeps time. And I'm late. It's been fun, Katie. Ta."

Stephen studied Kat's pale face as Tia left the room. "Obviously, I have some questions for you," he said gently.

"I need air." She looked faint.

"Come with me." He rose swiftly, guiding her along with him.

"Let me get the check. . . ."

"Hell with the check. We'll tip Tad and call it even." He threw a five-dollar bill onto the table and wrapped an arm around her shoulders.

She did not protest. It seemed too hard.

17

~~~

THEY WALKED SILENTLY UP FEDERAL HILL, CROSSING COBBLE-
stone streets until they reached the park at the top. The
day had grown warm. Stephen stopped walking and
rolled up his shirtsleeves.

Kat drifted toward the cannon perched at the edge
of the hill. Below her, the crowds at Harborplace
swelled in a moving mosaic of color. She didn't seem to
notice. Instead, her gaze floated toward the east, leaving Stephen no clue as to the object of their focus.

"Some of my cousins grew up in this neighborhood," she said. "On William Street. My uncle worked
at Key Shipyard. Are you from Baltimore, Stephen?"

"No. I was born in upstate New York."

"This neighborhood used to be pretty low-rent, but
we always had fun. My own house was so quiet with
just me, Dad, and Aunt Frannie living there. I'd come
here and whoop it up with my cousins until my aunt
got tired of the noise and threw us outside to play.
Then we'd play hopscotch and dodgeball until supper
smelled too good to ignore."

Stephen leaned against the cannon, folded his arms
across his chest, and waited.

"The neighborhood went downhill when the shipyard did," Kat continued, eyes still glued to some far-

away landscape. "Even my cousins eventually moved out to the country. Then the yups moved in, raring to rehab. Everything's so damned tasteful now. Repointed brick, woodwork slathered in pseudo-colonial colors. You never even smell supper anymore because sushi doesn't have a distinctive aroma."

Her voice trailed like a vapor on the air. A sudden gust of wind pushed through the humidity, sending the distant swings clattering into one another.

"So Peter Dulaney was your fiancé," Stephen said quietly.

She stood still, a statue of uncertain attitude. "Yes. If a few hours count as a valid engagement."

He rounded the cannon and studied the horizon. Kat remained an image of passivity. Stephen wondered if she knew that the rigid set of her jaw gave her away, that anyone who looked closely could detect the turbulence behind her wide, dark eyes.

"You're mad as hell," he said, "and you have every right to be."

She turned toward him. Those eyes nearly mowed him down with their intensity.

"I most certainly do," she said.

He appraised her clenched fists and the defiant thrust of her chin. At that moment she reminded him of a tough little urchin poised for a fight. He had no desire to serve as her scapegoat. Three or four biting responses crossed his mind, remarks he'd usually consider far too clever to lose. Somehow, though, none of them seemed appropriate.

"Funny thing about anger," he said. "For such a powerful emotion, it doesn't produce satisfactory results. It just eats away at you, drains you to your last ounce."

Kat's eyebrows raised in surprise as she took a tentative step in his direction. "I know that. But how am I supposed to stop it? When Peter died, there was no time for anger. I felt tossed in the middle of the sea without a raft. It took all I had to keep swimming for shore. I assumed that once I reached land everything would be okay. But I keep swimming and swimming, and there's never any land in sight."

Her shoulders sagged as she slumped against the cannon. "I always had my life so carefully mapped out. Now I can't even return to my original starting point. I have so much less than I had before I met him."

"You still have a family that loves you. And there's your law degree."

"That's not what I mean."

Stephen stroked his chin. "You wonder why you had to experience Peter if you were only going to lose him."

"Yes!" she spat fiercely. "Yes. If that path was never mine to keep, why did I have to walk any part of it? Why send me back to square one tormented by images of what I've missed?"

They fell silent as a young couple bicycled nearby. Both bicyclists wore helmets, and each carried a knapsack strapped across strong shoulders.

"Let's eat lunch by the playground," the woman called back over her shoulder.

As they rode past the cannon, Stephen saw that the sack on the man's back was not a knapsack after all. It held a baby, a giggling baby with a tiny bike helmet on her head.

"Oh!" Kat gasped, and Stephen knew that she'd noticed, too.

The baby, perhaps seven or eight months old, lifted its little face to the sun as if awaiting a benediction.

"Sounds like Samantha's enjoying every bit of this," the man called ahead to his partner. The two of them burst into laughter that harmonized with the baby's coos.

Kat stiffened. "I envy them. Look at them. They live in their own special world. They share everything with each other: hopes, fears, dreams . . . everything. Damn it, Stephen, I still can't believe that the one person on earth who knew me inside-out is gone." She quickly turned away, but he could see the force of her emotions in the ragged rise and fall of her shoulders.

He'd never before confronted pain this deep. He had no close friends and little experience in offering comfort. Part of him longed to bolt from the hill, leaving Kat to twist her life into some easy-to-digest form before he had to deal with her again. But she looked so small outlined against the city skyline, so alone.

He cautiously touched her shoulder. "It's okay if you want to cry, Kat."

"Don't worry. I won't cry. I didn't cry then, and I certainly don't plan to start now."

He processed her words slowly. "You didn't cry?"

She remained silent.

He took her by the shoulders and turned her to face him. She had regained total control of her emotions. Only a passive, calm mask met his questioning gaze.

He clarified his question in case she'd misunderstood. "You didn't cry when Peter died?"

She shook her head. "No."

"Jesus Christ."

The depth of her emptiness washed over him. He

didn't know how, for he did not consider himself a particularly perceptive man. But suddenly, as if someone had unplugged a clogged conduit, he felt himself buried under the force of her need.

"Kat, you've *got* to cry. How can you heal unless you do?"

"It's not necessary," she told him, but in spite of her words, her body began to shake. Stephen instinctively pulled her against his chest, then steadied them both against the cannon as wave after wave of shivering engulfed her. Finally the trembling stopped.

"I'm all right," she insisted, untangling herself from his arms.

They stared at each other, embarrassed. Then Stephen transferred his gaze to the toes of his scuffed boots.

"You mentioned something about returning to square one," he said. "You're wrong. There's no such thing as 'square one.' You aren't the same person you were before Peter, no matter what you think. If you loved him, Kat, then that love changed you somehow. You are undoubtedly much more because of it. It's the only way to make it all mean something."

To his surprise, she did not interrupt. He lifted his gaze to meet hers and, with an abashed shrug, continued.

"I'm not like you. I've never stayed in a relationship beyond that initial 'true romance' stage. Familiarity breeds vulnerability, and I'm not interested in that. It's too hard."

"You're smart." Kat kicked a pebble over the edge of the hill. "People who lose themselves in relationships are stupid."

"I disagree." He caught her hand. "I think they're brave."

Kat bit her lip. Then she gave his hand an awkward squeeze.

"Stephen, you've surprised me. You're a good friend. Thank you. I won't do this to you again."

No one had ever called him a good friend before. Of course, he'd never done anything to merit the compliment. He wasn't sure he deserved it now, either. He felt a blush cross his face.

"No problem," he said. "Any time, Kat, any time."

She removed her hand from his and shoved a strand of windblown hair behind her ears. "I want to go back to Tia's this week. Will you come with me?"

"Yes. But first we talk to your aunt."

"Done."

They started down the hill toward Angel Café in silence, but it was the least lonely silence Stephen had ever known.

18

DONALD'S EYES FLEW OPEN IN THE DARKNESS. SWEAT streamed down his face, soaking his pillow as he waited for the pounding of his heart to subside.

That damn dream. He'd lived through the horror of the accident once. Why did he have to retaste it again and again and again? Yet, every night for the past week, he'd drifted off to sleep to find it waiting for him, poised on the evening air as if someone had deliberately set it there. Each night he stepped into the passenger side of the stolen car. Each night he heard his friend gun the motor, saw the flashing police lights behind them, smelled burnt rubber as they rounded the sharp curve of the road . . . and awoke abruptly as the car crashed through the guardrail, silhouetted against the moonlit sky as police cars screeched violently to a halt at the edge of the precipice.

He reached out an arm for Dana. Only a smooth, cool hollow in the sheets met his touch. She'd apparently left his bed quite some time ago. A vein in his neck began to throb. It wasn't supposed to be that way. Dana was supposed to wash him, settle him in bed, and perform whatever fantasy he requested as a special bedtime treat. It was her job to sleep beside him in case he had a nightmare or required additional services during the night. Lately, however, he often awoke to find himself alone. Dana's story was that she suffered from insomnia. He suspected, however, that she waited until he dropped into a deep sleep, then left the bedroom to sleep on the couch.

The phone rang, piercing the stillness. Donald glanced at his nightstand clock. Three o'clock. Who would call at this hour?

Although he could reach the extension, he lay back against his pillow, waiting.

Another ring. He heard rustling from the living room, then Dana's soft cursing as she fumbled for the light.

He smiled in the darkness. Good. Proof that she'd been sleeping on the couch. She'd owe him big time for this latest breach of loyalty.

Dana's footsteps shuffled across the floor as the phone rang again. "Hello?" she mumbled groggily into the receiver. "Um . . . just a minute."

More shuffling. Then Dana appeared at the bedroom door, hair tousled and bedsheet wrapped tightly around her plump, naked body. "It's for you," she murmured.

"Is it, now?" Donald raised himself on his elbows, planted his palms firmly on the mattress, and hoisted himself to a sitting position. "I wouldn't go back to sleep if I were you. I need you, Dana. I need to show you why it's important to stay near me at all times."

She scowled. "I can always quit, Donald."

He shook his head in mock sorrow. "Poor, deluded Dana. Who else would pay our little ex-druggie so well? Get out of here. I'll call you when I'm ready."

She scampered away at the wave of his hand.

She probably *would* quit one day. That was fine with him. He'd grown tired of her anyway and thought that next time he'd recruit somebody with lusher lips and better measurements. Even if money wouldn't buy happiness, it could and did buy a great deal of pleasure.

"What is it?" he snapped into the phone.

"Now," a voice said. "You must come now."

Donald's eyes widened. "Tia? Tia, is that you?"

A deep, rippling laughter boomed through the phone. "Your stupidity continues to amaze me. Of course not!"

Donald straightened, then reached to pull the phone onto his lap. "Valentine," he whispered. Valentine had never called before. "Are you . . . alone?"

"Of course, imbecile!"

As far as he knew, Tia never channeled Valentine when alone. She'd always been able to hear him inside her head and allowed him use of her body only when somebody else required access to him.

He licked dry lips. "Where's Tia?"

"That's not your concern. She will return when I've finished with you. Now. You must complete your mission *now.*"

"Mission?" Oh, right. Katerina Piretti. Donald reached up to smooth back his hair. The room felt hot. He'd have Dana turn up the air-conditioner. "I remember. I'm working on it. Tomorrow's Sunday, so I'll—"

"You will come to my circle Wednesday night."

Great. All this and the moronic circle, too. "I'll do my best."

"You will be here." The line went dead.

Donald slowly returned the phone to the nightstand.

He couldn't remember the end of the accident. He'd lost consciousness as the car rolled over and over and knew that they'd slammed into a tree at the bottom of the hill only because he'd been told so. He was sure, however, that he'd been meant to die that night.

Valentine often intimated that only his intervention had kept Donald from tumbling into that final abyss of death. There was no reason to disbelieve this. Donald had accepted long ago that Valentine's powers transcended the ordinary.

"Faith," Valentine would say, "is the ability to believe without proof." Donald agreed wholeheartedly. He needed no evidence to convince him that Valentine alone had managed to keep him alive.

But, as he'd always known that Valentine could give, he was equally certain that Valentine could take away. Some night that horrible dream would win. On that night the car would sail effortlessly, majestically through the air, only to hit the ground and roll at the bottom of the hill.

And Donald knew that once this happened, he would never again awaken.

"Dana!" he called.

She took her time, but she came. "What?" she asked sullenly, clutching the sheet to her body in self-defense.

"We'll be taking a little trip. We're going to visit Tia in Baltimore. You will drop me off by one o'clock this Wednesday afternoon and then return here. I'll telephone you when I'm ready to come home. Understood?"

"Yes." She pushed out her lower lip.

She stood poised in the doorway, clearly hoping for

a sign of dismissal so that she could go back to sleep. Donald smiled coldly and patted the empty side of his bed.

"I've missed you," he said. "Suppose you take off that sheet and return to your proper place?"

Perhaps, he thought as Dana silently obeyed, he'd throw a few extra dollars her way this week. She wasn't his first choice, but she was at least available.

19

CHRIS LEANED OVER DEVON'S SHOULDER AND GENTLY BRUSHED aside a lock of her red-gold hair. It was still warm from the hot curler she'd just removed. The scent of apple blossom overwhelmed him. He longed to bury his face in the sweet, soft curl.

"You're beautiful," he murmured into her small, perfect ear.

A smile flashed across Devon's face as she reached across the bathroom sink for her comb. "And you're silly," she said.

"No. In love, maybe, but not silly."

He rested his hand lightly against her waist. She'd been his alone all weekend. If he could just keep touching her, maybe they would keep the connection he'd worked so hard to reestablish over these past few days.

"I realize that some of us are off today." Devon playfully brushed his hand away. "But I've got to get ready for work."

"Don't tell me the weekend's over already."

"Welcome to Monday, Loverboy." She breezed through the bathroom door and into the bedroom, leaving Chris to sink woefully to the rim of the tub.

The weekend had been blissful, but he could not

deny that it had taken hard work to make it that way. Loving Devon had been easy. He knew her so well, knew every languid curve and soft hollow of her body. And, as long as they were making love or holding each other close, Devon recalled all of him as well.

But despite Chris's stamina and Devon's will to conceive, they could not spend every minute of the day in their bed. And, once they'd climbed out of it, Devon's attention had wandered.

"Next time we make love," she'd begin, "we really should try to follow Valentine's instructions."

He'd wanted to shriek, "Screw Valentine!" Each time he'd passed the still-laden dining room table, he'd fought a nearly uncontrollable urge to sweep a savage arm down the entire length of it, crashing candles and bottles and balms into a heap on the floor.

"I love you, Devon," he'd told her instead, words true but forced from a parched, angry throat. "I've missed the hell out of you."

That had been enough to turn her focus back to him.

Then a phone call had shattered the delicately balanced peace.

"Tia!" Devon had cried with delight. "How kind of you to call!"

"Just checking, hon." Chris heard as he leaned into the other side of the receiver. "I wanted to make sure Valentine dragged you out of that funk you were in."

Devon had frowned at the strangled expression on her husband's face. A toss of her head had removed the telephone from his earshot.

The phone call had lasted only five minutes, but it had taken nearly an hour to talk Devon away from the subject of Valentine. Even when he'd finally pulled her close, Chris had known that his wife was no longer entirely with him. A part of her had been lured away, leaving him no choice but desperately to woo it back.

After that, he'd secretly silenced both the telephone ringer and the answering machine. He'd checked periodically for messages, constantly amazed by the fact that all of Devon's relationships now revolved around Valentine.

"Devon, it's Van from the Tuesday circle. You looked so low last week. Hang in there, sweetie. Valentine won't let you down."

"Devon, it's Marguerite from accounting. Can I join you guys for lunch at Angel Café this Monday?"

"Hal Banks here. Valentine gave me some work-related ideas. Why don't you meet me at eight-thirty Monday morning and we'll go over them?"

Eight-thirty. Chris jumped guiltily to his feet and followed his wife into the bedroom. He hadn't delivered any of the phone messages. Devon would miss the meeting, and he didn't even give a damn.

"How about I drive you to work today?" He struggled to keep his tone casual.

"No, thanks." She'd finished buttoning her pale pink coatdress and was stepping into a pair of white heels. "I'm driving to lunch with some friends."

Lunch. He remembered. They were going to Angel Café for lunch today . . . to see Tia Melody. An ember of anger kindled in the pit of his stomach.

"Want to meet me for lunch instead?" he asked.

"Oh, Chris, you're a honey, but I made these plans last week. I'd feel like a real jerk if I broke them."

He felt a nervous click in his jaw. The room grew

blurry. "Devon," he said, "don't go to Angel Café today."

Her hand flew to her hip as she appraised him from beneath lowered brows. "What exactly do you mean?"

"Please, Devon. We had a wonderful weekend without help from either Valentine or Tia. Don't ruin it for us."

She snapped to attention, gray eyes wide with amazement. Then she turned and strode from the room, the angry tap of each high heel muffled by the carpet.

"And here I thought you were actually progressing," she said bitterly. "You've been coming to the circle, listening to what Valentine has to say. I honestly thought we were getting somewhere. Now I see that Valentine's been right all along!"

"Right about what?" he demanded, close behind her.

Devon stopped so suddenly that Chris almost rammed into her. She whirled about to face him and, once again he found himself staring into the eyes of a woman he did not recognize.

"We'll never have that baby unless you change your mind about Valentine," she said. "He told me that weeks ago, but I didn't want to believe it. Instead, I've wasted my time sticking up for you, trying to make you understand!"

"Understand *what?*" His frustration rose in a white, hot cloud.

"That Valentine can guide you to perfect happiness if you'll just open up and let him!"

"But, Devon, how can you—"

"No." She held up a firm hand. "I won't let your

closed attitude suck me in. I plan to start this day with positive energy. We'll talk later, really talk. Because I refuse to live the rest of my life constantly falling short of my potential just because you—"

"Devon, what are you saying?"

She grabbed her purse, yanked open the apartment door, and flew down the hall in a flurry of pink and white. Chris remained glued to his spot, too stunned to follow.

His blissful weekend had been an illusion. He'd been a fool to think he could draw her back, keep her whole. Nothing in his life had ever prepared him to face as powerful a force as Valentine. Nothing.

With a howl of rage, he slammed the door so hard that a glass on the kitchen table tumbled to the floor and shattered to pieces.

"What *is* he?" Chris asked, still dazed. He glanced around his dining room table at Stephen, Kat, and Francesca. "What could he possibly be to have such power, such control?"

"Fortunately, God keeps information shadowed until we're ready to deal with it," Francesca said.

Stephen knew that she believed every word, but the comment smacked so soundly of platitude that it made him cringe. He warily eyed the pile of candles and aromatics in the middle of the table.

"Chris has a valid point," he said. "It would help if we knew what we were dealing with. Kat and I are going back to Tia's this Wednesday night with no more information than we had before."

Francesca lifted the sack of rose petals and passed it slowly beneath her nose, thoughtfully inhaling the sweet fragrance. Then she turned the bag over in her hand and allowed one finger to trace the little gold insignia of crescent horns embroidered on the muslin.

"The light should be stronger this time," she said. "Chris will help cover you."

"What about Devon?" Kat raised an inquiring eyebrow in Chris's direction.

He swallowed. "I'll tell her I'm working. She'll be just as happy to have me out of her way."

She placed a hand on his arm. He covered it with his own.

Stephen abruptly pulled a chair to Kat's free side. "No offense, but what do you mean, 'cover us'?"

"Prayer and meditation," Francesca said. "Light. I can't do it alone, but I think two of us can handle it."

His expression soured. "I'd feel a lot better if you could give me something tangible. Honestly, Frannie, how are we supposed to get anywhere without clues?"

"The clues seem to arrive when we need them. And as to what Valentine is, why don't you ask him?"

"Ask him?" Stephen leaned forward, amazed by her naïveté.

Francesca nodded. "Go ahead. Ask him on Wednesday and see what he says."

"What a great idea," Stephen muttered. " 'What are you, Valentine?' 'Why, pleased you asked. I'm diabolical scum. Any more questions?' "

Kat lifted a long, ivory-colored candle. It reminded Stephen of a horror-movie ritual prop. "I don't understand why we can't find more information about Tia and Valentine," she said.

"We haven't really tried," Chris said. "We could run a background check on Tia, maybe turn up some dirt."

Kat shook her head. "Don't you see? Peter would have already done that. He was a reporter, for heaven's sake, and he'd been working on this story since April."

"How do you know that?" Francesca asked.

Kat turned a rosy pink. "I came across some of his notes one night."

" 'Came across'?"

"I found a few notes and names of clients in that old green box I took from Peter's apartment. One note indicated that he'd planned to meet with Tia Melody on the night he died. But that's about all. It just doesn't make sense. Peter always researched every article he wrote. He had to have more on this one."

"Did he ever make it to Tia's that night?" Chris was momentarily pulled from his own problems.

Kat's fingers curled tightly around the candle. "I don't know. That reading Tia did at Angel Café on Saturday, the one where she saw Peter in his apartment, didn't provide any viable clues."

"You're wrong," Stephen said. He'd grown as pale as the candle in Kat's hand.

"It's happening again, isn't it?" Kat whispered. "You're getting another message."

"I prefer not to think of them in that fashion," Francesca said. "Tia and her fortune-teller friends get messages. Stephen just sees a broader picture of this very moment."

"What's the difference?" Stephen asked. "And, more important, how do I make it stop?"

Francesca ignored his second question. "Psychic messages feed on human desperation. Think of the usual questions: Will I get rich? Will I fall in love? Psychics often provide solutions, too. Of course, that encourages dependence on the psychic every step of the way, so you can forget about free will. I don't know why, but people seem more willing to believe that their destiny is controlled rather than inspired.

"What you hear, Stephen, is a deeper aspect of the present picture, the contained moment. Nothing you hear will predict the future or provide pat answers. Your destiny is still up to you."

Only Chris nodded in acknowledgment. Kat, trembling with anticipation, leaned in toward Stephen. "What do you hear?" she asked.

"Nothing, now."

"Give it back to God, then," Francesca said.

"What?" Why was it he never understood a word this woman said?

"Align yourself with the light, Stephen. Make it clear that you want to walk in that light."

"What?"

Francesca sighed as she met Stephen's confusion. "I don't get it. But there's got to be some reason you're the vessel for this information, so sit tight." She closed her eyes and sat motionless in her chair.

Stephen stared at her. He assumed she was praying, though he couldn't imagine why. It was so stupid, so archaic. There were psychiatrists who could handle this. People paid big money to rid themselves of neuroses such as these. He closed his eyes and, with a groan, cradled his head in his hands. Francesca spoke a foreign language, one that had long ago died a predictable death under the weight of its own irrelevance.

A current of energy snaked through him. A quiet, confident peace embraced him, radiating from his abdomen throughout his limbs.

This surprise was not entirely pleasant.

I'm not the one you want! he thought desperately. I have too many questions!

But the lightness stayed. The sense of well-being grew more firmly entrenched, urging him to discard his defenses and relax into it.

His mind screamed its protest, but his heart disassociated itself from the words even as they buzzed through his consciousness.

With unusual clarity, he recognized that there would never be concrete answers. Answers were changeable, altered by the breath of each moment, determined by the ever-changing tapestry of life.

No assurances. And yet, that was all right.

"My God!" he heard himself say. "Frannie, what are you doing?"

"I'm lighting you," she said. "I'm praying that your heart and mind be opened, that you start to understand how very rich you are simply by virtue of your humanity."

Strange. He actually understood that one.

Peace blazed tangibly within him. For a moment he thought he would open his eyes to find a world full of vivid color: green skies, pink grass, gleaming gold trees. For that brief, bright moment, everything seemed possible, all physical boundaries suspended.

His eyes flew open.

No otherworldly landscape greeted him. The room was as it had been before, except that Kat and Chris now stared at him in white-faced wonder. Francesca, too, had opened her eyes, though she didn't appear to have moved a muscle.

Stephen shifted in his chair. The blaze in his breast

had retreated to a quiet glow. "Kat, Tia saw Peter talking."

"So?"

"So there wasn't anybody in the apartment with him." He leaned forward. "There was a tape recorder running, though."

Kat's eyes widened as a bright pink flooded each cheek. "You think Peter was recording his own comments as he went to answer the door?"

"It's possible, right? Tia saw him stop by the end table. Did he tape interviews?"

She nodded.

"But I assumed he was interviewing Tia at her house that night." Chris said.

"That's what Tia told me," Kat added.

Stephen sat still. There was more. Cautiously he allowed himself to listen.

"Did anyone find a tape recorder in Peter's apartment while investigating?" Chris asked Kat.

"I don't know." She seemed annoyed by her lack of memory. "I was too upset to pay much attention."

"The police found it on the end table near the couch," Stephen said carefully. "There wasn't a tape in it, though."

"You're giving me goose bumps," Kat complained. "Are you sure about this?"

"Believe at your own risk. I'm only telling you what I feel."

"Stephen," Francesca said, "I think you know where to find the tape."

He swallowed back a slight swell of panic. Then the general feeling of peace reasserted itself. "It's somewhere in Tia's house."

"My God." Chris's jaw dropped. "Then Tia *did* kill him!"

"We don't know that," Stephen said. "We don't even know who stood on the other side of Peter's apartment door."

"Ask!" Kat urged.

But the flow of information had stopped, as if someone had shut a faucet.

Chris's fingers tapped an unconscious tattoo on the tabletop. "Think you two can search for that tape on Wednesday night?"

"We'll find a way," Kat said.

Stephen checked his watch. "Damn. I've got to get back to the restaurant." He stood and stretched. It felt as if they'd been together for only seconds, but his body, anchored to physical reality, knew otherwise.

Francesca's firm hand pulled him back into his seat. "Before you go, I would like to pray."

He grew uncharacteristically tongue-tied, not sure how to politely exclude himself from the command. Kat cleared her throat and studied the ceiling. Only Chris met Francesca's clear gaze, and he immediately reached to grasp her outstretched hand.

Kat squirmed in her chair and, with a sigh, took Stephen's hand. Embarrassed, he squeezed the small fingers now intertwined with his own.

"Gee, Frannie," he said, striving for sarcasm, "you should live in a convent. You'd fit right in."

Francesca threw him a dazzling smile. "Been there, done that."

He was startled into silence.

The late morning sun streamed through the dining room window as their hands met.

Francesca bowed her head. "Please guide us. Give us the discernment to recognize the right path and the strength to follow it."

Stephen glanced at Kat beside him. Her eyes were downcast; her eyelashes rested in feathery dark crescents against her cheeks. She looked positively demure, but he suspected that her mind was running miles away from the quiet dining room.

Francesca, too, fixed her niece with a subtle gaze. "Open our hearts to light and love in whatever form they may take," she said.

"Please bless Devon and keep her safe," Chris whispered, and Kat and Stephen exchanged a surprised glance.

"Amen," Francesca said.

May the force be with you, Stephen thought irreverently as they dropped hands.

And, from the recesses of his memory, shot back the one response he remembered from the Mass: *And also with you!*

20

TIA STARED IN OPEN DISBELIEF AS DONALD ROLLED HIS WHEEL-
chair to the foot of her doorstep.

"What the hell are you doing here?" she demanded.

"You're so gracious, Tia. You have a way of making a
guest feel completely welcome."

She squinted past him to the curb. There was Dana,
puffing in the morning heat as she pulled out one, then
two, suitcases.

"This isn't a good time," Tia said. "I'm leaving for
work in fifteen minutes, I've got appointments here
this afternoon, and my regular Wednesday circle meets
tonight."

"It's never a good time, is it?" Donald watched as
Dana deposited the suitcases at Tia's feet, then hurried
back to the van to fetch the ramp. "I'm here because I
was invited."

Tia's violet eyes, magnified by her thick glasses,
blinked rapidly. "I didn't invite you!"

"You're right. You didn't invite me. Valentine did."

Jesus Christ, when had that happened? Tia inadvertently grimaced as she tried to remember. It was useless. She'd never been able to hear Valentine as she
channeled him. In the beginning she'd set up a tape
recorder to play back his words once she was out of

trance. She'd grown spoiled these past few years. After all, she was usually surrounded by helpful admirers who were more than eager to repeat Valentine's words of wisdom to her.

But Donald was no admirer.

"When did he invite you? I haven't channeled him for you since . . ."

". . . your last visit to Ocean City. That's when he invited me." Donald smiled. "My mistake. I neglected to tell you."

"Why'd he want you here?"

But Donald was saved from answering by Dana, who arrived at that moment lugging the ramp. Donald and Tia watched in silence as she struggled to fit it into the grooves at the top of the steps. The ramp had been custom-made years ago, and it fit only Tia's stairway. Despite that, she refused to keep it. Storing it in her home smacked of acquiescence, and she didn't want to make herself any more accessible to Donald than necessary.

Dana finished securing the ramp and stepped aside. With a burst of strength, Donald propelled himself up the ramp and to Tia's side.

"You could open the door for me," he said.

Tia reached for the doorknob, gave it a savage twist, and cracked the door an inch. Donald plowed straight through. "I'll be in the kitchen," he said. "I presume you have something worth eating in there."

She glared after him, hands knotted into fists. Damn him! And, she thought disloyally, damn Valentine. What was going on, anyway? At first she'd assumed that her dislike for Donald was playing tricks on her memory, making it seem as though his visits had become more frequent. She quickly calculated. Nine visits over the past three years. No, it was not her own prejudice. Donald was definitely visiting more often.

Why, Valentine? she thought frantically. But if Valentine had an answer, he did not intend to share it now. Only a blank wall of silence met her question.

She glanced up and noticed that Dana still stood at the foot of the stairs. Tia tended not to pay much attention to any of Donald's nurse-companions. They all shared a vacuity she found annoying. Dana, in fact, was the most disconcerting of the bunch. With her awkwardly square body topped by that incongruous baby face and blunt haircut, she reminded Tia of a Kewpie doll on steroids.

Now the Kewpie doll was dangling car keys from an extended arm.

"What's that for?" Tia walked down a step. "You're not staying, too, are you?"

"No way," Dana mumbled. "I'm quitting. Take the keys so I can get out of here."

Confused, Tia cocked her head. "You can't do that. You've got to drive Donald back to Ocean City."

Dana vehemently shook her head. "That's your problem."

A spasm of panic shot through Tia's midsection. She forced a dry chuckle to her lips. "Hey, we can resolve this, I'm sure! What is it you want, Dana? Doesn't he pay you enough?"

The Clara Bow lips pursed, making Tia think of fish laid out on ice. "He pays me plenty," Dana said. "And he should, too."

"Well, then, what's the problem?" Tia allowed her

panic brief reign. Her voice sounded screechy even to her own ears. Dana recoiled.

She hastily lowered her decibels. "Dana, let's share some serious girl talk here. He pays you more than you'll make anywhere else, and probably for a lot less effort. I know he requires care, but he's fairly self-sufficient and . . ."

Her voice trailed as she caught the strangled expression on Dana's face. She'd seen that look before, usually on people about to reach for motion-sickness bags.

"You don't know." Dana's voice was low. It occurred to Tia that she did indeed know and that all her suspicions about Donald's demands on his care-providers were not only true, they were but the smallest tip of reality.

Dana stiffly raised her chin. "He's a nut."

"But"—Tia flailed helplessly against the inevitable—"he gave you a chance when nobody else would. He took you from a halfway house and . . ."

". . . made me what I am today," Dana finished bitterly. "Look, Ms. Melody. I made some bad decisions early on, but that doesn't mean I have to spend the rest of my life paying for them. I've got friends here in Baltimore. They're expecting me. Donald's your problem now. Don't even think of leaking my name as a reference, either, because I'll just spill my guts if you do. I'll tell about everything: the curses, the fetishes, that damn dream . . ."

"Dream?" Tia had no desire to deal with the fetishes, but dreams were her business. "What dream?"

"*The* dream." Dana drew in a dramatic breath. "He barely had it when I started with him last year. Then it got to be once a month, then every week. Now he wakes up nearly every night, scared to death."

"What's he dreaming?"

"He never says. He must be in a car, because he always screams 'Hit the brakes!' in the middle of it. Always."

Tia felt the blood drain from her face and knew she'd turned the yellowy color of old, dried parchment. "That all?" she asked shakily.

Dana shook her head. "No. That's just my warning. When I hear him yell about the brakes, I know he's about to wake up. He yells 'Damn you, Brenda!' and his eyes open. He's hellish then. I don't know if he's mad at the car or mad at that Brenda, but he's impossible after that dream. There are nights I don't get back to sleep at all."

Tia held herself immobile. When she spoke, her voice was softer than she herself had ever heard it. "You're right, Dana. You've got to go. Now. Get out."

Dana stayed glued to her spot, blinking in confusion at the summary dismissal. Tia raised both her eyebrows and her voice. "What are you waiting for? Get out!"

The Kewpie-doll mouth formed a round O. Then Dana turned and scampered to the van. Tia watched as she grabbed her suitcases and took off up the block. She'd packed lightly; the desire to rid herself of Donald carried more weight than did material possessions.

Tia's shoulders sagged. Where was Valentine? He was always around when somebody else needed advice. Where was he when she needed him?

His voice echoed through her mind. "I'm here," he said, and Tia gratefully closed her eyes.

There he was, beautiful as always. She often wished

that others could see him as she did in her mind's eye, magnificent and golden, astride that gleaming green-scaled dragon, asp coiled adoringly about his right arm. Valentine's hair was gold, and his eyes were turquoise. He wore a leather loincloth. Tia still swooned at the sight of his muscular chest and wondered why men like that didn't exist in the drudgery of physical reality.

"My dearest Tia, there is nothing to fear when I love you so."

Usually his words cured her deepest doubts. Today, they fell short.

He straightened with disapproval. His dragon pawed the ground, then tossed his head indignantly, ready to defend his master in the face of insult.

"Tia!" The chiding voice ricocheted through her head. "Is my love no longer enough?"

"But what's happening?" she asked him frantically.

"Peace, my dear one, for your fears are temporal. There is no reason to allow them birth. See yourself as I see you."

Tia, eyes still closed, smiled as she leaned against the doorpost of her house. "Oh, Valentine." A blush stole across her cheeks as she hungrily absorbed the image he sent.

There she was, running lightly toward the mounted Valentine. But what a different Tia this was! The violet eyes remained the same, but no glasses blocked their gleam. And her features! Somehow they'd been smoothed and softened so that she looked like herself, yet not quite herself. Long blond hair tumbled over her shoulders and down her back. Generously rounded breasts bounced as she reached up to Valentine, who wrapped a strong arm around her slender waist and lifted her behind him onto the dragon. He bent to kiss her lips; her slender legs brushed against his muscular calves as she wrapped her arms around him.

"Valentine!" she breathed.

"There is no other but you. Let that sustain you, for it is more important than the reality you endure. You have been chosen."

He was gone.

Tia opened her eyes and waited for the reassurance that usually swept over her after a visit from Valentine. She did feel better; there was no denying that. Still, she couldn't entirely shake the shadow of uneasiness which remained. Although the temperature had already topped eighty-five degrees, she hugged her thin arms against her chest and shivered.

"Tia!" Donald called from inside the house. "You'll have to buy a few things at the grocery store before you leave for work. Call your boss. Tell him you'll be late."

Tia gazed up at the blazing sun and wished that Valentine had let Donald die in the accident.

21

―――

"Now what?" Chris asked Francesca that Wednesday night.

She gazed up from her overstuffed armchair. "Sit," she said.

He obliged, though one foot continued to tap against the floor. "What do we do first?"

"We finish my cranberry juice. Are you sure you don't want any?"

"Very." Chris rose to stare out the window, fingers jiggling the loose change in his jeans pocket.

"Calm down," Francesca said.

"I can't. I don't know how you can."

She sighed. "Fine. You want an assignment? Sit down and picture yourself in the most beautiful, serene location you can imagine."

"Why?"

"Because it's hard to meditate through agitation. You sit and relax so I can finish my juice in peace. Then we'll move on to the next step."

"But Kat and Stephen . . ."

". . . just left. One step at a time, Chris."

He sank onto the loveseat. One step at a time. He squeezed his eyes shut, searching his memory for a calm image. He'd always liked the beach. That seemed a simple enough image to hold. Over there was the cool green ocean; here was the soft sand. He placed a couple of seagulls in the sky for good measure.

"Okay. I'm at the beach. Now what?"

"Enjoy it."

It was beautiful. He leaned back in the loveseat and fine-tuned the colors. The ocean was not just green, but silver and blue and gray. Each particle of sand grew distinct.

"Now ask God to join you," Francesca said.

"Ask God to join me?" he echoed bleakly. It was one thing to ask his mind to picture a place it remembered. It was quite another to force it into metaphysical contortions he'd never before required.

But Francesca apparently found this old hat. "Yes. Ask. Then trust that it will happen."

"But . . . will it?"

"Try it, believe it, Chris. It's been my experience that if you're willing to ask, God's willing to meet you more than halfway."

She waited for a few moments until his eyelids smoothed and his breathing slowed. "Do you feel calmer?" she asked.

"How am I supposed to tell if . . . uh . . . God is actually with me?"

"Just count on it." She rose and walked to the loveseat, where she sat beside him.

"I'll try."

"Keep your eyes closed. It helps. Your beach . . . are you comfortable there?"

"Yes."

"Imagine that Katerina and Stephen are with you. Ask God to keep them in the light, to protect and guide them."

"Okay." He ran the phrase through his mind. "Now what?"

"Just relax together on that beautiful beach. Feel the light cleanse each one of you."

"That's it?" His eyes flew open. "I thought we were going to pray."

"What do you think you're doing?"

"But don't you need words and stuff?"

"You can use them if you want, but this is the approach I've always liked best."

He did not respond, only stared at her from beneath lowered brows.

"I don't know any magical incantations," Francesca said. "You don't have to do anything special. Just open your heart. If you're supposed to do something, believe me, you'll know." She reached for his hand. "Let me know if your beach changes significantly."

Chris watched as her eyes closed. A gentle smile crossed her face. It occurred to him that Francesca had entered the familiar territory of a land she loved.

Warily he shut his own eyes and waited.

"Look." Kat tugged at Stephen's sleeve. "I'm a social pariah. They're all staring at me as if I ground Valentine up and stuffed him into a can."

Stephen followed her gaze to the group of Wednesday regulars. Sure enough, they stood clustered in a knot before Tia's collection of crystals, speaking in hushed voices as they cast surreptitious glances in Kat's direction.

"They're confused," he said, slipping an arm around her waist. "They won't know what to do until Valentine enlightens them."

At first she thought he was joking. One look at his

clenched jaw and cold, glittering eyes dispelled that notion.

"Are you angry at them or angry at Tia?" she asked.

"Both. It's despicable that Tia propagates this junk, but you can't let people off the hook for buying into it. Ultimately you're responsible for your own decisions in this world."

Kat turned her gaze back toward the members of the circle. They were well dressed, educated people. She could imagine them mingling at elegant cocktail parties. In fact, it was easier to picture them networking over glasses of white wine than it was to observe them extolling the virtues of herbal tea fasts and candlelit incantations.

She shook her head. "Poor Chris."

"Why?" Stephen demanded.

She looked up at him, surprised by the intensity of his tone. "It must be very hard to watch someone you love get sucked into this," she said.

He relaxed. "I see. I feel sorry for him, too. On the other hand, I can't imagine ever falling for a woman idiotic enough to believe such bull."

"Oh?" Kat raised a sardonic eyebrow. "You mean to tell me you're not besotted with the lovely Devon and her many obvious charms?" She savored the blush that crept across his face. "I beg your pardon, Stephen, but I assumed that was *your* tongue lolling on the table at Angel Café."

"That's entirely different. Sure, she's gorgeous. But I never pursued her."

"Only because Chris would have punched your lights out."

"And yet the specter of Devon's rage doesn't stop you from wanting her husband!"

Annoyed, Kat stepped away from the circle of his arm. "I don't! My feelings for Chris are not at all what you think they are."

"Odd. I'm not sure they're what you think they are, either."

They stared at each other, breathless with mutual amazement.

"How refreshing," a voice said. "I thought that all of Valentine's little acolytes preached love, love, love. What a delight to hear pure nastiness."

They turned to see a man in a wheelchair beaming up at them. He reminded Kat of a freshly polished figurine, for both his hair and his face seemed to shine despite the dim lighting in the room.

He studied her as if Stephen did not exist. "And you are . . . ?"

Kat opened her mouth to respond, but Stephen answered first. "This is Katie, my fiancée." He once again encircled her waist with a steady arm.

The man nodded solemnly. "Oh, yes, make sure you establish those property rights."

"For Pete's sake, Donald." Tia strode briskly to Stephen's side. "Stop badgering my clients. Especially this one. This here's Stephen Carmichael, my boss."

"Oh." Donald gave Stephen a clear and obvious once-over. "So you're the man who helps support me in style."

Stephen glanced toward Tia for clarification.

"Ignore him." She did not remove her piercing glare from Donald's face. "He's visiting, but not for long. Right, Donald?" With an authoritative shove, she guided the wheelchair out into the living room. "Come along," she called back over her shoulder. "We're late."

Kat and Stephen exchanged glances as Tia passed from earshot.

"Someday," Stephen said, "I'm going to write a book about this."

"Me, first," Kat contradicted as they drifted toward their seats in the circle.

"Did you feel that?" Francesca asked sharply.

Chris shook his head, then guiltily realized that he'd allowed his mind to wander. The beach, momentarily so vibrant, had receded behind idle thoughts of what Devon might be doing at the moment. "No," he admitted, embarrassed. "What happened?"

"I think we've come in direct contact with darkness," she said. His heart thumped. It sounded like a bad science-fiction script. If he hadn't experienced Valentine before, seen his own wife slip illogically away from him, he'd have dismissed the serious woman beside him as a kook. It was, however, hard to ignore what his eyes had seen and what his heart sensed was true.

With a gulp, he switched his focus back to the beach.

It was much harder to get there than it had been the first time.

"Ah, Mr. Banks," Valentine said. "Business, business, business. You worry too much about business. We will, of course, attend to it, I assure you. In the meanwhile, I am pleased that you've broadened our fellowship with candidates from your firm. The more of your colleagues who join us, the more profitable your firm will become."

Stephen let the words wash over him as he quickly reviewed the plan.

"I'll distract Valentine while you search for the tape," Kat had said. "Who knows? Maybe you'll get some . . . guidance."

"How do you plan to distract him?" he'd demanded, aware by now that Kat had a propensity toward thinking herself invincible.

"Valentine and I have such a great relationship. I'll ask questions. I'll pout. I'll do anything I have to do. Just move quickly."

How quickly was he supposed to move? He knew Tia, but he didn't know her house.

They couldn't do this alone. He watched nervously as Hal Banks straightened for more of Valentine's advice. They'd need help.

Please, help us.

He snapped to attention as he realized that, for the first time in his life, he'd actually appealed to a deity.

Jeez. This had to end soon.

But the familiar glow of serenity rushed through him as if it had been waiting in the wings, longing for an invitation. His apprehension slowly evaporated. He didn't know yet how to proceed, but that seemed relatively unimportant at the moment.

He glanced at Kat to see if she, too, had felt the breeze of relief. She stared straight ahead, eyes fixed on Tia's form, Valentine's mannerisms. Stephen reached impulsively for her hand. She delivered a tight little smile of acknowledgment before turning away.

How on earth could he make her pain go away?

This second surprise forced him bolt upright in his chair. Now, why would he ever think anything as dopey as that? He was no psychologist, and he'd always believed that the best course of action in human affairs was to stay out of them.

Kat squeezed his hand, hard. He jerked his head toward her. "Now," she mouthed. "Go."

Valentine had finished with Hal and was moving on to Madeline. Stephen would be next. With his place empty, Valentine would be obliged to move directly to Kat, who could buy extra time as needed.

Only the man in the wheelchair followed with his eyes as Stephen stood, stretched, and started casually toward the stairs. "It's upstairs at the end of the hall," Donald announced loudly, interrupting Valentine mid-sentence. Madeline pursed her lips in disapproval, but Valentine didn't skip a beat.

"The beach feels different," Chris said, surprised. "This sounds stupid, Frannie, but Stephen and Kat aren't together anymore."

"What do you see?" Francesca's eyes remained closed.

"Stephen's gone to gather shells. Kat's standing on the shore, watching the waves."

"Do the best you can. If you start to feel drained or exhausted, concentrate on Stephen alone. Leave Katerina to me."

He was too intrigued to question further. As he turned his attention back to his image, he noticed that Stephen seemed enveloped by a strong, white light. It danced about him, forming an aureole that surrounded his entire body.

Chris concentrated on this, so lost in the picture that he didn't realize he'd begun mouthing his old standby, the Lord's Prayer.

* * *

Tia's second floor held three small rooms and a bathroom. Stephen walked quickly through the hallway, peeking into each doorway as he slipped by. The largest bedroom was obviously Tia's. An antique four-poster crowded the room, but Tia had still managed to cram in two dressers and an armchair. A large closet, probably added long after the house's completion, spanned the entire length of the south wall. Two pairs of double doors folded back, revealing a tumbled heap of Tia's clothes. A pair of orange elephant bells protruded here; a shocking-pink paisley minidress hung twisted from a hanger there. Stephen shuddered. The room was a second-hand clothing shopper's paradise. There'd never be time to sift through all the rubble. He shook his head and quickly continued down the hall.

The only piece of furniture in the next room was a bookshelf, but the floor was littered with mail-order supplies. Stephen recognized the same type of candles that had rested on Chris's dining room table two days earlier. They sat in a large box in the center of the room, right beside at least two dozen bags of rose petals. There were stacks of products everywhere. A quick inventory yielded everything from toothpaste to teas to sexual aids. The bookshelf was piled high with mail-order catalogs. Stephen breathed a sigh of relief. There'd be no reason to search here. There were no drawers or closets in which to conceal anything.

The third room, though tiny, was another bedroom. A neatly made twin bed stood in the middle of the floor. A bureau rested against the wall. A suitcase sat open on a chair. Stephen stepped furtively into the room, half expecting to meet its occupant. Whose room was this? Tia, he knew, lived alone. He absently walked around the bed. A pair of men's shoes lay tumbled on the far side of it. One unscuffed sole stared up at him, as clean and smooth as if it had never touched the ground.

That's right. That man in the wheelchair was visiting. But how would he get up the stairs? Tia was hardly the strapping weightlifter type. Stephen couldn't imagine her hauling the man, wheelchair and all, up the steep flight of steps to the second floor.

He advanced quickly toward the bureau, aware that time was slipping rapidly away. The low hum of Valentine's voice floated up the stairs, punctuated by an occasional round of appreciative chuckles. Good. Valentine was playing to an adoring crowd. With luck, his vanity would keep him occupied.

The first dresser drawer opened with ease. Stephen carefully slid his hand under layer after layer of blankets. They were packed in so tightly that he had to remove the top few in order to thumb through the rest.

The second drawer contained sheets. He rifled through them, ear cocked toward the doorway.

All was silent downstairs. Too silent. He shut the drawer and hurried quietly to the head of the stairs.

Kat's soft voice drifted past his ears, but he couldn't decipher her words. Valentine boomed a response.

He turned once more for the bedroom, heading straight for the bottom drawer.

This one held towels. Stephen pawed through the stacks, no longer caring whether he left them in the same order in which they'd been found.

Nothing.

Frustration mounting, he slammed the drawer shut. Now what?

Why are all the linens in a bureau?

He couldn't have cared less. Glowering, he moved swiftly toward the door.

How does Donald get upstairs?

That stopped him. He stood in the hallway, absorbing the thought. It was a good question. His eyes darted from wall to wall, floor to ceiling.

Help me with this one, he thought awkwardly. I won't take the credit if it works out, I promise.

Slowly, following an inner compass, Stephen turned and walked toward the bathroom.

He nearly clobbered his knee on the old claw-footed tub protruding into the doorway. With more vehemence than necessary, he swung back the shower curtains. Only clean white porcelain met his scrutiny. Embarrassed, he let the curtains fall back into place.

Sink, toilet, linen closet . . .

. . . linen closet. If Tia had a linen closet, why were all her linens crammed into dresser drawers?

Holding his breath, Stephen reached for the closet door.

Valentine's piercing eyes flickered past Stephen's empty seat and came to rest on Kat. She drew herself up, arranging her expression into one of bland neutrality.

"Welcome," Valentine said, and she could not prevent the slight shudder of revulsion that raced through her. Didn't anybody else in the room think his voice sounded oily, slick rather than smooth, disingenuous rather than sincere? Apparently not.

They'd all turned expectant faces her way.

Damn. She was supposed to be grateful that Valentine had taken her back into the fold. "Grateful" was not an attitude she could pull off. Instead, she forced a smile to her lips and waited.

"We will douse the sparks which fly between us," Valentine said gently. "But, my dear, we must meet each other in truth. No more facades. A soul cannot be free until it takes responsibility for its reality."

An impressed murmur traveled through the circle as Madeline feverishly transcribed Valentine's words into her ever-present notebook.

Valentine paused and leaned back in his chair, eyes still fixed upon Kat's face. He obviously awaited a response.

"Agreed," Kat said, just to give him one.

"You, for example, have not been totally honest with us. I urge you to drop the fiction. You will find us all colleagues here, eager to help each other on the path."

Kat glanced toward Hal Banks. He gazed at her with an expression of mixed encouragement and sympathy. All members of the circle, in fact, looked as if they wanted to enfold her in their arms and simply were waiting for Valentine to say the word. Only Donald stared beadily from the depths of his wheelchair. She actually preferred the impersonal nature of his frigid stare over the earnest mushiness the others offered.

Once again, Valentine expected a response.

"Okay," Kat said.

"Let me help you be born anew into truth. You come to us as Katie, but you are in truth called Katerina Piretti, are you not?"

Donald straightened in his chair, swiveled his head slowly toward Valentine, then back to face her.

"Yes. 'Katie' is a nickname. There's not much fiction about it."

"Yet you use it as a shield. You've come here not for knowledge, but for information."

The challenge in his voice awakened the adversarial in her. She was a lawyer, for heaven's sake. She could play with words as well as any opponent, seen or unseen.

"They're the same thing," she said coolly.

She felt the reproachful eyes of the circle rest upon her, as if she were a naughty child responsible for making the entire class miss recess.

"They are not the same thing," Valentine said. "One enlightens. The other weights the soul."

"How so?" she demanded, irritated by the admiring sighs exhaled around her.

"Knowledge is absorbed and processed by the soul for the good of the entire entity. Information resides only in the mind, isolating it from the whole. The mind can become so engrossed in an informational nugget that it concentrates on it to the exclusion of wisdom. The soul cannot grow if it is mesmerized by one facet alone."

"Bullshit."

A collective gasp from the circle reminded Kat that she'd meant to hold her temper. Damn! But how could anyone listen to such drivel and not erupt? She studied Valentine with a touch of apprehension. If he had access to thunderbolts, now was his moment to throw them.

Instead, he spread his arms and gave a good-natured

shrug. "As you wish it. I am willing to aid those open to my message. I cannot, however, force you to believe. Know in your heart that I will always be waiting for you."

His eyes turned once again toward the empty seat at Kat's side. She followed his stare. Stephen had been gone long enough to raise anyone's curiosity, and Valentine was not just "anyone."

"Valentine!" she said.

The fathomless eyes swung back her way.

She tried to mask the challenge in her voice. "Valentine, I know a way you could help."

"Help, my child?"

"Help me believe."

"I have many with whom you can speak." His arm swept in a smooth arc across the circle. "Here are but a few who have known the truth of my words. Speak with them."

"I'm not interested in what they have to say."

"How can you say that?" Hal cried.

"I could tell you stories that would wipe away all doubt!" Madeline insisted.

Kat held up a hand to stem the flow of indignant testimony.

"Valentine is certainly capable of answering any questions I have." She caught the deep, dark gaze and held it. "Aren't you?"

He extended a languorous arm toward his water glass. "Indeed," he said, raising the glass to his lips.

The familiar light filled Francesca, bathing her in swirling energy that knew no bounds. There were never words to describe this swell of strength that flowed through her. It raced through her fingertips with incredible force, yet never smothered or swallowed her, simply invited her to rejoice in its presence.

How good this was! How could one not give thanks and praise in the presence of such love?

I need help and guidance, she thought. Please show me how to guide and protect Katerina.

A soft kiss rested on her eyelids.

In her mind's eye, at the edge of the mist, a figure rose. Francesca studied it curiously, knowing she was safe from harm in the circle of light.

The figure solidified but did not look her way. She saw a handsome profile, cut as sharply as the image of a Roman emperor on an old coin. Long blond curls tumbled halfway down the figure's back, held in place by a gem-studded golden band set firmly across a broad brow. The man rode upon a dragon and he clasped an asp in his right hand. As she watched, the figure raised his left hand above his head, a conductor orchestrating his own chorus of hosannas. He turned blindly toward her; his eyes were the glittering turquoise of a Caribbean island sea.

"Behold the glory of Asteroth!" he thundered.

Francesca's eyes flew open as she stifled a shriek. She raised a hand to her chest to quiet her pounding heart. All seemed well. Chris sat beside her, eyes closed, lips moving soundlessly.

But Asteroth, whoever he was, terrified her with his icy beauty. Though unseen in the mist, she'd sensed the outline of his army, dark, contorted beings astride the beasts of hell.

And they were legion.

* * *

"It's simple, really." Kat shrugged. "I just want to know what you are."

"What I am?" Valentine chuckled softly, then took another long swallow of water. "You are most amusing," he said, almost to himself. He replaced the glass on the tray beside him. "Truly, Katerina, your mind is a wonder. If you could but let go of insignificant details. What I am doesn't matter. We are all of one creation. It is the essence of my soul, my point of emanation, which defines me."

"Sorry. I can't handle abstractions. To the best you can define yourself, what are you, Valentine?"

Valentine's gaze took in each member of the circle. A broad, benevolent smile spread across his face. When he spoke, his voice fell as warm and rich as freshly made cocoa.

"My children," he said jovially, "you know in your hearts what I am. I am an angel."

Stephen swung open the wide linen closet door and stared into the space behind it. There were no medicines or linens stored on neat shelves here. There were, in fact, no shelves. His eyes met only an empty space surrounded by cracked plaster walls.

"Okay," he said beneath his breath. He reached his hand into a corner and touched metal. All four corners of the closet were rimmed vertically by a metal frame. At the bottom, where a linoleum floor should have been, an open shaft gaped several inches from his boot. He flicked a switch to the left of the door and watched as, with a slight clank, a metal platform began its slow, slow climb up to the second floor. A lift! Stephen stared as the heavy platform finally stopped before him. Then he stepped gingerly onto it, his mouth turning downward as the structure jiggled slightly beneath his weight.

There had to be a light in here. And since the lift had been made to hold a wheelchair, anything important would probably be placed low. He directed his search to waist level. Sure enough, a metal beam protruded slightly to his left, forming a small ledge. A large utility flashlight rested on top of it. Next to that, a lever jutted from a metal box welded to the floor.

Stephen grabbed the flashlight, clicked it on, and reached out to shut the closet door. Then he gripped the lever and tugged.

A soft whir filled his ears as the lift began to descend. He wondered whether the sound was audible in the living room, but there was no way out now. He could always plead curiosity. If he looked properly abashed, maybe Tia would let him off with only a scathing comment or two.

The elevator shaft inspired claustrophobia, and the damp, musty air reminded him that he was allergic to mold spores. The walls were painted only in the top portion of the closet, and now Stephen stared as wood, plastic, and brick passed before him. He glanced at a gold metal plate imbedded in the wall. It measured approximately eight inches all around and appeared to mark the change of stories.

The lift landed on the first floor with a soft thump. Stephen listened, trying to place himself in Tia's house. He could hear muffled voices . . . was that Kat? . . . coming from far away. Wherever he'd lighted, at least it wasn't smack in the middle of the living room.

He opened the door a crack and peeked out. An

unremarkable kitchen met his eyes. Other than the unusual height of the ceiling, there was nothing intriguing here. Tia hadn't even modernized the room. It looked like a relic from the forties with its freestanding sink and lack of counter space. There was even a stove perched precariously on short, uneven legs.

He groaned inwardly as he eyed a built-in china closet. He wasn't supposed to search through drawers and closets in the kitchen, was he? There certainly wasn't time for that tonight. He was amazed that the circle hadn't already organized a posse to track him down.

He closed the door and leaned quietly against the cold metal frame of the lift. There was no way to accomplish anything further this evening. Kat would be disappointed, but what more could he do?

Resigned, Stephen pulled the lever. The lift chugged slowly upward as he pondered excuses to explain his absence. The mail-order room. He'd tell Tia that the products fascinated him. Some day, he'd say, she'd have to explain their obvious benefits to him.

The platform shuddered and stopped.

"You've got to be kidding." Stephen squinted up into the mocking space above his head. The shaft rose clear up to the third floor. The top of the lift frame had just crested the second floor, leaving him suspended before the metal plate in the wall.

"Damn!" He gave the lever an angry jerk, then stepped back, surprised. It was in the proper position. Why, then, wasn't the lift moving?

The metal plate caught his eye. An assurance, quiet but undeniable, crept over him.

He'd asked for help. Help, he suddenly realized, could come in distinctly unexpected forms.

He drew in a deep breath and firmly grasped the edge of the plate with each hand. It came away from the wall.

Behind it, beneath the floorboards of the second floor bathroom, rested a stack of notebooks and a cassette tape. He grabbed the tape and tucked it into the inside pocket of his jacket.

As if on cue, the lift whirred into motion.

"Something's wrong." Chris gripped the edge of the couch.

"Is it Stephen?" Francesca opened her eyes, frowning. "Because Katerina seems safe."

"No, Stephen's okay . . . I guess. I'm so new at this, Frannie. God only knows what I'm doing."

"That's the point. What exactly do you feel?"

He shrugged helplessly, at a loss for words. "I don't know. It was just a feeling, that's all. Maybe it's my imagination."

Francesca sat still for a moment, then closed her eyes once more. "Keep me informed," she said.

"Our friend Stephen seems to have lost his way," Valentine said.

Donald watched a flash of crimson cross Katerina Piretti's face. He cocked his head appraisingly. His task wouldn't be difficult. This Katerina was a tiny thing with the fragility of a sparrow. A part of him wanted to laugh at the great and mighty Valentine. How on earth could he feel threatened by this mere slip of a woman? This seemed the sort of situation that a powerful entity should be able to handle alone, without the intrusion of anything as awkward as murder.

"Perhaps we should search for him," Valentine said.

"Oh, that's not necessary," Kat replied quickly. Her voice, Donald noted, was like velvet. It didn't seem to belong to that delicate body. "He didn't feel well this evening. I'll go check on him if you'd like."

Valentine nailed her with a steady, gleaming eye.

"Bzzz!" Donald said. "Laser beams. You're dead, Ms. Piretti." He realized he'd spoken out loud only when the members of the circle turned to stare at him. He'd have to be careful. He was not accustomed to this much blatant Valentine-worship crammed into one location.

Kat stood. "I'll go."

"No." Valentine's hushed voice made even Donald shiver. "Allow me."

Donald leaned back, dumbfounded. In all the time Tia had been channeling Valentine, he'd never seen him use her body for locomotion. It was somehow unnatural, as if a snake were rearing up on hind legs.

Valentine rose majestically and flexed his borrowed hands. "Ah," he said, studying the fingers.

Kat looked more distressed than the situation warranted. Her wide brown eyes had grown even wider and her skin had taken on the translucence of alabaster.

The front door opened with a bang. The most incredible woman Donald had ever seen dashed breathlessly into the living room. She was tall, with tousled red-gold hair and tear-filled gray eyes. But it was her body that hypnotized Donald: lush and curvy, narrow through the waist and ending with long, shapely legs.

"Devon!" Kat and Hal Banks said at the same time.

Devon. Even her name promised a retreat into fantasy.

Devon Alexander ignored them. Instead, she raced frantically toward Valentine as tears splashed down her cheeks. "Tia!" she cried. "Tia, you've got to help me!"

Tia's body drew itself up in haughty, angry lines. Cold, black eyes stared up into the woman's surprised face. Donald quickly read the situation and rolled his wheelchair to Devon's side.

"It's Valentine," he said, taking one of her hands in his own. How beautifully shaped her fingers were! And her skin! She smelled like an orchard and felt soft as fine silk. He stroked her palm.

"Oh! Oh, I'm so sorry." Devon took a step backward, mortified by her own brashness. "I had no idea!"

"We forgive you," Valentine said in stiffly formal tones.

"I didn't mean to intrude, honest. Tia told me that if I ever had to talk to her, I could just . . . and I. . . "

Kat suddenly appeared at Devon's other side. "Hey, Devon. Why don't you come with me? We can talk."

Donald glared at her, resenting the intrusion. He strained to hear as Devon allowed herself to be led to the loveseat. "Chris . . . told me he'd be at work, but . . ."

Stephen's footsteps clattered down the stairs. Valentine turned toward him. "We will resume shortly," he announced, obviously irritated by the turn of events. "Refresh yourselves that you may be prepared for deeper enlightenment."

Ever obedient, his followers rose to stretch, then trickled into the dining room for the herbal tea and cookies Tia always set out.

"Valentine," Donald whispered, clutching the edge of his chair.

Valentine's head swiveled toward him. "You have seen what is necessary. You should recognize the danger. I trust you will do my bidding quickly."

"I've changed my price." Donald nodded toward the loveseat, where Devon now sobbed on Kat's shoulder. Stephen stood beside her, occasionally patting her back with an awkward hand. The physical contact made Donald cringe. "I want her. Devon."

Valentine followed his stare, a smug smile playing about his mouth. "Money alone no longer amuses you?"

"I'll get that anyway."

"Ah, yes. Lust has always driven men to great feats."

"I want her. You tell me how powerful and influential you are. Well, prove it. I want that woman."

Valentine thoughtfully studied Devon Alexander. "You might at least have offered me a challenge," he said. "Very well. You dispose of my problem, and the supple Ms. Alexander is yours."

A beatific smile spread across Donald's boyish face as he watched Devon lean over her purse in search of a tissue. Jesus! That clear shot of cleavage was pure torture.

"Give her to me now," he wheedled in a strangled voice.

"Soon enough . . . Victor."

"Don't do that. I've told you before. Don't ever call me that!"

The echo of a deep, mocking laugh rang through the air as Tia's head dropped to her chest.

22

—⁓⁓—

"HOW COULD YOU JUST LEAVE HER THERE?" CHRIS'S anguished cry ripped through Stephen's ears.

"She wouldn't come with us." Kat reached for Chris's hand. "We tried to take her home, but she wouldn't budge."

"Shit." He ran a hand through his short blond hair and paced away from Kat's gentle hold. "Where did I put my keys? I've got to . . ."

Francesca stepped into his path. He came to an abrupt halt a split second before knocking her over.

"Chris." Her voice, cool and clear, penetrated the frenzy. "You're not alone in this. We want to help. But you've got to stop a minute and listen to me."

"Okay." He turned in the opposite direction. "Okay."

"What are you planning to do?" She hooked an arm through his, fell into rhythm beside him, and slowed the brisk stride to a walk.

"I've got to get her. I've got to go to Tia's and bring her home."

"Where do you plan to tell her you were this evening?"

"I'll tell her the truth, damn it! It's time she woke up. I'll tell her about Peter, about the cassette. Maybe it'll snap her back to her senses. Maybe she'll recognize once and for all how evil Valentine and Tia truly are, how—"

"Chris." Francesca placed a firm hand on each of his shoulders and swung him to face her. "You will do no such thing."

He stared into her eyes, mouth flapping wordlessly in search of a response.

"You can't," Francesca said. "They've got her hooked. Don't you understand?"

Kat flew to his other side, peering up into his face as she guided him to the loveseat. "Devon won't believe you. You know that. Oh, Chris, she couldn't listen to you before. Why would she listen to you now? All she'll do is tell Tia and Valentine that we're out to nail them."

"But I have to save her." His voice broke. "I can't leave her there with that woman."

Francesca nodded. "You're right. But not a word about what we're doing. Tell her that the person she spoke with tonight was mistaken, that you were, indeed, on duty. Tell her you were trying to surprise her. Tell her anything but the truth. Not yet."

He reached for his keys, biceps tightening beneath his T- shirt as a tremor raced through his body. Stephen watched his jaw clench. He himself had experienced this sort of anger only twice in his life. He remembered it as a blinding white rage that temporarily obliterated all reason.

"Hey," Stephen said, "how about I come with you?"

Kat nodded quickly. Stephen knew that she, too, harbored similar concerns. "That's a good idea," she said. "Stephen can drive."

"No." Francesca leaned wearily against the wall. "There's no way to explain his presence."

"Don't worry," Chris said in a monotone. "I can handle it. She's my wife. If what we've been to each other isn't enough, then. . . " His voice trailed into the air.

"Remember that she isn't herself," Francesca reminded.

He nodded, then reached for her hand. "Pray for me?"

"Of course."

"I'll call as soon as I can. Good luck with the tape." He closed the door gently, leaving them with the hope that he'd somehow restrain his temper.

"Damn," Kat said softly. "We've got to get to the bottom of this quickly."

Francesca checked her watch. "Let's move on to the tape. I'm too tired to last much longer."

Stephen withdrew the cassette from his pocket. Kat reached for it first, wincing slightly as she touched it. "You do it," she said, passing it to her aunt.

Francesca crossed the room to the compact disc-cassette player. "Which side of the tape?"

"Rewind side A, and let's hear what we have," Stephen suggested.

The room grew silent as Francesca inserted the tape, pressed the Rewind button, and stepped away.

"What's wrong?" Kat asked sharply.

"Wrong?" Francesca looked blank.

Kat hurried over to the tape machine. "It's not rewinding." She knelt to jab the Eject button, then lifted the tape toward the light, squinting to study it. "It's wound totally onto one spool."

Stephen sank to the floor beside her. "Let me see it."

He turned the tape over to side B and reinserted it into the machine. Only a slow, steady clicking met their ears.

"I can't believe it." Kat leaned her head against his shoulder in frustration.

"What's wrong?" Francesca wearily hugged her arms against her chest.

Stephen removed the tape. "It's like Kat said. The damn thing is wrapped totally around one spool. It must have overwound itself and snapped."

"Shit." Kat did not lift her head.

"Can we fix it?" Francesca asked.

"Most people throw cassettes away when this happens," Stephen replied.

Kat's head shot up, nearly ramming him in the chin. "Well, obviously we can't do that."

"Obviously," he said, pushing her head back down to his shoulder.

"Is this a problem we can solve tonight?" Francesca covered a huge yawn.

Stephen shook his head. "I'm afraid to touch it, frankly. It's too valuable to chance ruining. I have a friend who's repaired his own tapes before. Maybe he could do it for us. I'll drop off the tape tomorrow morning and get him to look at it by evening."

"Evening?" Kat groaned.

"That sounds like our best course of action," Francesca said. "We can't risk damaging an important piece of evidence."

"I wonder why Tia stashed it under the floorboards," Stephen mused.

"Well, it's not the sort of thing you'd want to set out on your coffee table." Kat dragged herself to her feet.

"Agreed. But why go to the trouble of concealing something like this when it would be easier simply to throw it away? And why not burn those notebooks?"

Kat shuddered. "Don't even put the thought into the air. We still have to get back into the house to grab those notebooks."

"But not tonight." Francesca leaned over to kiss her niece. "I'm going to bed. Tomorrow promises to be every bit as exhausting as today was."

She watched as Stephen rose to his feet. Then, to his surprise, she planted a light kiss on his cheek. "Good night, Stephen. Call us in the morning."

"Sure," he said, embarrassed. Even his own mother no longer kissed him.

Kat waited until her aunt's soft footsteps had faded above them. "Aw, shucks," she teased, reaching up to pat Stephen's head.

"Cut it out."

She plucked the cassette from his hand and sank thoughtfully down onto the sofa. "To think that so much rides on this tape. What if it turns out to be Tia reciting curses or something? What if it's a Valentine demo of demonic chants?"

Stephen sat beside her and reached for the tape. "It won't be."

"Is that you talking, or is it your . . ." she widened her eyes and passed a melodramatic hand across her forehead ". . .'special powers'?"

"I don't have any special powers," he said, setting the tape on the end table.

"Then what do you call these messages you're getting?"

Stephen leaned his head back against the sofa cushions and stared up at the ceiling. "Divine intervention, I guess."

"Really?" She twisted to stare at him.

"Yeah," he said defensively. "What's the big deal?"

"Nothing. You surprised me, that's all. You didn't used to believe in that stuff."

"Well, what do *you* believe in?" he asked.

She drew back, genuinely startled, apparently unaccustomed to personal questions. "I guess I believe in justice," she finally said.

"That's it? Generic justice?"

"Why? Isn't that enough?"

"What about 'God is love' and all that?"

She set her jaw firmly, and he suspected that he should shut up. He couldn't stop himself, though. He was inexplicably drawn to the walls that Kat had so carefully constructed around herself. Somewhere, somehow, there had to be a chink in their thickness, a way to burst through and let in some sunlight.

"You've been through such upheaval in your life, Kat. I just wondered whether you still believed that—"

"Upheavals are irrelevant," she snapped. "Suffice it to say that I don't get messages the way you do."

He raised an eyebrow. He'd hit a nerve a mile wide. Obviously, one thing Kat did *not* believe in was personal vulnerability.

"It's strange," he said, returning his stare to the ceiling. "My parents taught me to disbelieve anything I couldn't touch or see. But I've touched this now, you see . . . or rather, it's touched me. I've even seen it . . . or, at least, seen it in others. My senses have expanded beyond anything my parents ever imagined. Unfortunately, I can't explain what's happening to anyone, including myself."

A tentative smile pushed the brittle look from Kat's face. "You don't have to explain it to me," she said.

"Thank God. I'm exhausted."

It was hard to tell in the dim light of the room, but he thought she looked tired. She appeared to have lost a few pounds. Her cheekbones seemed more prominent, and the bones of her wrists looked downright fragile. She came packaged with more bravado than actual strength, and he wondered why someone didn't keep a better eye on her. She had no business fighting the world, seen or unseen, on her own. Despite her own conviction to the contrary, she was not invincible. Nobody was.

"What are you looking at?" she asked, eyes luminous in the half-light.

"You." He rested an arm behind her on the back of the couch.

"Why?"

"I'm wondering how you think, Katerina Piretti. I'm wondering if you'll ever decide to stop being such a stubborn loner."

"Takes one to know one," she said, and he winced. She was right, of course. He'd been extremely successful in maintaining an unencumbered life, a life devoid of serious human contact.

"I'm wondering, then, if you'll let me admit that I've been wrong." He slid her close to him in a loose hug.

Her body felt good against his. She leaned her head against his chest, and a silken strand of dark hair brushed against his neck with the soft tickle of a feather. He reached up to smooth it back into place. As if of its own accord, his hand continued down the back of her sleek head, then gently stroked her cheek. Kat gazed up at him, startled. He cautiously met her stare.

He didn't want to analyze the situation, didn't want to determine whether this was a move that could advance either his ego or his bank account. All he knew was that a persistent longing within him could find its answer in this woman.

He bent until his lips met hers.

Kat melted into him, her mouth searching his. He drew her onto his lap, suddenly overwhelmed by the need not only to consume her, but to be consumed by her. Her arms wrapped around his neck, pulling him close with the urgency of a lost sailor who has finally sighted land. Her ragged breathing matched his own. Stephen's hand slipped down her back and to her waist. Surprised, he realized that he was shaking.

He pulled himself away and stared helplessly into her flushed face. He'd taken other women in lust, even in curiosity, and the experiences had been undeniably pleasurable. But Kat . . . possessing her body alone would never quench the pull he felt toward her.

Trembling, Kat leaned forward and kissed him. One hand rested against his chest, the other played gently through his hair. The kiss grew deeper. She molded her body against his until he could feel the wild beating of her heart.

"My God," he whispered, kissing her neck. The lingering scent of her perfume teased his nostrils, pushed him forward. He brushed a hand lightly down the side of her body. Kat gasped, then guided his hand to her breast.

He needed no further urging. Toppling her down to the sofa, he stretched out beside her, one leg resting across hers, one hand smoothly traveling up the soft skin beneath her shirt. Her breasts were full under his touch. He groaned, wanting desperately to slow himself down.

"You're beautiful," he said.

She did not reply. Her eyes were closed; she'd become exquisitely pale. He wondered briefly if she was all right but, once again, her insistent little hand guided his. He did not, could not, stop himself from following her lead. He explored one breast with his mouth as his hand fumbled with the clasp of her bra. She was more than beautiful. She was heaven found in the least likely place, total joy when he'd given up on that emotion. "Oh, my most miraculous Katie," he whispered into the air.

The small hands resting on his shoulders tensed as she stiffened beneath him. "No," she moaned. "No, Stephen, we can't . . . I can't. . . ."

He drew back, uncertain that he'd heard correctly. Kat scrambled from beneath him, curling herself into a small ball at the end of the couch.

Confused, Stephen slowly pulled himself to a sitting position. Rebuffs were rare, but no big deal. One simply feigned huffy indignation and accused the other party of teasing or prudery. He gazed at Kat shivering against the arm of the couch. This was clearly new territory.

"Kat . . . I'm sorry."

She shook her head vehemently. "It isn't you. Oh, my God, Stephen, it isn't." She turned to him a face so full of anguish that he had no choice but to move swiftly beside her and gather her into his arms.

"I guess I misread my signals," he said, relieved that she'd at least let him hold her.

"No," she assured him miserably. "You didn't. You didn't do anything wrong."

He pulled back again to look at her, then followed her gaze to the cassette on the end table. "Oh. I see." How could he, who seldom lost against physical rivals, ever expect to compete with the dead?

"I'm sorry," Kat said in a tight, dry voice. "I was wrong."

She was fading away from him, rapidly retreating behind that smooth, controlled mask he so hated. If she succeeded, he'd be effectively closed out, unable to join her in the sterile cubicle she'd learned to create so well.

He held her at arm's length, shaking her slightly as he spoke. "Kat, please, listen to me. You can't live in a little box for the rest of your life. Do you honestly think he would want it this way? If he loved you, he'd want you to feel something again. Anything. He'd want you to cry again, even to get angry at him for dying. If he loved you, Kat, he'd want you to find some peace."

Kat stared at him, a study in alabaster. He half expected her to slap him across the face, then angrily order him out of her house.

Instead, she lifted a limp hand to her forehead. "I'm so tired," she said.

"I know."

"Could you just hold me? Please?"

He lay down beside her and wrapped her in his arms. Then they both drifted into deep, dreamless sleep.

23

CHRIS WEDGED HIS MOTORCYCLE BETWEEN TWO PARKED CARS, quickly dismounted, and raced up the four steps to Tia's front door. He raised a fist to pound on it but, at the last minute, uncurled his tight fingers and reached for the doorknocker instead. He'd originally won Devon with care and kindness. Rage, however righteous, would do nothing to remind her of that.

Tia answered the knock as if she already knew who stood behind the door. "Good," she said. "I knew you wouldn't let me down. You're just the man I wanted to see, hon."

"Where is she?"

He stormed into the room. The circle must have ended, for the house was quiet. The foyer blazed with light. He'd never before visited Tia for nonprofessional reasons. Her house, usually so dim and mysterious, appeared nonthreatening when bathed in brightness. The ordinariness made him feel grossly overdrawn, like a caricature of outrage.

"I want my wife," he said, sounding more like a hurt child than an angry man.

"As well you should." Tia soothingly stroked his arm. "She's in the kitchen. Look, hon, let me fill you in before you go to her."

She looked so earnest, not at all like a woman out to destroy his marriage.

"Tia, I'll handle this alone. Furthermore, I'd appreciate it if you spent less time with my wife in the future!"

"Face it, hon, there's not going to be a future unless you listen to me. I'm on your side, okay? You two kids are meant to be together forever. I believe that. I don't know why it's falling apart any more than you do. I *do* know that your little missus thinks you don't love her anymore, that you've got a honey on the side."

His eyes widened in disbelief. "That's insane."

"She can't think of any other reason why you won't do what Valentine says so she can have a baby."

"Damn Valentine!"

Tia pursed her lips. "There are times I'd like to agree with you. But he's always right. Truth is truth, no matter how unpleasant you find it."

"Valentine is not truth."

"Your wife's a believer. She wants you to experience the same joy she's found."

"Joy?" His voice cracked. "She's a walking shell. I haven't seen any joy in Devon since this horseshit with Valentine started!"

"Chris." Devon stood framed in the living room doorway, face waxen and eyes red-rimmed. She took a tentative step toward him. He raced to gather her into his arms.

"Devon," he whispered into her hair. If he let her go, she'd be gone forever.

"Introduce me," a hurt voice said. Chris opened his eyes to see a man in a wheelchair glaring up at him.

Tia ignored the command. She draped a firm arm around Devon's shoulder and helped Chris guide her toward the front door. "Devon, go home with your husband. Talk this out. You'll feel better in the morning."

New tears pooled in Devon's eyes as she nodded.

The man in the wheelchair straightened. "Don't go until he explains his whereabouts tonight, Devon. He lied to you."

"Donald!" Tia's violet eyes flashed. "Stay out of it!"

Devon lifted reproachful eyes to Chris. "You weren't at work."

Chris ran his tongue along his teeth. Lying did not come naturally to him, and he hated doing it. He could see very clearly, however, that he had no choice. "I was there. I was out on patrol. I wasn't originally scheduled, but Bill Archer's wife and kid had the flu and—"

"Should we verify that story?" Donald wheeled himself to Devon's free side. "I don't know, dear. You told us he's been acting strangely. It just doesn't make sense."

"Donald, I want you to read my lips." Tia bent until she was eye level with the man. "Butt out. You've got no business interfering between a husband and wife like this. They've got to work it out on their own."

"But, Tia," he said. "You're so very wrong. It's not only my business, it's my responsibility. We're part of the brotherhood of Valentine, are we not?"

Devon took a small step away from Chris, who instinctively tightened his grasp around her body.

"We should protect each other," Donald continued. "Especially in the face of outside intrusion."

"Outside intrusion?" Devon asked in a high, brittle voice.

Donald pointed an accusing finger at Chris. "He

doesn't believe. You told us as much, told us how it grieves you."

"He's trying." A wheedling note entered Devon's voice. "He comes to the circle with me."

"But he tried to stop you from seeing Tia."

"Enough!" Tia reached for the handles of Donald's chair. He turned and, with surprising strength, closed one hand around her forearm. She gasped in pain and relinquished her grip.

"I'm only repeating what you implied before, Tia. The truth isn't always pretty, but it remains the truth." He rolled himself slowly toward the sofa. "I've been a disciple of Valentine for a very long time."

Devon followed him with her eyes. "You have?"

"Tia and I met Valentine together. She never told you that, did she?" He patted the sofa beside his chair.

"Devon, please." Chris tugged gently at his wife's arm. "Let's go home."

Devon stared at Donald. Then, brushing Chris's hand away, she took a shaky step toward the sofa.

"Come." Donald once again patted the cushion. "Let me tell you my story. It won't take long."

She stumbled to the sofa to sit. Donald reached for her hand, then caught her stare and held it. "You want a baby," he said. "And you should have one. You're made for it. Look at you . . . a pure, sensual vessel of potential for every earthly experience. But Valentine is not only very good, he's very wise. He would never ask you to share your self and your possibilities with one who cannot comprehend their worth."

"I've heard enough of this." Chris stormed over to Devon and, with a mighty tug, pulled her to her feet. "We're going home!"

"Ah," Donald said. "When all else fails, use brute strength."

"Go with your husband, Devon." Tia rapidly guided the Alexanders to the front door. "We'll talk tomorrow."

"Wait!" Donald called from the living room.

Chris desperately threw open the door, sure of what was coming. He'd pushed Devon across the threshold when the expected words rained down on him, clogging his ears.

"Why don't we ask Valentine?"

"Not this time," Chris muttered, but Devon was already back in the foyer, a pleading look on her face as she turned to Tia.

"Please? You don't have to channel him. Just ask him what I should do."

"Oh, Devon, please." Chris turned her to face him. "Can't you decide this one on your own?"

"Why should she?" Donald asked. "Why rely upon our own fallibility when the perfect response is so easily obtained?"

Tia stood in the middle of the foyer, face white. She closed her eyes. As the seconds passed, two bright red splotches dotted her cheeks.

"Just so happens Valentine has his druthers." Her voice grew faint. "You're to stay here tonight, Devon. You can sleep on my couch."

"What?" Chris's head buzzed. An angry cloud rose before his eyes, making it difficult to focus.

Devon drifted toward the sofa, mouth turned downward as fresh tears began to fall. Chris rushed behind her and, with all the strength he had, pulled her into his arms. Forcing her head back, he kissed her, a deep, desperate kiss that longed for the power to yank her back, make her his. Even as he kissed her, he knew that everything was wrong. The kiss was not born of love, and she was already gone.

Hard rubber wheels rammed into his legs. He gave a howl of pain as he released his wife.

"How . . . how could you?" Devon sobbed, stumbling for cover behind the wheelchair.

Chris stared from his wife's heaving shoulders to the smug expression on Donald's face. Tia stood white and shaking, still planted in the middle of the foyer.

"Look what you've done," Chris hissed at her. "You're responsible for this. You and your monster, Valentine."

"Say good night," Donald commanded. "If you're a good boy, maybe Devon will call you in the morning."

The rage, barely suppressed before, now bubbled over. Chris toppled the wheelchair with one powerful shove. Donald spilled onto the floor, landing helplessly on his stomach.

"Police!" he howled, face red. "Call the police and lock him up!"

Devon jumped to his aid, but Tia remained frozen. Her voice followed Chris as he slammed out into the night.

"Damn you, Donald. Damn you to hell for all eternity!"

24

STEPHEN STRUGGLED AGAINST THE DARKNESS TO OPEN HIS eyes. For some unfathomable reason, he was still fully dressed. His eyes followed the length of his arm. It was wrapped around Katerina Piretti, an instant reminder of where he'd spent the night. Her breathing was soft and regular, the rhythm of deep sleep. He propped himself on his elbow and traced a gentle finger along the curve of her full lower lip. She looked so untroubled in sleep. He brushed a lock of long, dark hair away from her forehead, wondering how to transfer that peace to her waking hours.

"Good morning." Francesca stood above them, dressed to jog, an amused smile on her face.

Stephen guiltily extricated himself from Kat's warm body and swung around to sit on the edge of the couch.

"You can take it easy," Francesca said. "Her father won't be down for another hour or so."

"I didn't mean to fall asleep like that." He rested his head in his hands and strove for coherency. "What time is it?"

"Five-thirty. I didn't want to wake you, but I heard you had a business to run."

"Um . . . yeah. Yeah, I do." He colored as he realized she'd probably been standing there for quite some time. "I gotta get going. I need to go home, grab a shower, drop that cassette off . . ."

Francesca reached for his hand and helped him to his feet. "Come on. You have time for a cup of coffee. How about some breakfast?"

He suppressed a yawn. "Too early for breakfast," he mumbled, following her into the kitchen.

"This will help." She set a mug of coffee onto the table before him. "Drink it. I can't in good conscience let you leave this house until I see some signs of life."

She watched casually as he raised the cup to his mouth. He remembered Victoria doing the same thing, although her gaze had been more piercing, as if she meant to decode him. With Francesca, the action seemed noninvasive, somehow inviting. Or was it that he no longer considered isolation a virtue?

He cracked an awkward smile. "I . . . uh . . . think I'm in love with your niece."

She nodded in agreement. "I think you are, too."

His words rushed over themselves. "I don't know how this happened. I'm not sure I like it."

"It's frightening. You'll never be safe again."

Stephen wrapped both hands around his mug. "God, I hate this. Now everything Kat says or does will affect me. Everything that happens to her will happen to me, too. How did I let myself do something this stupid?"

"It doesn't sound stupid to me. It sounds as if you've decided to step into the flow of life."

He grimaced. "I had a choice?"

"You always have a choice, Stephen. Always."

She watched as he rose and headed for the coffeepot. She remembered him standing in her living room so many weeks ago, poised like a jaguar ready to spring. The tight lines of his lean body had shifted from rigidity to grace. Stephen Carmichael no longer looked like a man on the prowl, ready to fight for the right to reach the top. The subtle changes were promising.

"So, what was he like?" The nonchalance in his voice strained credibility.

"Who?" she asked, although she knew.

"Peter Dulaney." He kept his back to her as he topped off the coffee in his mug.

"He was a man like any other. He had his good points and his bad points."

"Tell me a good point."

She hesitated. It was difficult to encapsulate the essence of a man into one easily digested sound bite.

"He was nourished by life," she said finally. "He drew such energy from living that he was able to take a lonely, quiet girl and draw her out into the world."

"And a bad point?"

She once again examined the Peter of her memory, so open, simple, and robust. He'd been perpetual motion personified. She'd always liked him, despite the fact that she'd deduced his greatest flaw early on.

She sighed. "He himself never changed, and he probably never would have. He'd have been like a small town which shelters and inspires its children, only to see them move away when grown. That girl he helped nurture—Katerina, of course—grew into a woman he could never have kept."

Stephen turned to face her. "You really believe that?"

"Peter was uncomplicated. Katerina comes with textures and undercurrents that she's only just begun to explore. Hers will be a growing, straining life, the kind that requires more work than Peter could ever have understood."

Stephen stared into his coffee cup. "She still loves him, you know."

"And she always will. But you should know by now that there are different kinds of love. And God can work through each and every one of them."

He shook his head, smiling the broad smile he still used too rarely. "You always make it sound so easy. Just trust God and everything will be all right."

She shrugged. "Well, that's usually what I think."

"All I have to do is wait and watch."

"I never said that. Life isn't a spectator sport. You've got to participate, let the light flow through you. You know this stuff, Stephen; you've just forgotten."

"Forgotten?"

"Locked it away in your mind, back with the fairy stories and myths. It's always amazed me that people more easily believe in ghosts and goblins than they do in the glory of God."

"Oh! We were so distracted last night that we didn't fill you in. Kat took your advice and asked Valentine what he was."

She leaned back in her chair, surprised. "Did she, now?"

He bent toward her and dropped his voice to a whisper. "He says he's an angel."

"Hmmm." Francesca cupped her chin in her hand. "Interesting."

"I knew he'd lie."

She glanced up. "What do you mean?"

"I don't know much about this stuff, but he's certainly no angel."

Francesca mulled that over as he stood and stretched. "Be careful today," she said. "Remember your armor."

"Yes, ma'am," he said with a mock salute.

She watched idly from the kitchen door as he walked into the living room to fetch his jacket. He dropped the tape into the inside pocket. "See you later, Frannie," he mouthed as he slipped through the front door.

She stood in the doorway for a long time after he left, thinking. Valentine was obviously dark, as low in frequency and as far from the living light of God as one could get. But, somehow, she knew without a doubt that he wasn't lying.

He was an angel.

25

~~~

KAT STEPPED FROM THE SECOND-FLOOR SHOWER TO HEAR pounding on her front door.

"Damn." Dripping wet, she reached for her robe.

She'd awakened at eight o'clock to find herself alone. God only knew when Stephen had left, although she'd noted with relief that the cassette had gone with him. As for Frannie, she was nowhere to be found. Kat vaguely wondered what sort of excuse her aunt had manufactured for her father. After all, Joseph Piretti had never before come down to breakfast to find his daughter asleep on the couch.

The pounding grew louder. Kat quickly pulled on the robe and wrapped a towel around her hair. She hurried down the stairs and to the front door, where she didn't even need the peephole.

"Let me in!" Chris demanded.

She hastily pulled the door latch and unhooked the chain. Chris thundered into the house the second she turned the knob. He shook off her restraining hand and, brandishing a rigid finger in her face, backed her against the wall.

"You let this happen!" he shouted. "You and Stephen left her there!"

Kat registered the dark circles beneath his eyes, as

well as the blond stubble of beard on his jaws and chin. He'd obviously been awake all night, had probably never even made it home.

"What happened?" she asked, hoping that restraint would calm him.

Chris lowered the accusing finger, then staggered backward a step, bewildered. "She stayed at Tia's. She wouldn't come home with me."

"Oh, Chris! You should have called us."

"What could you have done? Attacked Tia's house? Stormed through her living room?" He dropped his head wearily into his hands.

"Why wouldn't she leave with you?"

"She nearly did. I had her out the door. Then this bastard in a wheelchair . . ."

"Donald."

He raised his head. "Donald convinced her to stay." His body tensed and his hands became hard fists. "He did it all in the illustrious name of Valentine, but that asshole wants my wife, plain and simple. You'd have to be blind to miss it. How on earth could Devon . . ."

His words limped to an end. Kat extended a hand. He stared at it without comprehension, then reached to clasp it.

"What am I going to do?" he whispered. "I've got to get her back."

"Maybe she's changed her mind," Kat said, though she didn't think it likely. Donald had cleverly chosen the bait his fish would eat. Devon was hooked on Valentine.

"I'm not sure she'll even want to see me." Chris looked at the floor. "I'm afraid I did some stupid things last night."

"You had good reason. You were upset."

His tired eyes met hers. "I went beyond reason. I couldn't help it. My God, I just love her so much."

He turned away from Kat, shoulders heaving with sobs she couldn't quell. She could hardly bear to witness his pain. Commiseration would force her to revisit the depths of her own loss, and she had no intention of ever opening those doors again.

She shifted from one foot to the other. "Chris. Maybe I can help."

His sobs began to subside. Kat glanced around for a tissue. Finding none, she unwrapped the towel from her hair and handed it to him. Chris wiped his face and drew in a deep breath.

"What can you do?" he asked.

"I can talk to Devon. After last night it makes perfect sense for me to check up on her. Are you sure she's not at work?"

He nodded. "I called. They were surprised to hear from me since she'd just called in sick."

"At least we know where she is. Listen, I've got to get into Tia's to grab those notebooks anyway. Devon's providing the perfect excuse."

"You won't be alone. My guess is Donald will be there, too."

"That's not a problem. He's scum, but he's not dangerous."

"I don't know. He gives me the creeps."

"Of course he does. It's your wife he wants."

He rubbed his chin. "I can't let you go alone," he finally said.

"You have no choice." She walked toward the kitchen with Chris at her heels. "If you go with me,

Devon will think it's a conspiracy. Besides, you need sleep. You're exhausted. Stay here and try to rest."

"Take Stephen with you."

"He's at the restaurant."

"How about Frannie?"

"I don't know where she is. Stop worrying about me." She handed him a mug of coffee. "Drink this and I'll be right back."

She dressed in a flash, pulling on jeans and a tank top. She ran a comb through her long, wet hair and expertly braided it into a thick rope.

It didn't take long, but Chris apparently hadn't needed much urging. Kat trotted downstairs to find him stretched out on the living room couch, arm flung across his face, full coffee mug on the end table beside his head.

"Good," she said out loud. She stopped briefly to scrawl a note for Frannie: "Gone to Tia's. Back soon." She placed it in the middle of the kitchen table and, without waking Chris, left the house.

Donald sat in Tia's dining room, his half-eaten breakfast on the table beside him. The pancakes had long ago become sodden with syrup, but he didn't care. From this spot, he had a premium view of Devon Alexander, still asleep on the sofa. That was all that mattered.

Poor thing. She'd been awake half the night, sobbing out her woes to Tia. Donald had wanted to stay, but Tia had been so adamantly opposed that he'd known it would serve his purpose better to acquiesce. He'd smiled pleasantly and allowed her to roll his chair to the lift. He'd even extended a willing finger to push

the call button. Sometimes giving in to the inconse-
quential mundaneness of life reaped great future
reward. He'd always known how to pick his battles.

There'd be no battle now. He could hear Tia's no-
nonsense heels in the kitchen as she clicked about on
the linoleum, only minutes away from leaving for
Angel Café. And Devon. Sweet Devon. She rested so
serenely, so trustingly on that couch. She was wearing
one of Tia's nightgowns, and while it had appeared
demure in the dimness of early morning, Donald
hoped it would prove more transparent in the
unflinching light of day. One tug of that top sheet from
Devon's luscious body and his eyes could feast.

Devon gave a little sigh and shifted position. Her
foot peeked out from beneath the bottom of the sheet.
Donald groaned. She was wearing pink toenail polish.
How cruel to throw a starving man a goddamned
crumb.

He placed a hand on each wheel rim and propelled
himself toward her.

"Not so fast." Tia's hand, bony but made of iron,
clamped down hard on his shoulder.

"I've finished eating," he said. "I'm simply moving
on."

"I suggest you 'move on' upstairs. She's off limits.
Hear me?"

"Why, Tia, whatever could you mean?" He gazed up
at her, prepared to feign shock.

He'd never seen Tia look so old. He was used to the
leathery quality of her skin, to the outdated hairstyles
and inappropriate clothing. His sister could never envision herself beyond the mid-sixties, the era during
which she'd first met Valentine. But Tia looked particu-

larly frightful this morning, nearly haglike with those tired lines etched deeply under her eyes and those slumped shoulders.

"I told you Dana quit," she said sharply. "I didn't tell you that I know why. I don't want to know your perversions, Donald. I don't give a shit. I just want you to understand that Devon Alexander is not your next toy."

"Why, Tia." He laid a hand over his heart and widened his eyes.

"You heard me. When her husband comes for her today . . . and he *will* come . . . you stay out of it. Either I get your word on that, or I'm calling in sick right now."

"Calling in sick? You can't do that. Who will make our millions?"

"Shut up, Donald. The money was never yours in the first place. You're just lucky I'm so good to you."

"No, sweetheart," he said in a low voice. "I'm just lucky that a touch of moral guilt has remained with you all these years."

She reddened. "Enough. I've paid my dues. I've got a call in to an employment agency. They'll find you a new nurse. I'll pay her wages, but that's it. I'm through with you. Do you hear me?"

"I hear you, but I know better. Look at me."

She turned her back to gather the breakfast dishes. He followed her into the kitchen, ramming her legs when she refused to meet his glare.

"Look at me, Brenda!" he commanded, and she whirled about in surprise at the name nobody used anymore. "Remember what I was before the accident?"

She swallowed and averted her eyes.

"Well, *I* remember," he said fiercely. "I was gorgeous, wasn't I. Captain of the football team, everybody's favorite date. I didn't have any trouble getting laid in those days, I can tell you that. They lined up for me, then. But look what you let happen to me."

He reached out and tugged insistently at her hand, squeezing her fingers until she gave a little yelp and stared woodenly into his face.

"It wasn't my fault," she said coldly. "I didn't tell you to get drunk and go joyriding with your buddies. Jesus Christ, Donald, you were nineteen, old enough to know right from wrong."

"As far as I was concerned, 'right' was whatever Valentine suggested. *You* taught me that."

Her skin had grown pallid beneath the tan.

"All I wanted," Donald continued, "was for you to channel Valentine. All I needed was to know whether or not I should go out that night. And what did you say, Tia? What did you say?"

"I'm not rehashing this again!"

"You said it was time to make up my own mind, didn't you. You said you thought we were relying on Valentine just a little too much, that maybe it was time to back off."

"And you know what?" Her voice was a violin E string careening screechily out of tune. "I was probably right! I should have followed my own advice and started closing the door on Valentine back then! I could have done it, too, if you hadn't gone and gotten yourself banged up in that car!"

"Oh, yes, Tia. Turning Valentine away was such a helpful idea. I'm the living proof. You could have saved me. All you had to do was channel him." He banged the arms of the wheelchair. "*This* is the result of your selfish experiment. This!"

She stood before him, still holding the plate of pancakes in one hand, the coffee cup in the other. "You know what, Donald?" she asked in a cracked voice. "There was a time years and years ago when I thought I heard somebody calling my name. Not 'Tia Melody,' mind you, but Brenda. Just Brenda. The voice came from deep inside me, somewhere Valentine couldn't touch. I wanted to hear more of it, but Valentine kept getting in the way. He'd talk over it. He'd laugh at it. He'd point out that I'd never get anywhere in this world without wealth or beauty."

"He was right," Donald said.

"Maybe. I can't honestly say that he's let me down. He promised money and delivered. He promised a loyal following and delivered that, too. But that other voice . . . I wanted to reach it. I could tell that whoever was calling knew every mistake I'd ever made, every weakness I had, all my faults, and it was okay."

"Get to the point, Tia. The convent doesn't become you."

She paused for a moment, then shook her head angrily. "There isn't a point. I just wanted Valentine to shut up for a while so I could think. Then you had that accident and there he was, the one offering all the advice for me to pass on. There isn't a point anymore except . . ."

"Forgive my boredom. Except what?"

Tia trudged to the sink and carefully lowered the dish and cup into it. "Except that I sometimes wonder what might have happened, that's all."

"Do you want me to tell you?" He fixed her with a

piercing glare. "You'd have lived the Harper history, hon. A bunch of brats in a too-small house. Never enough money. Real attractive, right? Check with your precious 'inner voice.' Maybe it does windows and provides groceries. More likely than not, it just tells you how flawed you are and lays a giant guilt trip on your head."

"Sounds familiar," Tia said acidly. "Sounds like where I am now." She glanced at her watch. "I mean what I say. You lay one paw on Devon Alexander, and you can kiss your ass goodbye. Got that?"

"I cringe in horror."

"You will. Believe me."

He rolled his chair into the dining room to watch her exit. He had to hand it to Tia. She'd always had a flair for the dramatic.

"Don't forget to slam the door," he said, but she upstaged him. The quiet, muffled click of the lock was positively eerie.

He swung his eyes back to Devon. God, she was gorgeous. She'd shifted position again so that one long leg crossed the other outside the sheet. The top of the sheet had pulled back slightly, and he cursed his sister's taste. Why couldn't Tia's flamboyance have extended to nightwear? This nightgown belonged in a girls' boarding school. The scoop neck stopped well above Devon's beautiful breasts, and he could see only the faintest outline of her body beneath the opaque material.

Well, he had time. He and this lovely lady were quite alone and would be for hours. He rolled closer to her, enjoying the familiar pull in his groin as he studied her. Sometimes, that sensation was the only thing that made his life tolerable. He allowed his eyes to rake across her. Her lips were pretty, but he'd never been much of a lip man. Her hair, on the other hand, was extraordinary. He shuddered at the thought of its silky softness traveling the length of his body.

He reached the edge of the couch. Hmmm. She had a pale sprinkling of freckles across her shoulders. He supposed he could live with that. The rest of her promised so much that he could afford to overlook her few imperfections.

He extended a hand toward the sheet. What harm could there be in wanting to see more, in wanting to touch . . .

A searing flash of light threw him backward in his chair. He closed his eyes to it, only to find that it had emanated from his mind in the first place, and now waited for him.

He was inside the speeding car, flying above the bushes below, plummeting downward. This time the vision did not stop in its customary spot. Instead, the car continued its wild free fall, and the earth grew closer and closer.

"No!" Donald screamed.

The image vanished, but words raced through his head.

First, you do my will. Katerina, then Devon.

Donald gasped for air, surprised to find it available. Cautiously he opened his eyes.

He was staring into Devon's frightened face.

"Ÿ . . . you screamed." She clutched the sheet beneath her chin.

"I apologize." His voice sounded shaky, but at least it still worked. "You looked so peaceful there that I must have dozed off myself. A dream. That's all it was."

"Somebody's at the door," Devon said. Her quick, shallow breathing reminded him of a trapped animal. "Could you answer it? I'm not dressed."

"Why answer at all? It will only be for Tia."

"Yes, but . . ." She blushed, and he bitterly realized that she fully expected her able-bodied husband to come and carry her home. He'd have to squelch that little flame quickly, he could see that.

He barreled angrily to the door, then boldly swung it open, bracing himself to meet the wronged and mighty Mr. Alexander. His line of vision dropped several inches before coming in contact with Katerina Piretti.

"I hope I'm not intruding," she said.

It was ridiculous, really. Hardly an even trade. This pretty little poppet in exchange for his elegant, beautiful Devon. But, then, that was Valentine's problem. Donald was obviously getting the better end of the deal.

"Intruding?" he said, sliding backward to let her in. "Nonsense, Ms. Piretti. We are delighted."

26

mm

"FRANNIE, IT'S BEEN ENTIRELY TOO LONG." SISTER ELISABETH Merchant rose from behind the oak desk of her university faculty office to warmly grasp Francesca's hand.

Francesca returned the handshake with a broad smile. "I meant to keep in touch, Elisabeth. I really did. Time just has a habit of slipping away from me."

Dr. Merchant tucked a strand of chin-length blond hair behind her ear and smiled. "It always did," she said dryly. "You were always late. Late for class, late for Mass, even late for meals. Fortunately for you, there's no time to scold. I've got a class in twenty minutes. To what do I owe the pleasure?"

"What are you teaching this semester?" It seemed rude to drop in after years simply to pump an old friend for information.

Dr. Merchant's face lit up, much as it had years ago when the two had debated philosophy while still in the novitiate. It heartened Francesca. They might be thirty years older, but the spark of knowledge could still ignite an enthusiastic flame.

"It's a good semester," Elisabeth said, cheeks as rosy as the deep red suit she wore. "Never mind the comparative religion survey course. It's a great course, if I do say so myself. Unfortunately, it's stocked with students more interested in the credits than the material.

I've got two upper level electives this year that are right up your alley, though. One is a study of women's role in the Judeo-Christian tradition. The other is my next class, and it's dear to my heart. Medieval Mysticism: the Sacred and Profane."

"I believe you're an answer to my prayers," Francesca said.

"Am I, now?" Elisabeth settled comfortably in her chair, a grin hovering about her mouth. "If memory serves me correctly, that used to be my line. And the phrase always meant trouble."

Francesca took in the office, from the crammed bookshelves to the richly hued oriental rug at her feet. "Apparently you've changed considerably. You've done better than I ever expected you would."

Her friend chuckled. "I've missed you, Frannie, you and your annoying honesty. It feels like decades since we plotted together."

"It *has* been."

"You must be happy. You look terrific."

"God has been kind to us both."

Elisabeth gave a satisfied sigh. "Yes, God obviously knew better than either of us where our paths should lie. If anybody had told me all those years ago that you'd be the one to leave the convent, I'd never have believed them. I was always the troublemaker. You seemed so happy, so content. Your faith was so strong."

"That's why I was able to leave," Francesca said gently. "You know the feeling. That call you can't hide from, no matter how hard you try."

"I know it well. It's why I stayed. How is Katerina?"

"She's in a jam. I'm afraid I've come with an ulterior motive. I need your expertise."

"Hopefully not in raising children."

"Believe me, Katerina is no longer a child. It was so much easier when she was. No, it isn't about raising children." Francesca leaned forward on the desk, meeting her old friend's gaze with solid candor. "Elisabeth, you're the only person I could think of who would know this. Who on earth is Asteroth?"

Elisabeth drew back. "Asteroth?"

Francesca nodded. "I think he's supposed to be an angel."

"He is indeed. A fallen one." She swiveled in her chair to reach for the coffeepot. "Does your question come from a sudden interest in black magic?"

"You know better. No, I'm afraid it comes from personal experience." She absently watched her friend pour two cups of coffee.

"Ever hear of grimoires?" Elisabeth asked, dropping two cubes of sugar into her cup.

"No."

"They're medieval. Basically, they're self-proclaimed treatises on transcendental magic. They give detailed information on the hierarchies of spirits, both infernal and divine."

"They sound silly."

"They weren't considered so, believe me." Elisabeth passed her a cup. "They were extremely eloquent . . . pompous, even. They spoke of spirit forms as if the entities were as solid and real as the peasant next door."

Francesca took a hasty swig of coffee to stop the chill crawling up her spine. "Go on."

Elisabeth eyed her sharply. "One of the most famous of these grimoires is called *The Lesser Key of Solomon*. It provides detailed explanations of about seventy-two spirits."

"Infernal or divine?"

"Oh, quite definitely infernal. They were supposedly locked in a brass vessel by King Solomon and then tossed into a lake. The legend is that a bunch of overzealous Babylonians, expecting to find treasure, dredged up the vessel and opened it. Out popped the spirits to return to their original spots of power in the world."

"Kind of like Pandora's box," Francesca said.

"Precisely. You've studied mythology. You know as well as I do that there's a strong link between pagan lore and religious . . ."

Francesca held up a weary hand. "Forgive me, Elisabeth. I know I owe you more than this, but we're running out of time, and I need to know more."

Dr. Merchant checked her watch and gave a resigned sigh. "You're right. At any rate, Asteroth is one of those spirits."

"I thought you said he was a fallen angel."

"People have tried to define angels for centuries. According to Milton, one-third of the heavenly host fell along with Lucifer. Asteroth, formerly of the angelic principality of Thrones, was among them. What else can a fallen angel be but a demon? Such a spirit has turned by its own will from the light of God. *The Lesser Key of Solomon* describes Asteroth as more than willing to discuss the fall. The catch is that he always pretends he himself was exempt from it."

Francesca frowned and set down her half-finished coffee. It hadn't helped. She still felt chilled to the bone. She wrapped her arms across her chest and rose to stare out the window.

There was no need to question the reality of Asteroth. She knew he was real, knew it dismally down to the core of her being. *The Lesser Key of Solomon* had only nudged forward what her heart had known for weeks: "Valentine" was a far greater evil than she'd ever supposed.

"Are you all right?" Elisabeth stood, brow furrowed with concern.

Francesca gathered her thoughts. "I will be. Is there more?"

"Not much. Traditionally, Asteroth has been traced in both male and female form, from Aphrodite to Tammuz to Astarte."

"He encompasses both sexes, then."

"Yes. Always beautiful and enchanting, but cruel and cold. The grimoire notes that he'll truthfully answer questions concerning past, present, and future. Given mankind's insatiable need to preview the future, you can see why he might appeal to the masses."

Valentine's predictions. Francesca once again turned from the scrutiny of Elisabeth's gaze, this time concentrating her attentions on a brass rubbing hanging on the wall.

"I like that," she said in a halfhearted attempt to divert searching questions.

"It's Saint George," Elisabeth said. "He's England's patron saint, you know, and I acquired it over there. I liked it because it's one of the few renderings of George without that damn mythical dragon. Though perhaps you could make use of a dragon-slayer where Asteroth's concerned. He supposedly manifests as a beautiful angel astride a dragon."

Francesca's head snapped around. "Tell me that again. Slowly."

Her friend studied her for a moment. "You're in deep, aren't you."

Francesca nodded. She felt sure that her own armor was strong, and she would willingly accept whatever action was required of her. But she feared for the three greenhorns by her side.

"Yes," she said in answer to Elisabeth's question. "It appears that I am."

"What can I do?"

Francesca smiled at her old friend. Elisabeth had thankfully maintained the charming trait of not requiring details before offering help.

"Prayer and meditation," she said. "Send me some light."

"I'll pass the word."

Both women glanced at the clock atop the bookshelf.

"You'd better go to class," Francesca said. "I'll call you as soon as I can. I owe you an explanation."

"Yes," Elisabeth agreed, gathering her notes. "You do. But until then, go safely in God. Close the door behind you when you leave. And for heaven's sake, Frannie, be careful!"

Francesca returned her gaze to Saint George as the office door shut softly. He gazed back from antiquity, his face grim.

"You'll need to come with me, you know," she told him. "Especially if you can truly slay dragons."

The clock began to chime eleven. Each sound of bells forced Francesca further back into physical reality.

She had to find Katerina.

27

~~~

WITH THAT STUPID SMILE AND THAT INSISTENTLY BOBBING head, Donald reminded Kat of a dopey, spring-necked novelty bouncing in the rear window of a car.

Delighted, my ass, she thought, stepping around the wheelchair to stand in the foyer.

"I've come to see Devon. She wasn't at her apartment or at work, so naturally I thought I'd try here."

"Naturally." He turned to face her.

"After last night . . ." She allowed the words to trail as she craned her neck to glance into the living room. Devon sat on the couch, a vacant stare on her face. Concerned, Kat hurried toward her.

Her secretary gazed up, gray eyes rimmed with pink. "Kat. How kind of you to come."

Kat grabbed her hand and sat beside her. "Devon, you've got to come with me."

She hadn't meant to start that way. The approach smacked of desperation, and she'd meant to radiate humanitarian concern. But Devon looked so much worse than she remembered, so listless and wan. And Donald, watching them with the eyes of a fish, gave off distinctly disturbing vibes.

The wheelchair rolled to her side. "Katerina, my dear, our friend is only following Valentine's advice. He told her to stay here with me—and Tia—until he says otherwise."

Kat unconsciously brushed away the hand he'd laid upon her arm. "Listen to me, Devon. Chris called me this morning."

A spark of interest lit Devon's face. "He did?"

"He's worried to death about you. Please, he loves you so much. Let me take you home."

"He was a bastard last night." Donald's voice cut through their conversation.

"He knows that." Kat refused to release Devon from eye contact. "He's so terribly sorry. He's ashamed. That's why he asked me to come."

Devon flushed. "I guess neither of us was at our best."

"Come." Kat tucked a hand under her friend's elbow and helped her rise. She could not stop herself from sending a disapproving sideways glance in Donald's direction. The expression of unmasked dislike she met there drew her up short. Well, she didn't like him, either.

"Where are your clothes, Devon?"

"Um . . . upstairs. I changed upstairs."

"Go get dressed. I'll wait here."

Donald's head swiveled as Devon floated past him and up the stairs. Then he turned back to Kat, an ingratiating smile on his face.

"You're such a good friend," he said.

She was only a little over five feet tall, and she was standing right beside him, quite alone. Donald's mind galloped behind his plastic smile. Devon was about to slip away with this pygmy-sized fly in the ointment, but he could prevent that. All he had to do was eliminate Katerina Piretti.

Damn it! Here was opportunity flung in his face, and he had no plan, no way to effectuate the necessary result.

Help me, Valentine! He was only trying to do the great lord's will, after all. *Come to me, Valentine. I'm summoning you!*

For a moment all remained still. Then, like an approaching wave, Donald sensed a curious roar at the edge of the stillness. The hairs on the back of his neck began to rise. A blast of cold air frosted his skin, as if a row of ice sculptures breathed behind him. He'd felt that cloud of frost before. Once he'd even caught the outline of creatures traced in the frigid fog.

He glanced at Katerina. She remained rooted to her spot, apparently unaware that they were no longer alone.

What an idiot. She was occupied with minutia, too stupid to realize that she stood in the presence of true and awesome power.

His smile grew more genuine.

He heard a bestial snort behind him, the pawing of a clawed foot on the ground.

Valentine's legions were arriving.

"Katerina," he said, "I would love a cup of tea, but I can't reach anything in Tia's kitchen. Would you help me?"

She wavered. He watched the indecision flicker across her face, but knew she'd do as he'd asked. Poor thing, the good Samaritan in her was going to win out over common sense.

"Okay," she said ungraciously, following him into the kitchen.

"Make yourself a cup, too. Tia wouldn't want a guest to leave without a cup of something."

"Hey." Stephen pushed open his office door to find Tia sitting in the midst of a blue haze of cigarette smoke. "You're on. Molly tells me you've got a long list of clients waiting for you."

She turned her violet eyes toward him. The corner of her mouth twitched. "Something's wrong," she said.

"Not yet. But it will be if you don't get out there. Come on, Tia, it's getting late."

"Columbine says something's wrong," she insisted. She cocked her head, as if listening. Stephen watched the color drain from her face. "Where's your girl-friend?"

"Katie?" He stepped all the way into the room, closing the door behind him with a solid bang. "Why?"

"I don't know why," she answered miserably. "It isn't clear. But something's wrong."

"Find out!"

Tia placed calloused fingertips on each temple and closed her eyes. She instantly clapped her hands over her ears. "Noise! There's just noise!"

She jumped as a rap sounded on the office door.

"What is it?" Stephen called, too preoccupied to turn around.

The door opened, but before Molly could usher in the visitor, Francesca Piretti swept into the room.

"Thank you," she told the startled Molly, closing the door in her face. "Stephen, something is very wrong."

Francesca's gaze met Tia's, and for a moment their eyes locked.

"You," Francesca said quietly.

Confused, Stephen gently touched her shoulder. "Francesca, this is Tia Melody. Tia, Katie's aunt, Francesca Piretti."

But neither woman seemed to hear. They stared toward each other, but not at each other. Stephen followed Francesca's line of vision and saw that it rested over Tia's shoulder, as if she saw a screen there. She'd grown pale. He turned toward Tia. On her face was an expression of such longing that it almost pained him to see it.

Francesca turned to him. "Katerina has gone to Ms. Melody's house. She left a note."

He nodded dumbly.

"I think she's in trouble. We'd better get there fast."

He knew by now that there was little point in arguing with her. Mechanically he reached for the doorknob.

Francesca once again studied Tia. Slowly she extended her hand. "Are you coming with us?"

Tia rose and followed them out of the room.

The entire house felt cold by now. In his mind's eye Donald saw them everywhere: creatures with webbed feet and tiny wings, emaciated human figures with contorted facial features, beautiful, strong angels with sneers of pure ice. They breathed frozen particles into the air. There were so many of them! It amused him that Katerina could see nothing. He suspected that she felt the cold, though. She shivered slightly as she impatiently shifted in her chair.

"I'd better check on Devon," she said.

"Oh, I wouldn't worry about her," Donald said casually. "She's probably washing, putting on makeup. She'll want to look good for her husband."

But Kat rose, determinedly wiping the palms of her hands on her jeans. "I'll go all the same."

Fear leaped within him like a bouncing ball. She'd trot upstairs, stepping unaware through the throngs of his unseen helpmates, and hurry Devon along. Then the beautiful Ms. Alexander would drift from his life forever, never to be enjoyed by him in any way, shape, or form. How sad.

It was worse than sad. It was unacceptable.

"Come," he said, grasping the delicate bones of her wrist. "I'll let you ride up in my lift. That's always a lot of fun. Children love it." Or would have loved it, had he known any children.

He propelled her toward the pantry door. She stumbled, causing him to slow his pace. He flashed a smile as he tightened his grip. "Sorry. I forget that my wheels are so much faster than feet."

Kat glared at Donald as the door to the lift closed before them.

"Let go of me," she said.

He did. She massaged her wrist, casting poisonous looks his way. Then she turned her attentions to the elevator shaft as he pulled the lever and the lift began its slow climb.

She glanced up. The shaft gaped above her, extending to the third floor. She was not the least bit claustrophobic and found this narrow tunnel fascinating. Ah, yes, there was the metal plate. Her fingers itched to pry it apart and grab the notebooks it concealed.

As if it could read her mind, the lift stopped, so suddenly that a shudder ran through the metal platform. Startled, Kat turned toward Donald. His hand rested on the lever. He'd pulled it. No wonder they'd stopped!

"Is there a problem?" she asked, arching an inquisitive eyebrow.

"Valentine seems to think so," he answered pleasantly. "Why does he dislike you so much, Ms. Piretti?"

Kat bristled. "I couldn't say. Maybe it's because I'm utterly unimpressed by his words of wisdom."

A chill wind whistled through the shaft. This surprised Kat, for she could see no space through which wind might pass. Even if a crack existed, the temperature outside was already steamy.

"Let's go," she said with a shiver. "We can talk upstairs."

He was still smiling that creepy grin. His teeth reflected what little light the stationary flashlight provided. He looked like the Cheshire cat in *Alice in Wonderland*.

"I like the privacy," he said, and she noticed his right hand travel down his useless leg toward the cuff of his jeans.

With a jerk, the lift began to move again. It caught Donald off guard, almost throwing him forward in his chair. He regained his balance and flailed once again for the lever, but it was too late. They'd already crested the second-floor doorjamb.

Devon Alexander flung the door open with a shy apology. "Oops. I didn't know you were on board. I was ready to come down and I thought I'd try the elevator. Sorry. I guess it's the kid in me."

"I guess it is." Kat stepped hurriedly from the lift, not even pausing to look at Donald. "We'll take the stairs, Devon. I want to get out of here."

28

DONALD SAW THE DARK, WRITHING CREATURES FAR MORE clearly on the second floor of Tia's house. He also saw why Katerina Piretti had managed to slip away. A narrow aura of light—a force field, almost—encapsulated her. Grotesque mutations surrounded her, their heads held between scaly hands. They blew barbed arrows of ice from between twisted lips. None of their grimaces, however, penetrated that glowing rim.

It was just as well. His plan had been clumsy, born of lust rather than thought. He'd have to curb his desire, although that wouldn't be easy with Devon in sight. He appraised her as he absently patted the knife tucked in his sock. She'd washed the sleep from her eyes, applied a hint of makeup. Ravishing.

But she and Kat were retreating now, down the hallway and toward the stairs.

"Come back," he whispered, stricken. The elfin beings nipping at Devon's heels turned to laugh at him, their glassy eyes filled with loathing. Goddamn hyenas. They laughed at anybody, even those on their own side.

But at least they were here, growing more visible by the minute, clinging to Devon like koalas to a eucalyptus tree.

Donald gasped and pulled himself straighter in his

chair. Valentine was indeed good. The slime couldn't touch Kat for some reason, but Devon . . . Devon was clearly accessible, an open channel through which he might break Kat's protection.

"Come back," he called.

Kat kept walking, but Devon, sweet Devon, turned on her heel mid-stride, just as he'd known she would.

"Let me say goodbye," he said, palms turned plaintively upward.

Devon floated back up the hall, hand extended in friendship. "Thank you for all your help," she said.

Donald grasped her hand and squarely met her gaze. "You know where to find me. Good luck, Devon."

"Thank you." She turned to leave.

He pulled her back with a light tug. "Forgive me. Maybe it isn't my place to speak, but I can't bear to watch this situation continue."

Kat had begun a slow, steady walk toward them. She glared at him with such intensity that he began to suspect she'd prove a more difficult adversary than he'd thought.

"I can hardly wait to hear your assessment of Devon's situation," she said acidly. He immediately pinpointed a major weakness. Kat possessed a finely honed sense of righteous justice. It made her tiresome. Far more important, it could easily push a less morally indignant individual completely to the opposing side.

"I'm sure you can't wait," he countered, "since my comments concern you."

Devon stood swaying between them, pretty mouth opened in confusion. Kat tossed her head and silently dared him to speak.

He'd never met a dare he didn't take.

"Devon, my dear, how did your husband know Katerina's telephone number?"

"Oh." Devon's brow relaxed. "Remember, I work for her at Harper, Madigan and Horn."

"That would explain how he knew her work number. But you told me she hasn't been at the office for a while."

"I guess he looked her up in the phone book," Devon said, but her sentence wobbled at the end, and a worried little pucker once again appeared between her brows.

"Maybe. But why? And how did he know where to find you last night? If he was at work and you left no message . . ."

"She's always here," Kat said. "Where else would he look?"

"How do you know she's always here?" Donald shot back.

"I . . . just do." Kat turned red.

"Know what I think?" Donald threw the full force of his accusation in Kat's direction. "I think the source of your husband's information is Katerina herself. I think she and your husband are closer than she cares to admit."

"This is bullshit," Kat said.

"You're sleeping with him, Ms. Piretti, aren't you?" Donald's eyes glittered.

"Bullshit!" Kat repeated through mounting fury. "Devon, you know better!"

But Devon, stunned by the chaos, stood frozen to her spot in the hallway.

"Poor Devon," Donald said softly. "I know you love him. And I know you trust her. But it's clear they've betrayed you."

A bright, hot pink flooded Devon's face.

Kat raised her voice. "Don't listen to him! It's a lie!"

"Look at her." Donald swallowed back a smirk. "Protesting loudly, the picture of righteous indignation. But he was waiting for her in their usual place last night, just waiting for the circle to end. This time, though, there was no time for a romp in bed. Instead, she told your husband where you were, warned him that you were catching on to their little game. *She* sent him to Tia's last night!"

It was an even better shot than he'd expected. Praise Valentine, Kat looked guilty, almost as guilty as if he'd pulled out incriminating photographs of a secret rendezvous between her and Chris Alexander. He didn't for a minute believe they were having an affair—he'd sensed a definite current between Kat and Stephen Carmichael—but her reaction provided more than enough fuel for the accusation. He rolled his wheelchair forward. Kat took a step backward. Devon remained planted, hands balled into hard fists.

"Ask her," he urged. To his right, a languid angel raised drooping indigo wings and smiled indolently through slitted eyes. "Ask her just how well she knows your husband."

Kat flattened herself against the wall. "Devon, can't you see what he's trying to do?"

"I speak in the name of Valentine," Donald said. "And Valentine speaks only truth."

"Kat." Devon held her chin high and advanced slowly. "How well do you know Chris?"

Donald watched, fascinated, as a tiny winged creature lit on Devon's right shoulder. It leaned toward her ear and whispered into it. Devon's eyes widened with shock, and he knew she'd been handed an image of

Chris and Kat together, entwined in a passionate embrace of pure lust. He could not help smiling at the simplicity of it. Feed a fearful, thirsty mind any thought, and not only would it leap to believe, it would rush to adopt the thought as its own.

Fear was working its way into Kat's heart as well. The light around her had dimmed somewhat, and Donald detected a definite chink near her shoulder. Then, she suddenly drew herself up to her full height— an ineffectual waste of energy, he thought—and the light brightened once again.

"Devon," Kat said in a clear voice, "you're right. Chris and I are friends. He came to me because of his love for you."

"Well, that's a new line," Donald drawled.

"Shut up!" Kat whirled toward him. "You've no right to do this! Devon, your husband came to ask my help. He's worried to death about you. He wanted—"

"I think we all know what he wanted." Donald rolled forward, blocking Kat into her spot against the wall. He took Devon's trembling hand. Her face had contorted into a mixture of anger and nausea. Her cheeks were red, and her eyes bulged slightly. He recognized rage in search of an outlet. Perfect. "I'm sorry, Devon. But it's better to learn bad news through friends than—"

"How could you, Kat?" Devon demanded, a dark, ominous undercurrent rimming her voice. "How dare you?"

The indigo angel Donald had noticed before drifted to Devon's left. It lifted a clawlike fingernail and gently, imperceptibly, pushed aside a strand of hair from Devon's ear. Its breath hung like steam on the air as it whispered. Donald caught the satisfied smirk on its face when it withdrew.

Devon clapped her hands over her ears.

"Obviously, she tempted him," Donald said. "She's beautiful in a mysterious sort of way, don't you think? There she was, so vulnerable and needy. And your noble husband is so easily taken by any damsel in distress."

Kat made a break for the stairs. Donald's eyebrows raised in pleased surprise as Devon blocked her path.

"Damn you!" Devon whispered through gritted teeth.

"But, Devon, I didn't—"

"The world outside the brotherhood of Valentine has no moral code," Donald said.

"How long has this been going on?" Devon demanded savagely. "All that time I worried about you, was afraid you were so lonely . . . you bitch!"

How lovely to watch. Donald folded his hands and gazed with rapt attention as more of Valentine's horde joined the fray, attracted by the tumult. The little beasts seemed to thrive on chaos. They loved it, were addicted to it. Donald had never before seen them this clearly, but he couldn't remember an earthly battle where he hadn't been aware of their participation. At least, he couldn't remember one since Valentine had entered his life.

He watched proudly as Devon grabbed each of Kat's wrists and pinned them to the wall. Perhaps on her own she'd never consider such drastic action. But, as he knew, Devon was no longer on her own. She had the aid of Valentine's acolytes, both seen and unseen. They were more than happy to stoke her rage.

"Valentine teaches justice," he said. "An eye for an eye."

An image of Devon clothed in a gladiator's short skirt and molded metal bra sent a wave of lust washing through him. It nearly knocked him breathless.

Kat was struggling now, kicking to break loose from Devon's grip. She was more in his way than ever.

"Bring her to me," he commanded.

Devon remained glued to her spot, firmly holding Kat's wrists. Donald impatiently rolled toward them. With a surge of strength, he grabbed Kat around the waist and plucked her from her place.

"Hold her hands," he ordered. The beautiful indigo angel raised her claws over Devon's head in some sort of benediction. "Hold her hands," the angel parroted, and her eyes, so dull before, glowed as two red-hot coals in the night.

A sliver of light fell across Devon, and Donald saw a look of dismay flash across the angel's face. He turned to see what had caused the light. Another angel, tall and nearly iridescent, floated several feet away. It glowed so brightly that Donald, with Kat immobilized across his lap, averted his eyes. Couldn't anyone else see this? He glanced quickly from Kat to Devon. Apparently not.

The new angel raised his sword. A second illuminating stripe of light shot from the tip. Devon looked away.

"The stairs," Donald said. "Get her to the stairs. It's got to look like an accident."

He gripped Kat's wrists tightly as Devon wheeled the chair toward the top of the stairs. She probably didn't realize that she was about to become an accomplice in Katerina Piretti's death. That was just fine. It would provide a little extra leverage should she ever try to refuse him anything. He noted their growing entourage of otherworldly courtiers. Valentine had certainly come through. He, in turn, would pledge eternal fealty in exchange for the gift of this woman.

The iridescent angel once again raised his mighty sword, flashing the light with increased urgency. This time he aimed it directly at Devon's heart. Donald, mesmerized, watched as the angel rippled with waves of violet, pink, and gold.

Devon glanced up, confused, and for a moment stopped pushing the wheelchair. The indigo angel sneered. Then she fanned her long fingers across Devon's chest, shielding her heart.

With a new burst of determination, Devon gave the wheelchair a mighty shove.

Kat opened her mouth and shrieked.

"Stop!" Donald shouted. "It's over, Ms. Piretti. Do you understand? The least you can do is face the inevitable with dignity!"

The front door banged open against the foyer wall.

"Kat!" a strong voice called.

As if awakened from a deep dream, Devon shook her head and released her grip on the chair. "Chris?"

Donald let out a reflexive roar. Kat took advantage of the distraction and rammed her elbow into his solar plexus. As he gasped for air, she leaped from his lap and dashed down the stairs.

Chris Alexander caught her at the bottom of the flight.

"They're . . . they're trying to kill me!" she gasped.

But when Chris looked up the stairs, he saw only his wife, tears coursing down her cheeks as she gazed down at them entwined in each other's arms.

The wheels of Donald's chair creaked as he made his slow, painful way back toward the lift.

29

~~~~

"ARE YOU ALL RIGHT?" CHRIS HELD KAT TIGHTLY.

She struggled to exhale. "Your timing is impeccable."

"I followed you." He stared at Devon while processing Kat's words. "They're trying to kill me," she'd said, but only his wife stood shivering at the top of the stairs. Surely, Devon wasn't part of that "they."

"I thought you were asleep." Kat steadied herself with a final breath and backed away from the protective circle of his arms.

"You're slipping, Kat. You're usually not that gullible. Where's Donald?"

"Probably heading for the lift."

"Wheelchair or no, I won't tangle with that maniac alone. Get out of here. I'll grab Devon and meet you outside."

"I can't leave yet. I don't have the notebooks."

"They'll wait."

"We can't be sure of that!"

Devon began to drift slowly, mechanically, down the stairs.

"Careful," Kat whispered. "She thinks you and I are lovers."

"What?" His head whipped around.

Wheels creaked across the linoleum kitchen floor.

"You and Devon get help," Kat said, racing up the stairs. "I'll be out as quickly as I can."

He'd known Kat long enough by now to recognize that look of tight determination on her face. There was no way to stop her. He could only pray that she'd be fast and careful.

Devon reached the final step and stood tearfully before him. "I can't believe it's come to this," she said in a low voice. "But I saw it. You and Kat . . ."

"You've seen nothing but shadows." Chris grasped her shoulders. She looked so drained. He peered into her eyes, searching for a spark.

The dining room floorboards groaned as Donald's chair rolled across them. Little time remained for explanations.

"Oh, my Devon." All the words in the world would not call back a spirit so shattered. Chris drew her close. "Don't you know how much I love you? I'd die for you, honey."

She relaxed in his embrace, head resting against him, arms wrapped around his neck as if she could no longer bear her own weight. His body felt electrified where it touched hers, as if he and his wife had somehow become one glowing being of light. He became aware that he was murmuring the same words over and over again, a mantra: "I love you, Mary Devon, I love you." He never used her given name, but this call to her flowed unbidden from the depths of his heart. He could not have changed it had he wanted to.

"What's happening to us?" she asked, gazing up at him in confusion.

He took her chin in his hand and caught a hint of promise in her brimming eyes. She was still there, and as long as even a particle of her heart longed to meet his, there was hope.

"It'll be all right," he said. "But we've got to leave this house."

Donald's chair halted before them. "Why? Am I really so poor a host?"

Still holding Devon, Chris turned slowly to face him.

The man's voice snapped through the room like the crack of broken icicles. "Where is our good friend, Katerina?"

"She's gone." Chris's mouth twitched as he willed himself not to look up the stairs.

"Such a high-strung young woman," Donald said calmly. "So quick to fly off the handle over nothing at all. She's still here. I never heard the front door."

"You must have been in the lift."

"Ah." Donald studied him for a moment. "So you know about the lift. How convenient. What else do you know?" He turned a soulful gaze toward Devon. "My dear, please don't make me rely upon the word of your husband. We both know how deceptive he can be."

A hot flush rose to Devon's face. "He's not!"

Donald straightened in his chair, surprised that he'd lost influence so rapidly. Trembling beneath his hard-eyed scrutiny, Devon burrowed further into the safety of Chris's arms.

"I certainly won't hold your thoughts against you," Donald said. "He is, indeed, the strong, handsome type, and I can see why you're so easily swayed. But don't lie to me. It would absolutely destroy my faith in humanity. You would never lie, Devon, would you?"

Her head jerked nervously from side to side.

"Good. Because Valentine, ever righteous, punishes

those who lie. Devon, I ask you in the name of Valentine, did Katerina leave?"

"Only God's name carries weight," Chris said through clenched teeth.

Donald shook his head as he leaned back in his chair. "Really, Mr. Alexander, your point escapes me. In the name of God, then, if that makes you feel better. Last I heard, your God didn't condone lying any more than Valentine does. In fact, I thought God-the-Father kept a nice, fiery hell for liars. All right, then. Devon, I ask you in the name of all immovable and imaginable deities, did Katerina leave this house?"

Devon hid her face in Chris's T-shirt.

"A charming picture," Donald said. "And, as they say, worth a thousand words." He swung the wheelchair around and headed back toward the kitchen.

Chris's chin jerked up. The lift. He was going upstairs.

"Devon." He gave his wife a little shake. "Devon, I've got to stop him. I need your help." He released her. She remained motionless in the center of the foyer, a dazed expression on her face. "Please, Devon. You've got to get help."

She observed him blankly, as if incapable of processing a thought.

"Devon!" Chris stared, not knowing an antidote for her lethargy.

She stared back.

He had no choice. Leaving her in the foyer, he raced into the kitchen after Donald.

"Look at the house," Francesca said quietly as Stephen parked his car across from Tia's home. "Do you see?"

He squinted, searching the scene for anything out of the ordinary. "I guess not," he admitted. The row house looked a little tacky and rundown, but perfectly normal.

From the back seat of the car, Tia gazed out her window. She said nothing, but her eyes grew round and her jaw dropped. Whatever Francesca saw, Tia saw it, too.

Francesca leaned over and placed a cool hand on Stephen's wrist. "We'd better check our armor and ask for protection."

He watched as she opened the car door and stepped briskly onto the sidewalk. She stood there with her eyes closed, meditating.

Armor. He stuck a finger between his neck and shirt collar and glanced awkwardly across the street at a woman walking her dog. All this time listening to messages about armor and he'd yet to actually envision himself wearing any. He closed his eyes for a moment and tried to slow the anxious rhythm of his heart.

The image was waiting.

His armor reflected the twelfth or thirteenth century. Delicate scrollwork was etched into the silver breastplate, and he saw that a full helmet, complete with visor, covered his head. He grasped a sword securely in his gloved left hand. (That made perfect sense; he was left-handed.) Emeralds rimmed the scabbard of the sword, glittering in a beam of light whose origins he could not trace.

He wasn't making this up. His mind had always moved mathematically, whether in the calculation of profit and loss or in the realm of spatial abstraction. He'd never longed to play any role other than successful businessman.

"Stephen." Francesca's soft voice interrupted his thoughts. "We need to go in."

He'd walked the path of the world all his life and could not deny his own financial success. The path was deceptive, however. It offered all the trappings of financial health, never once hinting that emptiness would gnaw inside the heart despite the outward treasures. The path of light offered no guarantee of worldly success. It didn't even offer explanations. But Stephen sensed a promise there: a promise to feed rather than simply to provide, a promise to keep him whole, no matter what the circumstances.

Suddenly he was incredibly tired of straddling the fence.

Eyes still closed, he surrendered. *You win. Tell me what to do.*

The words felt awkward and self-conscious. He had to admit, though, that they were heard. The warmth of a response encapsulated him. He added a hasty post-script: *Please, look after Kat!*

Drawing in a resolute breath, Stephen opened his eyes and stepped from the car. His eyes were riveted toward the house.

"Holy shit!" he gulped.

"Not quite how I'd phrase it," Francesca said. "But I catch your drift."

An aureole of elongated brown plumes surrounded Tia's house. It extended at least ten feet into the air and was still growing. The tips of the plumes streamed from dense, sooty bodies, dissipating through the air in feathery curls.

"What is it?" Stephen gasped.

Francesca threw him a startled glance, then followed his gaze. "You see it, then. Good. That will help."

Dazed, he stumbled around the front of his car to join her on the sidewalk. The passenger door slammed, and Tia stood beside him as well, eyes also glued to her house.

"What are we waiting for?" she asked. "Time to take action, I'd say."

Francesca blocked her way. "Tia, either go in with God's light or don't go in at all."

"I can handle it." Tia sidestepped her to lead them across the street. "Follow me, hon. I know the lay of the land. And stop worrying. Things look rowdy, but I can whip it all back into shape. I've done it before."

She trotted up the front steps and threw open the door.

"Careful," Francesca whispered, hooking her arm through Stephen's and half-dragging him across the threshold.

30

~~~

KAT MADE IT TO THE SECOND FLOOR BEFORE REMEMBERING
that she'd stay safe only as long as Donald didn't find
her. The realization made her racing heart pound even
harder.

Fear threatened to smother her like a heavy quilt.
She'd always prided herself on her ability to keep every
emotion at bay. This was one hell of a time to start losing control. She wrapped her arms across her chest and
waited for her teeth to stop chattering.

A creeping feeling of dread curled ugly tendrils
about her mind. Her thoughts turned to Peter. She
shook her head—hard—to dislodge his image. There
wasn't time now for a trip down memory lane.

Her head snapped around as Donald's wheelchair
rolled toward the foyer. For all she knew, that maniac
carried a gun. And there she was, fully visible, grasping
for sanity at the top of the steps! One glance up, and
who knew what would happen? Pulse throbbing, she
sprinted through the nearest doorway for cover.

The sight of Tia's wild clothing spilling from various
receptacles lent a weird sense of security. Here, at least,
was something solid in the midst of unreality. At the
very least, the colorful piles offered a place to hide
should Donald suddenly appear. Kat pressed flat

against the bedroom wall to listen to the voices down-stairs, waiting for a chance to make a clean break for the lift.

The image of Peter forced itself back into her mind. "No," she whispered, pushing it away. But it returned instantly, clinging with the tenacity of a stubborn weed. She tried to concentrate on the faraway conver-sation in the foyer.

In her mind's eye, Peter reached out a beseeching hand. He seemed to be calling her, pulling her closer to him. With a sigh, Kat relented. There could be no harm in a brief visit. It might even strengthen her.

"Oh, Peter," she said sadly, allowing herself a moment of rest with his familiar blue eyes and easy smile. What a story he could have fashioned from Tia's wreck of a room.

A new picture smashed through her consciousness. She nearly shrieked out loud. Peter lay dying, blood gushing from a gaping wound in his head, eyes wide open but unseeing. A deep-throated whisper ripped through her mind. "You did this. It wouldn't have hap-pened had you been less selfish, more loving."

She stood frozen as the blood drained from her head to her toes. The image wrapped itself about her eyes like a blindfold. Her throat tightened. Then the nasty little voice whispered another taunt into her ear. "You wanted him to die!"

Kat straightened as anger flooded her. How stupid! How utterly insane! Whatever that voice was, it had pushed beyond credibility. It spoke lies, nothing else. She glared reproachfully around the room, blaming the vibes of Tia's house, the residue of years and years of Valentine circles.

"Almost got me," she murmured, mainly to hear the encouraging sound of her own voice.

She could no longer hear Donald's voice in the foyer. She leaned her head toward the doorway. Was he gone? Where? Without waiting to find out, she held her breath and skittered down the hall to the bathroom.

The linen closet door gaped open. Kat stopped herself a split second before plummeting down the shaft. She'd nearly forgotten that the lift would be in the kitchen, right where Donald had left it.

She hastily flicked the call switch. With its usual soft whir, the lift began the slow ascent from the first floor.

"Devon!" Stephen exclaimed as they hurried into the house. "Francesca, that's Chris's wife."

Devon didn't answer. She stood alone in the foyer, face pink, eyes wide, mouth open. Something like a shadow hovered about her, but Stephen could not fathom why she seemed rooted to her spot. He started toward her. Francesca's strong hand pulled him back.

"What's going on?" he asked, confused.

Tia, too, stared directly at Devon. "Oh, for Pete's sake," she said into the air. "Leave her alone, will you?"

"Who's she talking to?" Stephen whispered.

Francesca had turned the color of chalk, but her manner remained reassuringly calm. "Try to see," she suggested, voice shaking slightly. "I think you can."

Stephen turned obediently back toward Devon and mentally lifted the visor of his helmet.

He instantly recoiled as the shadow surrounding her took shape.

Tia strode resolutely to the center of the room. "Get away from her," she commanded.

Feathers of indigo fluttered in a nonexistent wind. Great wings of shining purple, blue, and black framed Devon on either side, like gates in an unseen wall. Stephen stared, aghast, at the elegant, clawed fingers that rested atop Devon's head. A chiseled face, devoid of emotion, leaned close. He watched, nauseated, as a slender, lizard-like tongue flicked in and out of Devon's ear.

"I . . . I think I'm going to be sick," he gasped to Francesca.

"You're not. You're more than you think you are. Raise your shield."

But how could he defend himself with something that wasn't real? But, then, was this hideously beautiful creature stroking Devon's shoulder reality? And there, on the stairs, that writhing, grotesque gargoyle with the body of a snake, was *that* reality? All around him creatures began to take form, some of them ugly, some of them beautiful, all of them chillingly opaque. Stephen passed a shaky hand across his forehead.

"We carry the sword of spirit," Francesca said. "We can do this, Stephen, or we wouldn't have been called to it."

Tia had drawn herself up with the regality of a queen. Devon stared at her as if she offered the only possibility of salvation. The angel lifted graceful hands, extending pearly talons.

"Spirit, I command you to leave." Tia's grating voice fell hollow in the stillness of the room.

The angel defiantly bent toward Devon and pointedly kissed her cheek.

"My God!" Stephen twisted toward Francesca. "How can Devon stand this? Why doesn't she run?"

Francesca's cool gray gaze met his. "She doesn't know what's wrong. She can't see the demon, of course."

"She can't?"

"Well, *you've* never seen them before, have you? They're always around, Stephen. This is not a special appearance."

He stared, horrified. "How can that be? It can't be."

"But it is. They whisper lies into your ears, they fan your fears, they raise your doubts. You've heard them before; you've just never identified them. Unfortunately, Devon is an open, vulnerable channel."

"Then you've seen these . . . demons . . . before?" Stephen asked.

"No." Francesca shook her head. "I've heard about them, but I've never seen them. And I hope to God that this newfound vision is only temporary."

Tia slowly raised her right hand. She looked like a sorceress about to cast a spell.

"Do you know who I am?" she asked, and several creatures swiveled their necks to snicker at her. "I am Tia Melody, consort of Valentine. And it is in his name that I command you to release this woman."

The glowing eyes of the indigo angel dimmed. An expression of mocking comprehension veiled her features. With an obsequious bow, she backed slowly away from Devon, who lifted her head as if just awakened from a trance.

Stephen jumped as a chair crashed in the kitchen.

"Chris!" Devon cried, instantly alive. She grabbed Tia's hand and tugged her toward the kitchen. "Please, you've got to stop them!"

"Where's Kat?" Stephen called after them.

Devon stopped short, a pained expression on her face. "Upstairs," she managed to stammer as Tia propelled her away.

"Stephen, find her," Francesca ordered.

"Will you be safe here alone?"

"I won't be alone," she said as he raced for the stairs.

Francesca closed her eyes and turned her palms upward. The darkness in the house was stifling, nearly overwhelming. Even with her eyes closed, she could sense the beasts of hell surrounding her. They couldn't touch her unless she let them. She was safe as long as she ignored the fears and doubts of her mind. The trickery of Asteroth's minions couldn't be underestimated, however, for the crevices of entry within the human mind ran deep, indeed.

She steadied her breathing and tried to concentrate. Doubts pummeled her in a desperate attempt to interrupt her communion. A leering image of Kat, dead and disfigured in a bedroom upstairs, almost derailed her completely. She squeezed her eyes shut and forced her words through the swirling soot.

"Help us," she whispered fiercely. "Keep us safe. But above all . . . your way, not mine."

A tingling sensation began in the tips of her fingers, then traveled up her arms and throughout her body. The brightness of energizing light was so overpowering that, even behind closed lids, the effect was nearly blinding. Beyond those radiant curtains, Francesca sensed powerful figures of swirling iridescence.

She wanted to laugh, to shout with joy. Of course, she'd known that they'd never face the darkness alone. But even the depth of her faith had not prepared her for the glory of their comrades.

She opened her eyes and raised her arms in gratitude.

31

CHRIS INTERCEPTED THE WHEELCHAIR IN THE KITCHEN AS IT rolled toward the lift.

"I don't brake for animals," Donald remarked.

"Stop!" Chris leaped sideways before the wheels could collide with his legs. He grabbed a wooden chair from the table and reached the lift just ahead of the other man. Bracing his back against the door, he banged the chair squarely down onto the floor between them. Donald plowed into it. Chris winced as the back of the chair slammed into his midsection.

"Move it," Donald ordered.

"First, we talk!"

"Move it now, or I'll do it myself. It's only my legs that don't work. Every other muscle in my body is strong enough to compensate."

The gears of the lift creaked. With a groan, the platform began its measured climb upward.

"Ah." A crooked little smile pulled at Donald's mouth. "Perhaps my friend will save me the trouble of tracking her down."

"But why do you want Kat?" Chris shook his head, bewildered. "I don't understand."

"You don't have to." Donald's eyes followed the hidden path of the elevator. "Suffice it to say that it's Valentine's will."

"I'm no pal of Valentine's."

"So I've been told. It will cost you, but that's of no importance now."

The elevator stopped on the second floor. Both men paused, silent as the gears engaged again. Donald leaned back in his chair, relishing the moment his prey would step from the lift and into his custody.

"Are you telling me," Chris said slowly, "that *Valentine* wants Kat dead?"

The other man only smiled.

Chris stepped away from the door, crouching to meet Donald at eye level. "You killed Peter Dulaney!"

Donald's expression did not change. "Who?"

"He was a reporter from the Sunpapers. My guess is that Valentine wanted him out of the picture, so you obliged."

Donald shrugged. "Wasn't me. Honestly, Mr. Alexander. I'm not a crazed maniac on a rampage. I live a quiet existence, have very few demands. Valentine keeps me well enough. If he has occasional need of my services in return, I certainly don't mind. But going in for wholesale murder would only get me caught. I'm not that stupid."

The lift ground to a halt. Donald straightened in his chair. "It's between floors," he murmured, perplexed.

"I'll forget this conversation," Chris offered quietly, "if you forget about Kat. She's no threat to you. You have no reason to hurt her. Who cares what Valentine says? He's not the one who'll pay for it. You are. How can it be worth the risk?"

"Oh, I won't get caught. I'm physically disabled, you

see, unable to commit anything as strenuous as murder. Besides, Mr. Alexander, it's worth quite a bit to me. It's worth your wife."

The words hit like a blow to the midsection. Chris's body slackened as the other man's meaning reeled through his brain. "My . . . my wife?"

"Of course. Your lovely, lovely Devon. Or should I say *my* lovely Devon? She's my reward for the task. Don't worry; she won't miss you at all."

A cloud of rage engulfed Chris. He gasped for air, hands trembling as he balled them into fists. It was as if a protective veil had been torn from his mind. Image after image crashed upon him, turning his stomach and bringing bile to the back of his throat. He saw his wife astride Donald, her head thrown back in rapture. And there she was again, mockingly offering herself to her husband, only to pull away at the last minute, doubled over in scornful laughter.

"Over . . . my . . . dead . . . body!" he choked through the distorting smoke of his fury.

"That's the general idea." Donald's arms stretched outward in invitation. "Very well, then. Attack me. Turn my actions into self-defense."

Peals of laughter flooded Chris's ears. He reddened as he recognized the gales as Devon's. She floated before him, dressed in a filmy, gossamer gown which clung to the curves of her body. She paused before Donald's chair and slowly, carefully, loosened the delicate tie at the neck of her gown.

"No!" Chris rubbed his eyes to erase the sight.

Donald's gaze flitted from Chris's right shoulder to his knees, then traveled back to his face. His eyebrows raised in admiring comprehension.

The vision of Devon let the top of her gown drop to her waist, then leaned toward Donald. Band after band of nauseating jealousy pounded Chris's mind. With a grunt, he shoved the barrier chair away, toppling it with a loud clatter.

"Don't stop," Donald beckoned. "I'm waiting."

Chris lunged forward and grabbed him around the neck. Devon vanished. Only the man in the wheelchair remained, a blur of movement as he made a jerking grab downward. The knife flashed, and Chris staggered backward, bewildered, right hand reflexively covering the wound in his left arm.

"More," Donald said. "Come at me, Loverboy, and let me finish you off!"

The rage threatened to rise again. "No!" Chris gasped. To give in to the jealousy invited destruction. But Devon, his wife . . . he was helpless against the onslaught of mockery when she was involved, incapable of removing himself from the terror of losing her.

Donald leaned forward in his chair, the tip of his pink tongue protruding through his teeth. Chris closed his eyes and clapped his hands across his ears as the vision of that tongue nearing Devon's breast invaded his reason.

"No!" he shouted.

"Oh, my God, Chris!" Devon stood beside him, fully clothed, solid and real. She gasped at the blood running down his arm, then plucked a dishtowel from a nearby hook to try to stem the flow.

"Donald." Tia stood like stone in the doorway. "What have you done?"

Slowly, as if picking her way through a crowd, she glided majestically across the kitchen floor to stand before the wheelchair. Her gaze swept the entire room.

"Why have all of you come? You have no business here."

Chris and Devon exchanged uneasy glances.

"I summoned them," Donald said.

"Damn it, Donald. You were born to destroy everything you touch. In the name of Valentine, I command you to . . ."

Donald's laughter echoed throughout the room. Chris reached out his good arm and pulled Devon close.

"In the name of Valentine." Donald clutched his stomach in an effort to control himself. "Oh, Tia. By whose decree do you think I act? It's Valentine who arranged all this."

A look of confusion crossed Tia's face. "I . . . I don't understand."

"It's simple, really. Valentine wants certain people dead. But not Devon. Devon is mine. All mine. And you won't talk, Devon dearest, because you know you'll share the blame for anything that happens here. I need Valentine, Tia. Bring me Valentine."

Tia shook her head. "But Valentine is good. He speaks only truth. He would never bring violence."

Her brother rolled closer to Chris and Devon. "It's pathetic, Tia, how little you know your own master."

"My master?" Her voice slid up an octave. "My *master?*"

Donald reached out and ripped Devon from Chris's one-armed grasp. "Keep her for me," he ordered, thrusting her toward Tia. "We're not quite finished, are we, Mr. Alexander?"

"Chris!" Devon shrieked as Donald once again

reached for his knife. She stumbled forward, but this time it was her husband who motioned her away.

Kat felt safer with the control lever of the lift grasped securely in her hand. Donald had left the foyer, which probably meant he'd gone searching for **her.** She could envision him poised in the kitchen, salivating in expectation of the moment she'd innocently alight before him. Her grip tightened around the lever. Not in this lifetime. She'd grab the notebooks, park the lift on the second floor, and race like hell for the front door. The man was dangerous, but he had his limitations.

She yanked the lever and watched the walls pass slowly before her.

How fortunate that Stephen had discovered this lift. And the notebooks!

Stephen. Her heart caught in her throat. That kiss last night had come as a staggering surprise, wonderful and disastrous all at once. She'd wanted him, actually wanted him more than she'd ever wanted anyone in her life . . . including Peter.

She swallowed hard against a twinge of guilt, then forced her mind back to the elevator. The metal plate hovered at eye level. She tugged the lever and the lift squealed to a stop. Holding her breath, she dislodged the plate, setting it carefully onto the platform before turning to the contents hidden behind it.

There they were: two legal pads and a spiral notebook. Her stomach contracted at the sight of Peter's familiar scrawl. Hesitantly she lifted the top legal pad and drew it close to her chest.

"Talk to me," she whispered, hands shaking.

The first page was dated April seventh, about two months before Peter's death. Her eyes skimmed the scrawl:

Called David Toohey back—wants to discuss info re psychic circle—uses words like "darkness" re spirit and talks about God a lot. Thinks people who leave this "cult of Valentine" get knocked off by cult leaders. Is he nuts?

If she closed her eyes, Kat could see Peter sitting at his desk that day, grimacing into the telephone receiver while taking rapid notes of the conversation. Should he share this joke of a call with the reporter in the next cubicle? She knew him well enough to answer that one. Peter, despite his broad jocularity and ready smile, had possessed a keen sense of competition. He'd have kept the story quiet until checking it through.

She leaned her head against a steel beam. Why couldn't he at least have told *her?* Maybe she could have somehow prevented all this.

A crash from the kitchen made her jump, then instinctively press herself against a corner beam of the lift. The house had become eerily quiet, save for the sound of scuffling downstairs. What on earth was going on?

Her hands began to shake again as she reached under the floorboards for the rest of the notebooks.

The lift jerked upward. Kat hastily pulled her arm back, then glanced up. Light spilled into the shaft from the open bathroom door.

Donald!

That was crazy. He couldn't walk. He couldn't be the one who'd summoned her, the one now waiting for her on the second floor. But, then, there was nothing predictable about this entire situation.

She hastily dropped the legal pad onto the platform, then lifted the metal plate before her like a shield.

The crowd circling Donald and Chris reminded Tia of spectators at a bullfight, eagerly primed for a kill. She recognized some of them. The beautiful indigo angel she'd seen earlier in the foyer now stood by Chris's left arm. A rosy-cheeked cherub perched on the arm of Donald's chair turned to smile at her, revealing a surprising set of sharp little fangs. He'd been with her brother for years, although Tia had actually glimpsed him only on the night of the accident. She also remembered those muscular warrior angels near the table. They'd often accompanied Valentine, their broad, golden beauty a complement to his own. But these other creatures . . . she'd never seen them before. They were hideous. Slimy scales reflected the light where skin should have been. Flat eyes stared unblinkingly as Donald and Chris faced each other. Gash-like mouths twisted into smiles of delight. Who were these creatures?

"Tia." Devon's voice broke. "You've got to stop them."

Tia mechanically shook her head. "I can't. I can't act against the will of Valentine, and he hasn't told me what to do yet."

"But my husband, Tia. Please, you can't let this happen to him."

"Valentine will clear it up, I promise, hon. Just give me a minute to call him."

Donald gazed up at Chris, knife held loosely in his right hand. "Come on," he said. "You know what you want to do to me. Should I tell you my plans for your wife? You might enjoy them."

Tia watched as the indigo angel reached around to caress Chris's chest. Her forked tongue licked his neck, then disappeared from view as she whispered into his ear. A muscle in his jaw began to twitch.

Tia leaned forward, trying to hear the angel's message. At first, only a bee-like buzzing met her ears. She strained to decipher the words, then drew back suddenly, stung by the raunchy language.

She threw a sideways glance at Devon, who stood with her hands wrapped around her stomach, her mouth moving silently. Was she praying? Tia had never gotten the impression that Devon thought much of prayer. But the words falling from her lips were unmistakable. Tia herself remembered them from childhood. Devon was rambling through the Twenty-third Psalm, probably the only bit of prayer she could recall other than a table grace. Tia sighed. She'd hoped, of course, that Devon's faith in Valentine would be greater than this. Unfortunately, not everyone could be strong in the face of adversity.

The indigo angel had been joined by a flying gargoyle. He lit atop Chris's head and wrapped clawed hands across his eyes.

Tia concentrated. *Valentine. I need you.*

Suddenly a column of white light shot from ceiling to floor on Chris's right. Tia averted her eyes, unable to face the brightness. Through the vibrant curtains of light, she sensed a tall, powerful figure. Violet washed through the column as the figure raised its sword and aimed. Tia recoiled from the beam of light that shot from its tip. The beam, however, was meant for Devon. It diffused itself gently over her. Tia heard the melodic words that fell with it: *Met in love.*

Chris was trembling now, his fists clenched and ready for action. A naked male being, perhaps three feet tall, began to stroke his inner thigh. The indigo angel, thoroughly enjoying herself, gestured sharply as she whispered nonstop into his ear.

"Come at me," Donald taunted. "It's the only chance you've got to keep her for yourself."

Chris's face clouded with rage. He crouched forward, poised to spring, wounded arm hanging by his side.

The blinding beam once again flashed across the room, showering Devon in a shimmering rain.

"I love you, Chris," she called in a loud, clear voice.

Startled, he turned to her. She met his gaze squarely as tears flowed down her cheeks.

"I love you," she repeated, caressing each word. "Please, don't do this."

The indigo angel shrieked and leaped from Chris's side. The gargoyle tumbled from his head, landing in a broken little heap on the floor. The naked creature began to laugh hysterically, each burst bouncing him back toward Donald's wheelchair.

Chris slowly lowered his good arm and turned back to Donald. "You see how it is," he said quietly, all anger ebbing away.

Donald stared at Devon, his mouth pulled back in a grimace. "You love him. As if that mattered."

The indigo angel swept across the floor to Donald's side. Wrapping an arm possessively about his shoulders, she burst forth with bloodcurdling laughter. "She . . . loves . . . him!" Tia heard her cackle. "Of course she would. She'd never love you, you miserable, twisted excuse for a man! How did you ever dream you'd possess her? Only a golden knight can take her to bed, never a useless half-man!"

The cackle hurt Tia's ears. She hoped Valentine would hurry.

Donald's face grew purple. Chris stood his ground as the knife pointed toward his midsection.

An ugly hag hobbled up to the wheelchair. "Take me," she purred, kissing Donald's cheek. "I'm what you deserve."

With a guttural cry, Donald gave a mighty shove and propelled himself forward. Chris met him straight on, stopping the chair with a ready foot. He landed a solid punch to Donald's jaw, then kicked the knife from his hand. It slid across the floor, coming to rest beneath the refrigerator.

Donald fell gasping against the back of his chair. "Very impressive, Mr. Alexander," he panted, blood trickling from his mouth. His eyes darted toward his sister. "Valentine. Don't leave me alone!"

Chest heaving, Chris slumped against the elevator door. "Devon, call nine-one-one."

"Valentine, Valentine," Donald chanted.

Tia intercepted Devon's frenzied move toward the telephone. "Wait. He's coming!"

Every creature in the room turned to stare at her, mouths agape in expectation. Tia felt the familiar blast of cold air behind her.

"He's coming," she repeated triumphantly.

She dared not turn around. Valentine's arrival demanded humility. He'd manifest himself before her in his own time. Then she'd stand in his glory, bask in his magnificent beauty. That was enough.

The beings ringing the kitchen bowed low, their

grunts and groans silenced to an odd hum. The indigo angel sidled a step closer, her burning stare a lascivious invitation to erotic possibility. Tia smirked at her, confident of her own superior place in Valentine's affections. But even this sullen angel had bowed her head slightly, ready to pay homage to the great lord.

A gust of wind burst through the kitchen. Donald's smile grew broader as the breeze ruffled his blond hair. Chris glanced around in confusion, unable to trace the source of the gust. Frightened, Devon raced to his side. Tia's eyebrows raised. She'd never considered that the Alexanders might see only their physical surroundings. Pity. They'd miss the beauty of Valentine.

The column of light in the corner intensified. It illuminated the entire northeastern wall of the kitchen. The fang-toothed cherub shielded its eyes as the light grew brighter. The indigo angel turned her back. Tia squinted and shaded her eyes with her hand, trying to see the being within the light.

Suddenly she realized that the being *was* the light. She detected the curve of mighty biceps, the impression of strong, even facial features. A gentle question pervaded her: *Can you see me? Do you understand what I am?*

As she watched, the column metamorphosed into the tall, glowing figure of a man. He stood perhaps eight feet tall and reflected an endless mosaic of pulsing, sparkling energy. Tia slowly lowered her hand. Six huge, opalescent wings fanned open from the being's back, and the even features broke into a smile.

Tia stared up at this angel, mouth open.

Waves of cold lapped her feet.

"My Tia," a soothing voice said beside her and, with

the exception of the huge, shimmering angel in the corner, every nonhuman creature dropped to the ground in adoration.

Kat watched warily as a male figure appeared in the doorway before her, first feet, then legs, then torso.

"You're all right, then," Stephen said, relieved.

The metal plate slipped from her hands, hitting the platform with a clang. "Stephen! How did you . . ."

He grabbed her hand and tugged her from the lift. "We've got to get out of here."

"Something's wrong in the kitchen. I heard a crash."

"I know. Tia and Devon went to investigate."

"Tia's here?"

"Francesca, too. Please, Kat, I just want you safe. I'll check in on Chris, don't worry."

She stubbornly withdrew her hand from his. "I'm not leaving without Peter's notebooks. It'll only take a minute."

He studied her for a moment, apparently weighing his alternatives. Then his green eyes narrowed, and he nodded a brief acknowledgment. "I'll go with you," he said, guiding her onto the platform.

"I can handle this alone."

"Let's go." He shut the door. She reached to pull the lever, but found his strong hand on top of her own.

"Kat," he said, "please trust me. Nothing in this house is as it seems."

"No kidding."

"No." He grasped her shoulders and turned her to face him. "We're not alone in this house. Valentine's hordes are here."

She tried to decipher his expression in the half-light.

His face was drawn, his eyes serious. Suddenly she understood. For the first time since she'd known him, Stephen was terrified.

Her attempt at a careless shrug fizzled. "Sounds like a bad movie," she said weakly.

"I wish it were. But Valentine is coming. Stay with me. Guard your mind. I don't think you can be swept into darkness unless you allow it, but Valentine will try to distort your thoughts to the point where you don't even know you're giving in."

She remembered Devon's uncharacteristic violence and the grisly images of Peter which had assailed her in Tia's bedroom. "I believe you. My God, Stephen, I have no choice but to believe you."

He pulled the lever, but just as the lift began to move, a chill wind swept through the shaft.

"What is that?" Kat cried as her hair blew wildly behind her.

Stephen squinted into the wind and hastily tugged the lever. The elevator stopped, but the wind continued, growing colder by the second.

"It's coming from the kitchen," he said.

"That makes no sense. The platform would block the air flow."

He shook his head. "Its origins aren't physical. Something terrible is happening down there."

"Then Chris needs help." She bypassed him to yank the lever. This time, however, the lift jerked upward, chugging past the second floor door and toward the third story.

"What are you doing?" Stephen lunged for the lever.

"I didn't do anything different!" Kat reached it first. The lift shuddered to a halt.

"Let me try." Stephen sighed with relief as the platform once again moved downward.

It stopped short just above the second floor doorknob.

Together, Kat and Stephen stared at the blocked door.

The temperature in the shaft dropped another notch. Stephen wordlessly wrapped Kat in his arms as they sank down to sit on the platform.

"It's cold," she whispered.

"Listen." He placed a finger against her lips.

From the kitchen came a curious buzz, like the sound of a beehive. The wind increased, carrying with it a whiff of sulfur and tar.

"Remember that smell?" Stephen asked.

"You bet. We smelled it that first night we went to Tia's . . . when Valentine tried to choke me."

"Kat." He pulled her close. "Valentine is here."

She pushed back the terror rising in her throat. "What do we do?"

"Pray," he said, closing his eyes.

"But what good—"

His eyes flew open. "Look, I'm just the messenger, okay?"

She burrowed into his arms and rested her head against his chest. Then, as the temperature dropped another few degrees, she matched the rhythm of her prayers to the rise and fall of his breathing.

Tia had never before stood this close to Valentine. She had, in fact, never seen him other than astride his dragon. Now he stood within arm's length, glittering eyes fixed upon her. Oh, the beauty of him! She nearly swooned as the heady scent of musk threatened to overwhelm her. He had oiled the hairless skin of his chest. Each strong muscle glistened in chiseled definition. Other than the jeweled band circling his upper arm, he wore only sandals and a leather loincloth. Tia's gaze traveled hungrily from his narrow waist to the solid muscles of his thighs.

"Valentine. You're here."

His frosty smile engulfed her. "Of course."

Donald's eyes bulged. Tia suddenly realized that, in all the years Valentine had spoken to them, this was the first time her brother had seen him.

"Donald," she said smugly, "this here's Valentine." Her brother, she noted with satisfaction, remained speechless.

Chris and Devon edged toward the kitchen door.

"They must stay," Valentine commanded.

"Don't go," Tia called obediently. "Valentine is with us."

They stared at the space she indicated, unable to see. She stepped forward, backing them against the doorway of the lift.

"Wait just another minute," she pleaded. "Wait and see how Valentine keeps his promises."

Whimpering, Devon pushed herself against Chris. Chris met Tia's gaze with a cold stare. "Tia, it's over. Step aside. My wife and I are leaving now."

"I forbid it!" Valentine roared, and a new burst of cold air knocked the kitchen calendar from its place on the wall. Stunned, Chris and Devon stayed rooted to their spots.

Tia turned away from Valentine's ire and once again caught full sight of the luminous angel across the room. He extended a glowing hand toward her.

I bring God's message of love and light. Accept it and be free.

Free? Free of what? She turned back to Valentine, who stood glaring at the angel, lip curled in disgust. His expression softened as he returned his gaze to Tia.

"*I* am freedom," he said softly. "You know this is true. You called to me for help, and I am here. I will never leave you, Tia Melody."

The angel once again extended its hand, this time more insistently.

Return to love.

"*I* am love," Valentine said before the last tingle of the angel's message could leave her. "Look at me, Tia Melody, and tell me if this is not so."

Tia stared into his glass-cold eyes and saw herself scooped into his arms. He carried her toward a huge bed and, impatient with desire, dropped her into the midst of the pillows piled there.

"Oh!" Mesmerized, she wrapped herself in the image. Valentine swept away the pillows and roughly kissed her mouth. "Oh!" she gasped again, staggering backward against the kitchen counter.

"Take my hand," Valentine said, reaching out to her with a powerful arm. "Take my hand, and the vision is yours. The love I hold for you, and only for you, will be completely yours if you come with me. No other can give you this, Tia Melody."

The illuminated angel also extended both arms. *Come. Come and be made whole. Come.*

Valentine laughed. "Be made whole? As if you were scattered in tiny pieces. Tia, my own . . . you shall be worshipped, adored. Come with me and be satiated!"

Donald leaned forward in his chair, eyes wide with

comprehension. He looked like a child who'd just found the last piece of a jigsaw puzzle. "Take his hand, Tia," he urged.

She wondered how much he actually saw and blushed as she returned to the drama unfolding in Valentine's eyes. His incendiary kisses had moved down her body. His mouth rested against her breast. Strong arms were beneath her, around her, so that she was pulled flat against the hardness of his body.

She needed to sit. She had to sit or she would melt away onto the floor.

Valentine's hand moved up her thigh.

The image was gone. Tia slumped against the counter in disappointment.

"Take my hand," Valentine said, a teasing smile on his face.

"Yes, Tia, take his hand." Donald's eyes glittered in an unnaturally flushed face.

Chris and Devon stared, unable to interpret Tia's strange behavior. The angel beside them spread its magnificent wings, and the corner pulsated with a light so vivid that Tia preferred to look away rather than face its inevitable illumination.

Brenda, rest in forgiveness. Come to joy.

"Forgiveness." Valentine burst into scathing laughter. "As if you should feel shame, my beloved! There is no shame in living a life of self-discovery, in enabling others to do the same."

He stepped toward her, so close that she could see the bristle of beard on his jaw, could almost touch the fluid muscles rippling beneath the skin of his chest.

"Come," he said, face hot with desire. "Come to true love!"

He thrust his hand forward, palm turned upward to receive hers.

Tia took a breath to calm her pounding heart. She stared into the steamy promise of Valentine's eyes. Then, head held high, she resolutely grasped his hand.

She was falling, falling into an abyss so deep it seemed she'd never reach the bottom. The wind whistled past her ears as her body grew cold. Where was Valentine? He was not beside her, nor had he preceded her into this massive canyon. Far away, at the rim of the abyss, she thought she saw him staring down at her, Donald smirking by his side.

"Catch me!" she screamed.

But the dizzying fall continued, and no one came to her aid.

Chris watched Tia collapse in a heap on the floor.

"Let's go," he said, pushing Devon toward the door.

The wheelchair intercepted them. Chris tripped over it, stumbling to regain his balance. Devon collided into him, but it was Donald who steadied her. He clasped her hand firmly, smiling up at her.

Tia slowly rose from the floor, carefully checking her limbs for broken bones.

Chris whipped his head around as the now-familiar sound of the lift caused the wall to vibrate. The platform was descending to the first floor.

"We're out of here, Tia," he said shortly, reaching for his wife.

Tia flexed her fingers as she strode determinedly across the room. She stopped before him, then reached out with both hands and yanked him toward the lift. Chris gasped. He'd never encountered such strength in a woman. He raised startled eyes to hers and nearly choked in horror.

Black, fathomless eyes stared back.

Valentine kneed Chris in the stomach, then delivered a heavy blow to the side of his head. Chris sank to the floor, unconscious. Valentine opened the door to the lift, kicked the crumpled body inside, and deftly slammed the door behind him.

"Stop!" Devon shrieked as the heavy metal platform creaked toward its first-floor destination.

32

~~~~

ANOTHER BLAST OF FRIGID AIR SHOT THROUGH THE ELEVATOR shaft, dropping the temperature in the lift to around forty degrees. Stephen felt Kat's body tense against his. Suddenly she thrust her chin into the air and wrenched herself free of his arms.

"I won't be turned into a Popsicle," she muttered between chattering teeth. "Hoist me up."

He scrambled to his feet after her. "What are you planning to do?"

Kat peered into the dim tunnel above their heads, then pointed to the metal frame of the elevator. "If you lift me, I can pull myself up to that top beam there. I might be able to reach the third-floor doorknob and open the door."

Stephen paused, considering. "Then what? You don't even know where that doorway leads."

"Then I climb into whatever room it is and flick the switch to bring you up."

"I think it's safe to assume the switch won't work."

She fell silent for a moment. "Think you could reach the top frame if you boosted yourself up on the junction box? You're much taller than I am. Once I open the door, you can pull yourself over the threshold."

He'd already hiked one booted foot onto the junction box.

"Wait!" Kat protested. "I'll go first."

"You stay there."

He grasped a metal joist to steady himself. He might as well have grabbed a chunk of ice. The jarring cold snaked through his arm. It took pure willpower not to yank his hand away. He pulled himself to the narrow top beam of the lift and, using the wall for balance, shakily rose to a standing position.

Tia's house was old, built in an era when ceilings were high and walls were thick. The door to the third floor was flush with the wall, which left no ledge available for leverage in reaching the doorknob. Fortunately, the threshold of the door hit Stephen just below the chest, making the knob less than an arm's length away.

Kat could never have reached this, he thought, firmly grasping the knob.

Suddenly his feet were flailing through the air as the lift chugged downward.

The unexpected jerk of the lift knocked Kat forward to her hands and knees. Surprised, she froze for a moment before fully absorbing Stephen's predicament.

Damn! She stared up through the tunnel. Sure enough, he dangled above her, both hands tightly gripping the knob.

She struggled to her feet. "Hold on, Stephen. I'm coming."

"It's okay!" he shouted. "I think I can pull myself up."

"This is no time to play hero." How stupid they'd

been not to secure the lift in parked position before attempting any climbing stunts! The kitchen door crested the edge of the platform as she turned quickly toward the lever. The door suddenly opened, then closed with a slam. It caught her off guard. She stared blankly as the upper portion of the door grew larger before her.

"Stop!" she heard Devon shriek.

Reflexively Kat yanked the lever all the way back, bypassing the middle Park position and immediately reversing the direction of the lift. The gears protested with a loud squeal. She held on tightly as the platform began to shake. Then, like a boat regaining equilibrium after a mighty wave, the quivering stopped, and the platform glided smoothly upward.

Stephen waited until the lift was in jumping distance before dropping onto the platform. He quickly guided the lift back to the second floor.

"Did you hear Devon?" Kat scrambled across the threshold.

"Yes." He grabbed her hand. "Let's go."

"I think we'd better phone for help."

"And say what? That demons have taken over Tia's house?"

"Just do it, Stephen," she said, dragging him into Tia's bedroom. "There's got to be an extension in here somewhere beneath the wardrobe."

Tia's phone, a pink Princess dating from the sixties, sat on her bed stand. Kat grabbed the receiver from its cradle, then froze.

"Well?" Stephen asked.

"The line's dead."

* * *

Francesca's glowing armor had long ago become a part of her, so she seldom felt the need to make it tangible. Confining such vibrant energy to physical form seemed stifling. She preferred to feel her reality rather than to visualize it.

A circle of light surrounded her, radiating perhaps three feet in all directions. Creatures thronged the edges, squinting at her with a mixture of fear and dislike. Some had turned their backs. A few cowered in the corners of the room. Still others conferred in short little grunts, throwing scornful looks her way.

The jeering visages did not disturb her. Daily life harbored images every bit as disturbing as the hideous creatures now pacing before her. She was more concerned that these physical manifestations might merely hint at the evil stuff of which the monsters were made. The ice flowing through their veins was born of one darker than anything she'd ever before encountered.

She closed her eyes against them. Concentrating on their presence allowed them more tangibility than they deserved.

The armor, she heard, and a velvet warmth filled her. She felt familiar bands of light surround her arms and legs, noted the hard, weightless shell that encased her torso. The warmth of a helmet protected her head.

Her armor had never possessed a counterpart in physical reality. Instead of solid metal or woven mesh, her eyes met the quick, dancing movement of millions of light particles. Each particle radiated its own frequency, expressed its own color. Together, the spectrum of particles glowed with a fierce white light that nearly sterilized with its scorching intensity. Francesca found great beauty in this. Each color, so beautiful individually, became thoroughly enhanced by the brilliance of the whole.

She recognized the heft of her sword in her right hand.

She was ready.

A sizzling current spiraled through her body from a source behind her. She wouldn't turn to look. She couldn't. Her physical senses would never withstand the burning light they'd meet there.

In her heart she sensed the immense, whirring columns of energy gathered behind her, heard the timeless harmonies of praise, and absorbed the uncompromising love that encompassed her.

The angels of light had arrived.

Donald listened to the screeching gears of the lift, then turned an apologetic smile toward Devon.

"Oh, well," he said, shrugging. "Don't be too sad, darling. It was obviously Valentine's will. Your husband didn't believe."

Horrified, Devon stared wordlessly at Tia. Deep black eyes stared back. Donald wished that Valentine could have found a more impressive body in which to house himself. His sister's carnival-like clothing and bleached hair were not suitable complements to the awesome power the great lord possessed.

Valentine, still blocking the door to the lift, forcefully jabbed the air. "Katerina. I want Katerina."

"You can have her." Donald met his gaze. "She's upstairs."

Valentine's entourage drew closer, though none seemed willing to come too close. Donald smiled with satisfaction. He felt a paternal lordliness over these beings, recognizing in them a sense of the lost. They, like him, had been deemed unworthy, cast to the outer regions by those who thought themselves superior. Here in the darkness of the kitchen, they could join as one in the glory of Valentine, their protector. And he, Valentine's crown prince, would treat these misfits well, so much better than they'd ever been treated before. He smiled encouragingly at a misshapen little gargoyle. A hiss popped from its fish-mouth as it coldly turned away.

Both the light and the temperature in the kitchen had dropped considerably since Valentine's arrival. That suited Donald just fine. The room had taken on a subterranean feel, the dimness forcing everybody into an uncomfortable equality. The glowing angel who'd previously occupied the corner had vanished. Only a small dash of pure white light remained. Faint, it formed a wavering aura around Devon Alexander.

Devon took a step toward Valentine, her gray eyes wide with shock.

"What have you done?" she whispered.

Valentine drew back haughtily as she approached. The indigo angel tittered behind her hand, amused by the audacity of this human.

"Stop, Devon." Donald rolled to her side. "You're speaking to Valentine. Show some respect."

But Devon continued forward, stopping only when she came face to face with Valentine. She was several inches taller than Tia's angular frame. Donald was mesmerized by the ludicrous nature of the scene: Valentine, dwarfed by a mere woman. He sobered quickly as he caught the fury on Valentine's face. Devon was foolish, but he wanted her whole, not in pieces. He once again rolled toward her.

"Devon." He reached for her hand.

She brushed him away. "What are you?" she asked Valentine, voice trembling. "What are you that you can kill as if life meant nothing?"

"I am," Valentine replied succinctly, "your lord. You belong to me."

Devon stared at him as if he'd spoken gibberish. Donald took her hand again, wondering how long he had before the reality of her husband's death crossed the buffer of shock and sent her reeling. He'd have to act fast.

"Valentine," he said.

The great eyes turned to him.

Donald gestured toward Devon, eyebrows raised in inquiry.

"You have not done my will," Valentine said.

"But you're so much more capable than I. Katerina is here. You can go to her. And, in the meantime, I can remove this thorn from your side."

Valentine returned his gaze to Devon, who stood stonily before him. "My child," he said, voice smooth as silk.

"I am not 'your child,'" Devon replied, and though he couldn't be sure, Donald thought the aura about her brightened slightly. "I don't know who . . . what . . . you are, but you will step away from that door and let me reach my husband."

A corner of Tia's mouth turned up in an expression Donald had never seen on his sister's face. "You are my faithful disciple," Valentine said. "You have many times told me so. You came to me for help and I have promised to aid you. You came to me for a child. I promise you shall have one."

Her face crumpled in horror. "But my husband . . ."

"He was of no use to either of us. Your future is rosy, my dear. All who trust in me are rewarded. So shall you be."

He placed a hand on each of her shoulders and backed her away from the elevator door. Devon stared into his eyes, lips moving soundlessly, tears pouring down her cheeks.

"You've done what's right," Valentine said. "You've done my will." He gripped her wrist, then swung her around to face Donald. "Here is your destiny," he announced, pointing.

Devon stared from Donald to Valentine. Then, with an anguished cry, she drew back her hand and slapped Valentine across the face.

His eyes flashed. He lifted an arm and, as if she were a rag doll, sent her crashing into the kitchen chairs. She sank to the floor, staring in amazement as he stealthily approached.

"No, Valentine, please!" Donald cried. "Don't hurt her!"

Devon scrambled to her feet, breathing raggedly. "Kill me. At least I'll be with the man I love. And maybe, just maybe, God will forgive me for everything I've caused here."

The light surrounding her grew brighter. Even Valentine seemed to notice. He stood poised to spring, hands outstretched to grab her neck. He pulled them back hastily, as if burned. Devon bolted for the door of the lift. Valentine caught her as she passed, pulling her back in his iron grip.

"You would renounce me?"

"She's in shock," Donald interrupted frantically. "She doesn't know what she's saying!"

"No more!" Valentine thundered. He turned back to Devon who, shaking, met his gaze.

"I'm sorry I ever heard of you," she said in a low voice.

With a powerful shove, Valentine toppled her into Donald's lap. "I would end your miserable life, but you appear to have value to one of my faithful. Take her, Victor. Use her. And when you tire of her, I will destroy her." He turned and strode from the room.

Donald ran a trembling finger up Devon's shoulder. "Well," he said, entwining her in his arms, "it appears you owe me your life."

"I hate you." Devon struggled to rise.

She was his. Valentine had given his blessings, had even left them alone while he finished that disagreeable business upstairs. Donald tightened his grip, forcing Devon's head forward until he could taste her lips with his own. It was as he'd expected. The mere touch of her inflamed him. She'd been worth the wait, and as for tiring of her . . . as long as she cooperated, he was inclined to keep her alive for quite some time.

Devon let out a muffled shriek and tried to free her hands from his grip. Donald ignored her. The reaction was annoying, but it wasn't surprising. He had all the time in the world to make her want him as much as he wanted her.

Hungrily he traced her small ear with the tip of his tongue.

A low moan filtered through the elevator door.

"Chris!" Devon jerked herself forward. "My God!"

"No!" Donald protested furiously. How could it be? If this woman's husband still lived, still breathed, then surely Valentine would have known. Surely, he would have done something about it before delivering Devon for the taking, supposedly free and clear.

But there was that damn angel in the corner again, casting that contemptible light across the kitchen floor. Donald slumped against the back of his chair, staring at Devon in disbelief. Tears glistened on her cheeks as the angel's light illuminated her face. She was practically enraptured, damn it!

"Valentine . . ." Donald's voice trailed into the air. This woman would never do as he wished. She was in love with her husband, and he saw with sudden clarity that this love had not only opened her heart to the angel's glowing light, it had strengthened her as well. It wouldn't matter whether Chris Alexander lived or died. As long as even a spark of pure love for him lived within her, Valentine could never own her.

And he himself could never control her.

Devon tore his hands from her body and nearly flew across the floor to the elevator door. The aura of light around her grew stronger, bolder, so that Donald had to shield his eyes before following her with his stare.

She flung open the door and dropped to her knees beside the limp form of her husband. "Chris!" She pulled his head to her lap. Her soft hands stroked his damp forehead. "Sweetheart, it's me. Please, honey, talk to me. You'll be okay, I promise."

Donald's stomach rolled in disgust as Chris's eyelids fluttered open.

A beautiful smile broke across Devon's face. Donald felt the bile rise even higher within him. Swirling clouds of darkness hooded his vision, obscuring first one part of the tableau, and then another. Still, it was easy to see that the light now enveloped both Chris and Devon and that it was growing brighter by the second.

Chris struggled to sit, hand cradling his head. The wound in his arm no longer bled. The knife must have missed the artery. One side of his face had swollen, half-closing his left eye. Devon wrapped a supporting arm around his shoulders. Donald could not bear to witness the joy in her face.

"We've got to get out of here." Chris staggered to his feet and, with Devon's help, cautiously limped into the kitchen.

It couldn't end here. Donald frantically navigated his thoughts through his clouded vision. The woman was his. Valentine had said so. Certainly, this beaten lunk was no match for the power of Valentine.

He gripped the arms of his chair. "Valentine," he muttered. "Bring me strength."

An odd vibration ricocheted through his body. It filled his ears with a hum, obliterating all other sound in the room. Strength! Valentine had granted him strength, buoyed him up in the face of challenge. Donald raised his head in triumph and reached for his wheels.

Devon faced him now, eyebrows drawn together, mouth moving with words he could not hear. He lowered his head like a goat prepared to butt and aimed his chair directly toward Chris Alexander. Valentine was first and foremost a warrior. With his strategic help, this battle would be won.

Chris swayed, but Devon was ready. She waited until the barreling chair was within a foot of her husband before shoving him out of the way. Chris collapsed against the refrigerator. Devon sprang aside. The chair sailed into the lift, crashing against the back wall.

Devon slammed the door shut, then firmly pushed the call button.

The car was once again soaring through the night sky. Donald stared out the window in terror, his hands desperately scratching for the door handle. The green leaves of the trees gave way to empty sky, then to a blurry horizon where smoky low clouds met gently rising hills. The ground moved up to meet him. He could make out each rapidly approaching blade of grass illuminated in the high beam of the searchlights.

"Valentine!" he screamed as the car crashed to the earth.

Chris heard the strangled cry as the heavy platform chugged toward the first floor. Devon covered her ears to block out the clang of folding metal. The elevator gears churned and whirred in protest as the lift stoically plowed through its obstacle in search of its proper destination. Then there was silence.

Devon left her husband's side to vomit in Tia's sink.

33

_~~~~_

DESPITE THE CHILL OF THE FOYER, FRANCESCA SENSED AN EVEN
greater cold from the kitchen. Eyes closed, she tried to
define it. She felt something akin to a void, or even a
vacuum. Its outer fringes did not meet the light surrounding her. Instead, a gray chasm existed between
the clear frequencies of light and the heavy emptiness
of dark.

She opened her eyes. Most of the creatures lining
the room had lodged themselves firmly within the
bleak pull of the slow-moving darkness. A few, however, stood in the chasm between light and dark, staring with skeptical longing at the light.

She reached out a tentative hand to a trembling,
blue-scaled figure. It took a step backward. She
extended her sword until it wavered within claw's
length of the being. The creature drew in a rattling
breath, closed its eyes, and grasped the glowing tip of
the sword. Francesca watched, astonished, as light
swept through the raddled body. The current rushed
visibly through every limb, wrapping the head and
shoulders in brilliance. The little being rose from the
canyon, transported into blinding brightness. Only a
pile of spiky blue scales remained behind in the gray.

Francesca turned as footsteps clattered on the stairway. "Don't come any closer," she said, raising a hand to halt Stephen and Kat halfway down.

Kat continued down two more steps before Stephen pulled her back. "Aunt Frannie, we've got to find Chris and Devon!"

"Stay." Francesca's heart sank. Stephen, she saw at once, stood safe in the warmth of the light, armor intact. Kat, however, remained in the chasm of the undecided, probably with more company than Francesca cared to think.

Ever contentious, Kat began to protest. Stephen wrapped a secure arm around her. Francesca studied him for a moment. He'd grown very pale and looked ill. She suspected that he could see the creatures and feel the cold, but that he remained unaware of the gradations of dark and light swirling about him. He was traveling on autopilot, but that would be enough. What he saw didn't matter as much as how he reacted to his guided intuition.

She heard the gurgle of suction and raised her eyes to see Tia standing beyond the canyon, on the very edge of the darkness.

Tia, yet not Tia.

Francesca's palms tingled as she stared at the figure before her. An iron fear struggled within her, threatening to emerge as an endless scream. It wouldn't do. Not now, not when Kat's fate hung in the balance.

From across the canyon, Valentine bowed deeply. "I greet you in the name of all that is powerful and triumphant."

She was reminded of a noble courtier come to call in a foreign land. "I greet you in the name of Love and Light," she replied.

A corner of Tia's mouth turned down, but Valentine remained unfazed. His eyes darted from Francesca to the stairs, where Kat stood.

"I have come for one of my own," he said.

"She is not yours."

"She is, indeed."

"She belongs to God."

He pulled himself to Tia's full height. "Madam, she belongs to no one."

Francesca stood silent. The words were true.

Valentine acknowledged his victory with a condescending smile. "Do not attempt to cheat me of that which must be mine. My power will burn you. You know not to whom you speak."

Trembling, she set her jaw. "You've tried to make yourself more presentable to modern man, but your evil is old. You are Asteroth of the Crescent Horn."

A small demon shrieked, clutching his head and waggling a spiky tongue. Two broad, dark angels tensed, but they remained motionless.

Tia's body dropped to the ground with a thud. Kat muffled a scream as a huge hand punched the air several yards beyond Francesca's head. It vanished, replaced by locks of wild, yellow hair and the blurry form of a sandal-clad foot. They, too, dissipated into the air. Then a face floated before them, opaque, but clear enough to decipher the features. Turquoise eyes stared scornfully down at them. An arrogant smear of mouth fluctuated in and out of view. Finally the whole face faded away.

"You can't do it." Francesca squared her shoulders. "Despite your power, you can't inflict yourself on physical reality without the aid of a human channel."

"Yet *you* see me clearly."

She swallowed. "I do."

"Do I frighten you?" His deep voice rumbled in her ears.

"Yes. But God will protect me."

Asteroth smiled. "Perhaps. But, of course, God created me as well as you."

She licked her lips, determined to turn away. Asteroth muddied the clearest thoughts, weighted even the simplest words with unintended meaning.

She saw him all too clearly. He stood at least eight feet tall, icy in his beauty. Stephen's eyes were riveted to him, although his gaze seemed unfocused. He saw Asteroth as a disturbing shadow, nothing more. Francesca turned her troubled gaze to her niece. Asteroth was apparently invisible to Kat, who stared in shock at Tia's crumpled form.

Asteroth also appraised Kat, one large fist clenched. "Come closer, Katerina," he commanded softly.

Kat cocked her head slightly, as if a thought had flickered across her mind.

"Come," Asteroth said again. "Come to me."

With a determined nod, Kat started down the stairs, pointing to the body at Asteroth's feet. "Tia's hurt. We've got to help her."

"No!" Francesca shouted. "She's dead, Katerina. Stay back!"

"You can't interfere." Asteroth's jaw clenched. "You know this. The choice must be hers."

Stephen's hand closed around Kat's wrist, pulling her back from the bottom of the flight.

Asteroth raised a fist. "He will release her."

"But why?" Francesca asked frantically. "Why Katerina?"

He turned to face her, chin raised. "You wish to know?"

"Yes!"

His lips curled. "Very well. You are so proud of your studies, of your mystical knowledge. Step forward and I will enlighten you further."

She glanced from Tia's body on the floor to Kat shivering in Stephen's arms.

Asteroth's smile grew broader. "Come. You wear the armor of your God. Surely, you trust it to protect you."

That was so. Francesca glanced at the light that was her armor. All seemed intact.

"You have already chosen," he continued. "You would never switch your allegiance, never choose darkness over light. You would never even be tempted."

"You're right about that," she said and was instantly sorry. Only the most prideful, the most smug, would think themselves above temptation.

"You may wear your armor, Francesca. Step forward, and I will answer your question. Who knows? Perhaps you'll find a way to save her."

His words lingered in the air: *Save her.*

Francesca tightened her hand around the hilt of her sword and stepped into the chasm.

The *whoosh* of a vacuum clogged her ears. Her surroundings melted into liquid lines, then faded away. Where was Kat? Stephen? Where, for that matter, had Asteroth gone?

"What is this?" she demanded, lowering her shield.

Rows of energy particles swirled around her, rapidly changing form to create a different scene.

She was back in the convent, in the garden behind

the old stone building. There was the verdigris sundial, nestled amongst impatiens and petunias. The fragrance of basil wafted delicately from the herb garden nearby. Stunned, she stared down the familiar pebbled pathway. A woman ran toward her, auburn curls trailing on the wind.

"Frannie!" the woman called, and Francesca closed her eyes, pained.

Was that Asteroth's laughter she heard on the breeze, or had a touch of thunder rolled through the high afternoon clouds?

The figure drew closer, but Francesca didn't need to look. She remembered very clearly the way those cornflower-blue eyes crinkled in the corners, that dash of pink splashed across pale cheeks, the gentle curve of that lower lip.

And there was her younger self rising from the stone bench beneath the Japanese maple. Oh, the sheer invincibility of youth! It made her wince.

"This is trickery," she said through her confusion.

"No. It's truth." Asteroth suddenly towered a few feet away from her. "Do you deny it? Before your God, Francesca, do you deny it?"

"No." How could she ever deny the quickness of both heart and body that this young woman had inspired within her?

"Then face yourself, if you can. Or, my dear, is it easier to hide behind the shield of holiness?"

Young Francesca, long black braid hanging down her back, smiled broadly as the other woman approached.

"Is it any wonder we're always late, Moira?" she asked. "I'm going to stop waiting for you, let you face the consequences of your eternal tardiness alone from now on."

"You wouldn't." Even now, the melodic sweetness of Moira's voice sent shivers through Francesca. "You couldn't stand to watch me suffer alone. Besides, Frannie, you know you can talk us out of anything. Are we terribly late?"

"Not yet."

"Then can we stay here a minute? I read something wonderful today, and I can't wait to share it with you."

Even through closed eyes, Francesca could see both women sink to the bench. Dark head met auburn curls as they gazed eagerly at the book opened on Moira's lap.

"It was friendship," Francesca said, desperation tingeing her voice.

Asteroth smirked. "Oh, indeed. Wholly spiritual. As, of course, is your entire life."

"We shared a passion for the same things. It was nothing more."

His chilling laugh descended upon her as the image wavered.

"Oh, my dear Francesca. Is a liar such as you truly worthy of the Light?"

Oh, dear God! Her hands flew to her cheeks as the dancing particles transformed themselves into her narrow convent bed.

"I'm freezing," Moira said, slipping between the sheets like a wispy white waif.

"But it was nothing!" Francesca cried.

Her younger self held Moira close. Her present self remembered the softness of the other woman's body, the secure warmth of drifting off to sleep with a kindred spirit.

"Why protest this?" Asteroth asked. "This is merely an image from your own life. I have not altered it. Do you now, before your God, deny this?"

"No!"

"Then what of it, my friend?"

What of it? She stared at the bed, unable to remove her gaze from the accurate vision of her younger days. She'd insisted that nothing had happened, and she'd been technically correct. She and Moira had never exchanged more than the hugs and chaste kisses of friendship. They'd delighted in each other's wit and abilities, in the uncanny way each could unlock the other's soul. They'd reveled in true companionship.

But Francesca could not deny that she'd wanted so much more. She'd longed to spend uninterrupted, languid hours alone with this woman, to enjoy leisurely evenings exploring her mind, her soul, her body. She'd wanted to own every inch of her, to begin and end each day around her.

Asteroth's foul breath jerked her from her reverie.

"You have created such righteous reasons for why you left the convent. Oh, yes, my pious Francesca. Your poor, widowed brother needed help. You could best serve God if you rejoined the world's ranks. But this, Francesca . . . *this* . . . is why you left. Do you deny it?"

An empty, pulsing misery such as she'd never known poured over her. He was wrong. Her muddled brain couldn't remember why, but he had to be mistaken.

He folded his massive arms across his chest. "There is no precious spot for you in that heaven you've been taught to see. You will shrivel into nothingness like the poor, fallible weakling you are."

She turned to flee the chasm but found she could not move. An odd suction emanated from Asteroth, pulling her toward him even as she strained to break free.

She stared at him in disbelief. Droning noise crashed through her mind, making thought impossible. She shook her head to stifle the din.

There, in her peripheral vision, she caught a glimpse of light. It glowed as an incandescent question, waiting.

Of course!

"Help me," she whispered. "Please."

The light grew brighter.

As if on their own, her feet took a hesitant step backward.

Asteroth poised to spring. "You cannot leave me."

Warmth embraced her body, flowed through her limbs in a steady stream. Francesca gasped at the unexpected heat, then closed her eyes and extended her arms as the rising wave infused her. The drone in her head diminished.

"God loves all," she said, remembering.

"Even liars?" Asteroth's face clouded as she reached the edge of the chasm. "Even those made ugly by sin?"

"All," Francesca insisted, voice strong.

The light continued to race through her. A fine sweat glistened on her forehead as the heat intensified.

The image of the convent bed began to waver.

"No!" Asteroth roared. "Not yet! I command it!"

But the bed dissipated into billions of dancing particles that transformed themselves once again into Tia's foyer.

Through the curtains of light engulfing her, Francesca peered across the gray divide. Creatures pawed the ground, averting their eyes from the blinding torch she'd become. Devon stood in the doorway, white and shaking. Chris leaned heavily against her. Francesca realized that they saw nothing beyond her rigid physical form.

"It is I who controls this!" Asteroth shouted.

The lilting frequencies surrounding Francesca rose in volume and pitch. She heard the question: *Can you bear this?*

The light scorched by now, consuming all the air it could. Francesca drew in a ragged breath.

She had to know. Shading her eyes, she squinted at Asteroth. "Why Katerina? I command you to tell me. Can it matter so much that she destroyed Tia's circle?"

Asteroth turned slowly to face her. He was no longer beautiful. Twigs tangled his matted hair. His oiled chest smelled rancid. His face twisted into ugly hatred.

"The circle means little," he snarled. "She has, indeed, destroyed a fine channel, but there will be others. There are always others. They are easily found, easily cultivated."

All at once, recognition dawned through the radiance.

"Peter!" she cried out loud, and everyone turned to stare.

"A fool," Asteroth said with a sneer. "He was not meant to die. He was meant to draw Katerina into the circle, to bring her to me."

Francesca closed her eyes, steeling herself to withstand the burn of the protective light just one minute longer.

"Show me," she ordered from between clenched teeth.

A child sat before her on the floor, a rosy, smiling child with plump limbs and dark curls. Round eyes rose to meet Francesca's gaze. She gasped. The eyes resembled Katerina's, but they were the same pale green as Stephen's.

"The child," Asteroth said in a deadly whisper. "The child. Katerina must never bring to birth this cursed child of light."

The tips of Francesca's hair began to smolder, sending wisps of smoke curling past her nostrils.

"No more!" she cried.

The light vanished. Singed, she dropped to her knees, hands shielding her eyes.

"Concentrate on the light, Katerina!" she shouted.

34

KAT CLOSED HER EYES AND BEGAN A QUICK RECITATION OF THE rosary. Concentrate on the light, Francesca had said. Knowing her aunt, that meant prayer. As if it mattered anymore.

It was over. Tia was gone, and the answers to Peter's death had probably gone with her. Kat bit back an urge to shriek into the emptiness closing about her. What, then, had been the point of this futile mission? Why had she been allowed to undertake such an impossible task?

Damn it, she'd already lost her place in the prayers.

A cool breeze wafted across her clammy skin. Behind her closed eyelids, a beautiful image unfolded. An angel beckoned from beneath the shade of a large tree. Kat stared, dazzled by the angel's beauty. Iridescent feathers dripped gold like honey as soft wings fluttered in the wind. Golden curls tumbled about the angel's shoulders, and her perfect face resembled that of an antique china doll. She wore a simple white tunic, cut low across her neck and belted with a golden cord at her narrow waist. It fell in graceful folds to the grassy knoll on which she stood.

The angel extended her arms in welcome, plump elbows dimpling as she flexed long, elegant fingers.

"Come to me," she said softly. "So much has been asked of you, dear child, and you are weary. Drop your burdens in a safe place. No, my dearest, do not open your eyes. You know me well, for I am real to your heart, but you are not so schooled in spirit yet that you can see me in physical reality. Come."

Kat took a tentative step forward. "Who are you?"

"One who has known you throughout your walk on earth." The angel smiled, revealing small pearly teeth. "One who admires your inner strength. Much has been asked of you, but you have persevered and emerged victorious."

Kat did not reply. No answer seemed required.

The angel floated toward her, arms opened wide. "More will be asked of you, I'm afraid. I urge you, implore you, to choose the path of happiness, the way of the one who loves you."

"I don't understand."

"In this world, Katerina, we are known by our allegiances. They define us."

"I see." She studied the angel's perfect features. "Why have you come?"

"I've come to lend wisdom to your decision. Ask what you will. I shall answer truly."

Kat considered for a moment. "I want to know what happened to Peter," she finally said. "I need to know."

"Of course you do. How can you rest when you cannot silence the nagging of your heart?" The angel sank onto a large boulder, tucking her delicate feet beneath her. "Sit, dear Katerina. Watch. I will show you the truth."

"I'll stand." Kat wrapped her arms across her chest and waited.

* * *

Peter peered through the peephole of his apartment door, breathed an audible sigh of relief, and reached for the lock.

"Hey," he said, swinging open the door. "You scared me to death. What's going on?"

Tia Melody glided wordlessly past him. Peter glanced out into the hallway, half expecting to see her ever-present entourage trailing behind her. No, she was quite alone. He closed the door behind her.

"What gives?" he asked. "I thought we were meeting at your house. As a matter of fact, I was just about to walk out the door."

"What I must say can't wait," Tia said in a deep, urgent voice.

He'd been investigating this story for months now and knew that everybody involved in it was downright weird. First there'd been that poor Mr. Toohey, convinced that thunderbolts of justice sat poised to rain down upon him. Then there'd been those circle members. (Peter didn't know which aspect jarred him more: their conviction that Valentine was real or their willingness to do whatever Valentine said.) And now there was wifty Tia Melody. He'd been forced to endure two circle meetings before nabbing this interview. He'd come away convinced that Valentine was a clever performance, but that Ms. Melody's ability to speak truthfully of both past and future events in the lives of strangers verged on amazing.

"How'd you know where to find me?" he asked uneasily.

Tia paced the room as if her body could not contain the energy it held. "You supplied the address."

He hadn't. He'd listed the newspaper's address on Tia's information form. Pressing the point, though, seemed irrelevant. However she'd found him, she was here, her stare scouring every inch of his living room as if searching for something specific.

"I can interview you here," he said, loosening his tie. He ran a hand through his red hair and shrugged. "So, you want a coke or something?"

"Alcohol."

Alcohol? An unusual request, but perhaps not a bad idea. Tia struck him as the flighty type who might not hold her liquor well. That could make for an extremely fruitful interview.

"No problem. Any particular kind?"

"What is your preference?" she asked.

"Scotch."

"Then Scotch it will be."

Intrigued, Peter crossed the room to his liquor cabinet. "Oh, by the way, any objections if I record this interview?"

"Record?" She swung around to face him, expression blank.

He straightened, bottle in hand. Jesus, she was acting even nuttier than usual tonight. He pointed to his tape recorder. "On tape. I don't want to misquote you or anything."

Tia hesitated, then dismissed his question with a flourish of her hand. "It does not matter what you do."

Peter reached for a glass, puzzled. He had arranged his interview carefully, beginning with innocent queries about her methods of prognostication. He'd planned to slip in some questions here and there about the ethics involved in psychic readings and had even wanted to hit Ms. Melody with the far-fetched harassment claims of ex-cult members. He was a competent interviewer. This interview, however, was already off to an awkward start. Tia Melody strode through his living room, eyes raking the photos on his bookshelf. Why the hell had she come?

"Ice?" he asked, glass in hand.

"This picture." She pointed to a five-by-seven photograph on the shelf.

Confused, Peter set both the glass and the bottle onto the bar. "That's my girlfriend. I guess I should call her my fiancée. We've been engaged for almost two hours."

"Katerina." Tia drew out each syllable of the name.

Peter turned slowly to face her. "How did you know that?"

"She is in great danger."

A vein throbbed in his forehead. "Come again?"

Tia's gaze met his, drawing him into the depths of her dark eyes. With difficulty, he pulled his stare away.

"I have come to warn you," she said. "Katerina. She is in danger. You must bring her to me so that I can change this."

Peter shook his head, a dazed smile on his face. "Let me guess. She's in great danger, but if I pay you a sufficient sum of money, this danger can be avoided. Am I right?"

"No. She must come to me."

This was supposed to be an interview, not some creepy fortune-telling session. And Katie certainly had nothing to do with any of it.

"Look," he said, determined to seize control of his story, "some topics are off limits. My personal life has nothing to do with this. My girl has nothing to do with this."

Tia's laugh sounded like a short, sharp bark. "*Your* girl. She is not fated to be yours."

Peter automatically turned back to the bar, poured himself a Scotch, and hastily tossed it down his throat. He wasn't one to drink on the job, but Tia's unexpected prediction jolted him beyond professionalism. His own coughing provided a welcome buffer, an opportunity to clear the muddle this conversation had created in his head.

"I think," he said slowly, "that we'd better reschedule this interview for another time."

"There is no other time." She stood like a statue in the middle of his living room. "Katerina is not yours, but you will provide the line through which I can reach her. You must bring her to me. She must pledge herself to me."

"Ms. Melody, I hardly think that . . ."

Rough, raucous laughter assailed his ears. Tia was laughing, but the sounds coming from her mouth were distinctly male. Peter hastily poured another Scotch.

"You fool," she said. "You have been graced by my presence and have not even the intelligence to recognize it. I am Valentine."

Peter gulped a swallow of Scotch, careful this time not to inhale too much. "Ms. Melody, perhaps this act works for your followers, but I—"

"Listen closely, for you have seen that my predictions are accurate. You will never possess Katerina."

"Nonsense." He downed another swig. "We're in love."

"There will never be a wedding. I offer you a rare

opportunity . . . revenge before the slight. You will bring her to me."

The Scotch had flown immediately to Peter's head, but he was too good a reporter to let the obvious question pass unasked. "Why?" he demanded, shakily refilling his glass.

"I want her."

"Get out."

Valentine studied him for one long moment, then smothered a sneer beneath a disingenuous smile. "Forgive my temper. I have been . . . abrupt. We shall speak again, and sooner than you think."

"Get out of my apartment." Peter's voice cracked. He turned his back to Valentine, leaning against the bar for support. He heard a click, and then the slam of the front door. Rapid footsteps clattered down the nearby stairs. He was alone.

Yet he was not alone.

He swung around. Tia . . . Valentine . . . was indeed gone, but something still permeated the room. He could not say what it was, but the room felt greasy, as if a residue of Valentine had remained behind. Or . . . what if it were Valentine himself who'd stayed, unseen, but felt in every molecule of Peter's body?

He rapidly took another drink, then started to shake. He collapsed onto the couch and tightly closed his eyes, waiting for the trembling to stop.

What was happening?

His eyes fluttered open. There was no reason for the heavy fear growing in the pit of his stomach, no reason to feel as if the four walls of the room were suddenly closing him into a tight, inescapable cube. He would take a deep breath, calm himself, and then call Katie.

She'd be the first to tell him how stupid Tia's words had been.

But even as he formed the thoughts in his mind, they seemed to acquire tangibility. Drawn from his consciousness, Katie would not stay trapped within the confines of his skull but actually appeared to share physical space in the room. Everywhere he looked, he saw her smile, just like in the photograph. That smile had always warmed him straight through, but now it chilled. Had she always worn that mask to hide her true feelings toward him? Somewhere behind that painted smile, was Katie truly planning to break his heart, humiliating him in the process? A paralyzing dread stirred deep within him. His heart fluttered in panic.

If Katie was deceitful, perhaps Tia Melody could help. If he did as Tia asked and brought Katie to Valentine's circle, then maybe . . .

Peter groaned. What was he thinking? He had no sense of either the religious or the spiritual, but he had always considered his love for Katerina Piretti something holy. That love, after all, burned brightly within him, coaxing forth only the most positive parts of his personality.

He closed his eyes again, remembering the shy, pretty girl he'd courted in college. A faint smile curled his lips as he recalled their first kiss, how closely he'd held her after it. He'd wanted to tuck her into his pocket, to protect her always. Even the few times they'd made love had been buoyed by companionship. Peter had never required passion. The satisfying knowledge that Katie loved him had been more than enough to bolster every other aspect of living. And, in return for that love, he'd vowed to keep her safe forever.

He loved her. And love left no room for jealousy or fear.

He rose and headed nervously toward the bar. The Scotch bottle once again clinked against the rim of his glass as he poured an unsteady refill.

. . . you will provide the line through which I can reach her.

Was it really, truly Valentine? Could such a creature actually exist? David Toohey thought so. The ragged look on his face when first they'd met still haunted Peter.

"Mr. Dulaney," he'd said, "promise me you'll be careful. It's dangerous. You allow Valentine into your life, and all of a sudden he's working through you, wreaking havoc wherever he pleases."

What else had David Toohey said? Peter glanced toward the stack of notebooks he'd laid on the couch in anticipation of his interview. He'd taken copious notes throughout every conversation he'd had with Mr. Toohey.

The notebooks were gone.

He furrowed his brow, wondering where else he might have put them.

You will provide the line through which I can reach her.

His stomach suddenly felt lined with acid. What if, through his own brash stupidity, he'd opened corridors to Katie that could never again be closed?

He tossed the rest of his drink down his throat, then wiped his lips with a swipe from his sleeve. He needed those notebooks, fast. His fuzzy mind strained to piece together the events of the evening.

He'd had his back turned to Tia. He'd heard a click just before she exited his apartment. That click . . .

Eyes narrowed, he stumbled across the living room to the end table by the couch. Sure enough, the lid of his cassette recorder was flipped up. The tape was gone.

"Shit," he mumbled, unconsciously pressing the Eject button a few times. Tia Melody had pinched both his tape and his notebooks.

Well, she wouldn't get away with it. Peter slammed his glass down onto the end table, not noticing when it cracked. That was his work, damn it. This was theft. It was worse than theft; it was an assault on the First Amendment! In a cloud of self-righteousness, he reached for his car keys and staggered determinedly toward the door. He fumbled with the knob, then flung the door wide open.

Tia stood before him in the hallway.

"My notebooks," Peter growled, brows lowered. "My tape. Where the hell's my stuff?"

"It rests secure." The eyes, dark and luminous, glowed eerily in the dim light of the hallway. "You may have all once Katerina is brought to me."

"That's insane. I'll call the police."

"But she is in great danger. You must allow me to help."

Peter raised a weary hand to his forehead. Help? David Toohey's plaintive voice floated through his brain: *You allow Valentine into your life, and all of a sudden he's working through you, wreaking havoc. . . .*

What on earth had he done?

"You must bring her," Valentine repeated. "I insist."

And Peter was convinced; he would continue to insist until Katie's arrival was actually accomplished. It was foolish to think that he himself could hide from this. Somehow, Valentine had known not only his address, but also his fiancée's name. What other information had he unwillingly provided?

"What do you do?" he asked shakily. "Read minds? Absorb information like Mr. Spock's Vulcan mind meld? How do you do this?"

"I have no need to read minds. Don't you see? I am *part* of your mind, Peter Dulaney. *You* have allowed me birth."

Peter took a tentative step backward, eyes wide. Was this like a virus, then? Would the essence of Valentine thrive within him, manipulating his life, destroying not only his own decency, but everything he touched as well? He feverishly reviewed his past interviews. No one had provided an antidote. Nobody had mentioned a way out. His backward steps quickened. Then he turned and dashed into his bedroom.

He yanked open his nightstand drawer and pulled out the gun his grandfather had left him. Katie had always hated it, had always sworn that keeping a gun in the apartment was a dangerous thing to do.

But at the moment it smacked of incredible foresight.

Peter weaved back into the living room, gun pointed straight at Tia's heart.

Valentine laughed, that same harsh, horrible laugh Peter had endured earlier. "My poor, poor boy. Don't be foolish. You can kill this vessel I use, but you can never kill me. I am not physical. I can travel wherever necessary. Who knows? Perhaps *you* might even be the next to welcome me, my next physical host!"

Peter fought back an overwhelming wave of nausea. First him, then Katie?

He turned the gun toward himself, aiming at his right temple.

The grin left Valentine's face. He extended an entreating hand. "No."

Peter started to laugh, at last in control of the situation. "Not what you had in mind, eh? Because without me, of course, you'll never reach my Katie."

"No!" Rage clouded Tia's features.

"Never!" Peter's finger rested on the trigger. "You'll never destroy her!"

Valentine turned and dashed down the stairs as the blast of the gun echoed through the empty hallway.

The last of the vision died away, leaving only the angel in Kat's mind's eye.

"There," the angel said. The spun gold threaded through her wings sparkled as the wind kissed each feather. "You have seen the truth."

Kat nodded slowly, unable to speak. She'd been right all along, then. Peter had not willingly ended his life. He'd been coerced, goaded into taking the only exit his besieged mind could see.

Her throat ached with weary tightness. The knowledge would not resurrect him, could never replace what had been lost. Yet somehow, the missing puzzle piece fit the jagged hole in her heart. Her lashes grew wet with tears, and there no longer seemed any reason to stop them. She stood motionless as they trickled in rivulets down her cheeks.

The angel rose with a soft rustle of silk. "It was not your fault, Katerina."

Kat's chest heaved as a sob racked her body. "I know," she said, trembling as a second sob engulfed her. It felt good, as if a coil deep within her soul had finally sprung. The sadness jabbed like a dagger, but she reached to embrace it, wanting to feel it in every inch of her being.

"Goodbye, Peter," she whispered.

"He was a fool," the angel said placidly. "Through his foolishness, he caused his own defeat."

Kat stared through glistening tears. "Excuse me?"

"He was a foolish young man. Hardly worth your tears."

"He wasn't a fool. It wasn't his fault he couldn't understand. Valentine distorted his mind. Peter only did what he thought he had to do."

The angel extended her hand. "Come. Time grows short."

Kat drew back. "Where are we going?"

The angel sighed a pretty sigh, but the impatience behind it was palpable. "Come with me to the one whose strength prevails. Come to your master."

"And who might that be?"

"The mightiest of princes, of course. Asteroth, Lord of your heart."

Asteroth? Aunt Frannie had murmured that name in the foyer: Asteroth of the Crescent Horn.

Kat froze. "I don't think so."

"But it is already done. Just as your Peter could not escape his destiny, nor can you." The spectral hand drew closer, the fingers arching toward Kat. "Touch me," the angel commanded in a deep voice. "Touch me and be mine!"

Kat pressed cold fingertips against each temple. Frigid air emanated from beneath the angel, rising in curling vapors as the flow increased. A magnetic pull beckoned, drawing her despite her reluctance.

"Come," the angel said. "You owe no allegiance to

the Light. Renounce the God who allowed death to snatch both your mother and your lover. Avenge them now!"

The pull tightened around Kat like a rope, urging her forward.

Her right hand grew heavy as her fingers instinctively closed around a metal object in her palm. She glanced down. Her sword! She'd forgotten all about it.

Desperately Kat reviewed her armor, mentally flinging each piece of it onto her body. It had protected her before; she hoped it could do so again.

Helmet of salvation, shield of faith, truth about the waist . . .

"Armor makes no sense," the angel said sweetly. "It's nothing but a stupid image, an archaic fantasy."

But Kat's body warmed as each piece flew rapidly into place.

Sword of spirit . . .

She remembered using the sword back at Tia's, back on the night of that thick, dark cloud. Archaic fantasy or not, there was something about this that somehow strengthened her. Now was not the time to decide if any of it made sense.

The angel was within arm's reach now, a plastic smile pasted on her face as she relentlessly approached. Kat raised her chin and stared into the dark eyes. Through them, she saw writhing creatures in torment, jeering grotesques. She saw emptiness which knew no end, gaping nothingness.

Peter had died to spare her this.

"No!" she shouted. With a powerful thrust, she shoved the sword into the angel's abdomen.

For a split second the angel stood motionless. Black

tar boiled from the gaping wound. Then a loud crack snapped through Kat's consciousness. A huge, plaster-like hunk broke from the angel's face. Another toppled from the middle of her robe, revealing a strong, hard chest. Wings fell with a crash to the ground, vanishing in a cloud of hissing steam.

Asteroth emerged from the core of the angel, face twisted in rage. Muscles rippled beneath his flesh as he clenched his mighty fists.

Kat frantically opened her eyes.

But even with eyes wide open, the horrible image of Asteroth remained, growing great and terrible in size. He loomed before her, nearly purple with fury.

"I will have you!" he thundered, raising a powerful arm. A chilling gust of wind whipped through the foyer.

Stephen was beside her now, one arm around her waist, the other gripping her hand. "Block him out, Kat!" He raised his voice to be heard above the howls of wind and creatures. "You've made your choice! He can't invade you unless you let him!"

Asteroth's outline blurred as he whirled toward Stephen, eyes piercing. Stephen grew white and looked away. Kat wondered what thoughts raced through his mind. Whatever they were, they allowed Asteroth no quarter. The demon faded slightly as yet another human channel was denied him, and the knickknacks on the mantel crashed to the floor as greater gusts of wind swirled through the room. A low, buzzing hum started near the ground.

Asteroth strode across the floor to face Chris and Devon Alexander. Devon nearly swooned as his image grew clear to her.

Weak but determined, Chris grasped his wife's hands in his own. "Look away, Devon! Don't listen!"

She gave a wild sob and buried her head in his shoulder.

Asteroth stared at them, eyes bulging. "You cannot keep me at bay. You can never keep me out!"

But apparently they could, for again he uttered an angry cry before turning toward his last hope.

Francesca followed his moves with her aching eyes, scorched hands cradled in her lap.

"Allow me access," he wheedled. "I will grant whatever you ask. The world will be yours for just five minutes' use of your human body."

She examined him closely. "Five minutes? It's worth this much to you?"

"It is." His image grew more solid as the hum reverberated against all four walls. Sweat dripped from the ends of his matted hair. "You can never win, Francesca. This battle is eternal."

Eyes glued to his, she slowly raised her right arm. Kat noticed a light grow bright behind her.

"Go," Francesca ordered her companions. "Get out of this house. Quickly!"

Dazed, Devon and Chris staggered toward the door.

Kat shielded her eyes from the still growing light. It burned so brightly that she wondered why her aunt was not engulfed by it. The buzz had become even louder, making her head ache.

"What's happening?" Stephen asked.

Francesca lowered her voice. "Asteroth is buying time. He can't find an available channel, but the darkness in this room is growing stronger. The frequencies here are so low that physical reality is nearly accessible to him. He'll be able to manifest himself shortly unless something is done, and we're not the ones to do it. Go!"

Through her fingers, Kat saw a fiery form emerge from the intense light. It stood nearly nine feet tall, blazing with energy she could barely comprehend. Its face seemed made of fire, and it burned so brightly that she couldn't decipher any features. She stared, mesmerized, as the angel hoisted a flaming spear. It sailed through the air, falling to the ground with a soft thud. Immediately a small fire burst into life at the point of contact.

Asteroth unleashed a mighty roar. "To battle!" he commanded hoarsely, and to Kat's incredulous horror, creatures and angels of light fell upon each other. A spear whizzed past her ear. The acrid smell of smoke plugged her nostrils as fires erupted throughout the room.

"Let's go!" Stephen hollered. Chris and Devon fumbled for the front door. Coughing from the sulfuric fumes, Francesca limped to join them.

Kat stood, hypnotized by the otherworldly battle unfolding before her. Stephen grabbed her by the arm, yanking her away as a small fire ignited at her feet. He half-dragged her to the door, tugged it open, and shoved her out to the sidewalk.

"Don't stop!" he shouted. "Get away from here!"

All five of them dashed across the street, then turned to stare at Tia Melody's house.

Fingers of flame leaped through the second-floor windows, while sooty black smoke stained the blue sky above. Kat clapped her hands over her ears to block out the wailing shrieks and groans seeping through every window of the building.

"Jesus!" Devon collapsed against Chris as sirens wailed in the distance.

"Excuse me," Kat said, and fainted dead away.

She was floating, weightless and bright, miles away from any recognizable landscape. At first she thought that if she looked down, she might glimpse the Earth as the astronauts did, a shining, blue sphere reflecting the sun's brilliance into space. But looking down offered no clues. Pink and white swirled clouds veiled her view.

Kat wanted to laugh with the bubbling joy that only small children possessed. No other reaction seemed suitable. It was so peaceful here, and her own buoyancy struck her as the most natural thing in the world.

But suddenly, all too soon, her feet were back on solid ground. She stood again at the edge of the sparkling brook she'd dreamt about so many months ago.

Peter! She'd seen Peter here last time! She glanced up expectantly, not at all surprised to find him standing on the other side of the water. He smiled as if they'd parted only an instant ago.

"Katie." The caressing tone of his voice warmed her, but it no longer sent spasms of pain coursing through her.

She wistfully met his gaze. "I think I've done what you wanted."

He nodded. "You did good, Kate. But, then, I knew you would."

She looked down at her feet, then back up into his blue eyes. "So I guess there's nothing left for me to do."

His smile broadened. "Now, there's where you're wrong."

"Pardon?"

He blew a kiss across the stream. "My lips are sealed," he said, turning to leave.

"Peter, wait! You can't . . ."

He stopped and turned to face her, one hand on his hip, the other casually draping his suit jacket over his shoulder. "Hey," he said, suddenly serious. "He's a good man, Katie. And with you along for the ride, he's going to be an even better one. Go in peace and live your life to the fullest. I'm rooting for you."

Kat's face flamed red as she fumbled for a reply. But he was gone again, lost in the swirling clouds.

35

~m~

"THANKS," CHRIS SAID AS KAT SLOWED HER CAR. "I NEEDED to see this one more time."

"You're sure?" She threw him a sideways glance. His left arm still rested in a sling and his face remained slightly purple where the bruises had yet to fade. This was his first visit to Tia's house since the fire a week ago.

Kat had visited twice. Each time she'd stoically faced what was left of the structure, only to reel back against the sturdy wall of the building across the street, overwhelmed by images she'd yet to absorb.

"Hey." Chris laid a hand atop hers. "It's over, Kat."

She swallowed hard as Tia's house came into view. Only the front wall remained standing. It looked like a Hollywood movie flat. The stoop, still intact, was strewn with flowers and bouquets. Valentine's followers were in mourning.

Chris barely blinked as he surveyed the ruin. "Kind of hard to feel sorry," he said as Kat clicked on her flashers and double-parked.

"How's Devon?"

"It's going to be a long haul. I'm in it for the duration, though. And once we're settled in Atlanta, she'll have her family's help, too. We'll pull her through."

Kat shook her head. "I wish you weren't leaving."

"Devon will never recover if we stay."

"I know, Chris. Of course, you need to go."

"What about you? You had me worried. When your father said you wouldn't take my calls . . ."

Kat turned toward Tia's house. "I didn't take anybody's calls. I needed time to think."

"It's good to see you out again, that's all." He studied the house as if committing it to memory. "I've seen enough. We can leave whenever you're ready."

She gave an inadvertent shiver and tightened her grip on the steering wheel. "I confess. I can't wait for the wrecking ball to level this place."

"I wonder who won the battle?"

The words chilled her straight through. "I think it's best to assume that the battle is still being fought."

He remained silent as she eased the car into the flow of traffic.

"Mind if we stop at Angel Café before I take you home?" Kat asked casually.

She had the distinct impression that he was studying her, weighing the true meaning behind her words.

"I haven't taken Stephen's calls, either," she said. "I owe him a visit."

Chris smiled slowly. "Let me out at the corner."

"Oh, no, if it's inconvenient, then—"

"Let me out. I have a sudden urge to walk to a pay phone and call my wife."

"Chris, I can't . . ." But it was a moot point. He unlocked the door as the car slowed for a red light, and he was on the sidewalk before she knew it.

"Give Stephen my regards," he said. "I'll call you tomorrow."

She stared as he trotted up the block. Only a toot from the car behind her made her notice that the light had turned green.

Molly manned the lobby of Angel Café, a fragile, wan Molly who looked as if it required concentrated effort just to lift her head. It was nearly two o'clock. What was left of the lunch crowd sat tucked away in the dining rooms. The lobby was empty.

"Hi," Molly said in a subdued voice. "One for lunch?"

A soft blush crossed Kat's cheeks. "Actually, I'd like to see Mr. Carmichael."

Molly nodded, and it occurred to Kat that many people had asked for Stephen this past week. She herself had read a few quotes from him in newspaper accounts of the fire. His comments had been circumspect, never venturing beyond his role as Tia's employer.

She glanced around the lobby as Molly paged Stephen. The angel memorabilia remained in place, but the meditation stones were gone, along with the crystals and the feathers. The room felt serene. It made her want to curl up in the large sofa by the fireplace and sleep peacefully for the rest of the afternoon.

"Kat."

He stood in the hallway, face drawn, green eyes questioning. He looked impossibly familiar, though she couldn't say exactly when he'd left his imprint on her heart.

Without a word, Kat walked steadily across the room and into his open arms. "I'm sorry, Stephen. I should have called."

"It's okay." He took her hand and, with a glance at the obviously curious Molly, led her back to his office.

"How are you?" she asked as the door closed behind them.

He hesitated. "I'm better than I have a right to be. I feel . . . alive. That's the only way to put it. It's more than I can say about Tia's followers, by the way. They've been drifting in and out of this place for days, looking like a herd of lost souls."

Kat shook her head. "Jesus, Stephen, what will they do?"

"Find some damn good therapists, I guess."

"It's going to take more than that."

He did not meet her eyes as he reached for something on his desk. "Here. You'll want this."

Kat stared at the cassette tape in his hand.

"It's yours, after all," Stephen said. "Take it, Kat."

She'd forgotten all about the tape. She reached for it gingerly, no longer connected to it. "Have you listened to it?"

He shook his head. "That's your right."

"Well." She didn't know what else to say.

"Here." He plucked it from her hand, then walked across the room to the boom box on his bookshelf. "You can hear it now if you'd like."

She drifted to his side as he inserted the cassette.

"Do you want me to leave?" he asked, searching her expression.

There was no more to know. The tape felt like a relic from the past, and Kat was no longer sure of the wisdom in disturbing the past.

She reached for Stephen's hand. "Stay with me," she said.

He pushed the Play button.

click . . . click . . . click . . .

They stared as one at the tape, and then at each other.

"Damn!" Stephen slumped against the wall. "I wasn't here when my friend dropped it off. I just assumed he'd fixed it. I'm so sorry, Kat. I had no idea."

She stared at the recorder for a second, remembering that Peter's notebooks had gone up in smoke as well. She had no evidence of anything. The attorney in her howled at the fact that there was no proof. The rest of her understood clearly that experiences of the soul could never be proven, anyway.

Stephen peered at her. "Are you okay?"

She was more than okay. She was finally whole.

With a sigh she wrapped her arms around his neck. His arms instinctively flew around her, and they met halfway in a long kiss.

Epilogue

MEDITATION NO LONGER CAME EASILY. AT FIRST FRANCESCA was distracted by her sunburned skin and aching eyes. But two weeks after the ordeal with Asteroth, her skin no longer itched, and her eyes no longer required sunglasses. Why, then, was she still unable to immerse herself in spirit as completely as before?

Her soul felt pried open. She was aware of a darkness hovering at the edge of the light, as if a door had been left ajar. Even physical reality seemed overly vivid and coarsely drawn.

Today she was determined. She sat cross-legged in the living room, eyes closed, breathing measured.

Finally, behind her closed eyelids, she caught the beautiful image of light she'd so missed. She nearly laughed with relief.

But something was different. She was not alone.

In the center of the pulsing sunburst sat a baby. It cooed, its green eyes smiling out at her. She instantly recognized the child as the little one she'd seen at Tia's.

But why?

"Yes, child," she said cautiously. "I remember who you are."

A cold wind swept through the living room, rustling the leaves of the ferns on the windowsill. Francesca's eyes flew open at the sound of a deep, mocking voice.

"*And so,*" it said, "*do I!*"

JILL MORROW has enjoyed a broad spectrum of careers, including practicing law and singing with local bands. She has just completed a sequel to *Angel Café*. She lives outside Baltimore, Maryland, with her husband and two children.

DON'T MISS THESE OTHER FASCINATING PAPERBACKS FROM
PARAVIEW POCKET BOOKS

THE SEVENTH SENSE
The Secrets of Remote Viewing as Told by a "Psychic Spy" for the U.S. Military

LYN BUCHANAN

"Remote viewing"—the psychic ability to perceive the thoughts and experiences of others through the power of the human mind. Now, for the first time, Lyn Buchanan, a world-renowned expert on remote viewing and its potential, tells the complete, candid story of his experiences.

0-7434-6268-8 • $14.00 ($22.00 Can.)

BIGFOOT!
The True Story of Apes in America

LOREN COLEMAN

In this fascinating and comprehensive look at the fact, fiction, and fable of the North American "Sasquatch," award-winning author Loren Coleman takes readers on a journey into America's biggest mystery—could an unrecognized "ape" be living in our midst?

0-7434-6975-5 • $14.00 ($22.00 Can.)

STRANGE SECRETS
Real Government Files on the Unknown

NICK REDFERN AND ANDY ROBERTS

Containing the actual government "X-Files"—revealing the mysteries behind the world's greatest phenomenon—*Strange Secrets* will turn even the most skeptical reader into a believer.

0-7434-6976-3 • $14.00 ($22.00 Can.)

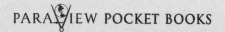

PARAVIEW POCKET BOOKS

3200.00